CARDBOARD SOULS

Bonnie E. Perley

Contents

Acknowledgements

I want to thank the people who, over the years, encouraged and believed in me - Thank You. I also want to give thanks to my friend Andre Faust who set up my computer so I could write offline and who also encouraged me in this work.

About the Author

Bonnie E. Perley is a multidisciplinary talent with a deep commitment to understanding the complexities of human society. She holds a Master's degree in Sociology from the University of New Brunswick and a B.A. Honours in Sociology from Saint Thomas University. Her academic pursuits also include graduate-level studies in Criminology at the University of Toronto.

Bonnie's intellectual curiosity and passion for exploring human behavior are not limited to the written word. She is also a gifted artist and musician, drawing on her creative instincts to express the same depth of emotion and insight found in her scholarly work. Whether through pen, brush, or instrument, Bonnie brings a distinctive voice and perspective to everything she creates.

A Word To The Wise - Be Aware of Tangled Webs.

Chapter One

Company is Coming

"No one ever taught me how to spit," Rita said as she pulled over to open the car door to release the spit in her mouth. Her husband Joe laughingly said, "What?"

"Yeah," Rita said. "I don't know how to spit the way men do, I just drop it," she added, and they both cracked up laughing.

"You're funny tonight," Joe said.

"I'm always funny," Rita replied, smiling.

It had been quite a few years since Joe had seen his friend Frank. Joe and his wife Rita had now driven for hours to get there. There, being a backwoods town in the middle of nowhere, at least that is how they both viewed it. There, is where Frank had chosen to live his later years. Joe and Rita were city dwellers and didn't quite understand the finer things of country living. Nor did they care much to find out about them, so to speak.

However, Joe had promised Frank that he would pay him a visit this coming summer. With summer now turned into early fall, Joe was keeping that promise to Frank, come hell or high water because Joe was the kind of person who hated to break a promise, since he hated it when people broke promises they made to him. *"Do onto others as you would have them do onto you!"* he would always say to Rita, his wife of sixteen years. And Joe tried his best to live his life by that teaching.

At this point, Rita had heard every story at least once, if not more, of the adventures of Joe and Frank during their time in University together. Rita had never meant Frank, and all she knew of him was through her husband Joe and his stories of the two of them. Joe and Frank had met in University and attended some of the same classes. They partied together and had become good friends, staying in touch over the years.

Rita figured this would be a boring visit vacation for her, since she was not much interested in the things Joe and Frank liked to discuss. She knew this from Joe having his phone on speaker when he and Frank would be talking. World politics, local politics, religions and what they both like to refer to as "the big picture" were the topics they liked to discuss. And Rita was not interested in any of it, until she was. She would sometimes find herself being pulled into the conversation by accident and simply out of interest.

Still, she fancied herself to be 'not interested' in such matters. "I am content to live my life and not worry about such matters," she would say, pushing her nose up in the air. As if to say, her interests were superior to what was happening around her. "Head in the sand," Joe would say to Frank regarding Rita's apparent disinterest, and Frank would always agree. "Yup, and she's far from being alone in that," Frank would respond.

Both Frank and Joe, however, sometimes wished they did not see and know all that they did about the world around them.

Sometimes, it seemed overwhelming and even depressing. Yet, they felt it was better to know than not.

"Ignorance is not bliss. It is simply ignorance," Frank would say during their discussions.

And Joe would always retort with, "It seems to work for lots of people, though Frank!"

"Seems is the operative word," Frank would respond.

Conversations like these were now rolling around in Joe's mind in anticipation of seeing Frank face to face after all these years.

"What was the address again, Rita?" Joe asked. "One forty six Clarendon Drive," Rita said in an annoyed tone of voice. She was getting agitated by Joe repeatedly asking her for the address. It seemed to her that he'd asked for it not minutes after they left their house and several times since then. Of course, that wasn't the case, but it felt like it was to Rita.

They had Google mapped the location of Frank's house and Frank had sent them pictures in the past, so they figured they wouldn't have any problems finding the place.

"It's an old farmhouse on a hundred acres of land," Joe said, thinking about Frank's place. "Frank must be out of his mind to buy a big place like that," Joe continued.

"At his age, what did he want with such a huge property?" he said to Rita. Rita had no reply. She didn't know Frank personally, and thus, asking her the question seemed inept to her. So she didn't bother to respond.

But Joe already knew why Frank had opted to buy that property. "I know why he bought it," Joe said, looking over at Rita. "We must prepare, or we will all be doomed," he added and chuckled. "It's the end of days," he continued in a sarcastic tone, and he and Rita both chuckled a little.

The whole doomsday thing was a bit much for Joe. Still, he was interested in what Frank had to say about it all and was looking forward to the great conversations they would have in the coming days. He smiled a huge smile as he envisioned being at Frank's place, where the two of them could sit around having great discussions and debates about current and past events in the world.

He was looking forward to it because, in Joe's experience, there were very few people who would or could, or even desired to, speak about these important matters. Frank, Joe knew, was a deep sea diver and preferred to look at subjects from all angles and objectively as possible. This was a rare quality of Frank and one Joe very much enjoyed and found refreshing because he loved intellectual discussions of this nature. Thus, he was looking forward to spending time with Frank for that very reason.

It was Joe's turn to drive and Rita could now relax and look out the window of the vehicle. She liked to analyze the houses and sites as they passed by. She wondered who the people who lived in the houses were and what they were like. She figured she could assume many things about who lived in what house just by how the house and yard looked. She wasn't a Sociologist. Still, she had read a few books on it and she enjoyed thinking in abstract ways.

From there, her mind went back to memories of when Joe and her were first looking to buy a home and how the outside of the home was not always indicative of what the inside looked like. And to Rita, this was a good analogy for people as well, for she knew that just because someone looks good on the outside doesn't mean they are good on the inside. However, she also realized these were not steadfast rules regarding either houses or people. Yet, it was a part of reality that she herself had witnessed in situations and experiences over time.

"What are you thinking about?" Joe finally asked.

"Oh, I'm just thinking about when we bought our first house and how the houses often looked good on the outside, but not so much on the inside and how that also applies to people in many instances as well," Rita replied.

"I have to agree with you on that, Rita," Joe responded.

"Good analogy," he continued. "Thanks," Rita replied, smiling. "I do come up with some interesting thoughts once in a while," she added and chuckled.

"Yes, you sure do," Joe replied, smiling back at her.

Joe had great affection for his wife, Rita. He was sexually attracted to her like on one's business. *"You are delicious Rita,"* he would always say to her. And Rita would always smile at the comment. Rita was well aware of her husband's great affection and sexual attraction towards her. Even after all their years of marriage that level of attraction had not waned. In fact, Joe was so attracted to Rita that it sometimes became annoying to her. Sometimes, she felt that Joe's incessant sexual attraction to her was all there was to their entire relationship, and that made her feel sexualized and misunderstood on every level.

"We can't have it all," she'd say to herself when thinking about it. Because Joe was a successful business man and had built a very profitable company, of which Rita had reaped the benefits. And she was well aware of that fact.

When Rita meant Joe, she had just finished her degree in Psychology, and planned on opening her own practice. However, when she married Joe everything changed.

Rita became what society refers to as a 'kept woman,' and she was okay with that label, because it meant she didn't have to work outside the home and she could enjoy her time to herself. It also meant she didn't have to do the dreaded house labour, because she could hire people to do all of that for her.

She also had a hired cook who cooked ninety nine percent of their meals, as well as someone who did her grocery shopping, someone who drove her to her appointments, someone who washed and took care of their vehicles and so on. Rita had many helpers in her life, all afforded her by her husband's great financial success. And she had grown very accustomed to that way of life.

"I have a very blessed life," she thought to herself, which was a thought she had on many occasions over the years of her marriage to Joe. "I've been so fortunate to marry a man like Joe," she said to herself and smiled as they drove down the highway.

But in many ways, it was a lonely life for Rita. She made friends with her staff just to have someone to talk to, to eat with, or go for a walk.

It wasn't that she didn't have friends. She did, but they were all people in the same situation as her. People who did the same things and contended with the same issues, and that got boring for Rita after a while. She wanted to meet different people, and she was looking forward to finally meeting Frank for that reason.

She wanted to meet people who were not like the people she knew. The wives of the husbands who were Joe's business associates. 'Kept women' like herself.

 She now found them to be boring. They always talked about the same things over and over. It all felt so plastic to her. It seemed that all they cared about was competition with others and getting one up on the next person. "All they want is a bigger house, a nicer vehicle, more clothes and another vacation," she'd say to herself.

And while Rita enjoyed and appreciated the high-status life afforded her by her husband, she didn't feel she was better than other people. She had never been into competition. And all of this luxury had come at a price, for she barely saw her husband most of the time.

He was always working and striving to make more and more profits. And she wondered if the trade off was really worth it.

When parties or events occurred, Rita never felt like she fit in. She hated going to these events for that reason. She felt like she wasn't allowed to just be herself and that she had to pretend she was in conformity to what they all believed in, when she knew she did not believe as they did. In fact, she saw it all as shallow bullshit, but she felt obligated and compelled to conform for the sake of her husband and his business connections.

Joe knew Rita was not happy being around what she called 'the important people.' He knew she found them to be shallow and plastic; but he would always encourage her to try to like them and see life from their perspective.

"Look at all the privileges you have compared to millions of other people in this world due to our social status," he would say.

"I know, I know," Rita would reply. "I'll try to be nice and inviting to them for your sake," she would add. Then Joe would smile, kiss her on the forehead and thank her.

So Rita became very good at playing the part of strict conformity when needed. She would dress the part and speak in ways she knew they wanted to hear. She always made sure to repeat back to them the same-things they were espousing. This way of being and speaking, she knew, would give them a sense of being supported in what they were saying at any given time. Rita considered her behaviour in those times as going in what she called, *'the phony plastic mode.'*

Still, she did not like being that way. She knew she was lying to herself and to those around her when she forced herself to behave in ways that were contradictory to her own beliefs. And it seemed to Rita that every time she had to act phony and plastic, denying who she really was, she lost a little piece of herself. And she had become increasingly lonely in her material world of financial success.

"What would life be like," she wondered, "had I not married Joe?" "I wonder, if I continued on with my own dream of opening my own Psychology practice, what my life would have been like."

But it was all speculation because that was not the path she had chosen. And to wonder about it in her current life, only made her feel uneasy and restless. So she tried not to think about what ifs and instead focused on what is. After all, it wasn't like she was living some poverty existence of struggle and hardship. She was a princess, living in a mansion castle, with staff to work for her and with everything she could ever want or ask for. She was, she knew, very fortunate.

And Joe was not the type of man who lorded any of it over her. No, Joe did just the opposite. He always insisted to Rita that she was the reason he worked so hard to become the successful person he was. "Without you by my side, I'd be nothing and have nothing; it is you who motivated me to do so well in life, Rita," he'd say. "I do all of this because I want to make you happy and provide the best possible life for you," he'd continue. These words made Rita feel important and assured her that she had played an important part in the accumulation of the great material wealth they both enjoyed. She very much appreciated and loved Joe for the life he provided for her, but she also knew that despite all the materialism, she didn't feel fulfilled, happy or content inside, and this perplexed her to no end.

"You're awfully quiet," Joe finally said, looking over at Rita. "Yea, I'm just thinking about our life together over the years," Rita replied.

"So, what's the verdict?" Joe asked, still smiling. "Have I been a good husband to you?" he continued. Rita smiled and took Joe's free hand. "Yes, Honey," she said. "You have been a most excellent husband, and I appreciate you very much. You are a great provider, and you always make me feel like I am the only woman in the world," she continued, still smiling and looking at Joe.

"I did it all for you, Babe," Joe replied, squeezing Rita's hand a little. Rita smiled warmly, pulled Joe's hand up to her lips, and kissed it. "Thank you my sweet love," she said, putting his hand back down on the seat. Silence now filled the car once again as they continued down the highway.

Joe looked at the gas hand in the car and realized he had better stop and get some fuel at the next station he saw along the road. And just then, the sight of a gas station popped up in the distance. "I'm going to pull over and get some gas, Honey," he said to Rita. "We should take a pit stop anyway; I really need to stretch," he continued.

" I hear yea," Rita said, pushing her back against the seat.

Joe pulled into the gas station/convenience store. "How many more miles do we have to drive before we arrive at Frank's house?" Rita asked in a tired tone of voice. Joe then looked at the map and estimated that they were now approximately an hour and a half away. "Wow, only an hour and a half now!" Rita exclaimed. "That's great," she continued, now feeling relieved that the long drive was almost over.

Joe got out and proceeded to gas up the car. While he was waiting for the car to fill up, he asked Rita if she wanted anything in the store. But Rita wasn't hungry for anything in a convenience store. She hated junk food, and if given the choice, she would refuse to eat it. She also needed to pee something fierce, but she hated using public washrooms.

"No," Rita replied. "I'll pass unless they have fresh fruit," she continued. "Oh yea, and get me a bottle of water too, please," she added.

"Will do," Joe said, putting the gas nozzle back in place and closing the lid. He headed toward the store to pick up some snacks and pay for the gas while Rita got out of the vehicle to stretch. But it wasn't long before Joe was back, so she returned to the vehicle when she saw him coming.

"Here yea go, that was all the fruit they had in there, but it looks fresh at least," Joe said as he passed the items to Rita.

"Thank you," Rita replied, taking the banana and bottle of water.

Joe then started the vehicle and proceeded down the highway. "I have to pee something fierce," Rita finally said. "What! Why didn't you use the washroom at the gas station?" Joe asked.

"You know me," Rita said. "I am averse to using public washrooms," she added.

"Yes, right," Joe said, smiling. "So what do you want to do?" he asked.

"Just look for a spot to pull over on the side of the road. Like maybe a side road that we can pull off into," Rita replied. "Oh, okay," Joe said and chuckled. "If the important people could only see yea now, eh Rita," he said, and they both started laughing.

Joe and Rita enjoyed making fun of 'the important people,' behind their backs. It was one of their favourite things to do. They figured it was harmless as long as 'the important people' were never to find out.

"Oh, that looks like a good spot right there," Rita said, pointing to a side road.

"Okay," Joe said, slowing down and checking to see if anyone was behind him. "The coast is clear," Joe said as he pulled off the highway. "Where are you going to go?" he asked, smiling.

Rita looked around, and suddenly, she saw the perfect spot. "Right over there behind that little tree," she said and smiled. "What are you going to use for toilet paper?" he asked.

"Right!" Rita replied, now looking around the car to see what she could find.

"Here," Joe said, passing Rita a box of Kleenex that was on the floor of the backseat. "Oh, perfect," Rita replied while taking several pieces of Kleenex out of the box and exiting the car. Joe watched on as Rita headed to the spot she had pointed out to him. He looked around to ensure no one was around and waited patiently in the car.

It wasn't long before he saw her head pop up with a big smile on her face as she walked back towards the car. "Feel better now?" he asked, smiling. "Yes, much improved," Rita said, still smiling as she got into the car. Joe then backed up onto the highway, which had now turned into a road more than a highway, and they continued their journey.

Rita and Joe were both tired of driving at this point in the journey, and the anticipation of finally getting to Frank's house was on both of their minds. "Only another hour and a half eh?" Rita said, smiling.

"Yup, it won't be long now, Honey, and we will be there," Joe replied. "I am so looking forward to seeing Frank after all these years," he continued. "I am also looking forward to seeing his place and his land. He has told me so much about it," he added.

"He lives in an old farmhouse, right?" Rita asked. But she already knew what Frank's house looked like because she and Joe had Google mapped it and street viewed it before they left on their journey. Plus, Frank has sent pictures.

"Yes, that's right," Joe replied. "I have to tell you, Rita," Joe went on to say. "It's not going to be the mansion you are used to living in," he added, looking over at Rita and smiling.

"Oh, I know," Rita replied. "You already warned me of that before we left. I'll manage, I am sure," she said and chuckled.

There were no more houses along the side of the road for Rita to look at and analyze. The scenery was now all wood. "We are in the boondocks now, eh Honey," Rita said smiling. "Yup, we sure are," Joe replied, smiling back at her. And the closer they got to Frank's house, the more the anticipation and excitement grew within them.

"I can't wait to meet Frank," Rita said as they got closer and closer to his place.

"I can't wait for you to meet him either," Joe replied. "He's a really down to earth person. Not like 'the important people' friends we have," Joe said and smiled. "I think you will really like him, Rita," Joe continued. "He's a smart guy, really smart, in fact," he added. "But he's not arrogant about it, and he doesn't put the same importance on social status and wealth accumulation that the people we know and associate with do," he continued.

"Well, I sure don't have any problem with that," Rita replied. "It will be like a breath of fresh air to be around someone who is down to earth and real. I am looking forward to it," Rita said and smiled.

"What is the address again?" Joe asked, now leaning forward to look out the windshield window. Rita rolled her eyes and looked at the paper with the address written on it and told Joe, once again, what the address was.

"Okay," Joe replied, "I think we are on the right road. We must be getting close to Frank's house now. Keep your eyes peeled," he continued. So Rita was also looking around to see if she could spot Frank's house from the pictures they had seen of it. "We are looking for a big white house with a big field around it," Joe said, slowing down to enable them to see better.

Then suddenly they both saw Frank at the same time standing in his yard waving his arm. "Oh my gosh, that is Frank right there!" Joe exclaimed in excitement and he quickly pulled into the driveway and exited the vehicle.

Frank had already commenced walking toward the vehicle when Joe came around the back of his car, and they embraced one another. "Good to see yea buddy," Frank said, patting Joe on the back. "Really good to see you too Frank," Joe said and then he stepped back a little to take a look at Frank after all their years of separation.

Just then, Rita was standing there beside the two of them. "Oh," Joe said, putting his arm around Rita's waist. "This is my beautiful wife, Rita," he continued and smiled at Frank.

Frank extended his hand to Rita. "Well, it is finally good to meet your beautiful wife," Frank said and smiled. "Likewise," Rita said, shaking Frank's hand. Right away, Frank could see that Rita was as hot as heck, and he was thinking what a lucky man Joe was to have such a fine looking wife.

"You haven't changed a bit, Frank," Joe said as they all walked towards the front veranda of Frank's house. "Neither have you," Frank responded. But inside, he was thinking how much Joe had aged since the last time he had seen him. "I wonder if I look worse than I realize," Frank thought as he and Joe were close in age.

"Can I get you guys something to eat or drink?" Frank asked once they were all seated on the front veranda.

"A coffee would be nice," Joe said.

"What about you Rita? Would you like a coffee or something else?" Frank asked, looking Rita in the eyes.

"Yes, a coffee sounds wonderful," Rita replied, smiling and looking Frank in the eyes.

"But we don't want to be any bother," Joe said. "Oh, it's no bother," Frank replied. "You two just sit here and enjoy the nice country air and scenery, and I will go and prepare us all a coffee," he said as he got up from his seat and entered the house to make a pot of coffee.

Once inside the house, Frank couldn't help but wonder how Joe had ever got such a beautiful, sexy woman for a wife. "He really hit the jackpot on that one," Frank thought to himself and smiled. "Good for him," he continued. "I'm happy for him. He deserves a good woman," Frank thought.

While the coffee was brewing, Frank went back to the veranda to sit with Joe and Rita. "Really nice place you have here, Frank," Joe said, looking around.

"Yea, it's coming along," Frank replied. "I still have a lot of work to do, but it is much improved from when I bought it four years ago," Frank continued.

"No man," Joe replied. "I like it. It suits you," he added. Frank wasn't quite sure what Joe meant by that statement, and he didn't really care. He liked his house and land and that was all that mattered.

"I know it's not the mansion you guys are used to," Frank replied and smiled. "But hopefully, you two will feel comfortable here," he added.

"Oh, I am sure we will," Rita responded. "I can use a break from all of that, and I am sure Joe can as well," she added.

Frank then got up and peered in the kitchen door to see if the coffee was brewed yet. "Coffee's ready," he said. "Sit still. I will bring everything out here to the veranda, and you guys can prepare your own the way you like it," Frank continued and then he entered the house to retrieve the coffee pot and all the fixings.

He put the cream, sugar, and cups on a tray and took them to the veranda first, sitting the tray on the table on the veranda. Then he went back and got the coffee pot full of coffee and grabbed a cutting board to sit it on the table with.

Frank then motioned them to go ahead and make themselves a cup of coffee. Rita got up first and made herself a cup and Joe followed. After that, Frank made himself a cup, and the three of them sat on the front veranda relaxing and enjoying the beautiful surroundings and fall day. "This coffee is delicious," Rita said, taking a sip. "I agree," Joe said. "Thanks," Frank responded.

So they sat on the front veranda and had a casual conversation for the rest of the afternoon catching up on each other's lives. Rita listened somewhat to what they were talking about. But mostly, she was off in her own mind, thinking of how nice it was to be away from the city and how good the air smelled in the country. How peaceful it was and how pretty the land was surrounding Frank's home. "I could easily get into living in a place like this," she thought to herself.

Chapter Two

Settling In

Frank was up early and had gone to the kitchen to make coffee and check out the news of the day on his computer. Afterwards, he sat at his kitchen table thinking. It had only been a day since Rita and Joe had arrived, and Frank was already wondering how he was going to deal with the sexual feelings he was having towards Rita.

He was also thinking about how much he was enjoying the company and the great conversations he and Joe were having. He hadn't realized how much he had missed having a good friend's company. The only friend Frank had in the area was Louise, and while Louise was intelligent, Frank just felt more relaxed conversing with Joe, whom he'd known for a lot longer.

But Rita, she was a different story altogether. The way she dressed, the way she walked, wiggling her butt. The very low-cut tops she wore. The short skirts that barely covered her private parts. Frank wondered why Joe didn't seem bothered by any of it. "If she were my wife, I wouldn't want her to dress like that around other men," Frank thought to himself. But Rita wasn't his wife, and he had no say over the way she dressed.

Frank had been trying not to stare at her, but he found it hard when she seemed to always be bending over in front of him. When she winked and smiled at him all the time, he could swear she was flirting with him. But then he'd think it was just his imagination and that maybe that was just who she was, how she acted normally.

Rita was lying awake in bed, thinking about how great it was at Frank's place. She really liked Frank's routines and his way of doing things was something she had not witnessed before. And his mind, oh yes, she really liked his mind. "He is just so damn intelligent," she thought. She also liked his strong, manly body and hands. Joe was always so pristine and clean. She hadn't been around a man who actually smelled like a man in years. It was doing something to her and she knew she was sexually attracted to him.

She could hear Frank downstairs moving around. She was hoping he had made a fresh pot of coffee. She didn't want to disturb Joe, who was still fast asleep, so she slowly and quietly slipped out of bed, put on her robe and headed down to the kitchen. Truth be told, she wanted to spend time alone with Frank.

Frank was sitting at the kitchen table, coffee in hand, when she entered the kitchen.

"Good morning, Rita," Frank said, looking up at her as she entered the room.

"Good morning, Frank," Rita replied and smiled.

"There's a fresh pot of coffee on the counter, and the cream and sugar are there as well. Help yourself," he said, smiling.

"Don't mind if I do," Rita replied, walking to the kitchen counter to prepare herself some coffee.

Frank couldn't help but gaze upon her as she stood there making her coffee. He could see the outline of her figure, and he already knew she had a very nice figure underneath that robe.

Rita took a seat at the side of the table, facing Frank.

"Oh, this coffee is so delicious," she said as she took a sip.

"Ahhh," she said after taking a sip. "Not sure why, but everything seems more wholesome and delicious here," she added, smiling and looking Frank directly in the eyes.

"What?" Frank said, wondering if he had heard her correctly.

"Oh, nothing," Rita replied. "I was just thinking out loud. I have a bad habit of doing that sometimes," she added and smiled.

"No problem," Frank responded. "I'm happy you like it here," he continued.

"Oh, I do," Rita said, pushing her breasts out a little as she raised her arms to have a morning stretch. The action caused her robe to fall open, exposing her breasts under her sheer nightgown.

Frank couldn't help but look, but he tried to pretend he didn't notice what she was doing. Rita knew Frank was looking, and she didn't want to be too obvious, so she slowly lowered her arms. Frank quickly looked her in the eyes.

"So, what would you guys like to do today?" he asked.

"Oh, I don't know what Joe wants to do. He was still fast asleep when I got up just now," she replied. "I'm sure he will tell us when he gets up," she continued.

"Yes, he probably has a plan, knowing Joe," Frank replied and smiled.

Just then, Rita leaned forward toward the table and pushed her breasts up on the side of the table. They might as well have been naked, as the nightgown she was wearing was sheer. But she pretended it wasn't. She was acting as if nothing was happening. At that, Frank was feeling nervous. "What is she trying to do here?" he said to himself. "She is Joe's wife!" he thought. "Is she trying to test me? Set me up? What?" he thought. And he couldn't help but look at her breasts, which were now, quite literally, laying on his kitchen table in front of him.

So he pretended to be looking at something else on the table, but Rita knew he was fixated on her breasts, and she was loving every minute of it. She knew what she was doing was wrong, but she couldn't seem to help herself. She was attracted to Frank, and she wanted him to know it.

Just then, Frank heard Joe stirring upstairs. "I think I hear Joe coming down the stairs," he said, hoping that those words would encourage Rita to take her breasts off his kitchen table.

"Yes, I think I hear him as well," Rita said, and she suddenly changed her position and removed her breasts from the table.

"Thank God," Frank said to himself. "What would Joe think if he walked into the kitchen and saw what she was doing?" he thought.

"Good morning, my friend," Joe said as he entered the kitchen.

"Good morning, Sir," Frank replied, smiling.

"Oh, good morning, Honey," Rita said.

"Good morning, my love," Joe said as he leaned over and kissed Rita on the cheek. Then Joe went to pour himself some coffee.

"Help yourself," Frank said. "There's still enough coffee in the pot for a cup for you," he continued.

"Thanks," Joe replied as he continued to the kitchen counter to prepare his first cup of coffee of the day.

Having prepared his coffee, Joe took a seat at the kitchen table with Rita and Frank.

"You're up early, Honey," he said to Rita. "How long have you been up?" he asked.

"Oh, not that long," Rita replied. "You were fast asleep when I woke up, so I decided to come downstairs and get a coffee," she added.

"Right!" Joe replied and let it go at that.

"What are you reading these days?" Joe asked, looking at the stack of books sitting off to one side of the table.

"Oh, various things," Frank replied. "These books are just some of the ones I keep handy. I have tons more upstairs," Frank continued.

At that, Joe began to look through the stack of books. Then he chose one and said, "I'm going to take this book and retire to the washroom for a bit."

"Oh, okay," Frank replied, smiling. "I'll make another pot of coffee, as you probably all want more than one cup first thing in the morning," he added.

"Right," Joe replied, smiling as he got up from his chair and headed to the washroom.

Frank got up from his seat at the table and began making a fresh pot of coffee when suddenly he felt Rita standing close behind him.

"What is she doing?" he thought to himself. "Is she trying to get me in trouble with my friend?" he wondered. But he wasn't sure what to say or do in that exact moment.

She was standing so close to him that he could feel her breast against his back.

"Ah, can I help you, Rita?" he asked, without turning around.

"I don't know, can you?" Rita asked in a sexy tone of voice.

"You know you're a married woman, right?" Frank said, still not turning around to face Rita.

"Yes, I am well aware," Rita replied, and pushed her breasts even harder into Frank's back.

Frank continued making the new pot of coffee, then turned around to face Rita, at which point she was right there in his face.

"Listen, Rita," Frank said. "You are a beautiful woman and sexy as heck, but I don't think the way you are acting is appropriate. Joe is my good friend of many years, and your actions are causing a problem for me. Can you please stop what you are doing?" he pleaded in a gentle tone of voice.

"What?" Rita said, looking up at Frank with her piercing green-blue eyes, lips pursed as if begging to be kissed. "I'm very attracted to you, Frank," she said, not moving an inch.

"I get that," Frank replied. "And I am very attracted to you as well, but there's only one small problem: you are married," he continued. "And not only married, but married to my good and longtime friend. Now please, get a grip and stop flirting with me," Frank said, now in a more stern tone of voice.

Rita pouted. "What? You don't want me?" she asked.

"That's not what I said, Rita," Frank replied, gently moving her backward and away from standing so close to him. "It's not that I don't want you, it's that you are married to my friend, and I don't think it is cool for you and I to be doing things like this behind his back, if you see what I mean," he continued.

"Yes, you are right," Rita said in a disappointed tone of voice. "I'm sorry," she continued. "I don't mean to put you in an uncomfortable position. I know you and Joe are good friends of many years. I just don't know what has come over me. I have never felt so attracted to someone in a long time," she added.

"Well, I'm flattered," Frank said. "But truly, I see you as someone who is out of bounds for me. As much as I want to take you and make sweet, passionate love to you, I know that is not possible under the circumstances. You do understand, right?" he asked.

"Yes, I understand," Rita said, pouting. But all she really heard was, "I want to take you and make sweet, passionate love to you."

"So he does really like me," she thought to herself and smiled. "He does want me," she thought. "So, it is just a matter of time before I have him," she said to herself.

Just then, Joe returned to the kitchen. "That's a great book, Frank," he said, sitting the book down on the kitchen table.

"Yeah, it is very interesting for sure," Frank replied. Frank was relieved that Joe was back in the room.

"What's on the agenda today?" Joe asked, looking at the two of them.

"Well, first I am going to smoke some medicine," Frank replied, reaching for the box where he kept his cannabis herb stored.

"Medicine"?" Joe replied and chuckled. "You still smoke that stuff?" he continued.

"I sure do," Frank replied and smiled as he began preparing a joint to smoke. "I can roll you each one, if you'd like," Frank continued.

"I'm up for it," Rita said and smiled.

"Sure, why not," Joe replied. "After all, we are on vacation, what the hell," he added and smiled at Rita.

And while Frank was preparing a cannabis joint for each of the three of them, Joe said, "I was thinking we could take a walk on your land today."

"That sounds like a great idea," Frank replied. "I'd love to show you around and take you both down to the river," he continued.

"Sounds good to me," Rita replied, smiling.

"Yeah, that sounds perfect," Joe responded.

"Okay then, that is what we will do," Frank said as he licked the glue on the paper of the joint he had rolled.

Frank then passed both Joe and Rita a joint of their own.

"What kind of smoke is this?" Joe asked, picking the joint up from the table.

"Oh, it's not really strong stuff," Frank assured him. "I grow it myself, so I can control what is in it," he continued. "It is all organic," he went on to say. "I don't trust the weed you can buy in the stores these days. Even the stuff the government sells, I think they put too many chemicals in it now," Frank continued.

"Right," Joe replied. "Well, Rita and I don't usually smoke it, but we are making an exception today," he added.

"I use a special mixture of soil, and I use only organic plant food for fertilizer," Frank replied. "I'm not kidding when I say it's my medicine," he continued. "Even society recognizes it as medicine nowadays," he added, lighting up his joint as he spoke.

"Okay, Frank, I think you are taking it a little too far in calling it medicine," Joe said and chuckled.

"Well, whatever it is, it is good stuff," Rita said, blowing the smoke out of her mouth after taking a big haul on the joint Frank had given her.

"I have to agree, Rita," Joe replied, taking a big haul off his own joint. "It is smooth, and I am feeling the effects already," he added.

"Good," Frank replied and smiled. "I'm glad you guys like it."

"Yeah, it's really good," Rita said, taking another haul off the joint. "I'd like to buy some from you, if you don't mind. I'd like to take some back home with me when we leave. Could you sell me some?" she asked.

"Oh, I don't sell the weed I grow, but I will give you some before you leave if you want," Frank replied.

"That would be awesome," Rita responded and smiled.

"Did you guys know that the cannabis herb is in the Bible?" Frank asked.

"What!" Joe said and laughed. "Really!" Rita chimed in.

"Yes, really," Frank responded.

"Where?" Joe asked. "I have to see this," he continued.

"Yup," Frank replied. "Genesis 1:29," he added.

"Do you have a Bible, Frank?" Joe asked. "Because I really need to see that with my own eyes, as I'm finding that hard to believe," he continued.

"Yes, of course I have a Bible, Joe," Frank said, getting up from his seat to retrieve his Bible.

Once Frank left the room to retrieve his Bible, Joe looked at Rita and said, "I've got to see this!"

"Me too," Rita agreed.

It wasn't long before Frank returned with his Bible in hand. "Look right here, read it for yourselves," Frank said, laying the Bible on the table in front of them, pointing to the Scripture, Genesis 1:29.

Joe and Rita both leaned forward to read the Scripture, and they were amazed that the Scripture did speak of God giving the seed-bearing herb and how it was to be meat for the people.

"That's amazing," Rita said in a surprised tone of voice.

"Yeah, really," Joe agreed.

"See, I told you guys," Frank said, smiling.

Neither Joe nor Rita could believe their eyes, and they then had nothing more to say on the subject.

"You know, most people don't have a clue as to what is actually written in the Bible," Frank added. "There are a lot of things in the Bible that no one knows about because it hasn't been taught to people by religions. Most folks have no idea what is actually written in the Bible," Frank continued.

"You're getting kind of deep here now, bro," Joe replied and smiled.

Frank chuckled. "Don't worry, I'm not going to start preaching," he said. "I'm just saying," he continued.

"More coffee, anyone?" Frank asked as he walked to the kitchen counter and poured himself his second cup of the day.

"No, none for me," Joe replied. "I can't drink too much coffee; it makes my stomach hurt," he added.

"Yes, please," Rita said, turning to hand Frank her empty cup.

"Are you sure you should have another cup of coffee, Rita?" Joe asked. "We should be getting ready for the day now, so we can go and walk the property and get in some nature while we're here," he continued.

"I'll drink it fast," Rita said and smiled.

"You'd better drink it fast," Joe replied. "Because I know you, it will take you at least an hour to get ready for the day," he continued and chuckled.

Rita didn't respond. She hated it when Joe tried to order her around, and she was determined to have one more cup of coffee before she went to take a shower and get ready for the day.

But Rita opted to drink her second cup of coffee quickly, as she had said she would, and she and Joe both retreated upstairs to get ready for the day. Once alone in the bedroom, Joe was quick to take advantage of the alone time.

"You are so damn sexy," he whispered in Rita's ear as he groped her breasts. Rita smiled and struggled to get loose from his grip.

"You're always so anxious," she said in an annoyed tone of voice. "You don't give me any challenge!" she added. "Sometimes, it feels good to have a challenge," she continued.

"I'm sorry baby," Joe replied in a sulking tone of voice. "I just can't help myself when it comes to you. What can I say? I'm pussy whipped," he added and laughed.

"I'm going to take a shower now," Rita said as she grabbed her clean clothes and exited the bedroom.

"Okay, don't be long. I have to take one too, and maybe Frank does as well. So don't use all the hot water, Honey," Joe said.

"I won't," Rita yelled back as she walked down the hallway to the bathroom.

Sometimes she felt smothered by Joe. It seemed to Rita that he was always telling her what to do, like she didn't have a mind of her own, and that annoyed her to no end. "I know he's a good husband and an excellent provider and all, but sometimes I just can't stand him," she thought to herself as she jumped in the shower.

She quickly took a shower, as Joe had instructed her, and returned to the bedroom to finish getting ready for the day.

"Good girl," Joe said as she walked into the bedroom. He was lying on the bed waiting, so as soon as she entered the room, he got up and headed to the bathroom.

As Rita was getting ready, she admired her own body in the mirror. "I am a sexy mama," she said as she slid her hand down over her own body. "I even turn myself on," she added and chuckled.

Then her thoughts turned directly to Frank, and she realized she had to stop flirting with him after what he had said to her that morning. "What if he tells Joe that I was flirting with him?" she thought. "I'm going to contain myself from now on," she said to herself as she put on her clothes and prepared for the day. "He is right, I'm a married woman, and I should behave like one," she said to herself in a determined tone of voice. Yet, she knew inside that she was very attracted to Frank, and truly she wasn't sure she could follow through with all she was saying to herself in that moment.

Once Joe was out of the shower, Frank took his shower and got ready for the day as well. Then they all met in the kitchen.

"Are we all ready now for the adventure?" Frank asked, looking directly at Rita.

"Yes," Joe replied. "I just have to get my hiking boots from the trunk of the car," he added as he exited the kitchen to retrieve his boots.

Frank couldn't help but notice how sexy Rita looked with her short skirt and top that revealed three-quarters of her breasts. "You might be cold dressed like that," Frank said to her and smiled. "I suggest you bring a warm jacket," he added.

"No, I'll be fine," Rita said, smiling and looking Frank in the eyes. "Don't you like what you see?" she asked.

Frank smiled back at Rita. "Of course I do," he replied. "What man wouldn't like a sexy woman like you, Rita?" he added. "I am just thinking you might be cold, as it is not that warm a day out. I just want you to be comfortable on the walk, is all," he continued.

"Oh, don't worry about me, Frank," Rita replied. "I assure you, I am all good," she continued. "But since you insist, I will grab a warm coat just in case," she said and smiled.

Then suddenly, Rita blurted out, "I masturbated over you in the shower this morning, Frank."

"What?" Frank responded.

"Don't say such things, Rita, Joe might hear you," he continued.

"Joe can't hear me," Rita said. "He's out getting his boots from the car."

Frank knew she was right, but he also didn't want to take any chances. "Did you hear what I said, Frank?" Rita asked.

"Yes, I heard you, Rita," Frank replied.

"Does that turn you on, Frank?" Rita asked.

"Of course it turns me on," Frank replied. "You turn me on, but I can't have you. I already told you that, and you know as well as I do that it is wrong. So please stop with the flirting, I can't take it," Frank continued in a pleading tone of voice.

And just then, Joe returned from getting his boots from the trunk of the car. He sat down at the kitchen table and put his boots on, stood up, and said, "Okay, I'm all ready now. Are the two of you ready?"

"Yup, I am," Frank replied.

"Yes, all good," Rita replied.

"Good, let's get this show on the road then shall we?" Joe said, smiling.

And the three of them exited the house and commenced walking on Frank's property.

Frank's property was magnificent, that much was obvious to Joe and Rita as they walked. It was clear to them that Frank had taken very good care of his land.

"You own all of this land, eh Frank?" Joe asked.

"Yes, I do," Frank replied, smiling.

"Wow, what a nice piece of property you have here," Rita said.

"Wait until we get to the river," Frank said. "It is very beautiful," he added.

"Can't wait," Rita said, smiling.

"How far is it to the river?" Joe asked.

"Oh, not far. Just a few minutes walk," Frank replied as they continued walking.

It wasn't long before they were at the river's edge, and Joe and Rita both realized Frank had not lied to them, for it was exquisite. Frank had brought snacks for the three of them and had rolled a joint for each of them as well. So he pulled out the joints and passed two of them to Rita and Joe, who were both enjoying the natural beauty that now surrounded them.

Rita found a nice rock to sit on a short distance away from Frank and Joe, and she took off the coat she had opted to wear since she now felt warm and cozy. Frank looked over at her sitting there, and he could see the nipples on her breasts were now protruding.

"Oh my goodness. She is one damn sexy woman," he said to himself, and he could feel himself getting turned on.

"Let's make a small fire," Frank said to Joe in an effort to distract himself from staring at Rita. So Joe and Frank made a fire in the fire pit Frank had made. They smoked their individual joints and hung out at the river for a couple of hours. Rita stayed to herself while Joe and Frank had their usual type of conversation. The day felt so relaxed, and Rita was really enjoying herself. "I could most definitely live in a place like this," she thought and smiled.

Once back at Frank's house, Frank made a nice meal for the three of them. He was thinking of calling Louise to see if she would like to join them, but he decided to wait and call her the next day instead.

"That meal was absolutely delicious," Rita said.

"I agree," Joe added.

"Thanks," Frank replied, smiling.

"Not only is he handsome, he is also a great cook," Rita thought to herself.

"Do you guys want to watch a movie?" Frank asked. "I have a ton of movies to choose from," he added.

"Sure, that sounds like a great idea," Joe replied.

So the three of them went to the living room to relax and watch a movie.

"What kind of movie do you guys feel like?" Frank asked as he looked through some of his movies.

"Nothing too heavy," Joe said. "Maybe a comedy," he added.

"A comedy it is," Frank said, taking one of the movies and putting it in the machine.

The three of them commenced watching the movie, but it wasn't long before Joe could feel himself drifting off to sleep.

"I'm exhausted from all the fresh air today, plus that beautiful meal you made for us," Joe said, looking at Frank. "I think I am going to retire to bed. I am falling asleep here in the chair," he added.

"Oh, okay," Frank replied.

"Come on, Rita," Joe said, getting up from his chair.

So Rita got up and followed Joe upstairs. She was tired herself, but she knew Joe would most likely want to have sex once they were in bed.

Frank shut the movie off and returned to the kitchen to clean up from supper.

"I know it's late, but I feel like making myself a coffee," he said to himself.

So he made a coffee and sat down and rolled another joint.

"I'll smoke this and drink my coffee and then I'll head to bed."

Once finished with his coffee and smoke, Frank headed upstairs to his bedroom. The old house didn't have the best soundproofing, and suddenly Frank could hear the bed springs singing.

"Oh no, I'm going to have to listen to them having sex," he thought. "Maybe I should get my earplugs, or better yet, get my iPod and listen to some music to drown that out," he said to himself.

But he didn't want to move. It was as if he was frozen to his bed.

Just then he could feel himself getting turned on.

"Stop it," he told himself.

But it was to no avail as his penis was now starting to respond to the sound of Joe and Rita having sex. Then, he began to masturbate, imagining that he, not Joe, was the one having sex with Rita.

Finally, the noise stopped, and Frank, once finished masturbating, fell quickly asleep.

When he awoke in the morning, all was silent, and he realized he still had his penis in his hand and it was hard. But this hard was from the fact that he needed to take a morning piss. He figured it was safe to scoot out to the washroom without getting dressed, as Rita and Joe were both obviously still sleeping, and he wouldn't be surprised if they slept half the day after their night of profuse sex.

He opened his bedroom door and peered out. No one was in sight. So he made a run for the washroom, penis in hand. Once in the washroom, he was quickly releasing his pee when in walked Rita.

"Oh, I'm sorry," she said. "The door was open and I just thought, well, you know, I thought no one was in here. I'm embarrassed now," she added.

Frank wasn't sure what to do. He couldn't let go of his penis as it was hard as a rock, and if he let go, he knew urine would go flying everywhere. So he just stood there with his penis in his hand, looking at Rita, who had made no effort to leave. It was at that moment that he realized Rita was staring at his penis.

"Look at that nice penis," Rita was thinking to herself while licking her lips without realizing it. But then she realized what she was doing.

"Sorry again," she said as she walked out of the bathroom and closed the door behind her.

Frank didn't even respond. He was just interested in finishing peeing and getting back to his bedroom.

Once back in his room, he began thinking about how Rita was staring at his penis, and the thought was turning him on.

"Oh no, not this again," he said to himself. "I really need to start thinking about something else, anything else. I need to get her out of my mind," he told himself as he commenced getting dressed and headed down to the kitchen to make a pot of coffee.

However, upon entering the kitchen, he found Rita standing there in her robe. She had already made coffee and was offering him some.

"Right on, thanks," Frank said as she passed him a ready-made cup of java.

"I figured you'd be down for a coffee soon," she said, smiling.

Her robe was loosely tied, and when she moved in a certain way it exposed her naked body underneath.

"Oh my gosh, she is naked under that robe," Frank realized. "How am I going to contain myself and deal with this?" he asked himself. "I wish Joe would wake up and get down here," he thought.

But on the other hand, he was counting himself lucky to be there alone with Rita. He knew it was wrong to think that way, but he couldn't seem to help himself. He was human, after all.

"She must know what she is doing," he thought.

And just when he was thinking all of that, Rita bent over right in front of him, shaking her breasts, letting them loose from inside her robe.

"How do you like these?" she asked, smiling and looking Frank directly in the eyes.

"I like," Frank replied, staring at her naked breasts.

"Want to touch them?" Rita asked.

"Do I ever," Frank replied, now feeling very turned on.

"Go right ahead then," Rita said, smiling. "I won't tell if you won't," she continued.

So Frank reached out and took her breasts in his hands, but he was feeling anxious about the fact that Joe was right upstairs.

"I can't do this," he said suddenly, pulling his hands away from Rita's breasts. "It's not right," he added. "And what if Joe were to wake up and hear us, or worse, come down here and catch us. All hell would break loose and I just can't chance it," Frank continued. "Are you not worried about that?" he asked.

"No, not really," Rita replied. "I gave him two sleeping pills. Trust me, he is not going to be waking up for a while," she added.

"Did you plan this?" Frank asked, suddenly wondering if Rita had an agenda.

"Oh no, I never plan anything," Rita replied. "Joe was overtired and he couldn't get to sleep, so he asked me for a couple of sleeping pills. That's all, no big deal," she continued. "So that gives us time to have some fun," she added. "That is, if you want to have some fun," she continued, smiling at Frank.

But Frank wasn't convinced.

"I do want to have some fun, don't get me wrong, but I'd feel horrible if Joe knew we were acting like this behind his back. And I'd feel even worse if he caught us having sex. He may want to shoot me, and I can't say I would blame him if he did."

"Listen," Rita responded. "I know he is sound asleep and will be for some time. Now, if you want to enjoy this," she opened her robe, revealing her naked body, "then I suggest we make hay while the sun shines."

Frank wasn't sure what to do. He knew what he *wanted* to do, but he was feeling very apprehensive about Joe being right upstairs.

"I want you so bad it hurts," he said.

"Then take me," Rita replied. "I want you too," she added and bent herself over the table. "I like it from behind."

So, against his better judgment, Frank got up from his chair and entered Rita from behind. Rita moaned as Frank entered her, and at this point, Frank had forgotten all about Joe being right upstairs. They continued having sex until both of them had ejaculated.

"That was amazing," Rita said, smiling and taking a seat at the kitchen table.

"I agree," Frank said, also sitting back down at the table.

"You're an excellent lover," Rita added, smiling.

"Likewise," Frank replied, smiling back at her. "But we were lucky this time and we can't be doing this again," he added.

"Okay, if you say so," Rita replied, but in her mind, she had no intention of giving up that easy.

"I'm going to go and take a bath," she said, getting up from the table.

"Okay, I think I will cook up some breakfast," Frank replied. "Is there anything special you would like?" he asked.

"No, I'm good with whatever you cook," Rita said as she exited the kitchen and headed to the bathroom.

Once Rita was out of the room, Frank just sat there, mesmerized by what had just happened. He couldn't get Rita out of his mind.

"Has she possessed me now?" he asked himself.

And if so, what was he going to do about it, he wondered. But he had no immediate answer. He wasn't sure he could control himself around her, but he thought surely he could manage to control himself when Joe was present.

And with that thought, he suddenly felt tremendous guilt. He had always valued his friendship with Joe, but now he had lost control and betrayed him, and there was no going back.

Chapter Three

Who Knows What?

It's a strange thing in life, but sex has a way of changing things even when people don't think it will. It has an energy all its own and exposes things that simply cannot be hidden. And this was certainly true of the situation between Rita, Joe, and Frank.

Joe finally woke up and headed to the kitchen to get a morning coffee. He could sense a change in the atmosphere, but he wasn't sure where exactly it was coming from. Things seemed normal enough and nothing was out of the ordinary, but something just didn't feel right.

"What did I miss?" he asked as he entered the kitchen and took a seat at the table.

"Oh, nothing much," Frank responded. "Can I get you a cup of coffee?" Frank asked.

"Yes, please," Joe replied. "My head hurts. I took a couple of Rita's sleeping pills early this morning and they knocked me right out. I needed the sleep, but now my head is hurting," he added.

"Do you want an Advil or something?" Frank asked.

"Yeah, I'll take one if you have some handy. My head is pounding for some reason," Joe replied.

Feeling mega guilty, Frank got up and made Joe a coffee and got him an Advil from the bottle in the cupboard.

"Here you go, my friend. Hope you are feeling better soon," Frank said, passing Joe the fresh cup of coffee and the pill.

"Thanks," Joe said, popping the pill into his mouth and taking a drink of coffee to wash it down. "I think I'll be fine here in a minute," he added.

"Where's Rita?" Joe asked finally.

"Oh, she was down here earlier and she said she was going to take a bath. So I think she's still in the bath, but I'm not sure," Frank replied.

"Oh, she is taking a bath. I know I shouldn't be telling you this, but my wife is the best sex I have ever had. I could, I swear, make sweet love to her all day and night long, she is that good," Joe said and laughed. Frank just sat there smiling and listening. *Oh I know,* he was thinking, but of course he didn't say that.

"Did you hear us having sex last night?" Joe asked. But before Frank could answer, Joe continued. "I'm sure you did, we had sex for what seemed like hours. I love having sex with Rita. I don't think I will ever get tired of sex with her, you know what I mean?" Joe asked. "I mean, when you find a woman you love having sex with that much, you can't let her go," Joe continued, still smiling.

"I can only imagine," Frank responded.

"You old devil," Joe said. "You were listening to us last night, weren't you? I know you were. Did you jack off? You can tell me, I won't be offended. I get it. I'd probably do the same if the situation was reversed," Joe added.

Frank could now feel his face getting hot with embarrassment.

"Oh no, I tried not to listen. I put my iPod on and listened to music until I fell asleep," Frank replied. "So no, I never heard much, but I hope you guys had fun," Frank added.

"Fun, is that what you call it?" Joe asked. "Yeah, we had fun alright," Joe continued and chuckled.

Sex talk with Joe was making Frank feel nervous. He had sex with his wife in that very kitchen that very morning, and here his friend was telling him about the great sex that his wife was. What was he to think? What was he to say? He had to stay cool and try to change the topic. Get Joe off the subject matter of sex before Rita returned.

"Don't you just love her ass?" Joe asked.

"What? Her ass"?" Frank replied.

"Yeah, I love her ass, man. She has the nicest ass I have ever seen. And her boobs. Oh, her boobs are to die for, don't you think?" Joe asked.

"Oh, well, I never really noticed, and I wouldn't really know," Frank replied. "I wasn't really looking at her in that way. She is your wife, after all," he added.

"Yeah, sure," Joe said. "I know you, buddy," he added. "I know that a woman who looks like Rita and dresses like Rita, with her boobs three-quarters out of her bra, is not going to go by unnoticed by you. Don't give me that line of bullshit. I know my wife is hot, and so you don't need to feel shy about telling me you think she is hot. I'm not offended. I like that other men are drooling over her. I see them all the time, gawking at her and looking her up and down. And I'm a man. I know how I feel about her, so I am sure other men are horny for her as well. You can admit it, it's really okay. I am very open about such things, and so is Rita. We have a very open relationship that way," Joe continued.

Frank wasn't sure how to take any of what Joe was now sharing with him, and he wondered if Joe somehow knew that he had crossed the line with Rita.

Just then Rita entered the kitchen.

"We have a very open relationship about what?" she asked.

"Oh, Frank and I were just discussing man stuff. You know, guy talk. That's all," Joe explained.

"Yeah, okay, but you said we have a very open relationship, and I am wondering in what regard you meant that statement?" Rita asked again.

"Oh, just that you are so sexy and men are attracted to you, and that I don't get all bent out of shape over it, that's all," Joe replied.

"Oh, that's good news," Rita said, winking at Frank.

Rita smelled amazing after her bath. Her scent followed her right into the room and went straight into Frank's nostrils. And she looked amazing as well. She dressed very provocatively, and Frank wasn't used to that style. He was used to women who dressed modestly. This new style of dress for women, he wasn't sure he fancied. His friend Louise was sexy as heck, but she always covered herself up, making it hard to see her womanly parts. And that was the kind of dress Frank was used to.

But not Rita. Rita was daring with the way she dressed. She hung her boobs right out there, and Frank wasn't used to seeing women dressed like that. Although he wasn't complaining, he also didn't want to get caught staring at her in front of Joe.

"Well, what do you guys want to do today?" Frank asked.

"Not sure," Joe replied. "With my head feeling the way it does, I don't think I am up for too much," he continued.

"I'm good with whatever," Rita responded.

"Well, I was thinking of inviting my friend Louise over for a visit. I think you guys would like her, and I'm pretty sure she would like you guys as well. She's a buddy of mine and we hang out from time to time. She's a really sweet person and highly educated. Her and I have some great conversations and discussions on things. She's definitely one of the smartest people I know. I think you guys would enjoy hanging out with her. I was thinking of inviting her over and asking her to stay for supper. I have a roast out thawing, and I was thinking we could all have a nice dinner together. What do you guys think?" Frank said.

"Oh, that sounds lovely," Joe replied. "I'm feeling hungry just thinking about it," he added and laughed.

"It won't be supper time for a few hours. If you're hungry, I can cook us some breakfast," Frank responded.

"I was going to cook breakfast earlier, but Rita went to take a bath and you were still sleeping, so I decided to wait," he added.

"Oh no, don't put yourself out. I am good with just having some toast, if you have any bread," Joe replied.

"Yeah, I have homemade bread and homemade jam if you would like some jam on your toast," Frank responded.

"Sure, that sounds good," Joe said.

So Frank got up and put two slices of bread in the toaster.

"What about you, Rita? Would you like some toast or eggs or anything?" Frank asked.

"No, I'm good. Actually, I'm not really hungry this morning for some reason" she said and smiled.

Frank immediately felt pangs of guilt remembering the morning coffee between him and Rita. He wanted to push it out of his mind, but it was hard with Rita sitting right there, smelling so sweet and looking so damn sexy.

"How's a man supposed to stop thinking about sex with her?" Frank thought.

He was trying, but it was hard. "Then Joe with all his sex talk about Rita is only making matters worse," Frank said to himself. And with that thought, feelings of guilt consumed him. "I had sex with my friend's wife and my friend has no idea... or does he?" Frank wondered.

Frank was hoping Joe had not picked up on anything between him and Rita. He was trying his best to act "normal," pretending in front of Joe that he had no interest in his wife. He would catch himself staring at her boobs, which seemed to Frank to be staring him in the face at all times — even when he wasn't looking. Even when Rita wasn't in the room. Having now seen them naked, Frank had a picture of them in his mind. It was a picture he now wanted to delete.

So, in an attempt to forget things, he brought up his friend Louise again.

"Okay, I'm going to give Louise a call," Frank said. "It's Saturday and I should call her early, as who knows what she may have planned for the day. She may be busy and not able to come over," Frank said, getting up from his seat and leaving the room to retrieve his phone.

He wanted to speak to Louise in private.

"How am I going to approach this?" he thought. "What exactly do I say to Louise?"

He knew that his friend Louise was very astute, and he worried that if she were around, she would pick up on the vibe between him and Rita, and he most definitely didn't want that to happen. But he said he was going to call her, so he felt he couldn't back out of it now.

"Hello," Louise said on the other end of the line.

"Hey," Frank said. "What are you doing?" he asked.

"Oh, not much. I just got up not long ago. Don't really have any plans for the day," Louise replied.

"Good," Frank said. "My old buddy Joe is here with his wife Rita visiting, and I thought maybe you would like to come over and meet them. They're real nice folks, and I think you would like them. I was thinking you could come over later, and the four of us could have supper together. I'm cooking a roast. What do you think?" Frank asked.

"Oh, that sounds delicious, and I'd love to meet your friends. I've heard you speak so often about your friend Joe and the old times the two of you had. What time should I come over?" Louise asked.

"Well, you can come anytime, but supper won't be ready until around five. But I was thinking we could all hang out before supper, so come over early afternoon if you want. Well, come over whenever you want, actually. It's all good," Frank replied.

"Okay, I'll be over at some point. I have a few things I have to take care of, but I'll try to make it over around mid-afternoon," Louise responded.

"Sounds great," Frank said. "Looking forward to seeing you," he added.

"You too," Louise said. "I've not been by your place in a while. I'm looking forward to seeing you. I miss you," she added.

"Miss you too," Frank replied. "Okay, see you later then," he said, and the two of them ended the call.

Frank returned to the kitchen, but Joe was absent.

"Where did Joe go?" he asked.

Rita was sitting there rolling a joint. "Oh, he went to take a shower. Said his head was aching and he thought taking a shower might help," she replied. "I hope you don't mind me rolling up some of your delicious medicine. It was sitting there and I didn't think you would care. I wasn't going to smoke it until you got back," Rita added.

"Oh, that's no problem," Frank replied, smiling. "I was planning on rolling one up anyway, so all the better that you already started," he added and smiled.

"Good," Rita said. "Didn't think you would mind. I really like this pot. You're a good grower," she added.

"Thanks," Frank responded.

"You're also a good lover," Rita said, winking and smiling at Frank.

"Shush..." Frank said, putting his index finger up to his lips. "Don't talk about that, and you never know who might hear you. They have ears, you know!" he said, smiling.

"Yeah, well, I don't think Joe can hear me. He's in the shower," Rita said, smiling back at Frank.

"Come on, let's have a smoke and maybe you could put another pot of that delicious coffee on too," Rita said. "I never got to drink much of it this morning. I was too preoccupied with other things," she added and winked at Frank.

"Yeah, I know what you mean," Frank replied and chuckled a little.

But wasn't really funny, because he knew he had crossed the line with his buddy's wife, and the guilt he felt inside was tremendous— almost as strong as the passion he felt towards Rita. Now that they had had sex, he was even more attracted to her than before.

"What am I going to do?" he asked himself. "How long can I keep this up?" he thought. "How long are they planning to stay here?" he asked himself.

They had not discussed how long they planned to stay, but regardless, Frank knew he had to try to restrain himself from his desire for Rita.

He wondered why he had not even asked them how long they planned on staying, but he figured chances were they would not be staying more than a week.

"A week is a standard visit," he thought. "Yeah, a week is probably how long they plan to stay here," he said to himself.

And it was already day three now, so he figured he should be able to contain himself for the remainder of the time they were there.

"Maybe I should just ask her how long they plan on staying," he thought. But then he opted not to, thinking Rita might think by him asking that, that he wanted them to leave. So he opted not to ask her.

Frank made a fresh pot of his organic coffee that Rita enjoyed so much, and the two of them sat at the kitchen table having their coffee and smoking the joint Rita had rolled. "Man, do I ever dig this pot," she said again. "It's so smooth and I love the stone I get from it," she added.

"Oh, yeah, it is pretty good stuff, even if I do say so myself," Frank said and smiled.

Once the joint was finished, Rita began asking about Louise.

"So, who exactly is this Louise woman?"

"Oh, she's a good friend. I met her when I first moved here. She's a really nice person. Really smart," Frank answered.

"Yeah, but what does she look like?" Rita asked.

"Oh, Louise is a good-looking lady and very well put together," Frank said and smiled. "And she is really down to earth. I think you and Joe will really like her," he added.

"I'm looking forward to meeting her," Rita said, but inside she was already feeling a sense of competition.

"Good," Frank responded. "She said she'd be over sometime this afternoon," he continued. "She's looking forward to meeting Joe, as she has heard me speak of him before. I've told her about the adventures Joe and I had in the past, way before he met you," he added and smiled.

"Yeah, Joe has told me a few stories as well," Rita responded.

"Yup, we go back a long way," Frank added.

Just then, he remembered again that his friendship with Joe had always been solid, always good, always loyal. And feelings of guilt once again welled up inside him.

"I feel terrible that I had sex with you," he suddenly blurted out.

"What!" Rita said. "Really? You feel terrible? Why?" she asked.

"Well, because you're my friend's wife, for one thing," Frank replied.

"Oh, that," Rita said. "Don't worry. He is never going to know. I sure as hell am not going to tell him, and I don't think you are either. So don't worry about it. Trust me, with the amount of sleeping pills I gave him, he never heard a thing," she added and smiled.

"You're terrible," Frank said. "How can you just brush it off like that?" he asked. "He's your husband! Don't you care about being loyal to him? Don't you care that you and I crossed the line?"

"Not really," Rita answered. "Joe knows I have a very healthy appetite when it comes to sex," she continued.

"Yes, but with him," Frank added.

"Yeah, well, things happen," Rita responded. "And I hope they happen again," she added, pushing her chest out.

"Stop it," Frank said. "He could be down here at any minute and I don't want to have a hard-on when he walks in the room."

"It's just that easy, eh"?" Rita said and laughed out loud.

"Yes, unfortunately, it is," Frank replied. "What can I say? You turn me right on. I can barely contain myself. I would love to bend you over this table and have sex with you right here and now," he added.

He couldn't believe he had just said that to her. What was he thinking, talking to her like that with Joe just upstairs? He had to do better. Maybe when Louise got there, it would help.

"I can hope," he thought.

Rita loved hearing him speak that way. She only wished they were alone and could carry out his suggestion. It frustrated her that Joe was there, even if he was her husband. She envisioned living there, yes, living there alone with Frank. But then she realized that was most likely not going to happen given her current circumstances.

"No, we can't be doing that. It is too close for comfort, if you know what I mean," she said, winking at Frank.

"Oh, I know," Frank responded. "I was just dreaming, that's all," he added and smiled.

"Dream away," Rita replied. "There's nothing wrong with dreaming," she said, smiling.

She was dreaming too, but she dared not express what she was dreaming, as she didn't want to scare Frank off by her thoughts of staying and living there with him. It was one thing to have a fling with him while visiting, but she wasn't sure moving in was part of Frank's agenda. And she wondered about his friend Louise coming over.

She didn't like other women being present in her world. She preferred to have all the attention to herself. But she would play along and try to be nice to Louise. She just hoped she wasn't too beautiful or sexy.

Already she was feeling a little jealous of Louise, and she hadn't even met her yet.

"She is most likely just some plain-looking country girl and nothing to worry about," Rita thought.

Still, she was nervous about meeting her and would have preferred that Frank had not invited her over. But she knew she couldn't say that. Joe would wonder why if she protested her coming over.

"Are you off in la la land?" Frank suddenly asked, as she had been sitting there silent and appeared to be off in another world.

"Oh no," Rita said. "I was just thinking about your friend coming over this afternoon, is all. You're sure she's just a friend, right?" Rita asked.

Frank smiled. He knew what she was getting at.

"Yes, she is a good friend," he answered.

"Have you slept with her?" Rita asked.

But just then, Joe walked into the kitchen.

"Slept with who?" Joe asked.

"Oh, no one," Rita responded.

"No, no... who were you talking about?" Joe demanded.

"Oh," Frank said, "we were talking about my friend Louise. She is coming over around mid-afternoon and will join us for supper."

"Excellent," Joe replied. "I'm looking forward to meeting her. I've heard you speak of her when you and I were talking on the phone. So I am looking forward to actually meeting this wonder woman," Joe continued and smiled.

Frank smiled as well, but Rita was struck by the words "wonder woman."

"What?" she wondered. "Does that mean exactly?"

Then she thought, "Who is this chick? Do I have to worry?"

And with those thoughts, she suddenly felt anxious and felt like she wanted to go fix herself up more.

"Maybe I should change my clothes," she thought. "Wear something more revealing to make sure I keep Frank's attention focused on me and not 'wonder woman' Louise," she said to herself.

She didn't want Louise taking the show from her, nor did she want Frank paying more attention to Louise than he was to her. She needed Frank's undivided attention, but how was she going to achieve that with Joe in the room, she wondered.

"That will be tricky," she said to herself. "Should I give him more sleeping pills?" she thought. "No, no, I can't do that," she thought. "I need those for nighttime, when I can sneak into Frank's room and fuck him for real," she said to herself.

And suddenly, she was turned on just thinking about having sex with Frank in his bedroom, on his bed. She could not wait for nighttime because of it.

"Are you with us, Rita?" Joe asked.

"Oh, yeah, I was just thinking about something," Rita said, smiling. "Actually," she added, "I was thinking I should go and do some things before Louise gets here. If you guys don't mind, I'm going to go upstairs for a bit," she continued.

"No problem, Honey," Joe responded, tapping her on the butt as she walked past him and exited the kitchen.

"Can I help you with dinner?" Joe asked.

"Sure," Frank replied. "You can help me peel some veggies if you want."

"Sounds good. Bring them to me," Joe said, smiling.

So Frank brought the carrots and potatoes over to the kitchen table and the two of them began preparing the vegetables for supper, talking about old times and laughing.

"I'm really looking forward to meeting Louise," Joe said.

"Yeah, she's really great," Frank responded.

Once the vegetables were prepared, Frank took the pots and put them on the stove.

"My head is still hurting," Joe said. "The shower helped somewhat, but I still have a faint ache. I think I will go rest for a while before Louise shows up," he added.

"Okay, cool. I hope your head feels better. Did the Advil help?" Frank asked.

"Yeah, I think it did for sure," Joe responded. "I'm just a little wheezy for some reason. I think if I rest for a time, I will feel much improved," he added and got up to leave the room.

"Okay, have a good rest. I am just going to finish preparing for supper and then I think I will rest as well," Frank responded. "And thanks for all your help with the veggies," he added.

"Oh, you're most welcome," Joe replied and waved his arm back as he exited the kitchen.

Once Joe was out of the room, Frank began thinking about how fun it was having Joe around, and he felt so guilty about what had happened between him and Rita.

He loved his friend Joe. He always had. He was one of the best friends Frank ever had. And the guilt grew more and more as he thought about how much Joe really meant to him over the years.

"How could I have had sex with his wife?" Frank asked himself. "How can I be drooling over her? What is wrong with me?" he thought. "Am I that big of a fucking wimp?" he asked.

He never considered himself to be a whore before this, but what he had done was now making him wonder. He felt like crying. He was so hurt for what he had done. How he had lost control.

"How could I have done this to my longtime buddy? A man who has always been there for me?" he thought.

And with that, tears started to well up in his eyes. Then tears rolled down his cheeks and leaked onto his neck. He felt like a piece of shit in that moment.

He himself could not understand how all of this had happened, and he resolved right there and then to put a stop to it for real. He would resist Rita no matter what it took, he said to himself.

"Thank God Louise was coming over," he thought. He would use her as a buffer. Maybe he would ask her to stay the night. They did have a "stay over night" thing that they did once in a while. It was just a thing they shared between the two of them, no strings attached. So maybe that would be the thing to get Rita off his mind and to prevent her from sneaking into his room once she had drugged her husband.

Drugged her husband. The words suddenly hit Frank.

"What in fuck am I doing? I had sex with my friend's wife, while he was out cold from the sleeping pills that she gave to him!" he said to himself in dismay.

He could not believe the situation he was suddenly in. "So much for having people come visit," he thought. "I'd never have invited Joe if I knew all of this was going to happen," he said to himself. Still, he could not deny that he had so enjoyed having sex with Rita that very morning.

He was a man, after all, and Rita was a knockout.

"Joe should tell her to dress better and cover herself up," Frank thought. "If she were my wife, I would want her to dress differently, and I wouldn't want her exposing her chest around other men, friends or not," he thought.

"But she's not my wife, she's Joe's wife, and really it is none of my business, I guess.".

Plus, he could not deny that he loved the show Rita was putting on in the way she dressed. Even if he couldn't have sex with her anymore, he figured there was no harm in looking.

"That's what I'll do," he said to himself. "I won't touch her again. I will just enjoy looking at her and thinking about what is underneath those clothes. I will fantasize about her and masturbate, but I won't have sex with her again," he swore to himself.

The house was quiet now, so quiet Frank could hear the ticking of the clock on the wall in the kitchen. He had prepared everything and suddenly felt like he too should take a rest before Louise showed up. But first, he wanted to jump in the shower.

"If Louise wants to stay the night, I want to be clean," he thought to himself. "I sure as hell don't want Louise smelling Rita on me from the sex we had this morning," he said to himself as he headed upstairs to the bathroom.

He finished his shower and went directly to his bedroom to read and rest, and maybe even sleep for a time. Dinner was all prepared, so he had nothing to worry about there, and it wasn't long before he had fallen asleep.

And he must have fallen into a deep sleep, because the next thing he knew, Joe was standing over him.

"Frank, wake up. Your friend Louise is here."

"Oh fuck," Frank replied, being jolted awake. "I fell asleep. What time is it?" he asked.

"It's four p.m., my friend. You must have been tired, you've been asleep for quite a while," Joe replied, smiling.

"I'm sorry," Frank said. "I was more tired than I realized I guess," he continued, now getting up from his bed.

"You go ahead, I'll be right down," he told Joe.

"Okay, we are just all hanging in the kitchen. I'll tell Louise you'll be right down," Joe replied as he left Frank's bedroom and headed back down to the kitchen.

Frank headed to the washroom and splashed some water on his face. His hair was messed up from having fallen asleep with it wet.

"Thank goodness I came to the washroom before going downstairs," he thought. "I wouldn't want them to see me with this crazy looking hairdo," he said and smiled. He wet his hair and fixed it as properly as he could.

"That's good enough," he said. "I'm not trying to impress anyone," he thought.

Frank had the kind of good looks that it didn't really matter if his hair was messed up. His handsomeness was natural and he knew it. He knew women were always checking him out and he quite enjoyed all the female attention he got based solely on his good looks.

One time a woman told him he could have been a movie star if he had wanted to be. He smiled thinking about that compliment. He had never forgotten it, even though it was quite a few years ago.

He smiled at himself in the mirror.

"Remember now... no more fucking around with Joe's wife. You are a solid friend and you need to act like one. Behave yourself. Focus on Louise and ignore Rita as much as possible," he told himself.

He was trying to brace himself for the situation of having now three people in his home, and especially not giving away, in front of Louise, his lust for his friend's wife.

Slowly, he walked down the stairs towards the kitchen.

"Be good," he kept on repeating to himself as he walked.

Chapter Four

The Other Woman

Once in the kitchen, Frank went directly to Louise and gave her a huge hug. "So good to see yea," he said, giving her a peck on the cheek. Louise looked amazing. "What has she done to herself?" Frank thought upon seeing her. He hadn't seen her in a while as they both had been busy.

"You look amazing," Frank said.

"Oh thanks," Louise responded, smiling. She was aware she looked good. She had been taking extra care of herself, and she was happy that Frank had noticed. She had a crush on Frank, but she never let him know it. She thought it might ruin their friendship, so she opted not to say anything. Plus, she figured deep down he already knew anyway.

"I guess you guys have already introduced yourselves," Frank said, pointing to Joe and Rita who were seated at the kitchen table.

"Oh yes," Louise said, smiling. "I have officially met your house guests and friends," she continued, smiling at Joe and Rita.

"Good," Frank replied. "Let's have a smoke of medicine and maybe a glass of some wine I made," he added, smiling.

"Your homemade wine is to die for," Louise responded. "I just love it. What kind did you make this time?" she asked.

"Well, I have wild strawberry, I have wild blueberry, and I have dandelion as well," Frank replied. "Which one would you guys prefer?" he asked.

"Wow!" Rita exclaimed. "You are just full of surprises. You even make your own wine, you grow your own medicine, and your own food. Is there anything you don't do?" she asked, laughing.

"Oh, he's a very talented man," Louise replied, smiling at Frank.

"Come on ladies, you're embarrassing me now," Frank said, looking shy.

"You're making me look bad," Joe said. "I have tons of money, but not all the skills you have," he added. "But that's okay, right Rita?" he asked.

"What?" Rita replied. "Oh yes, Honey, you have talents too," she continued.

Rita was now distracted by Louise. She was sizing her up and down. "She is pretty for sure and sexy too, even if she is covering up her figure with the clothes she is wearing. I can tell that much," Rita thought to herself. And she was sure both Joe and Frank could tell as well.

"Well, since you guys haven't said what kind of wine you prefer, I am choosing the wild strawberry," Frank finally said.

"Yes, please," Louise replied. "I love your homemade wine. I swear I'd be a full-blown alcoholic if I lived here with you," she said and laughed.

"You're too kind," Frank replied while pouring them all a glass of wine.

"Cheers everyone," Frank said, picking up his glass in a toast. "Here's to good friends and good times," he continued.

"I'll drink to that," Joe said.

"Me too," Rita and Louise both said at the same time, and they all took a sip of Frank's homemade wine.

"Um mm," Rita said after taking a sip. "I see what you mean now, Louise. It is delicious," she added.

"Yes, it is very good," Joe agreed.

"Awww, thanks," Frank responded.

"When is dinner going to be ready?" Louise asked. "I don't mean to sound rude, but I hardly ate anything all day in anticipation for dinner here," she added.

"Well, it is all prepared," Frank replied. "And the roast has been cooking on low for a while now," he added. "Speaking of which, I hope one of you guys checked on it while I was sleeping. I didn't mean to sleep that long," Frank added.

"Oh yes, no worries my friend," Joe responded. "We've both been keeping an eye on it. It's all good and looks absolutely delicious," Joe continued.

"Good then, and thank you," Frank replied. "I feel bad that I slept so long, so rude of me with house guests," he added.

"Not a problem my friend," Joe responded. "You must have needed the rest."

Immediately Frank's mind went to thinking of him and Rita, how they had sex in that very kitchen that very morning. He was tired alright, but he dared not say why.

"Okay then, all I need to do is cook the veggies," he said and went over to the stove to turn the pot of veggies on.

"Can I do anything to help?" Louise asked.

"No, everything is taken care of, but thanks for asking," Frank replied. "For now, let's just enjoy our wine and a smoke of medicine, shall we?"

"Yes," they all agreed.

As the food cooked and they enjoyed their wine and smoke, Rita was again drawn in by Louise. She was smart. Rita could tell by the way she spoke. And Rita was feeling a little intimidated.

"Plus, she has nice boobs, even if they were covered up," Rita thought to herself. "She also has a half-decent ass," she thought.

"What if Frank is in love with Louise and just hadn't let on," she thought. "Naw, that can't be the case. If that were true, she'd be living here with him, wouldn't she?" she thought.

Rita looked even more amazing than usual. She had spent extra time making herself look as good as she possibly could, and she was already a complete knock out. Still, she was already feeling jealous toward Louise. The way Frank hugged her when he saw her and kissed her on the cheek. The way he had told her how good she looked. But she didn't want to let her jealousy show, so she tried her best to be as sweet as possible to Louise. Plus, being sweet to Louise might get her brownie points with Frank, she was thinking, and take away any suspicious thoughts Joe might have about her and Frank. So she attempted to engage Louise in conversation, but Louise, it was obvious, was more interested in talking with the men.

Soon enough the veggies were cooked and they all sat down to eat.

"This is soooo good," Louise said, taking a big scoop of food.

"Yes, yes, it is... I agree," Rita added.

"For sure," Joe agreed. "Frank and I did the veggies," he added in an attempt to take at least some credit for the delicious meal.

"How's your head feeling?" Frank asked Joe.

"Oh, it is better now, thanks," Joe replied. "The pain seems to have gone away for now anyway," he continued. "It was really bad when I woke up. But the Advil you gave me and the shower I took, plus resting, really did the trick," he added.

"Right on, happy to hear," Frank said, as he and Rita both looked at each other. They both knew why Joe had a headache. It was due to the sleeping pills Rita had given him. And with that thought, the guilt started to well up inside of Frank again.

"Oh no," he said to himself. "Focus on Louise... Focus on Louise," he told himself. And so he started asking Louise what she had been up to since he had last seen her.

Louise was happy to oblige Frank and happy for his attention. She went on and on about all she had been doing until Rita spoke up and said, "Okay, this is boring! Let's put on some music and dance."

"That's a great idea, but let's finish eating first and clean up the mess," Frank suggested.

"You're a party popper," Rita said, pouting.

Rita was getting a buzz on and Frank could see it.

"Oh no," he thought. "I've never seen her when she is drinking. Maybe bringing the wine out was a bad idea," he thought. "What if she has loose lips when she's drunk and says something in front of Joe?" he thought. "Fuck, this could be horrible," he said to himself. "Maybe I had better put the wine away before she has had a chance to have any more," he thought. But then he thought that if he did that, it would make him look rude.

"What am I going to do?" he asked himself. "Pray. Pray for the best. Pray for the best," he thought to himself.

As soon as they had finished the meal, Rita brought up dancing again, and this time Frank was all good with her suggestion. He himself, as well as Louise and Joe, were all getting a good buzz on and dancing sounded like fun.

"Sounds like fun," Louise said, getting up from her chair at the table.

Louise was a good dancer, and she loved to dance, especially with Frank. She figured Frank would dance with her since Rita was married to Joe, so she was all game for it.

But Rita had the idea of doing some dirty dancing with Frank. "It's okay if I do it while dancing," she thought. "Joe won't mind and will get a kick out of it," she said to herself.

The kitchen in Frank's house was large enough for the dance party, so Frank put on some music and the four of them began to dance. Before long, Rita was bending over while pushing Louise aside and sticking her ass up against Frank. Without thinking, Frank put his hands on her waist and motioned as if he was making out with her. Then suddenly he realized what he was doing and quickly removed his hands. Louise and Joe were both busy dancing and hadn't noticed.

"Thank goodness no one saw that," Frank thought.

But Rita was looking at him, still bent over and wondering why he had stopped all of a sudden.

"Come on baby," she said to him, "what's your problem?"

"Shut up," Frank was thinking in his mind, but he laughed and gently pushed her away.

Rita looked around and suddenly realized she was out of line. Her husband and Louise were both right there, so she straightened herself up and started dancing normally. She then began flirting with her husband, and when she did, Louise was quick to do likewise with Frank. Frank grabbed Louise and brought her close to him, but Rita was not happy with what she was seeing. She wondered if Frank was getting hard, like he did when she rubbed up against him. She looked at his penis to see if she could notice any difference, but she wasn't sure. His pants were loose, so it was hard to tell. However, she could tell Louise was thoroughly enjoying all of Frank's attention.

Joe was enjoying the attention from Rita. "You are so sexy, Babe," he said to Rita, holding her close and feeling her ass. Pushing on her ass, making her body come closer to his. "Do you feel that?" he asked Rita. "That's my penis getting hard for you," he said and smiled. Rita could feel his penis up against her, and so she answered, "Oh yes, baby, I can feel it." But it wasn't the penis she wanted. And truly, she was more interested in what was happening between Frank and Louise than she was in Joe's lust for her.

Rita couldn't help but stare at Frank and Louise, who were all up close and personal now, and seeing the two of them made her jealous and angry. Suddenly, she pushed Joe away from her. "What in fuck are you doing?" she said, breaking up the party all of a sudden.

"What? What do you mean, what am I doing? I'm enjoying my sexy wife," Joe responded and grabbed her to bring her back close to him again.

"Stop it!" Rita exclaimed. "I want to dance with Frank for a while," she said. But both Frank and Louise pretended not to hear her and kept on carrying on with each other.

Joe just stood there, bewildered looking. "What is wrong with you, Rita?" he asked. "Are you not turned on by me anymore?" he added.

"Of course I am turned on by you," Rita responded. "Just not here and now, is that okay?" she said sarcastically.

"Fine!" Joe replied. "I'm going up to bed. Are you going to join me, or are you going to sit here staring at Frank and Louise making out?" he asked.

"You go on ahead, I'll be up shortly," Rita responded. "And I'm not staring at Frank and Louise either. I just want to finish my wine and maybe have another smoke, if that is okay with you and with Frank, since it is his wine and smoke," she said.

"Whatever," Joe replied. "Don't be too long. I'll be waiting for yea," he added and winked at Rita as he exited the kitchen and headed upstairs.

As soon as Joe was out of sight, Rita made her way over to Frank and Louise and tried to impose herself in between them.

"Share, girl," she said to Louise. "Don't yea know how to share?" Rita continued, smiling at Louise and pushing herself in between them.

Louise was a little taken back by Rita's actions and words and wasn't quite sure what to say. "Isn't she a married woman?" Louise thought. "Is she trying to hit on Frank?" Louise wondered. But Louise, being Louise, backed off and let Rita move in closer to Frank.

"Oh now ladies, relax," Frank said, and it was obvious he had a good buzz going at that point.

"Who wants to relax?" Rita asked. "When there's a handsome dude like you around," she added, while putting her hand up against his penis, checking to see if he was hard.

"Louise must have turned him on," she thought. "Fucking bitch." "But she doesn't make him as hard as I do," she thought and smiled.

"Where did Joe go?" Frank finally asked.

"Oh, he went up to bed," Rita responded. "He was tired and horny," she said, laughing. "He is waiting for me up there now. So I suppose I should go service him," she said, smiling.

"Okay, yes, you should," Frank replied, holding onto Louise around the waist. "You shouldn't keep him waiting," Frank added.

"It was nice to meet you," Rita said to Louise. "Maybe we will see you again before we leave," she added, indicating that she didn't expect Louise to be there in the morning.

"Oh yes, nice to meet you as well," Louise responded. "No doubt you will be seeing more of me before you guys leave," she added.

That was not what Rita wanted to hear, but she forced a smile anyway. Then Louise asked, "By the way, when are you guys leaving? Frank never said how long you were going to be here."

Rita had not thought of leaving. She didn't even want to think of it.

"Who knows," Rita replied. "No specific plans as of yet. I guess we will be leaving when Frank kicks us out," she said and laughed a little.

"I'm not going to kick you guys out any time soon," Frank replied, but he wondered, truly, what Rita meant by her remark.

Rita wasn't happy. She didn't really want to go and "service" her husband, but she felt it was her wifely duty, so off to the bedroom she went. "See you all later," she said and winked at Frank, and he knew exactly what she meant.

Once Rita was out of the room, Frank began kissing Louise hard and passionately.

"OOOO," Louise moaned. "I like it," she continued. "Where is all this passion coming from?" she asked. "Never mind," she added. "I don't care... I like it. Give me more," she said. So Frank continued kissing her passionately, while rubbing his hands all over her body.

"Want to stay the night with me?" Frank whispered in her ear while they were making out in the kitchen.

"I'd love to," Louise said, now breathing heavily and feeling sexually aroused.

"Let's go to bed then," Frank said.

"Yes, let's," Louise responded. And off they went to Frank's bedroom.

Once in the room and lying on the bed, they could hear Joe and Rita having sex.

"Wow, they sound like they are having some wild sex," Louise said and smiled.

"Yea, that is how they go on every night," Frank replied, smiling back at her.

"How do you get any sleep?" Louise asked, laughing.

"Oh, I put in these," Frank said, holding up the earplugs to his iPod.

"Oh right. Yea, you would need those with those two having sex down the hall," Louise responded, still laughing.

But the truth was, the sound of Rita and Joe having sex was turning both of them on. Frank quickly slipped out of his clothes and got under the covers. Louise stood by the side of the bed undressing, as Frank watched her. She was sexy, there was no doubt about it.

"How can a woman who looks like that stay single?" Frank wondered to himself, as he gazed at her naked body. He had seen her naked before, but it had been awhile. And every time he saw Louise naked, it seemed different somehow.

They were both undressed and naked now under the covers, and suddenly Frank remembered what Louise felt like when she was naked next to him.

"You feel so good," he said to her.

"You do too," she responded.

Frank was happy just to have access to Louise's breasts. He swore he could amuse himself with them for hours, he liked them so much.

"You really love my boobs, eh?" Louise said, smiling.

"You're right, I do," Frank replied, smiling back at her. "I wish they were mine," he said and laughed. "If I had boobs like that, I'd be busy playing with them all the time and never get anything done," he continued, and they both struck up laughing.

"I always say, 'show a man a boob and he'll follow yea anywhere,'" Louise said and laughed.

But Frank somehow didn't find her statement all that amusing. He knew it was true. "But did women realize things like that?" he wondered. "Apparently, they do," he thought, "at least some of them anyway."

"Enough talk," Frank said, putting his hand on her ass, pushing her vagina against his hard penis.

"I was hard watching you undress," Frank said.

"You really know how to turn a woman on, I'll give you that," she added, smiling and pushing her vagina up against him.

Then they began having sex and enjoying one another, but Frank kept on being distracted, thinking of Rita.

"Stop thinking about Rita," he told himself, and it would work for a while, but then the thoughts of Rita would come back again.

"Wow, that was great," Louise said with a big smile on her face.

"It sure was," Frank responded, smiling back at her.

They both noticed that the house was now silent.

"Are you still frisky?" Louise asked.

"I'm always frisky around you," Frank replied, kissing her on the lips.

But the truth was, both of them were now tired, and it wasn't long before Louise had fallen fast asleep. But not Frank. Frank couldn't seem to get to sleep. He was worried about Rita showing up.

"What if Rita comes to my room? What am I going to say? How am I going to explain it to Louise?" These thoughts were now running through his mind.

"This can't be happening," he thought. "Surely Rita has had enough sex for one night if the noise coming from their bedroom is any indication," he said to himself.

But he also knew that Rita seemed to have an overactive sexual appetite.

"Shit, this is not good. I have to stay awake and head her off," he thought. But his eyes were growing tired, and he could feel himself drifting off. He was losing the fight to stay awake, and it wasn't long before he was snoring to beat the band.

Rita wasn't sure if Louise was there or not, but she so wanted to head down to see Frank. All the time Joe and she were having sex, she was imagining she was having sex with Frank. Joe thought she was enjoying him and was feeling all proud for how she was reacting to his thrust, but Rita was dreaming of Frank the entire time.

And when she'd open her eyes and see Joe there, she'd quickly close them and brush it off, and she didn't even feel guilty about it. She had sex with Joe so many times now, it was custom for her to fantasize about something. But it wasn't a fantasy this time, it was a real thing. He was a real person.

"Maybe Joe does the same thing?" she thought, and she didn't even care if he did. But he acted like he was still very attracted to her. He was constantly grabbing her and telling her how sexy she looked. So she figured he was still very turned on by her. She just kind of wished she could say the same.

She'd never been turned on by a guy the way she was by Frank. Even the smell of him turned her on. He smelled like a man, and she'd not smelled what she considered a "real man" in years. She'd almost forgotten what a real man smelled like.

Joe, and all his business associates, always smelled like cologne. Rita liked some of the smells, but some of them she found repugnant. Frank, on the other hand, had a scent all his own, and it wasn't from a bottle bought in a store. No, it was the smell of sweat and pheromones—pheromones that sent Rita into a horny fit every time she smelled him.

She wondered if Frank was asleep yet, and she really wanted to go to his room. She had given Joe more sleeping pills, but she didn't feel guilty, as he had asked her for some, saying he wasn't sleeping well. But she knew, in the long term, she couldn't just keep feeding pills to him. Sooner or later, she was going to have to stop doing that. But for now, it was working just fine, and so she wasn't going to worry about it. For now, all she could think about was having sex again with Frank.

And as the thought grew, before she knew it, she was at Frank's bedroom door. Frank was fast asleep, she knew, because she could hear him snoring.

"Is Louise in there with him?" Rita wondered. She slowly and as quietly as possible opened the bedroom door. She tried to look to see if she could see anyone in bed with him, but it was too dark in the room to see. So, she opted to venture in further, and when she did, she saw Louise lying there in bed beside Frank.

"That fucking bitch," Rita said, as she gazed at the two of them lying there naked. She could see Louise's boob hanging out from under the covers. It was making her horny, but mad at the same time.

She knew, logically, that she had no grounds to be angry at Frank. She was, after all, a married woman, and he was a single guy. But the fact that they had already had sex, in Rita's mind, meant that it counted for something at least. She couldn't believe he would invite Louise to stay the night—and obviously had sex with her too.

"What a guy," she said to herself. "Maybe he's not the man I think he is," she thought.

"I know what I'll do," she said. "I'll seduce Louise," she added.

And so, she gently climbed in bed beside Louise, Frank on the opposite side. She cupped Louise's exposed breast in her hand.

"Oh nice," she thought to herself. "No wonder Frank wanted to have sex with her. She is sexy," Rita thought as her hands roamed Louise's body.

Louise suddenly felt aroused and started responding to Rita's sexual touch. Then she looked up and saw it was Rita fondling her, not Frank.

"What are you doing?" Louise whispered in a surprised tone of voice.

"What does it look like I'm doing?" Rita replied, kissing Louise's neck. "I'm attracted to you, Louise," Rita said. "I want to have sex with you. I was turned on by you the minute you walked in the house today," she added.

"How did you know I was here?" Louise asked.

"I just figured you were. I saw how horny the two of you looked when I left the kitchen to go to bed," Rita replied.

Louise was satisfied with the answers Rita provided, and she had to admit Rita was turning her on. The attraction was mutual. And so Louise laid back and let Rita do her thing.

"I've never been with a woman before, and I'm just so excited I feel like I could explode. I don't think I have ever been this turned on with a man. Now I am thinking maybe I am gay!" Louise said.

"Relax," Rita replied. "It's just because it's your first time. The first time is always exciting, because it's new and mysterious. Don't worry, you're probably not gay," Rita added.

"Okay, I'll take your word for it," Louise replied. "But I'm telling you, I have never ever been this turned on with any man, first time or not," she added.

Just then Frank began to stir from his sleep. He opened one eye and saw the two of them there in bed beside him. At first he was unsure exactly what he was seeing, because it looked like the two of them were making out.

"Could it be?" he thought. "Naw, it can't be," he answered himself. But then he realized he was seeing what he thought he was seeing.

"Holy shit," he thought. "I had no woman, and now I have two beautiful, sexy chicks in my bed! Did I die and go to heaven?" he thought to himself and smiled.

Just then Rita noticed that Frank had woken up and was looking at her and Louise making out.

"Hey baby," Rita said to him softly. "I see you have company in your bed," she added, while at the same time shoving her boobs in his face.

Louise, at this point, didn't know what to think.

"What in fuck is going on here?" she thought. "Why is Rita now hitting on Frank and acting like it is normal? She is married to Frank's friend. Have the two of them been having an affair behind

Joe's back? Where is Joe? And why is Rita not worried about getting caught?" All these questions were now running through Louise's mind.

"Come over here," Rita said, motioning to Louise. "We can share, can't we?" she asked. "He's got enough for both of us," Rita added, grabbing Frank's penis.

Louise couldn't resist. She'd never been with a woman, and she'd never had a threesome, so she figured this might be her one and only chance to have that experience. And for good or for bad, she was going for it. She'd think about the consequences, if there were any, tomorrow or whenever. Right now, she was just going to go for it, she told herself.

Frank was laying there in quasi shock over all that was happening.

So the three of them had sex, and all three of them seemed to be enjoying themselves immensely.

"Oh wow," Louise said. "That was awesome, Frank," she continued.

Underneath Rita's breath, she was telling Louise to fuck off. She hated seeing Frank having sex with anyone but her, even if she was married.

"I need to go to the washroom," Frank said and quickly exited the bedroom and headed toward the bathroom.

Louise laid back on the bed.

"That was so fucking amazing," she said to Rita with the biggest smile on her face. "I don't know what you did to him, but sex was better tonight than it has ever been," Louise said to Rita.

Rita had no response. She didn't want to hear it. All she could think about was having Frank all to herself. She didn't want to share him.

Soon Frank was back from the washroom.

"I need to get back to my bedroom," Rita said as she got up from the bed to leave. She bent over on Frank's side of the bed and kissed him on the lips.

"See you at breakfast," she said, shoving her boobs in his face, just to remind him.

"Yes, you'd better get back to your room," Frank said. "See you next time," he said as Rita exited the bedroom.

Then suddenly, he realized he was now alone again with Louise and that she probably had a ton of questions for him.

"I know you probably have questions for me right now," he said. "But I am beat tired from all the sex we all had, and I really need to sleep. We'll talk about all of this tomorrow, if you want. Or we don't have to talk about it at all, if you don't want to," he continued.

Frank was hoping she'd say she didn't want to talk about it at all and that she was willing to just let it go. Chalk it up to experience. But inside he knew better. Louise was not the kind of person to just let it go. But she was tired too, and so she agreed that they would talk about it the next day. For now, they both needed sleep. So they snuggled up together and fell asleep.

Rita was now back in the bedroom with Joe. She slowly climbed back into bed. She'd get up early and take a shower before Joe woke up, she thought.

"I can't take a shower now. I'm just too exhausted," she said to herself. And she had no worries, because Joe was out like a light.

She was exhausted, but she couldn't get to sleep. All she could think about was Frank being in bed with Louise right down the hallway. She hated Louise already.

"Fucking whore, why did she have to show up here?" Rita thought. "Now she is ruining everything! I don't like her. I wish Frank had never invited her over here. Who was she anyway? And if she was so great, why wasn't Frank in a relationship with her already? She must not be that great," Rita thought.

"She's just a fuck buddy. That's all she is," Rita concluded. "I don't have to worry about her. She'll be gone in the morning, and I'll tell Frank not to invite her back here again while Joe and I are staying here. I'll make up some excuse why I don't want him to have her over again. And I'll fuck him so good tomorrow night that he'll never even think of her again," Rita told herself.

But she wasn't convinced it would work. Louise was Frank's good friend, and the two of them had apparently been friends for a long time. So getting rid of her might not be as easy as getting rid of women around her husband. Yet, Rita was determined to somehow get her gone, and the faster, the better.

She knew she was being a hypocrite and unfair to Frank in thinking that way, but she didn't care. She just wanted Louise out of the picture. She wanted Frank all to herself, even if she was a married woman. Finally, Rita fell asleep, and all was quiet in the house until morning.

When Rita woke up, she went directly to the shower. She wanted to look good in case Louise was still there.

"I have to show Frank that I am much prettier and sexier than Louise," she thought. "I need to make him desire me and not even think about her," she said to herself.

Joe was still fast asleep and would be for some time. Rita wasn't sure how many pills he had taken—she had just handed him the bottle. He was, she thought, responsible for himself. She wasn't his mommy. And it seemed to Rita he was dead asleep, so she figured he must have taken a few of them.

Once cleaned up, she headed down to the kitchen. She was hoping Louise had already left, and she listened to see if she could hear her talking as she started down the stairs. She'd looked in Frank's room briefly as she passed by his door, and they both were gone, so she knew they were most likely in the kitchen having coffee. Or maybe, if she was lucky, Frank was down there all alone and Louise had left.

She could hope. But to her disappointment, when she got to the kitchen, Louise was sitting there at the table with Frank.

"Good morning, beautiful," Frank said to Rita as she walked into the kitchen. She had done herself up real nice. She wasn't going to be outdone by Louise.

Rita smiled a big smile. "Good morning, handsome," she said back to Frank. "Oh, and good morning, Louise," she said, looking at Louise.

"Good morning," Louise responded, smiling at Rita. Louise thought Rita was sexy. Heck, who didn't think Rita was sexy? She was sexy, that was obvious to anyone who had eyes.

"There's a fresh pot of coffee there if you want one. Help yourself!" Frank said, pointing to the full pot of coffee on the kitchen counter.

"Don't mind if I do," Rita replied, going to make herself a coffee.

The room was silent, as if none of them knew quite what to say. Then Rita asked, "What's on the agenda today?" to break the silence.

"Oh, I'm not sure," Frank responded. "I never really thought too much about it. What would you guys like to do?" he asked.

"Well, Joe is still sleeping and looks like he'll be sleeping for a while, so I'm not really sure," Rita replied. "What about you, Louise? Do you have to go to work or something?" Rita asked.

"No, I'm off work right now," Louise responded, smiling.

Louise sensed that Rita wanted her to leave, and it made her want to stay all the more.

"She's a married woman," Louise thought. "What is she doing having sex with Frank anyway? Slut. She should be happy with her own husband," Louise said to herself. "And what is Frank thinking? Joe is supposed to be his friend," Louise thought.

But she knew she was just as guilty, as she too had messed around with Rita sexually. So she felt it wasn't her place to judge too harshly. Still, she wondered what exactly was going on between the two of them.

"Obviously Joe is not aware of what is happening, and if he finds out, I'd hate to be around," she thought to herself.

But that was really none of her business, she realized.

"Frank is just my friend," she reminded herself. "We are not in a relationship, so I have no grounds to ask too many questions or to be jealous," she said to herself.

She had never gotten involved with Frank because she didn't want to ruin their friendship. Plus, Frank had never indicated to her that he wanted more than a stay-over once in a while. So, even though she was super attracted to Frank, she knew she had no claim on him.

Plus, Louise was content with the way things were between the two of them. Plus, Frank had never had any other woman over to his place to stay the night—that she knew of—and so she felt that he was hers in a strange kind of way.

But now Rita was in the picture, and Louise had not been threatened by Rita, as Frank had told her she was married to his friend Joe. However, now she knew that Rita was cheating on her husband with Frank!

"But how is she pulling that off with Joe being right in the house?" Louise wondered. "I'll question Frank about it all later, once we're alone," she said to herself.

"Do you ladies want some breakfast?" Frank asked.

They both said no, they weren't hungry—maybe later.

Frank wasn't sure what to do. Suddenly things felt really awkward. Sex has a way of making things feel awkward the next day, especially under these circumstances.

He wondered if he should leave. Go cut some firewood. Go take a shower. But he didn't want to leave the two of them alone, and he wasn't sure exactly why.

The atmosphere was heavy and strange feeling. So Frank tried to break the ice by asking about Joe.

"Is Joe okay? Is he still asleep? Maybe you should wake him up and ask him to come down and have some breakfast, or at least a coffee," Frank said to Rita.

"Oh, Joe's fine," Rita replied. "He'll be asleep for a while yet, I think. Don't worry about Joe. He does this all the time," she added.

Chapter Five

The Aftermath

Louise suddenly remembered she had some important things she needed to take care of, so she stood up suddenly and announced she had to leave. "Are you sure?" Frank asked. "Yes," she said smiling. "I have some things I have to take care of. I'll give you a call a little later," she added, bending over to kiss him on the cheek. "Bye for now," she said to Rita, waving her hand. "Bye," Rita said smiling. She was having a hard time containing her joy over the fact that Louise was leaving. Now, she would have Frank all to herself, and that was exactly what she wanted.

Once Louise was gone, Frank asked Rita if she felt like having a smoke. "Sure," Rita replied. "Wake and bake, right!" she added and laughed. "Yea, I guess," Frank responded. "I like the first smoke of the day," he added. "It kind of puts a different light on the day, I find," Frank continued. Rita smiled and sat patiently as Frank rolled two joints, one for each of them.

Louise pulled out of the yard and began driving home. "What in fuck just happened?" she asked herself and she couldn't help but smile. Yet, she was plagued with more questions than answers. "Was Frank having an affair with his friend's wife?" she wondered. "Obviously, he is!" she thought. "That's a dangerous game," she said to herself. "Especially with Joe right there in the house!" And with that thought, her thoughts took a serious turn. "What if...." and she found herself thinking of all the possible sineros that might happen, and she didn't like the sounds of any of them. She needed to call Frank and ask him to come over to her place. She needed to talk some sense into him. He was, after all, her long time friend. "I have to at least try to get through to him," she thought.

In the meantime, Frank and Rita were smoking a J and remaining silent, but there was an elephant in the room and they both knew it. Finally Rita spoke. "So, how long have you been having sex with Louise?" she asked. "What!" Frank replied. "Oh, Louise. Ummm, we have stay over nights every so often. I'm not sure exactly how long it's been. Three years maybe, something like that," he answered. "Oh, really," Rita replied. "And you asked her to 'stay over' last night, knowing full well that I would be coming to your bed! Why would you do that?" she asked. "It freaked me right out when I went to get in bed with you and she was laying there. I didn't know what to do, so I started making out with her," Rita added and laughed. "Yea," Frank replied. "I saw that, and I don't think I will ever get the image out of my mind," he added, winking at Rita. "Seeing that was a serious turn on," he continued. Rita didn't respond, she just smiled.

"Are you jealous?" Frank asked. "Yes, of course I am," Rita replied. "And I don't want her 'staying over' any more while I am here," Rita added. "I think it is sexy that you are jealous, but remember, you're a married woman!" Frank replied. "And married, no less, to my buddy. And you and I shouldn't even be doing what we have been doing! So maybe it is good if Louise does stay over while you guys are here!" Frank added. "Stop it!" Rita responded. "Don't you enjoy having sex with me?" she asked. "You don't have to answer, I know you do," she continued. Then she suddenly put her finger over his lips. "Shush, I told you, no more 'stay overs' while I am here. You can go back to your 'stay overs' after we leave. I need you all to myself while I am here, understand!?" she continued.

Frank was amused by Rita's jealous insistence and possessiveness. He thought it was cute, and he had to admit she had a point. However, he also enjoyed having two beautiful women in bed with him, and if 'stay overs' meant he could have both of them at once, well, he couldn't see the issue with it.

Just then the phone rang, Frank picked it up and looked at it. "It's Louise," he said to Rita. "Oh great," Rita responded. He pushed the button to answer, "Hey...What's up?" he said. "I need you to come over to my place," Louise replied. Why? What's up?" Frank asked. "Is everything alright?" he added. "I think so," Louise replied. "But I really need you to come over. I won't keep you long, I know you have house quests. Trust me, I need you to come over as soon as you can, okay!" Louise continued. "Okay, no problem. I'll be right over," Frank replied and ended the call.

"What does she want?" Rita asked. "She wants me to come over to her place right away, but she said everything is okay. I'm not really sure what she wants, to be honest. But it seemed pretty important whatever it is," Frank replied. "She probably wants to get you alone," Rita responded. "No, don't be silly. That wasn't the way it sounded," Frank replied. "Yea, but who knows," Rita continued. "She may want to get you away from me. Get you all alone to herself. I bet that is it. She is probably jealous now because I am here and because of what happened last night between the three of us. I hope she's not thinking of ratting us out!" Rita said. "Oh no," Frank assured her. "Louise is not like that at all. She's a solid Chick. I've known her long enough to know that. No worries there," Frank replied. "Yea, she probably wants more sex," Rita said. "I can't say I blame her," she added, touching Frank's penis as she spoke. "Ummm," Frank said smiling. "But you have to stop that now, because I told Louise I'd be right over." "Oh yes, you better jump and get right over there," Rita replied in a sarcastic tone of voice. "You have to calm down Rita," Frank said, trying to be a little stern with her. "You're married to my friend and right now he is sleeping upstairs, remember?" Frank added. "Oh, I remember only too well," Rita responded, hanging her head a little as she spoke.

Frank kissed Rita on the cheek. "I'll be back before you know it!" he said. "And don't worry, I'm not going to have sex with Louise. I am saving it all for you," he added. "Okay, hurry back," Rita replied, pouting. "What am I supposed to do here while you are gone" she added in a whinny tone of voice. "Entertain yourself," Frank replied. "I don't know, but I have to go now," he replied while heading out the door.

As he got into his truck and pulled down the driveway, he wondered what Louise wanted to see him about. What it could possibly be that she was so determined to get him to her house. Then it struck him, "She's freaked out about Rita and I! I bet that is what this is about. Fuck, what am I going to tell her?" Frank asked himself as he drove.

He arrived at Louise's and entered the house. "Hey," he said, opening the door. Louise was sitting at her kitchen table. "Hey Handsome," she said smiling. "So what's so important that you needed me here right away?" Frank asked. "You," Louise replied. "You are what's important!" she added. "Me?" Frank asked. "How so?" he asked. "Well, I'm very worried about you," Louise replied. "You're having an affair with your friend's wife! And if that's not bad enough, he's right there in the same house! Aren't you the least bit afraid of being caught?" Louise asked, but before Frank could respond she continued. "My gosh, last night the three of us were having sex, and here her husband was just a couple doors down! I never thought of it then, I was having too much fun, but this morning it hit me like a ton of bricks as I was driving home, and I knew I had to call you and talk to you about it. I'm afraid for you Frank! What if her husband finds out you are having sex with his wife?! You guys are playing a very dangerous game. And I am sure you know all of this, so why in fuck are you playing around with your friend's wife?" Louise asked.

"It's complicated," Frank responded. "I figured on the way over here that was why you wanted to see me alone. And I don't really have any good answers for you. I'm sorry. It just happened. I never planned it, and I don't think she did. I never meant her before this trip, and I had no idea any of this was going to happen. I feel bad about it, for sure; but it is, what it is, I guess," Frank replied, shrugging his shoulders.

"Is what it is!" Louise replied, raising her eye brows. "Can you hear what you are saying?" she asked. "Yes," I know," Frank said. "I know it's wrong. I know I shouldn't be doing it. I know I should put an end to it before, like you say, we get caught. I hear yea. And that's exactly what I will do. You are right," Frank continued. "Good," Louise replied with a serious look on her face. "It's the right thing to do Frank, you know that," she added. "Yes, yes, it is," Frank agreed.

Then Louise continued, "What if something really bad happened? Like Joe finds out and shouts you both?" she asked. Frank grinned. "I don't think Joe has a gun and mine are all locked up," he replied. "But I know what you are saying, it could be, yes, high drama for sure," Frank agreed.

"I'm glad you called me and got me to come over," Frank continued. "Talk some sense into me. I've been trying to control myself, but it hasn't exactly been working, and I've been feeling guilty as well. Like you say, I know it is wrong. So from here on in,

I am going to stay away from her. They are not staying much longer, I don't think anyway," he added.

"Good," Louise replied. "Because I am very worried for you in that situation. You never know how situations like that can turn out. Many have been murdered in such situations as you know!" she said sternly. "I know, I know," Frank replied. "Don't worry, I'm going to take care of it. I appreciate you talking to me about it," he said and leaned over and kissed Louise on the cheek. Louise blushed and smiled. "You handsome devil," she said. "No wonder Rita can't keep her hands off of you," she added. Frank smiled a wide smile. He was loving all the attention he was getting. He was alone for months, and now suddenly he had two beautiful women both giving him attention.

Louise got up from her chair and sat on Frank's lap. "What are you doing now?" Frank asked her, smiling. "What's it look like?" Louise said, kissing his neck. "That was so much fun last night," she whispers in his ear. "It sure was," Frank said. "I'd love to have some more," Louise added, pushing her breasts into his chest.

Suddenly Frank was feeling anxiety. "How did Rita know that Louise was going to hit on me?" he thought to himself "She didn't know," he thought, "she was just guessing, but she was guessing right," he said to himself. "There's no one here but you and me," Louise said, still kissing his neck and pushing against his chest. "What am I going to do now?" Frank wondered. If he had sex with Louise, Rita would know, as he would be gone too long. But if he left, Louise might get offended and suspicious as to whether he was being honest about his situation regarding Rita.

Finally, Frank said. "Listen Baby, you're a hot, sexy mamma and you know I love having sex with you, but I do have house guests who are at my house by themselves right now and I feel like I am being rude not being there. You understand, right?" he asked in a quasi pleading tone of voice. "No, I don't understand," Louise replied, still kissing his neck and trying her best to seduce him. "They are adults, I'm pretty sure they can entertain themselves for a while without you there," she insisted. Seeing that Louise was not going to take no for an answer, Frank decided to just agree with her. "Okay, you win," he said. "But it's not going to be a long haul, it's going to be short and sweet, okay?" he added. "I'll take whatever I can get," Louise said smiling. So they headed upstairs to Louise's bedroom.

They had just started having sex when suddenly the phone started ringing. "FUCK," he thought. "I bet that's Rita wondering where in fuck I am! Fuck, what do I do? I can't, obviously, answer it, this isn't my house. I'll just have to ignore it and get this over with as soon as possible and get back there," he thought.

Louise looked briefly in the direction of the ringing phone, she could hear if anyone was leaving a message, but she figured it was Rita as well. "She's jealous," Louise said to herself. "She knows Frank and I are having sex right now," she thought and smiled. "Fuck her, she's a married woman. She shouldn't be worried about what he is doing. She can fuck off," Louise thought, trying to ignore the sound of the ringing phone.

Frank couldn't help himself to want to see who called, so he interrupted the situation and went to check the phone. Yup, just as he thought, it was his number, so he knew it was Rita who had called. "Sorry Honey," he thought to himself, "you're gonna have to wait this one out." He put the phone back and turned to Lousie. "Now where were we?" he said, smiling.

"I'll try to pretend I'm having sex with Rita. That way, I am sure to get off fast and then I can get out of here," he thought. And it wasn't long before they both ejaculated. The two of them laid there on the bed exhausted. Frank was covered in sweat and wondered how he was going to explain all of this to Rita who was sitting at his place waiting for him. "Maybe Joe is awake by now," he thought. He hoped that was the case, because if it was, he could go and take a shower as soon as he got home and Rita wouldn't be able to stop him.

"That was great," Louise said, kissing Frank on the cheek. Frank agreed and smiled. "But, I really have to go now, as you know I have visitors there waiting for me," he said. "But it was fun, and we must do it again soon," he added, getting up from the bed and kissing Louise with a quick peck on the lips.

Frank began getting dressed to leave, but Louise was still laying naked on the bed. "I wish you didn't have to leave," she said pouting. "I know, me too" Frank replied. "But duty calls," he added, as he continued getting dressed. Finally Louise got up and put on her housecoat. "I'll see you to the door," she said and walked with Frank down to the kitchen and back door. "Give me a hug before you go," she said, pulling Frank close to her. "Do you want me to come back over tonight and have another stay over?" she asked. Frank wasn't sure what to say, he didn't want to offend Louise, she was, after all, his steady once in a while sex. The only one he had, in fact. "Ah, no, that's okay. I got this," he said smiling at her. "But thanks for the offer. I appreciate it," he added. "No problem," Louise replied. "I am here – any – time you need me," she added smiling. Frank smiled back and headed out the door to his vehicle.

Once in his vehicle and driving back home, his mind was going a thousand miles an hour. "What am I going to tell Rita?" he asked himself. "I will tell her the truth," he thought. "She's not my woman!" he said to himself. "I don't owe her anything!" he thought. "She's a married woman, she has no claim on me," he said as he drove. "I'm going to tell her where to go, if she puts the questions to me," he thought as he drove into his driveway.. "She has no right to question anything I do. I am single and so is Louise and it's really none of Rita's business," he thought, trying to muster up the strength and courage he needed to greet Rita.

Rita and Joe were both sitting at the kitchen table when Frank entered his house. "Morning to you Sir," Joe said right away. "Morning my friend," Frank responded. He didn't even want to look at Rita who he could feel was staring a hole right through him. "I trust you slept well," Frank continued. "Yea, a little too well," Joe responded. But Frank didn't ask for an explanation to Joe's comment, he knew Rita had given Joe sleeping pills so she could sneak off to his bedroom, and he clearly didn't want the conversation to go in that direction. So he opted to let the comment die.

"Everything okay over at Louise's?" Rita asked, staring Frank directly in the eyes. "Yea, yea, everything was fine. Louise just wanted to talk to me about something personal, that's all," Frank replied. "Sorry I took so long, but Louise had a big issue she was dealing with and it took some time. I tried to get back here as soon as I could, but you know, friends; when they need yea, they need yea," Frank replied.

Joe smiled from the end of the table. "You went over there to have sex with her, didn't you?" Joe accused. Frank could feel his face getting hot. "No, no," he said. "Like I say, she had an issue she needed my help with is all," Frank continued. "Sure," Joe said in a sly tone of voice. "If you say so," Joe continued grinning from ear to ear. "Do I look like I just had sex?" Frank wondered. "Maybe the sweat was apparent," he thought. Then he told himself, "No, Joe is just being a typical man. Making assumptions. Don't let it bother yea."

"Well, I'm going to go jump in the shower. I never had a shower yet today and I need one," Frank said. "You guys help yourselves to coffee and anything else you want for breakfast. There's bread and eggs and some bacon in the fridge," Frank added. "Thanks,"

Joe replied. "But we already had toast and eggs while we were waiting for you," he continued. "While you were over having sex with Louise," Joe added and laughed. Frank looked at Rita, and Rita looked at Frank with daggers in her eyes. "Oh fuck," Frank thought. "She is pissed," he said to himself. Then he quickly exited the kitchen and headed upstairs to his bedroom to get some clean clothes and underwear for his shower.

Once in the shower, his thoughts began to race again. "How am I going to deal with this situation?" he wondered. "I promised Louise, I think I promised, or at least I told her anyway, that I was going to stay away from Rita. And yes, I have to stick to that, no matter how badly I am attracted to her. She is married to my friend, like Louise reminded me, as if I needed reminding. But Louise is right, I have to stop this nonsense before it gets out of hand. Or even worse, we get caught," he said to himself as he showered.

He quickly washed the sex smell off his body. He figured he need not feel guilty about having sex with Louise as they both were single consenting adults. And so he was determined not to let Rita make him feel guilty because he had a sick feeling in his gut that told him she was going to try.

Frank got dressed and went back down to the kitchen, but Joe was absent and only Rita was sitting there at the table. "Where's Joe?" Frank asked. "Oh, he's on a private call," Rita said. "Something to do with his business. He is all about his business, you know," she continued. Frank smiled. "Yes, and his business has taken very good care of you as well," Frank reminded her. "Indeed it has," Rita agreed. "But it's like he has another relationship. It's just not with another woman, it's with his business and making money," she replied. "Awww, poor you," Frank responded smiling. "Poor little Rita, so deprived," Frank added still smiling. "Fuck off," Rita said. "You have no idea and don't judge," she continued. "Hey, I'm not judging," Frank responded. "I'm just thinking you are one spoiled little bitch, who is one of the horniest people I have ever meant. Doesn't Joe satisfy you? From the sounds coming from your guys bedroom every night, it sure sounds like he does," Frank continued and chuckled.

Rita smiled a big smile, "Whose jealous now?" she asked "What!" Frank exclaimed. "I'm not jealous, I'm just sayin," he added. "Yea, well, you have no idea. So don't assume things you have no idea about okay," Rita added. "And by the way, what took you so long over at Louise's? Hey!" Rita asked. "Oh, she was in a pickle, and needed my help is all," Frank responded. "What kind of pickle?" Rita asked. "Oh it's personal," Franks said. "I can't discuss her personal business with you. That wouldn't be right. I am sure you can understand that," he added. "Sure," Rita replied. "I can understand only too well. Just like Joe said, you were over there having sex with her weren't you?" Rita asked with a serious look on her face staring directly into Frank's eyes.

"Tell me, come on now. I know that's what she wanted you for. She just did that because I am here. You said you guys only have sex once in a while, and she was just here last night. Now all of a sudden she wants you again today! Yea, right. Don't tell me your lies, I know what is going on," Rita said. Frank smiled a nervous smile, he knew Rita was spot on; but he couldn't tell her that. "No, No" Frank insisted. "Like I said, she was having an issue that she needed my help with. Now let it go, please," he continued.

And just as he was saying that, Joe walked back into the kitchen. "You're never going to believe this Rita, but there is a huge issue at the firm and we have to leave sooner than planned. I know it sucks, but what can I do?" Joe said. "What!" Rita and Frank both said at the same time, which kind of startled Joe, but he continued. "Yea, there's a major issue with a huge contract and I just cannot leave it to my underlings, it's just too important," Joe went on to say. "Sorry," he added.

Chapter Six

Sudden Departure

Rita looked horrified. She'd never even thought of the aspect of leaving. She was just getting used to being there.

"It feels like you guys just got here," Frank said. "And you're leaving already!" he added.

"Sorry, buddy," Joe replied. "But duty calls, my friend. I am sure you get it and understand," Joe continued.

"For sure," Frank said. "Just sorry you have to leave is all. I was really enjoying having you guys here," he added.

"Yes, and we really enjoyed being here, right, Rita?" Joe said.

"Yes, of course," Rita replied, smiling. She was still in shock over the idea of having to leave.

"When are you planning to go?" Frank asked. "We have to leave tomorrow, unfortunately," Joe replied. "I want to be back by the next day at the latest, and it will take quite a few hours to drive back home," Joe replied.

"But you're spending another night here, right?" Frank asked.

"Yea, it's too late in the day to leave now," Joe said. "So yea, we'll have to spend another night. I hope you are all good with that," he added.

"Of course I am," Frank replied. "I wish you guys didn't have to leave at all. Like I say, I am really enjoying your company. I am usually alone in this big old farmhouse, and it's kind of nice to have other adults around to talk to and hang out with, "Frank continued.

"Yea, last night was really fun," Joe responded. "I really enjoyed myself. And I really dig your friend Louise. She is a sexy Mama," Joe added and winked at Frank.

"Yea, she's cool for sure," Frank replied

"How come you're not more involved with her on a steady basis?" Joe asked, smiling.

"Ah, that's not the kind of relationship we have is all," Frank responded, smiling back at Joe.

"Each to their own," Joe replied. "But if she was my 'friend,' I'd be having sex with her on a regular basis," he added. Then he looked at Rita, as if he suddenly remembered she was present.

"No offense to you, Honey. You know you are my main and my only squeeze. I was just saying, if I were Frank, you know," Joe added.

Rita smiled. "No worries," she said. "I know how you men think," she continued, looking over at Frank. But Frank let on he didn't see her and instead went to pour himself another coffee.

"So, what time do you think you'll be heading out in the morning?" Frank asked while pouring himself a coffee.

"Well, the earlier the better," Joe replied. "I'd like to get an early start on driving. Rita doesn't like to drive much, so I have to pretty

much do all the driving. And as you know, it is a very long drive,"
Joe continued.

"Yea, for sure," Frank responded. "Well, maybe you guys can make it back to visit me again sooner than later," Frank added.

"Oh, for sure," Joe replied. "I'll be back to see yea, buddy, don't worry," he added. "We'll be back before long, right, Honey?" he said to Rita.

"Sure," Rita replied. "I really love it here. It is so much nicer than the city. I wasn't sure I would like it here, and to be honest, I thought I'd be bored stiff; but now that I've been here, I have to say, I really like it," Rita replied with a big smile on her face.

"See, even Rita the city Chick likes it here," Joe said, smiling at Frank.

"Right on," Frank said. "It grows on yea, that's for sure," he continued. "I wasn't sure I would like it here, but it grew on me pretty quickly. And I can't say I miss the city anymore," Frank added.

Joe then stood up from the table. "Well, Honey, I have some calls I have to make regarding this issue I am dealing with, and so I am going to go make them from the bedroom. I'll be back down to hang out as soon as I am able to. Sorry for this, but I truly have no choice in the matter," he continued. Then he gave Rita a quick peck on the lips and headed upstairs.

Once alone in the kitchen, Frank and Rita were both dumbfounded. Neither of them had thought about the leave day. They both knew it was inevitable, but not this suddenly.

"What are we going to do?" Rita said to Frank.

"What do you mean, what are 'we' going to do? You're Joe's wife, and so you are going to leave with your husband," Frank responded.

"I should have known something like this would happen," Rita said. "It's always business, business with Joe. I'm so sick and tired of it," she continued.

"Oh well," Frank said. "You guys will be back again, and trust me, I'll be waiting for yea," he added and winked at Rita.

"You won't be waiting for me," Rita said. "You'll be busy having sex with the whore up the road," she added in an angry tone of voice.

Frank smiled a big smile. "There's that jealousy again," he said. "Come on, Rita, you're a married woman. And married to my friend, no less. Now lighten up," Frank continued.

"Yea, whatever," Rita replied. "You don't have to remind me, I am well aware," she continued and sighed.

Suddenly, gloom had entered into the atmosphere, and both Rita and Frank could feel it. So, in an attempt to lighten things up, Frank suggested having a smoke of his medicine.

"This stuff is what keeps me from getting too lonely or depressed," he said, holding up his glass jar of organic buds.

Rita smiled. "You're sad," she said. "That is what keeps you company. How pathetic," she added, smiling.

"Yup, that's right," Frank replied, taking out a couple of choice buds to roll up.

"What does she know," Frank thought. "She's not living my life. She just came here for a visit, she has no idea what my life is like, and from the sounds of it, she's not too happy in her own life. So she ought to not be judging mine," Frank said to himself. But he never said anything to Rita. He was afraid she would bring up Louise again, and he didn't want that to happen.

So he lit the joint, took a couple of drags, and passed it to Rita.

"Hey," she said. "You said you would give me some of this to take home with me," she reminded Frank.

"Oh sure," Frank said. "I'll give you and Joe an ounce to take with you. I have lots, as you know. That's the beauty of living out here and having land, it's no problem to grow my own supply," he added.

"Well, you sure are a good gardener," Rita replied. "Because this is some mighty fine smoke," she added, taking a haul and blowing the smoke in the air.

"I'm glad you like it," Frank said, smiling.

"That's not all I like," Rita added, smiling.

Frank knew what she was getting at, and he wondered how he was going to get to have sex with Rita one more time before she and

Joe left. Then he remembered, he had told Louise he was going to stay away from Rita. And he thought, "Maybe it is good they have to leave tomorrow. It will make it much easier for me to keep my hands off Rita."

"I know what you're thinking," Rita said.

"What... What am I thinking then?" Frank asked.

"You're wondering if we are going to get to have sex one more time before we leave tomorrow," she replied with a big smile on her face. "I think you're in love with my pussy," she said and laughed.

"Well, what's not to love," Frank replied, smiling a big smile. "And yes, that is exactly what I was thinking. You read my mind," he added.

"I read your mind," Rita replied. "Because I was thinking the exact same thing. And I'm wondering myself how we are going to pull that off. I can't give Joe sleeping pills tonight, as you heard him, he has to get up early and drive. And I'm not driving in a vehicle with him when he is strung out on sleeping pills from the night before. And I know him, even if I did give him pills, which he, by the way, asks me for, he will still make himself get up to the alarm clock because he has to, you know, take care of business. That is very important to him, too important if you ask me, but then no one ever asks me," she continued.

Frank's heart sank in thinking he may never get to have sex with Rita again. Suddenly, he felt devastated at the prospect.

And it was at that point that Joe entered the kitchen.

"Everything okay?" Frank asked, trying to act concerned.

"Oh yea," Joe replied. "These things happen and are to be expected, right, Honey?" he added, looking at Rita.

"Oh yea," Rita replied. "These things are always happening," she continued and frowned.

Joe, in seeing Rita's frown, kissed her on the cheek.

"Don't worry, Honey, I promise I'll make it up to yea. I know I promised no work on our vacation coming here, but this is a very important contract, and it just can't be helped. You know how these things go," he continued.

Rita didn't answer. She just looked at him with half a smile on her face.

Joe felt bad for disappointing Rita, but he felt disappointed too, as he too liked hanging out with his longtime buddy Frank. But business was business, and it had to come first. That was the motto Joe lived by and believed was the reason he was so economically successful.

"You may not like the business end of things," he said to Rita, "but think of all the rewards you get," he continued.

Frank smiled and looked at Rita, but Rita was not amused.

"So, what would you guys like to do for your last day here?" Frank asked.

"Something low key," Joe said. "I need to save up my energy for the long drive tomorrow," he added.

"Hey, we could all watch a movie!"

"That sounds like a great idea," Joe replied.

"Sounds like a plan then," Frank replied.

So the three of them headed to the living room where Frank had a big screen television and a literal ton of movies.

"Who wants to pick one out?" Frank asked.

"Oh, you go ahead," Joe replied. "You have a better idea of what you have for movies than we do, and I don't feel like looking through all of those," Joe responded, pointing to the stacks of movies.

"Any particular genre you guys prefer?" Frank asked.

"No, we like most everything," Joe said.

Rita was just sitting there silent, like she wasn't even there at all. Like whatever was happening, was happening without her, even though she was present. She had a blank look and stare on her face, and Frank didn't want to disturb her. He was imagining she was thinking about leaving and not getting to have sex with him anymore. He knew that's what was paramount on his mind, anyway, and he hoped it was the same for her.

"I like the old westerns," Frank said. "I find them kind of interesting and funny, as compared to today's society," he added.

"Sure, I like old westerns too," Joe responded. "Sounds good," Joe said. "Pick one and let's get to it," he added.

So Frank picked out one of his favorite old westerns and put it in the DVD player. The film consisted of the typical old western movies: gunslingers and heroes, good versus evil. But it was something neutral to watch, and that was all that mattered.

Frank knew he wasn't going to be interested in the movie when he put it in the machine. His mind was elsewhere. All he could think of now was the fact that as of tomorrow morning Rita would be gone, and he had no idea when he would see her again. The mere thought of it pained his heart. And he could see from looking at Rita's expression that she too was no more interested in the movie than he was, and he was somehow certain she was thinking the same things he was.

Both of them tried to pretend they were interested in and watching the movie, so as not to make Joe suspicious when he made a comment about something in the movie. Both of them were quick to comment back and laugh when appropriate.

After the movie, Frank volunteered to make supper for the three of them and put in another movie for them to watch while he cooked. He'd make something quick, he thought, because he didn't really have time to cook up a big meal, although he wished he had. He was a good cook, and he felt he'd not really had the opportunity to show his cooking skills in full to Rita and Joe. But now wasn't the time, so he opted to add ingredients to a frozen pizza he had in the freezer.

That was always his go-to in a pinch, or if he was too hungry to prepare what he considered a proper meal. He tried to eat healthy most of the time, but there were times, like tonight, where he felt it was okay to cheat and eat a store-bought pizza. Besides, the pizza was good with all the extra organic toppings he put on it.

When the pizza was cooked, he called for Rita and Joe. "It's all ready," he yelled into the living room.

"Come and get it," he added.

And the two of them sauntered into the kitchen, hungry and ready to munch out.

"It smells really good," Rita said as she entered the kitchen.

"I could smell it all the way in the living room, and yes, it does smell mighty fine," Joe added. "I'm starving as well," Joe added.

"Me too," Rita added.

"Well, that makes three of us," Frank said, smiling.

And the three of them chowed down until the pizza disappeared.

Joe leaned back in his chair and rubbed his stomach.

"I have to say that was delicious and really hit the spot," he said.

"Yea, well, I added some toppings," Frank responded, "and that makes all the difference, I find," he added.

"Good idea," Rita replied. "And I agree, that was the best frozen store-bought pizza I think I have ever had," she added.

"Thanks," Frank said, smiling. "Happy you guys liked it," he added.

"Don't worry about cleaning up," Frank said. "I'll take care of that. I know you guys probably have to pack and prepare for leaving in the morning," he continued.

"Thanks, buddy," Joe said. "Yes, it is going to take a while to get packed up and ready, for sure. And it's a good idea to do it now versus waiting until later, right, Honey?" he said to Rita.

"Yea, I guess so," Rita responded.

She was no more interested in packing to leave than Frank was in watching her go. But she knew she had to do what she had to do. So both Joe and Rita retired to the bedroom to start the process of packing their things and preparing to leave in the morning.

Just as they left the kitchen, Frank's phone rang. Rita looked back at Frank as if she knew it was Louise. Frank looked down at his phone, and sure enough, it was Louise.

"Why is she calling me again?" he thought. "She's getting a bit hard on my head. She was never this clingy before. Maybe Rita is right, she is jealous of Rita."

He picked up the phone.

"Hey... what's up?" he asked.

"Oh, it's just me," Louise said, sounding kind of shy all of a sudden, as if she could tell that Frank was getting annoyed with her sudden insertion into his life. "I was just calling to see how you are making out," she continued. "Or rather not making out," she added and giggled.

Frank was now a little agitated, feeling that Louise was sticking her nose into his business, but he tried to contain himself.

"Oh, things are fine," he replied. "I told you already, I'm done with that, and I meant it. No reason for you to worry, my dear," he replied. "Was there something else?" he asked. "Because we just finished supper and I'm kind of busy right now cleaning up," he added.

"No, no," Louise replied. "I was just wondering how you were doing with the whole situation. I'll let you go, so you can get back to what you were doing," she added.

"Sorry I bothered you. I'm just worried about you is all. You sound annoyed with me," she continued.

"Oh no," Frank responded. "I'm just kind of busy is all. You caught me off guard. Plus, you really have no reason to worry. Joe and Rita are leaving tomorrow anyway. Joe has to get back to take care of some important business that came up. So you see, you have no reason to worry anymore. So stop worrying and forget about it, okay!" Frank replied.

"Really, they are leaving tomorrow? Wow, they haven't been here that long, have they?" Louise asked.

"Yea, they have been here a few days now," Frank said. "And Joe says he has no choice and I respect his decision. He is a very successful businessman, you know!" Frank added.

"No, I didn't know, but I kind of assumed from the money they seem to have," Louise said.

"Yea, well, they are leaving first thing in the morning, so you have nothing to worry about, okay!" Frank said once again, trying to reinforce to Louise not to bug him anymore about it.

"Okay, Love, I'll let you go. And I hope we can have a 'stay over' sooner than later," she added.

"Okay, bye for now and have a good night," he said and ended the call.

"Where was I," he thought to himself once off the phone. "Oh right, cleaning up," he remembered.

Then he returned to the task of doing the dishes and cleaning up from supper. And while he was cleaning up, he couldn't help but think about how Louise was suddenly inserting herself into his life. He understood that she was a good friend and that maybe her worry about his involvement with Rita was warranted, but it bugged him that she was now bothering him about it.

"I'm a grown man. What business is it of hers what I do?" he thought to himself as he washed the dishes.

He was feeling annoyed by all of what Louise had said to him and how she seduced him, and how she wouldn't let him leave without having sex with her. Suddenly, it was all making him not like her.

"Maybe she is jealous of Rita. Women know things that men are oblivious to. Rita even knew Louise was going to want to have sex with me!" he thought.

"Women are complex creatures," he said to himself and smiled. "And right now, Louise is far too complex for me to even think about, so I'm just going to forget about it and let it all go," he thought.

Just then, Rita entered the kitchen.

"Do you have any plastic shopping bags by chance?" she asked. "I need one to put my dirty underwear in," she added, holding up several pairs in her hand.

"Ah, yea, I think I do," Frank replied, opening the door under the sink to check. "Yup," he said. "Here's one right here," he added and passed the plastic shopping bag to Rita.

"Would you like to smell them?" Rita asked, smiling and holding them up to Frank's nose.

Frank smiled and leaned into the handful of panties, taking a deep sniff.

"Ummmm, now those don't smell like dirty panties to me," he said, smiling. "They smell like the sweetest pussy," he added.

"Humm, the 'sweetest' pussy, eh," Rita replied, winking.

"Yes indeed," Frank responded. "The very sweetest pussy," he added.

"Would you like to keep a pair of them for remembrance of me?" Rita asked.

"What! Sure, thanks. I'd love to keep a pair. Glad you asked," he replied and smiled.

He then looked over the various pairs of panties Rita was holding and chose the one he thought held the most smell.

"I'll take these ones," he said, picking the black ones out of the many colors she had in her hand.

"Nice choice," Rita replied, smiling. "Those are one of my favorite pairs," she added.

"Well, I don't have to take these ones," Frank said. "If they're your favorite ones, I mean, I can pick another pair!" he added.

"Oh no," Rita replied. "I have tons of underwear, and I can always buy more anytime I want. Don't worry about it. I am happy to give them to you. I hope you sniff them all the time and think of me," she continued and smiled.

"Oh, I will," Frank assured her. "Don't you worry about that," he added and smiled a big smile.

Rita then turned to leave to go back to the bedroom to finish packing. Frank was then wondering what to do with the pair of panties Rita had just given him. He looked for a safe place to put them until he could take them to his bedroom. Then he quickly stuffed them into a drawer in his kitchen and continued cleaning up. He wondered why Rita never mentioned the phone call and/or quizzed him about who it was, but he was relieved that she hadn't.

Once the kitchen was cleaned, Frank took Rita's underwear up to his room and put them under his pillow. If he couldn't have sex with her tonight, he could at least smell her sweet vagina while he slept. He wondered if he should put them in plastic in an attempt to encapsulate the smell for longer. But then he thought he was just being creepy in thinking that. Still, he was wondering how to best preserve the smell of them, seeing that he may not see Rita again for a long while. He and Joe had been friends for years, but this was the first time Joe had opted to come and visit him since he moved to his place in the country. Granted, Joe and he lived thousands of miles apart. So he got it.

After putting Rita's underwear under his pillow, he went back down to the kitchen. He figured the three of them could hang out for a while since he may not see either of them again for some time. And it wasn't long after that, that both Joe and Rita showed up.

The three of them sat around the kitchen table talking, having a glass of wine and a smoke of medicine.

"Well, I have to get to bed," Joe said. "Long drive tomorrow, right, Honey?" he added, looking at Rita.

"Yea, I'm not looking forward to it," Rita replied, looking sad.

"Come on, Babe, we need to hit the hay now," Joe continued. "Good night, Frank, and thanks again for everything. You've been a great host and I appreciate your hospitality, buddy. It was really good to see and hang out with yea," Joe added, reaching out to shake Frank's hand and give him a man hug.

"Yea, for sure," Frank replied. "It's been a real pleasure having the two of you here," he added.

"Good night, Frank," Rita added.

And Joe and Rita headed upstairs to retire for the night.

Frank sat at his kitchen table wondering how it was going to feel being there alone again in his house. He was used to being alone, but now that he had company for a few days, he knew it would be an adjustment getting used to being alone again. Plus, and it was a big plus, he had never had a woman like Rita before, and he knew damn well he was going to miss her. Even if what they were doing was wrong, it felt so damn good.

"How," he wondered, "can something so wrong feel so damn good. It doesn't make sense," he thought.

But he knew it was wrong, and he concluded, or at least tried to, that it was a good thing Rita was leaving. He would no longer be tempted to have sex with her, and maybe his feelings of guilt would also go away once she was gone. He hoped they would, at the least.

He sauntered up the stairs to his bedroom. He hoped Joe and Rita were done having sex, as he didn't think he could bear listening to them. He knew, or thought anyway, that he was not going to be getting any sex with Rita that night, or maybe ever again, and the thought of listening to Joe having sex with her, even if he was her husband, was just too much for him right then.

He got to his room, and all was quiet.

"Good, they are not having sex, or they had sex already and they're done now. Thank goodness," he thought.

He got undressed and climbed into his bed. Suddenly, he remembered Rita's panties under his pillow, and he reached under his pillow to find them.

"Ah, there they are," he said to himself. "How thoughtful of her to give me these," he said to himself as he laid them over his nose, sniffing them as he breathed, laying there on his back on his bed.

"Really, these are a tease," he thought. "Because the real thing is right down the hall and yet I can't have any," he pouted.

He wished he had known that Rita and Joe would be leaving tomorrow, but then it really wouldn't have mattered. But maybe he and Rita could have had sex in the morning, in the kitchen as they had done before, while Joe was still sleeping. But stupid Louise had to call and get him to leave during that time.

Suddenly, he hated Louise for being all up in his business. A side of her he had not seen before.

"And who is she to judge me, or Rita, when she herself engaged in sex with us just the night before!" he thought.

Anyway, he didn't want to think about it all right now. He knew Louise had a point and he truly wasn't mad at her, nor did he truly dislike her; he was just angry and frustrated over the entire situation and the fact that Rita was leaving in the morning.

He laid there thinking of Rita and wishing she could somehow make it back to his room. "Just one more time before she has to go," he thought.

Rita and Joe were in bed in their own bedroom. Joe didn't want to have sex, as he said he had to save up his energy for the long drive the next day.

"You don't mind, do you, Honey?" he asked Rita. "I am just too tired and I need to save up my energy," he continued.

Rita didn't care. She was relieved that Joe didn't want to have sex. It was a very rare occasion when that happened, and something to do with business was always the reason when it did.

"No, that's fine, Honey," Rita replied.

Joe laid there trying to get to sleep. He wasn't used to sleeping on his own accord. He was used to having help to sleep via Rita's sleeping pills. But he didn't want to use them for fear he would oversleep in the morning. Still, he couldn't for the life of him get to sleep. Thoughts of the business deal, the issues he had to deal with, trying to find solutions to them, ran through his mind.

Rita laid there silent with her back towards Joe. All she could think of was Frank and how she might never get to fuck him again. It was making her sad and angry, and she wished Joe would ask her for some sleeping pills, but she told herself she wasn't going to offer.

"I'll wait for him to ask me for some," she said to herself.

And, sure enough, it wasn't five minutes later that Joe tapped her on the shoulder.

"Rita! Are you awake? I need some of your sleeping pills. I can't get to sleep," he said.

Rita turned and got out of bed to fetch her pills, passing Joe the bottle.

"I'm not going to take too many tonight," Joe said, opening the bottle. "I don't want to oversleep in the morning, as I always do when I take too many," he added. "How many should I take, do you think?" he asked Rita.

"I don't know," Rita replied. "You know your tolerance better than I do. Take as many as you need, I guess," she continued.

So Joe dumped some pills out into his hand and then he took out two and swallowed them down without even a glass of water.

"Wow, you sure are used to taking those," Rita said, watching him. "You don't even take a drink to wash them down anymore!" she continued.

"Yea, yea," Joe replied. "I'm going to sleep now. Don't bug me," he added and rolled over on his side with his back facing Rita.

And it wasn't ten minutes later that Rita could hear him snoring to beat the band. In hearing Joe snoring, Rita smiled the biggest smile, realizing she could now sneak down to Frank's room and have sex with him.

"Hooray," she thought. "I get to have sex one last time with Frank before I have to leave here," she said to herself as she slowly got out of bed and quietly tiptoed down the hallway to Frank's room.

Frank was fast asleep with Rita's underwear still on his face, and when Rita saw that she began to quietly laugh to herself.

"Oh my goodness," she said to herself. "He's got it bad," she thought.

She was delighted to see that Frank was so obsessed with her, because she was just as obsessed with him.

Rita was naked under her housecoat, and so she simply slipped it off and crawled into bed with Frank. She lightly touched him on the end of his nose through her underwear, laying there on his face, which made him stop snoring for a moment but didn't wake him up. So, she opted to just lay there beside him for a few moments.

She wondered what it would be like to lie there with Frank every night. To live in his house. It was so different from the world she was used to in New York. Yet, she felt it may be a good change for her. She never dreamed she'd like life in the country, but since she had gotten there, it has seriously grown on her. Yet, she figured Frank was a huge part of that, since she was somehow sure she had fallen in love with him.

"Oh my gosh," she thought to herself. "I can't believe I just thought that," she said to herself and then she smiled a huge smile and opted to wake Frank up.

She pushed her naked body up against Frank, pushing her vagina against his leg. Then she reached down and took hold of his manhood.

Frank opened his eyes in surprise and looked over at Rita.

"What in fuck are you doing here?" he asked her. "I thought you'd not be able to make it down to my room tonight. How in hell did you pull that off?" he asked. Then he grabbed her, pulling her close to him, kissing her neck and aiming down for her breasts.

"Never mind with that," Rita said. "We have business here to take care of," she continued, without answering Frank's question on how she was able to make it down to his room. "This may be the last time I get to have you for a while," Rita said. "So let's concentrate on that, shall we?" she added and smiled.

Frank smiled a big smile and agreed.

"You're so right," he replied. "I'm so happy we got to be together one more time before you leave. I was so sad thinking I was never going to get to make sweet love with you ever again, or at least not for a long time," Frank added.

Rita liked that Frank seemed to know exactly what to do to please her. Frank knew all the right moves for what Rita liked. She didn't even have to tell him. Honestly, he was the kind of man who just knew these things. He hadn't been with that many women, but he spent a lot of his time fantasizing about them nonetheless. Hence, he felt that he was experienced regardless.

So before they knew it, they were having sex and getting lost in the moment, making a ton of noise in doing so. Never once giving thought to the fact that Joe, Rita's husband, was asleep right down the hall. What would they say if he suddenly woke up and went looking for Rita, never entered their minds. All they could concentrate on was how good they were making each other feel in the moment.

They had sex in every position they could think of. They were trying to make the most out of their last night together, seeing as they had no idea when, or even if, they would ever have the chance to be together again.

"I can't get enough of you, Rita," Frank whispered in her ear. "I think I might be falling in love with you, and that scares the shit out of me," he continued.

Rita smiled a big smile. "Oh Frank," she replied. "You're just pussy whipped, is all. I am sure you'll forget about me in no time. You'll probably have Louise over here before too long," she added in a sarcastic tone of voice.

"Shush, Frank said as he turned Rita around and began having sex with her from behind.

"Man, I love his penis," Rita thought as she enjoyed every second of Frank's manhood.

They continued having sex until the two of them were completely worn out from exhaustion. Then they laid there on the bed not moving, just relaxed and calm.

"I really should get back to bed with Joe," Rita said finally. "I sure as hell don't want to fall asleep here! That wouldn't be good," she added, smiling at Frank.

"Yea, you're right," Frank conceded. "But I really wish you didn't have to go. If you stick around a while longer, I may just get hard again," he said, smiling, hoping to entice Rita to stay a bit longer.

"Maybe we can have sex right up until almost morning, just in time to make sure we don't get caught. Because I should take advantage of this situation while I can," he thought.

And just then, he reached for her hand and put it on his now soft penis.

"Feel that?" he asked. "Don't you want some more of that?" he added, looking Rita in the eyes.

He was pretty sure the answer was a resounding yes, but he wanted to hear her say it.

"You know I do," Rita said, kissing him on the lips and squeezing his penis at the same time. "But I really should get back to my own room. I'd hate for this trip to end badly," she said and winked. "I'd rather play it safe, so I can bug Joe to come visit you again sooner rather than later," she added.

Frank understood her reasoning, but he didn't like it.

"Listen," he said. "We've been doing this every night since we first had sex in the kitchen that morning, plus we had a fucking threesome. Can't you just stay a little longer? I'm not finished with you yet," he added while putting his hand on her vagina.

At that, Rita was instantly feeling aroused by his gesture and words. It made her feel aroused to know that Frank desired her so much.

"Well, maybe just a little while longer then," she moaned. "I do love having you," she added and smiled.

Then she decided she would dominate Frank and show him a few tricks she had not yet let him see.

"That was amazing," Frank said.

"Yea, you liked that, eh?" Rita replied, looking at him and smiling.

"I more than liked it," Frank said. "I fucking loved it," he continued with the biggest smile on his face he could muster.

"Okay, big boy," Rita said. "I really do have to get back to my own room now. It's coming on daybreak," she added.

Then she kissed Frank on the cheek.

"Okay," Frank said, pouting. "I'm gonna miss you, baby," he added with his lip hanging down.

Rita stood up by the bed.

"Take a good hard look, Frank. Take a picture in your mind, right now, of what you are seeing before you. I want you to freeze-frame me in your mind. All of me. So that you don't forget me when I'm gone tomorrow, so that you think of me every time you have sex with Louise," she continued and laughed.

"And I really wish you would stop having sex with her, because you never know who else she might be sleeping around with besides you," Rita added. "Have you ever thought of that?" Rita asked.

Frank smiled. It turned him on to think that Rita was jealous. He liked it.

"Don't worry," Frank replied. "It will be a long-ass time before I can get you out of my mind. Plus, I have your panties to help me along," he said and chuckled a little.

"Okay, I really have to go now," Rita said.

"One last kiss?" Frank asked.

"Okay, one last kiss," Rita said, leaning over and kissing Frank on the lips.

She hated to leave him. She wanted more of him even though they had just had sex for what seemed like hours. She had lost track of time.

"What is this guy doing to me?" she wondered as she got up from kissing him to leave the room.

She hurried down the hallway to sneak back into bed with Joe, but when she got there, Joe wasn't in the bed.

"What the fuck!" Rita thought, and her heart began to pound hard in her chest.

"Was Joe awake? How long had he been awake? What did he hear?"

A thousand different thoughts were now running through her mind, and fear was gripping her hard. Anxiety was pouring out of every fiber of her being. What was she going to say? What was Joe going to do?

She was suddenly terrified of what could happen.

"Where in fuck is he?" she wondered as she crawled into bed as quickly as she could and pretended to be asleep.

"Maybe he didn't realize I wasn't in bed," she thought. "No, don't be silly, the bed is not that big," she corrected herself.

Suddenly Joe walked into the bedroom. "Oh, there you are," he said. "I had to get up to take a piss. I didn't take as many pills as I usually do, so I woke up with a piss hard on," he continued. "Where were you?" he asked.

"Oh, I woke up too and couldn't get back to sleep. So I went downstairs and made a tea and just sat at the kitchen table thinking," Rita replied.

"Really!" Joe said. "Is that where you were? I figured as much," he added.

And just when he said that, Rita's anxiety began to dissipate a little.

"What were you thinking about?" Joe asked in seeing Rita was not quite herself.

"Oh, nothing really," Rita said. "Just about life. How strange it all is. You know, stuff like that. And I was thinking of the long drive tomorrow and what I might do during the drive. And what snacks should we prepare to take with us? You know, stuff like that," she added.

Then Joe said, "You're gonna miss Frank, aren't you? I can tell you really like him, and the two of you seem to hit it off."

"What!" Rita said. "Yea, he's okay, I guess. He seems nice enough for sure. He's been a very good host to us. And I've learned a lot from him with his hippy lifestyle here, for sure," she said and chuckled.

She was wondering what Joe was getting at, or if he was getting at anything. Her heart was still in her mouth with anxiety.

Joe smiled and said, "Well, I am going to try to get back to sleep. I'm glad you like my buddy Frank. He's been a really good friend to me for years and I figured you would like him, just like I do," he said, climbing back into bed turning his back to Rita.

Rita let out a huge sigh of relief. "That could have been sooooooo bad. Thank the Lord he was just using the bathroom and I came back here when I did," she said to herself.

She could only imagine what might have been the case had Joe gone looking for her and couldn't find her! "If he had looked into Frank's bedroom and seen her sitting on top of Frank..." she thought. "Oh my goodness. I am freaked right out now," she realized

Her heart was still racing even though the danger had passed. It was the what-ifs that were now plaguing her mind, but she was relieved to know that none of them had occurred.

After a time, her anxiety began to dissipate, and finally she fell asleep. She was exhausted from all the sex she and Frank had had.

Chapter Seven

Not Ready To Go

The next morning, neither Rita nor Frank were up early, but Joe was up raring to go. He made coffee and toast for everyone and woke both Rita and Frank up to come and have some. He had even set the table for the three of them.

Both Rita and Frank were tired from the night before, but neither of them wanted it to show for obvious reasons. Frank was awakened by the noise Joe was making in the kitchen. Once awake, he went quickly to the washroom to splash some water on his face, and when he was almost to the bathroom door, Rita was just coming out and they pretty near ran into each other.

Rita backed off, "Sorry, I didn't see you there," she said.

Frank smiled. "No worries. I just wanted to splash some water on my face to look half alive before going downstairs to face Joe," he replied.

"You wouldn't believe what happened after I left your room last night," Rita whispered to Frank.

"What?" Frank asked, all curious.

"I don't have time to get into it right now," Rita said. "But once we are back home, I'll call yea and fill you in," she continued.

"What, I have to wait that long?" Frank asked. "You've got me all curious now!" he added.

And just then Joe hollered up the stairs to the two of them. "You guys better get down here, the toast and coffee I made for the two of you is going to get cold."

"Be right down," Rita yelled back. Then she tapped Frank on the ass. "You best get some water on your face and get your ass downstairs," she said, smiling as she headed toward the bedroom to get dressed.

Frank quickly splashed some water on his face and examined his face in the mirror.

"Man, you look like you've been screwed, blued, and tattooed," he said to himself.

He tried to fix his hair that was sticking up all over the place by wetting it down and running a comb through it. He was feeling pressure as he knew Joe was in the kitchen with food and drink waiting. Suddenly, he felt nervous inside.

"What had happened? What was Rita talking about? Did Joe know something? Did he hear them having sex?" Suddenly, all these thoughts were going through his mind and his anxiety was rising.

"Do I even want to go downstairs and face Joe?" he thought to himself. "Was this some kind of set up?" he wondered. But then he remembered that Rita seemed all good and relaxed when he had just seen her, so he probably had nothing to worry about.

"Whatever it was about, she must have dealt with it effectively," he thought to himself.

Then he quickly headed downstairs to the kitchen.

The table was set and the coffee was poured and Joe was already seated at the table.

"Good morning, fine sir," Joe said as Frank entered the room.

"Top of the morning to yea," Frank replied and smiled. "This looks great," Frank added, looking at the food on the table. "Thanks so much for making us a bite to eat," he continued, pulling up a chair at the table.

"Yea, it's the least I could do," Joe replied. "Seeing as you have put Rita and I up for the past few days. Rita and I were talking about it just last night, and we both agree, you're a mighty fine host, my friend," Joe added.

Frank smiled and took a gulp of coffee. He wasn't quite sure what to say as Joe sat there watching him.

"Is he suspicious?" Frank wondered. "Does he know something, and he is just not saying anything?" he thought. "What was Rita talking about when she said I'd never guess what happened?"

All these thoughts were running through Frank's mind as he ate the toast that Joe had prepared for all of them. But he concluded that Joe must not be aware, because if he was, he wouldn't be being this nice to him or Rita. So he must not know that anything went on between the two of them, he surmised.

Just then Rita entered the room.

"Ah, there's my beautiful, hot, sexy wife," Joe said, smiling at Rita.

"Good morning," Rita says, smiling and leaning over to hug Joe around the neck from behind, while looking directly at Frank as she did.

She was dressed in her usual attire, with three quarters of her breasts exposed. Tight pants that showed every curve of her sexy body and high heels to extenuate her long slender legs that went up to make the sweetest ass Frank swore he had ever seen.

"How in fuck am I ever going to forget that?" Frank wondered as he gazed at Rita's beauty.

"Good morning to you too, Frank," Rita said, as if she knew what he was thinking and was bringing him out of his gaze.

"Oh, good morning," Frank replied. "Have some toast, it is really good with the homemade jam on it," Frank said, pointing to the stack of toast Joe had made that was sitting in the middle of the table.

"Don't mind if I do," Rita said, sitting down at the table, reaching for a slice.

Like Frank, Rita didn't really want to talk much, so she stuffed her mouth with toast and went on about how good the jam was and how the coffee Joe had made was spot on, just the way she liked it.

"Are you all packed?" Joe asked.

"Yea, pretty much," Rita replied.

"Okay, good," Joe responded. "I'm going to go finish packing and I think I will jump in the shower as well. But don't worry, I'll be quick to make sure I leave enough hot water for you to take one too," he said, looking at Rita.

"Thanks," she said, smiling. "You're the best, Honey," she added.

Joe leaned over and kissed Rita on the cheek and then headed upstairs.

"Thanks again for making toast and coffee for us all," Frank yelled to him as he was leaving the room.

"My pleasure," Joe replied and kept on walking.

Once alone in the kitchen, Frank asked Rita what she was talking about earlier.

"Oh, it was nothing, really," Rita said. "But then, it was," she added.

"Which is it?" Frank asked. "Come on, tell me what you were talking about," he demanded.

"Well," Rita said. "We almost got caught last night!"

"WHAT!" Frank responded, his heart starting to beat faster. "What do you mean, we almost got caught?" he asked.

"Well, it was really lucky that I went back to the bedroom when I did, because when I got there Joe wasn't in the bed!" she continued.

"Where in fuck was he?" Frank asked, suddenly starting to feel very nervous.

"He was in the bathroom," Rita replied. "But I didn't know that at first. I wasn't sure where he was and I was freaking out. All these thoughts were running through my mind and I could see a horror story unfolding before me. My anxiety was through the roof and I thought my heart was going to beat right out of my chest," she added, looking Frank directly in the eyes.

"But finally he came into the bedroom and said he had been in the bathroom taking a piss. Apparently, he had woken up with a piss hard and had gone to relieve himself. But I didn't know that, until I did. And in the meantime I was freaking out," she continued.

"No kidding," Frank agreed. "Fuck, that is freaky. Man, that could have turned out real bad for both of us," Frank added.

"You don't have to tell me," Rita said. "I know," she added. "But luckily it didn't," she continued.

"So he must have known you were not in bed when he got up," Frank said.

"Yes, of course he did," Rita responded. "I told him I couldn't sleep so I came down here to the kitchen and made a tea and was just sitting at the table thinking to myself," Rita added.

"And he bought it?" Frank asked.

"Obviously, yes," Rita replied, smiling.

"Oh my gosh," Frank said. "Just hearing about all of this is giving me anxiety," he continued.

"Tell me about it," Rita said in agreement. "We were damn lucky, I can tell you that," she added.

"I guess we were," Frank agreed. "Thank God he never heard us. We, no doubt, were making a lot of noise. Probably more than we even realized," Frank continued.

"Yes, I know," Rita said. "I am so grateful that it worked out and Joe is none the wiser," she added.

"Well, I better get up there and get packed and ready to go," Rita said, getting up from the table to leave to go upstairs.

"Man, I hate to see you leave," Frank said, staring at her and looking her up and down.

Rita looked down at her sweet breasts and then looked up at Frank and smiled.

"You really like those, don't you?" she said, smiling and moving them side to side.

"You know I do," Frank said, smiling. He wanted to reach out and touch them, but he knew that wouldn't be cool in the moment. He didn't want to get sexually aroused. So he refrained himself and opted to just stare at them instead.

Rita seemed to know what he was thinking and leaned over and whispered to him, "Don't worry Baby, I'll be back" she said and chuckled.

"But I do have to get going and get ready. Joe will be in a big hurry to leave here soon and I don't want to deal with him nagging me and being pissed that I'm not ready when he is, so I have to go, sorry," she added, pouting.

"Give me one more private hug and kiss before you leave to go upstairs," Frank said.

"I can't," Rita said. "We came close to getting caught last night and you never know when Joe could come walking in here. It's not like he is out of it on sleeping pills. He's wide awake. Big difference. So we have to cool it, okay," she said.

"Okay," Frank said, resigning himself to the truth of the situation.

Rita was not his woman. She was Joe's wife. Joe, his good buddy of many years. He had to remind himself and bring himself back to reality. Soon she would be gone and he had no idea when or even if he would ever see her again. It pained him to think of it, but he tried to push it out of his mind. He didn't want Joe to pick up on his feelings, and he was feeling like they were laying right there on the table for all to see. Still, he would deny them if Joe were to say anything to him about it.

Rita left to finish packing and just as she was about to close her suitcase, Joe came into the bedroom. He was naked but for the towel around his waist. He opened the towel in front of Rita and shook his penis.

"You want some of this before we leave? I never got to give you any last night as I was too tired and needed my rest for the trip today; but I feel like I could definitely use a little love right now," he said, smiling.

Rita looked at him and smiled. "You're okay," she replied. "We don't have time right now, we have to get packed and on the road. I thought you were in a rush to get going!" she reminded him.

But Joe ignored Rita's reply and moved up close to her, putting his penis against her leg.

"I want some," he whispered in Rita's ear.

"Sorry Babe, but we really don't have time. We'll have awesome sex when we get home. It will give you something to think about and anticipate on the drive," Rita said and smiled.

Then she tapped his ass and said, "Come on, get your shit together so we can get on the road."

"Okay, okay," Joe said and moved away from her. And it wasn't long before they were packed and ready to go.

Frank was still sitting at the kitchen table when Joe and Rita came back downstairs, suitcases in hand. Frank had started reading one of the books sitting on his kitchen table in an effort to distract his mind while waiting for Rita and Joe.

"Well, we're off," Joe said, smiling and giving Frank a man hug. "Thank you so much for your hospitality. We had a great time and I wish we could stay longer. You've been a great host and we thoroughly enjoyed our visit here with yea, and hope to get back to see yea again sooner rather than later," Joe said.

"Oh, you're very welcome," Frank responded. "It was real nice having the two of you here. I'm gonna miss you guys," he added.

"Especially Rita," Joe said, smiling and winking at Frank.

"What! Rita, oh yes, of course," Frank replied, smiling back at Joe.

Rita just smiled and didn't say a word.

Frank nor Rita were sure what Joe meant by that statement, but neither of them were prepared to question it. Joe could see the statement made both of them uncomfortable, so he opted to provide them with an explanation.

"Well, what I meant was, having a sexy woman around the house like Rita, a man has to love that. Especially one that lives alone and is single. That's all I meant," Joe said.

"Oh right," Frank replied. "Of course," he added and smiled.

"I'm going to go pack up the vehicle," Joe said, picking up the luggage and heading out the door with it.

Once Joe was gone, Rita looked at Frank. "I'm going to miss you," she said. Then she moved close to him and put her hand on his penis.

"I'm especially going to miss this," she added, looking up at Frank and smiling.

"Stop that," Frank replied, smiling back at her. "You don't want to get me all horny now, do yea?" he added.

"No," she said. "Bad timing," she added, still smiling.

Frank hugged her tight. "I'm going to miss you too, more than you probably know or realize," he said.

"Oh, I have a pretty good idea," Rita replied. "I'll call as soon as we get home and let you know we made it all good," she continued.

"Great, yes, please do," Frank replied.

By this time, Joe was back in the house. "Car is all packed and ready to go," he said as he walked in the door. He reached out his hand to Frank.

"See yea later buddy," he said. "Thanks again for everything," he continued.

"Yes, yes," Frank said. "No problem, come back anytime. You guys are always welcome here," he added.

Rita and Joe both said thank you once again as they left to get in their vehicle to leave. Joe drove off and tooted the horn as he left the driveway. Frank had gone outside to see them off with a wave and a smile.

As Frank entered back into his home, he suddenly felt a great emptiness. Rita, he realized, was now gone and it made him suddenly feel very sad. The house felt empty and cold, Frank did not like the feeling at all.

"It's going to be an adjustment now," he thought. "It always is, when people come here and then they leave. It takes time to get back into my own rhythm and used to being alone again," he realized.

And so, he sat down at his kitchen table and rolled up a doobie to ease his troubled mind.

Just then, memories of Rita sitting at that exact table came into his mind.

"Hey," he thought. "I don't have Rita here anymore, but I still have some awesome memories to keep me happy," and that thought made him smile even though inside he was feeling sad that Rita was gone.

Chapter Eight

The Long Way Home

It seemed to take what felt like forever to get back to their home in New York. Time just seemed to drag on, as did the miles of road.

Rita reminisced about Frank in her mind for almost the entire time, but she didn't want to think too much about the sex part, as she didn't want to get herself aroused in front of Joe. So she kept her thoughts to things like the way Frank looked at her, the way he walked, the sound of his voice, his eyes, his intelligence. The stories he told her and Joe, the land there, the river, his house, his life.

Then she thought about Louise, his friend with benefits, and she started to feel worried that Louise would move in on Frank now that she was gone. Yet, she knew at once that there was nothing she could do about it. Frank was not hers and was free to do as he wished. Still, it made her feel worried, yet she knew she had to face the fact that she was Joe's wife and that Frank was a single guy. She had no claim on him, and it was, she knew, wrong of her to even think such things.

Still, she was only human, and the jealousy she was feeling over Louise showing up at Frank's was starting to consume her. So much so, that she was feeling that somehow she had to make sure Louise did not steal Frank from her. Even though, at the same point, she knew Frank didn't belong to her. She didn't care. In her mind, Frank did belong to her, and she aimed to keep it that way despite the fact that she was a married woman who was now hundreds of miles away from him. Somehow, she was determined to keep him in her grip despite the circumstances.

"You're not talking much, Honey," Joe finally said to break the silence.

"Oh, yea, I'm just relaxing and thinking," Rita replied.

"What yea thinking about?" Joe asked.

"Oh, not much, just our visit and how nice it was at Frank's house. The land and the way he lives, it's all new to me and quite nice, I now realize," she said. "I had always thought that living in the countryside would be a complete drag and not something I would ever want to even consider. I've always been a city person, but since being at Frank's place, I see living in the country in a whole new light," Rita continued.

"Maybe it's because I am getting older, that the country seems like a nicer place than I had ever imagined it to be. I'm really not sure; I just know that it did my soul good to spend time there at his place. Being in the fresh air and nature, you know, it rejuvenated me in many ways," Rita continued.

"Yes, I have to agree with you," Joe replied. "I too feel rejuvenated from spending time there, and Frank is a swell guy. Can't say a bad word about the dude. He's always been there for me, and I'm happy I finally got to go and visit him after all the years of just talking to him on the phone," Joe replied. "I'm also glad I got to introduce you to him, as I talked so much about you to him before he ever meant you," Joe added.

Then he asked Rita, "What did you think of Frank? Did you like him?"

"Oh Frank... ah, yea, I like him. Like you said, he is a great guy. He was very pleasant and sweet to us the entire time we were at his home. Yea, no question, he's a sweet dude," Rita replied.

"I can't believe he is still single," Joe said. "He's smart, he's got his own home and lots of land. He's hardworking and looks to be in good shape. Plus, he's a good-looking guy. Makes yea wonder why he is alone. I thought he'd be married with children by now," Joe continued.

The mere thought of Frank being married, or having children of his own, made Rita feel sick. She was happy he was single and not saddled down with a wife and children. If he had been, she could have never had all the awesome sex she had had with him.

"What a relief," she said out loud, without thinking.

"What do you mean?" Joe asked.

"Oh, nothing, just that it was a relief that there were not more people to deal with when visiting is all. I'm happy it was only Frank and not a wife and kids also," she added and laughed.

So Joe laughed as well and let it go at that.

Finally, after hours of driving, they were pulling into the driveway of their mansion home in New York.

"Home sweet home," Joe said, smiling as he pulled into the driveway.

"Yes, my own bed is going to feel good tonight," Rita said and smiled.

They parked and unpacked the car. Rita was exhausted from the trip.

"I'm going to go take a nice bath, Honey," she said.

"Go right ahead, Dear," Joe replied. "I'm going to go make some phone calls and get on top of the situation at work," he added.

So Rita retired to the bathroom that was connected to their luxury bedroom and drew herself a bath. As she undressed to get into the bathtub, thoughts of Frank came into her mind. She wondered what he was doing at that moment. If he missed her. If he was also thinking about her. And she wanted to call him, but she felt it was too soon. Then, she remembered she had told him she would call when they had arrived home. So, before she got into her bath, she went to her phone and called him.

"Hello," Frank answered.

"Hi Frank, it's me, Rita. I just wanted to call to let you know we made it back home, all good. I remembered that I'd told you I would call, and so I'm calling yea now. We just got here about a half hour ago," she said.

"Oh, that's great," Frank replied. "Happy you guys made it home safe and sound, and thank you for calling to let me know - Appreciated," he added

"No problem," Rita said, and then she was at a loss for words.

"How was the trip?" Frank asked.

"Oh, it was good, uneventful, but long," Rita replied.

"That's good," Frank said. "Happy you guys made it back safely," he continued.

"Thank you," Rita said.

Then she decided to tell Frank, "I was thinking of you the entire drive back here. I couldn't get you out of my mind, Frank! I miss you so much already," she said.

"Yea," Frank responded. "I know what yea mean. I've been thinking a lot about you as well and missing you being here. But we both knew this was the situation and so that's the way it goes... right!?" Frank said.

Then Frank realized he'd best be careful what he said on the phone because Joe could be in the vicinity.

"Where's Joe?" Frank asked.

"Oh, he's downstairs making phone calls to do with the situation at his work," Rita replied.

"Oh, okay," Frank said. "We have to be careful how we talk on the phone, Rita. We don't want Joe to overhear us," Frank added.

"Of course," Rita responded. "I knew he was not within earshot when I said those things to you," she continued.

Then Rita started again.

"But the truth is, I do miss you already, and I am feeling jealous of Louise. She is right there. Right up the road from you, and I know she has a major crush on you. I'm worried she is going to steal you from me now that I am no longer there! I know, I have no right to feel that way, you are single and so is she, and I am married, but I just have to tell you that is how I am feeling. I am worried about it, and I can't help it," Rita said.

"Hahaha!" Frank laughed.

"Why are you laughing?" Rita asked. "Do you think my feelings are funny?" she continued.

"Yes, I do," Frank responded. "Because Louise and I are just good buddies. We've been friends for years. If I was going to hook up with her, as in a relationship, it would have happened a long time ago. So I don't think you have any worries, Rita. Relax," Frank replied.

Rita took a deep breath and smiled.

"Okay," she said. "I will try not to worry about it," she added.

"Good," Frank said.

"But are you still going to be fuck buddies with her and have stay overs?" Rita asked.

"Well, that remains to be seen," Frank responded. "But most likely, to be honest, yes, we probably will. It's just sex, Rita, you know. We've been getting together for years. I don't see why I should stop now. I mean I am still single after all, and a man does need some lovin every now and then, you understand that, right?" Frank asked.

"Yea, I get it; but I can't say I like it," Rita replied.

"Listen," Frank said. "You're a married woman and you're having sex with your husband. How do you think that makes me feel?" he asked.

"Oh right," Rita said. "I'm sorry," she added.

"It's quite all alright," Frank replied. "I knew what I signed up for. I knew you were married and to one of my best friends, no less. So don't worry about it. I understand. But also, don't bug me about Louise. She is my longtime friend and yes, we have sex from time to time. It's not a big deal, okay!" he said.

"Okay," Rita replied.

"I should get going, I can hear Joe coming up the stairs and I have a bath drawn and waiting for me. I'll call yea soon, take good care," Rita said.

"Okay, later then," Frank replied. "Enjoy your bath. I wish I were there to take it with yea," he added and laughed.

Just then Joe walked into the bedroom.

"Who are you talking to, Honey?" he asked.

"Oh, I called Frank to let him know we made it back okay."

"Oh, hey Frank!" Joe yelled.

"Hey," Frank said back.

Then Rita handed the phone over to Joe.

"Yea, just happy you guys made it back safe and sound," Frank said right away.

"Yup, we're all good," Joe responded. "And thanks again for the great visit," he added.

"No worries, anytime," Frank replied.

"Okay, talk to yea later, or did you want to talk to Rita again?" Joe asked.

"No, no... I'm good. Talk to you guys later," Frank replied, and they ended the call.

"That was nice of you to call Frank and let him know we made it back home safe and sound," Joe said to Rita.

"Yea, I told him I would before we left, and so I did before I got into my bath. Now I am going to go and take my bath as the water is probably getting cold," Rita said.

"Enjoy your bath, Honey," Joe replied. "I need to get back to the office. This situation is worse than I thought, and I'm glad we came back when we did," he continued.

Then he kissed Rita on the cheek and left to go back to his home office in the downstairs of their home.

Rita got into her bath, laid back and relaxed. She thought about what Frank had said about Louise, and she hoped that Louise would stay away from him. But she had grave doubts that that would happen. She could tell that Louise had a major crush on Frank, and knew all Frank would have to do would be to open the door to her, and she would be there living with him as his full-time woman. And that was the last thing Rita wanted. Yet, she knew there was nothing she could do about it, so she resigned herself to trying not to worry about it. She tried to just relax and enjoy the quietness of her bath.

How all of this was going to pan out, she had no idea. She was not prepared to leave her husband, nor her life in the city, and so she would just have to get over her feelings of worry and jealousy when it came to Louise and Frank, she concluded.

Time went by, and life seemed to be a drag to Rita. She missed Frank's smell. She missed his voice. She missed his ways. She missed his home. She missed his penis, the way he made love to her. She missed it all.

Joe was never around. He was always working. The only company she had was the hired help. She continued fantasizing about Frank while having sex with her husband. She found it helped in terms of missing him, but it didn't really work because sex with Frank was not sex with Joe. So even that was not working very well for her now.

She'd call Frank, but there would be no answer, and then she would fret that he was with Louise or maybe some other woman he'd met. She was, she knew, just about driving herself crazy over it all.

She felt like she was living in some sort of mystery novel, the end of which even she was not sure of, despite being one of the main characters. At times, she wanted to jump in her vehicle and drive back to Frank's place! Just show up out of the blue! But she knew that was not reasonable thinking. First off, she had a husband to consider and he would not be too pleased with her if she were to do such a thing. How would she explain it? Yet, these were her thoughts and they were common and recurring.

She also didn't want to call Frank too often, because it would show up on the phone bill and Joe may see it and become suspicious of why she would be calling "his" friend all the time. So, she was attempting to think of more creative ways that she could maintain communication with Frank.

Then it occurred to her that she could always write to him! Sure, it was considered old-fashioned, but in her situation, it seemed perfect… almost, too perfect. No one would have to know, and she could stay in touch with Frank. Plus, it would allow her to express her desires without fear of anyone overhearing her.

She now had a new mission, and she was excited about it.

Chapter Nine

Life After Rita

The house seemed empty now that Rita and Joe were gone. Frank was used to living alone, and he was very content with that lifestyle. It always seemed to him that when people came into his world, after they left, he would have to adjust to being alone again. He hated that feeling, but he also knew that it wouldn't be long before he was back into his comfort zone once again.

Every time he entered his bedroom, he thought he could smell Rita's scent. He imagined her on his bed, laying there naked and sexy as fuck. Just the thought of it made his penis move with excitement. Then he remembered the underwear Rita had given him, and he smiled and went and retrieved them from his dresser drawer. He pushed them up to his nose and reveled in them for a moment. "Ummmm," he moaned. "She smells soooo good." And before he knew it, he was on the bed masturbating, fantasizing she was there with him.

He wondered if she could feel him thinking about her. And this sort of action was becoming a habit with Frank. At least once a day, but usually more, he was masturbating in his bedroom and fantasizing over Rita. Then he would feel ashamed knowing she was, after all, his good friend's wife. Then he would feel tremendous guilt. It was one thing to have sex with someone who is single, but it's another to be screwing around with a married woman and even worse, married to a great friend like Joe had always been to him. "Have I turned into a complete lying asshole?" he wondered. But he couldn't seem to help himself. So he concluded that his lust for Rita was stronger than his moral fiber.

He'd not gone to see Louise since Rita left. It had been a while, but he wasn't sure exactly how long. To Frank, it already seemed like an eternity. He had thought about Rita being jealous and asking him not to have casual sex with Louise anymore. And while he knew he had set Rita straight on that situation, he realized he had in fact been avoiding seeing Louise, and maybe that was the reason why. He didn't want to have sex with Louise; he didn't think, but he thought he would venture over to her place to pay her a visit just for something to do and to see how she was doing.

He arrived at Louise's house, but her car was not in the driveway. There was another car there and he figured it must be Louise's daughter's. He wasn't sure if he should go in or not, but since he was already there, he opted to go and knock on the door. Louise's daughter Lacy came to the door.

"Oh, hi Frank. Long time no see," Lacy said, smiling. "Come on in, Mom's not home. She had to run out to do errands. I'm not sure what time she will be back; she just left not long ago," Lacy continued.

Frank entered the house but stood by the door. "Oh, that's cool. I was just dropping by to say hi. I should have called first. I usually do, but I just got the urge to come and visit and went for it," Frank said, smiling.

"Oh no, you can't leave," Lacy said, smiling. "I've not seen you in a long time. Come in and sit down, I'll make you a coffee," she continued.

"Are you sure?" Frank asked hesitantly.

"Yes, of course I'm sure," Lacy replied. So Frank took a seat at the kitchen table.

Frank could not help but notice that Lacy had turned into a fine-looking young woman. "You're all grown up now," Frank said, looking her up and down

"Yup, I sure am," Lacy said, leaning over in front of Frank, showing her breast to him while putting his cup of coffee on the table. "What do yea think?" she asked. "Did I turn out alright or what?" she asked, smiling.

"Oh, yea, you turned out mighty fine," Frank said, smiling back at her.

Frank had seen Lacy here and there over the years from being friends with Louise, but he'd not seen her since she graduated high school and moved to the city to go to college. She was away most of the time, and it seemed she rarely came to visit. So she had changed quite a bit from the last time Frank had seen her.

"How long has it been since I saw you last?" Frank asked.

"Oh, it must be two or three years anyway," Lacy replied. "I don't get to come home much as I am so busy with work and school. Mom understands, but I know she wishes I was here more often. I just had some time off this week and thought I would surprise her with a visit. She didn't even know I was coming, and it didn't work out so well as she had things she had to take care of today, for instance. But she says she is free for the rest of the week, so thankfully we will get some time to hang out together," Lacy continued.

"That's nice," Frank said and smiled. "You don't have any children, right?" Lacy asked.

"No, no... it's not that I didn't want kids, it just never happened is all," Frank responded. "And I'm all good with that. It would just give me something more to worry about," Frank added, still smiling.

"I'm not having any children," Lacy agreed. "I don't think I would be a good mother. Plus, I don't see any men I would want to create a child with," she added and laughed, hitting her leg.

Frank laughed as well. "Slim pickings out there, eh," he replied.

"You got that right," Lacy said. Then she said something that Frank did not see coming. "I'm attracted to older men," she added.

"Is that right? Wow," Frank responded. "Like how old?" he asked.

"Like your age," Lacy said and winked.

Frank could now feel his face getting hot and he wondered if he was blushing, but he couldn't stop it. He was sure Lacy noticed as

well. Then he suddenly started feeling hot, so he decided to take off
his   jacket.

Frank was sexy himself and well-built. He didn't work out
as such, but he worked hard on his land and house and it kept him
in tip-top shape. Plus, he was very easy on the eyes, even as an older
man.

"I think men my age are a little too old for you," Frank finally
said.

"Oh, I don't think so," Lacy replied, getting up and walking over
to the kitchen counter. "I'm a woman now, Frank, not a little girl. I
have lady parts and they all work!" she said, looking Frank directly
in the eyes and smiling.

"I can see that," Frank replied, admiring her while she stood by
the kitchen sink.

"Would you like some more coffee?" Lacy asked, bending over
in front of Frank, exposing her underwear under her short mini skirt.

Frank couldn't help but stare; it was right in his face.

"Ummm, sure," he said without even thinking. He was
mesmerized, and Lacy was aware of it, which was the true reason
she had bent over in front of him.

So she stood there bent over for a time, even though it wasn't
logical. Finally, she stood back up and pretended she hadn't noticed
what she had just done. The coffee was ready, so she went to retrieve
Frank's empty cup off the table, and when she did, she made sure
she leaned way over, exposing her breasts as best she could. Then

she wiggled her way back over to the counter to prepare another coffee for him.

This whole scene felt strangely familiar to Frank. Rita used to do a lot of those same things, and he knew where that had led to. But this was his friend's daughter, and hence she was off limits, even if she was a sexy young thing who was into older men. He couldn't dare to cross that line with her, could he? he asked himself.

"Here's your coffee, Frank," Lacy said, leaning over in front of him once again. She knew Frank was looking at her chest, and she was happy about it. In fact, she wanted Frank to have sex with her, but how was she going to make it happen?

Suddenly, before she even knew what she was saying, she blurted out, "Listen, I want you to take me. I'm really turned on by you. I've had a crush on you for years, and now that I am older and of age, I want you to have sex with me," she said.

Frank was stunned, and at a loss for words. "You want me to what?!" he asked in a surprised tone of voice.

"You heard me," Lacy said, smiling.

"Yea, I heard yea, but I'm not sure what in hell you are talking about. I'm your mom's friend. Your mom would flip if I had sex with you. You do realize that, don't you?" Frank continued.

"She doesn't have to know," Lacy said. "I don't plan on telling her, and I am quite sure you wouldn't, so what is there to worry about?" Lacy asked and smiled.

"Maybe you don't understand the type of relationship your mom and I have," Frank said. "We are more than just friends, we have sex together from time to time and have had for years," Frank continued.

"Oh, I'm well aware," Lacy replied. "I know you guys have sex, but I want you to have sex with me," she continued.

"WHAT!" Frank replied. "You've got to be kidding me right now," he added.

Then Frank continued. "This is just too much for me. You really need to stop this nonsense. I can't sleep with you, your mom would probably never speak to me again. Plus, you are way too young for me. I like women my own age or around my own age anyway."

Lacy looked Frank directly in the eyes and started removing her shirt and bra, exposing her bare breasts in front of him. "You don't want to play with these?" she asked, holding her naked breasts in her hands and looking down at them. "They are so cute, don't you think?" she said.

Frank was stunned and suddenly very horny. "Stop it," he told her. "Put your shirt back on. I can't do this," he continued.

But Lacy was not about to give up. She got up from her chair at the table and went directly over to where Frank was sitting. She pushed herself onto his lap and, with her hands, put her boobs in his face. "Here," she said. "Suck on these for a minute; they need some attention," she added and smiled.

And before Frank could even think about it, he was doing as she asked and loving every second of it. And while he was enjoying her boobs, she was grinding on his penis, which she could feel getting harder and harder through his pants.

"We can't do this," Frank said, coming up for air.

"Yes, we can," Lacy replied.

"What if Louise comes home and catches us here making out, then what?" Frank asked.

"We don't have to stay here. We can go over to your house and lock the door. No one around here recognizes my car, as I am not around here very often. I could follow you over to your place," Lacy suggested.

"Now things are getting complicated," Frank thought. "Listen, it is probably best that I just leave before we both do something we will regret. I'd better just go before your mom gets home. I'd hate to be sitting here with a hard-on when she walked in the door," Frank said.

Lacy smiled and got up off of Frank's lap. "Okay, have it your way then. I can't believe you don't want to have sex with me. I've waited all these years to grow up so I could get you in bed and now you are turning me down," she said, pouting.

"I'm really sorry," Frank replied. "You are wicked sexy and all, and I'm not saying I don't want to; I'm saying it is probably not a good idea given the context. I am sure you understand," Frank added.

Then he continued, as if he was trying to defend his position. "Don't get me wrong, I would love to make out with you, no doubt about it. And I wish I could, believe me. I am horny as hell right now, but it just seems too complicated and risky, and so I am thinking it is probably not a good idea.".

Then Frank immediately thought of how he and Rita were having sex just down the hallway from Joe, and he realized he sounded like a hypocrite. Yet, this was different—this was his friend's daughter, even though, technically, yes, she's a grown woman. Still, it just didn't feel right. "How could I look Louise in the eyes again if I had sex with her daughter?" he thought.

Frank left with his penis so hard it could be seen through his pants. Lacy stood at the door bare-chested in her miniskirt. "Sure you won't reconsider?" she yelled as Frank was walking towards his truck.

Frank just waved his hand at her and got into his truck, turned it on, and got the hell out of there. "WHAT was that?" he thought, as he drove back to his place. He had never seen any of that coming. That was totally unexpected. "She had a crush on me all these years! That is news to me," he thought to himself.

Then he took a deep breath and smiled. "Thank goodness I got out of that one. That could have been bad and real bad," he thought. "Even though it most likely would have been good and real good at the same time," he countered and smiled.

Frank had just entered his home when the phone started ringing, so he went to answer it. "Hello," he said without looking to see who was calling.

"You were right, Frank," Lacy said right away. "Mom just got home. We would have been right in the middle of you-know-what when she got here. So you made the right call, and I just wanted to tell you. I have to go, she is coming into the house now. Talk to yea later," Lacy said and then ended the call.

"Hi Mom," Lacy said, trying to make sure she had put herself back together properly and that nothing looked out of place. Lacy felt she knew her mom was crazy about Frank and had desired to have a real relationship with him for years. She assumed it was the only reason her mom had stayed single, just so she could be free to have sex with Frank.

"How did you make out with all your errands and stuff?" Lacy asked.

"Oh, good," Louise responded. "But I'm happy they are done, that is for sure. Now I can relax and spend some time with my sweet daughter who I rarely get to see anymore. I'm so happy you got to come and visit with me for a time, I know how busy you have been. It is so nice to have you here dear," Louise said, giving Lacy a hug.

"Ah, thanks, Mom," Lacy replied and smiled.

And just then Louise noticed the empty cup of coffee on the kitchen table where Frank had been sitting. "Who was here?" Louise asked.

"Oh, Frank dropped over. He didn't realize you weren't here," Lacy replied. "I invited him in for a coffee," she added. "I hope you don't mind."

"Oh no, of course not," Louise responded. "You've known Frank for years. It is good you invited him in. I bet he was surprised at how grown up you are now," Louise added.

"Yes, I think he was," Lacy replied.

But then Louise said, "I hope you weren't dressed like that when he was here!"

"Like what?" Lacy asked. "Yes, I was dressed the same way I am now! Why, is there something wrong with the way I am dressed?" Lacy asked in a demanding sarcastic tone of voice.

"Well, that outfit doesn't leave much to the imagination, is all I am saying," Louise retorted. "And Frank is a man, after all, Lacy. You ought to know that dressing like that is not appropriate around older men, especially," Louise continued.

Suddenly, Louise could feel herself feeling jealous of her daughter. She didn't want to feel jealous, but it was there whether she wanted it to be or not. She could just imagine Frank gawking at Lacy in that outfit that barely covered her private parts. She didn't blame him, she understood he was a man and men gawk at such things; she blamed Lacy for having been dressed like that in front of him, of all people. Frank was, after all, her man; even though he wasn't, he was in her mind in a sort of way. And as such, he was off limits, especially to her own daughter.

Then she changed gears. "What am I saying," Louise finally said. "I am sure it was all fine. Don't worry about it. I'm sorry I said anything about your outfit. It's no big deal," Louise continued.

"Thanks Mom," Lacy said. "For a minute there, I thought you were judging me for how I dress. All the women my age dress this way these days. And you're right, it's not a big deal," Lacy added.

Louise smiled and hugged Lacy. "Don't worry about it. I'm just happy you are here to visit and hang out. I miss you being away and hardly ever getting to see you," Louise said and kissed Lacy on the forehead.

But she couldn't let it go, not just yet. "So, how long was Frank here for?" Louise asked.

"Oh, I don't know really. Maybe half an hour or so. I made him a couple of coffees and we talked here at the table," Lacy replied.

"Oh really," Louise responded. "What would you and Frank have to talk about? You barely know him, really. I mean, you've seen him around with me for years, of course, but I don't think you really know him very well. So, I am curious as to what the two of you talked about," Louise continued.

"Oh, not much. Just small talk, you know, the weather and such. Nothing too serious. He asked where you were and how I was doing in school and how I like living in the city, just stuff like that," Lacy replied.

"Oh, right, that makes sense," Louise responded. She now was feeling satisfied and willing to let it go.

"What do you want to have for supper sweetie?" Louise asked.

"Whatever you like. You choose, I'm easy. I always love your cooking, Mom," Lacy said and smiled. "But I have some calls to make, so call me when supper is ready, okay," Lacy added, leaving the room and going upstairs to the room that was once her bedroom.

"Okay honey... I'll let you know when it's ready," Louise replied as she began preparing supper for the two of them.

While she cooked, she thought, "Hmm, Frank came by, he must want some love. This is great. I must go over and see him after supper, if that is okay with Lacy of course. I don't want to run out on my daughter when she is here visiting. She doesn't get home all that often anymore." Then she thought, "Oh, maybe I'd better just stay here and spend time with Lacy. It might be rude of me to leave and go to Frank's place tonight. I'll call him and set something up for when Lacy leaves," she thought. Still, she was so excited that Frank had dropped by.

She'd not seen nor heard tell of him since Rita and Joe had left and she was wondering if Frank was now all hung up on Rita and hence was not interested in their 'stay over' nights any longer. So she was relieved that he had dropped by and it made her feel happy, for she took it to mean that he still wanted her.

After supper, Louise called Frank. "Hey, it's me, stranger," she said on Frank's answering machine.

Frank was busy when the phone started ringing so he didn't bother to answer. But when he heard Louise's voice, he ran for the phone and picked it up. "Hey there," he said. "I stopped by earlier today to see yea but you were out," he continued.

"Yea, I heard," Louise replied.

At that, Frank immediately felt tension in his body. "Oh yea, what did you hear?" he asked, chuckling a nervous chuckle.

"Oh nothing really, just that you had dropped by while I was gone," Louise replied. "Lacy said you and her had a nice talk and that she made you a couple of coffees," Louise continued.

"That's right," Frank said. "I couldn't believe how much she changed since the last time I saw her. Time flies I guess, eh," he added.

"It sure does," Louise agreed. Then she asked, "Soooo, were you coming by for some loving, Frank?"

"Oh no," Frank said. "I was just coming by to say hi and to see how you were doing. I realized it had been some time since I had seen or talked to yea, so I figured I'd drop over. I should have called first, sorry about that," he continued.

Louise was saddened to hear this. She was thinking he wanted to have sex, but all he wanted was to say hi and chat.

"Oh no, no problem," Louise replied. "You know you are always welcome at my home anytime. No need to call first, but I might not be here is all, as you found out today," she continued.

"So when are we going to get together again? I miss you. I need some lovin,' Louise added. "I want to come and see you, Frank."

"Right now?" Frank asked.

"No," Louise replied and laughed. "Not right now, but in the near future. I would come over right now if my daughter wasn't here, and trust me I thought of it; but I don't get to see Lacy that often anymore, so I figured I should spend as much time with her as possible," Louise added.

"Oh right," Frank responded. "Makes sense," he agreed.

"But I do want to see you very soon," Louise continued.

"Okay, well I'm not sure what is going on right now. You know, with Rita just leaving and all; but give me some time and I'm sure we can get back into the swing of things again," he said and chuckled.

"I sure hope so," Louise replied. "I really miss you," she reiterated.

"Okay, I have to get going," Frank said. "Talk later," he added, and with that they ended the call.

Frank then sat down at his kitchen table and rolled a joint. The house was quiet. No one was there but him. He liked it. Then he smoked his homegrown weed and thought about the strange day he had had. He never dreamed Lacy would come on to him, or that she was a woman now. It had just never occurred to him. And what a woman she was. "Wow, those boobs, ummmm," he thought as he remembered her putting them in his face while grinding on his penis.

"She's a naughty little one," he thought and smiled. "Maybe a little too naughty," he thought. "What in hell was she thinking coming on to me like that? She knows her mom and I are good friends and involved," he said to himself. "So what was she thinking, or doing in trying to seduce me in her mom's house of all places?" he asked himself

It was all too much to get his head around right now. Too many women coming at him at once. "What is all of this about?" he wondered. Not so long ago it was just him and Louise once in a while, but now it was Rita, Louise, and now Lacy! "What," he wondered, "is going on?" But he couldn't figure it out and he didn't even want to bother trying.

He was stoned now and he just wanted to relax and watch a movie. It was too hard on his head to try to figure it all out. So he put a movie in his DVD player and laid down on the couch and it wasn't long before he dozed off. He was just nicely asleep, when he was awakened by a loud knock on the door.

"Who could be at the door at this hour?" he wondered. Still feeling half-asleep, he got up from the couch and sauntered to the door.

"Who's there?" he asked.

"Open up, it's me, Lacy,"

"Lacy!" He opened the door. "What in fuck are you doing here? Where's Louise?" he asked. He looked out the door and didn't see any car. "Where's your car?" Frank asked.

"Oh, it is still at Mom's place. I walked over here, so as to not cause any suspicion!" Lacy said and smiled.

Frank smiled back at Lacy without thinking. All he could think about in that moment was that maybe they were going to have some fun even though he knew it was probably not the best idea considering the circumstances.

Lacy was soaking wet from walking to Frank's house as it had started pouring rain outside.

"You're drenched," Frank said. "Do you want to put your clothes in the dryer? I can give you some clothes to put on while yours dry, if you'd like," he offered.

"Oh, no," she replied. "It's not a problem. You see, it's only my coat that is drenched, I'm naked underneath it," she said, smiling a big smile, pulling her coat open exposing her naked body underneath.

"WHOA," Frank replied, looking at Lacy standing there naked. "What are you trying to do to me? Are you trying to get me in trouble with your mom?" he asked.

"Yea, and don't forget she is also your fuck buddy. You can't forget that part," Lacy replied in a sarcastic tone of voice. "You guys have been fuck buddies for how many years now?!" she asked.

Frank smiled. "Yes, Louise and I have been having sex for some years, you are right about that. But we have gone for periods of time where we really didn't see each other much. Louise had a few other dudes along the way; but me, I've pretty much stayed to myself; and now I suddenly have not one, not two, but three women wanting to have sex with me. I have to wonder why," he said and chuckled.

"I know why," Lacy said, moving closer to him and pressing her naked body up against him, while looking him in the eyes. "You're a sexy fucking dude, that's why," she continued. "Sure, you may be older, but I don't care about that. I want some of what has been keeping my mom on the hook for all these years," she added and laughed a little.

"Oh, that's what this is all about," Frank replied. "The cat is out of the bag, huh," he continued and rubbed his chin with a smile on his face.

"Does that bother you?" Lacy asked.

"No, not really," Frank replied. "But you might be disappointed," he added, still smiling.

"I don't think so," Lacy responded. "I have dreamed of a day when I would be old enough to get some of that for myself," she continued.

Frank was at a loss for words. He wasn't quite sure just how to deal with this situation. On the one hand, he had this hot-looking young woman wanting to have sex with him; but she was also the daughter of his friend and off-and-on lover Louise. "What am I to do in this situation?" he asked himself.

Lacy picked up on his hesitancy, so she reached down and touched his penis, and when she did, she was pleasantly surprised to see that Frank was already somewhat sexually aroused.

"Now," she thought to herself. "I just have to get his mind on board."

"No one will know," she whispered in Frank's ear while she stroked his penis. "Come on, Frank, have sex with me. I'm hungry for it. Come on," Lacy pleaded. "I promise I won't say a word to anyone and my mom will never even know I was here," she continued. "She was sleeping when I left the house, and my vehicle is there, so she is not even going to know I left the house. And I'll go right back and I will be there before she even wakes up," Lacy added. "You have nothing to worry about, I promise," she continued.

Frank was getting weaker by the second. "Okay," he finally said. "You win, you make a convincing argument, and I am horny as fuck for you right now," he added.

Then he picked Lacy up and carried her upstairs to his bedroom and threw her gently on the bed. He took off his shirt and pants and admired Lacy's body laying naked there on his bed waiting for him. The anticipation on both their parts filled the atmosphere in the room.

"You want some of this, do you?" Frank said

"Yes, please... oh yes, I do," Lacy said in a sexy tone of voice.

And at that, they began having wild sex.

Frank had staying power and Lacy was greatly impressed by that. Most young dudes she had sex with only lasted a few minutes. "Now, I'm having sex with a man," she said to herself and smiled.

The two of them were so enthralled in the sex that time had passed without them even realizing it. Suddenly, it became apparent that the sun was up!

"Oh, shit," Frank said. "The sun is up. Your mom is going to wonder where you are! Fuck, we lost track of time. You better get up and get going right now! FUCK!" Frank exclaimed.

Lacy suddenly looked worried as well and got up quickly, putting her coat on.

"Yes, you're right, I'd better get going right now. But before I leave, I just want to say, I had the best time ever with you tonight," Lacy said as she leaned in and kissed Frank on the lips. "And I have to tell you, I want more," she said, smiling.

"No, no," Frank replied, smiling. "This was a one-time deal," he added. "You said you wouldn't say anything, remember?!" Frank reminded her.

"Oh, I know I did; but fuck, I loved it so much, didn't you?" Lacy replied and asked.

"I have no complaints," Frank replied and smiled. "But it's the situation, you know – I don't have to tell you," he added.

"Okay," Lacy said, putting a frown on her face and pouting. "But just in case you change your mind, I'm leaving you my number and address in the city. So, if you are ever in town, you could come on by and see me and no one would know!" she said and smiled. "Just think about it anyway, but I should get going," she continued.

And at that they started down to the kitchen, when suddenly there was a loud knock on the door.

"Frank, are you in there? It's me, Louise. I need to talk to you," Louise yelled from the other side of the door.

Chapter Ten

Excessive Complications

Frank was now faced with answering the door to Louise, who was still knocking. "Hide and stay quiet," he said to Lacy as he went to answer the door.

"Hey, good morning. What are you doing around so early in the day?" Frank asked and smiled.

"Oh Frank, I'm in a state, I don't know where Lacy is. Her car is in the yard, but she is nowhere to be seen. I called her for breakfast, but when she didn't show up, I went to her room and she wasn't there. I can't imagine where she would be this early in the morning. You haven't seen her, have you?" Louise asked.

"No, I haven't seen her, but she probably just went out for a walk or something. I wouldn't worry too much about it, she's from these parts and knows her way around. I'm sure she's not too far away," Frank reassured her.

"Oh, I hope you are right. I'd die if something happened to her and I just can't imagine where she would be at this early hour of the morning, plus it was pouring down rain earlier. Why would she be out walking in the pouring rain?" Lousie asked.

"I'm sure she is all good. I bet if you go home now, she is probably already there waiting for you and wondering where you are," Frank said and smiled.

"Do you think?" Louise asked.

"Okay, that's what I'm going to do then. Thanks, Frank, you really helped to settle my nerves. Hopefully, you are right, and she is back at the house already. I'll call and let you know if that is the case. If not, can you please help me search for her?" Louise asked.

"Yes, please do call and let me know and of course I will help you search for her if she's not there," Frank responded. "But I have a feeling she's going to be there when you arrive," he continued, smiling as he spoke.

"Okay, thanks again, Frank," Louise said as she left to get back into her vehicle.

Frank watched her drive away and waved. Just then Lacy popped around the corner.

"Is she gone?" Lacy asked.

"Yes, she's gone, but you have to get back to the house ASAP, because I convinced her that you would probably be there by the time she got back home, so she is expecting to find you there. If not, she is going to start a search for you, for which she asked me to be a part of. So, get your ass back to the house right now," Frank told her.

"Okay, okay," Lacy responded. "Just give me a few minutes to get myself together here. I didn't expect her to wake up and look for me. I don't even have any clothes on underneath this coat! How in hell am I going to explain that one?" Lacy asked.

"She's going to think I've gone mad or something, if she finds out I am out walking around naked under my coat," Lacy said and laughed. She was attempting to make light of an otherwise tense situation.

"Well, just don't take your coat off is all," Frank said. "But you really need to get going before she calls here and says she wants me to help her search for you," he continued.

"Okay, I will get going then, but first I want a kiss from you, and I want you to tell me when we can meet up again," Lacy replied, looking Frank directly in the eyes.

"I'm not sure when, or even if, I can do this with you again," Frank responded. "It is risky, and to be honest, I don't want to get in trouble with your mother. I'd hate to ruin our friendship over this. So, I think maybe you and I should cease and desist, even though, yes, I did really enjoy our time together last night," Frank continued.

"I am sure you can understand where I am coming from," he added.

"Yea, I know where you are coming from," Lacy said. "You and Mom are sex buddies, and so, you don't want to chance losing that situation. I get it, but I'm also not taking no for an answer!" she added.

"Listen, we don't have time to have this discussion right now. Your mother is looking for you and is probably about to call me to get me to help her search for you, so you really have to get going!" Frank replied in a stern tone of voice.

"Yea, yea... I know, I'm going okay; but here's my number and I want you to call me soon," Lacy replied, passing Frank the piece of paper with her address and phone number on it.

Frank took the paper from her and pushed it into his shirt pocket. "Okay, fine, I'll take your address and number, but I'm not making any promises that I am going to contact you," Frank cautioned.

"Fine," Lacy said as she opened the door to leave. Then suddenly she realized it was now daylight and that meant Frank's neighbors would all be able to see her leaving his house.

"I can't leave!" she exclaimed. "People are going to see me!" she added.

"Fuck," Frank exclaimed. "I didn't even think of that aspect. Damn, what are we going to do?" Frank asked, now feeling frustrated.

And just then the phone rang. Frank looked and saw it was Louise calling to say that Lacy was still not home.

"Fuck, what the fuck do I do?" he said.

"Answer it," Lacy said. "Just tell her to give it a bit more time, that you are sure I will be home before long," she added.

So, Frank answered the phone and tried to stall Louise, saying give it more time... In the meantime, Lacy was trying to think of a way to leave Frank's house without being spotted by the neighbors, and she had come up with a plan. So she wrote a note to Frank while he was on the phone with Louise and passed it to him.

"We can go in your truck. I will scrunch down so no one can see me."

Frank told Louise he had to go, but to keep him posted on any new developments, and he ended the call.

Then he and Lacy proceeded to drive away from his place in his truck, with Lacy not visible to anyone. He drove down the road a ways and let Lacy out in a spot where no one was around. Lacy jumped out and smiled at Frank as she closed the door.

"See yea later," she said and winked.

"Get going, you," Frank replied, smiling back at her.

So she shut the door of his truck and stood there waiting for him to drive off before she started walking towards her mother's house.

Frank continued down the road awhile before he headed back to his house. He was mesmerized by everything that had taken place and how he ended up with Lacy, his friend's daughter! "What was I thinking?" he wondered as he drove.

Lacy slowly entered the house and did not see her mom right away, which made her feel somewhat relieved. She tiptoed through the kitchen and was at the foot of the stairs when Louise caught sight of her.

"Oh my gosh, Lacy," Louise exclaimed. "Where in hell have you been? I've been looking all over for you!" Louise continued in an alarming tone of voice.

"What!" Lacy replied. "No big deal, Mom, I just woke up really early and decided to go for a walk is all. Why were you so worried?" Lacy asked in a curious tone of voice.

"Well, I didn't know where you went, and it seemed unusual for you to be out for a walk when it was still dark out and it was pouring rain earlier! So, I just never assumed you would be out for a walk. You must have walked a long time, because I've been looking and waiting for your return home for about two hours now. Well, ever since I woke up and realized you weren't here. How ever long that has been now," Lousie added. "Where could you have possibly walked for that long? I think you are bullshitting me, and I want to know what is going on," Louise replied.

"I wasn't walking the entire time. I walked down to the park and sat on a bench by the river there for a long time. I just needed to clear my head and take some time in nature, it's really not a big deal," Lacy responded. "Maybe you don't realize, but I do that kind of thing a lot in the city. I leave my apartment at all hours, take walks, and spend time in nature where I can find it, that is, in the city," Lacy continued. "And you walked and sat in the pouring rain," Louise added. "Yes mom, the rain doesn't bother me. I like it," Lacy replied.

"Okay," Louise replied. "If you say so," she continued. "I'm just happy you are back home safe and sound," she added, and then made a motion to give Lacy a hug. But Lacy saw it coming and quickly ascended the stairs, pretending not to notice her mom's motion. She didn't want Louise realizing that she was naked underneath her coat.

Lacy went directly to her old bedroom and decided the best thing for her to do before engaging with her mother was to take a shower. So she headed down the hallway to the bathroom to take a shower and get ready for the day.

In the meantime, Louise called Frank to let him know that he was right and that Lacy had returned, and how relieved she was. She thanked him again for being the voice of reason.

"No problem at all," Frank responded. "Happy to be of assistance and happy she is back home all safe and sound," he added.

"Yes, yes," Louise replied. "I am just so relieved she is home again. She's in the shower now. Apparently, she was at the park sitting on a bench by the river," Louise continued. "I didn't know she was such a nature lover! She never used to be, but I guess people change over time," Louise added. "Plus, it was raining hard for a time, but she said she likes the rain," Lousie continued. "Who knew," she added.

"See, I told you there was nothing to worry about!" Frank responded.

"Yes, yes you did," Louise said. "And you were right," she added.

Then they ended the call.

Louise and Lacy were having breakfast but they didn't speak much to each other. Louise was still shaken up by the morning's events and Lacy was preoccupied thinking about the sex she had with Frank—wondering what her mom would do if she knew the truth about where she was and who she was with. Thinking about all the times she saw her mom and Frank together over the years of her growing up. "Now, I understand what my mom has been getting from Frank all these years," she thought to herself and smiled.

"What are you smiling about?" Louise asked. "Do you care to share?"

"Oh, nothing," Lacy replied. "I was just thinking about how nice it is, and has been, to spend some time with you, and hang out, and it made me smile is all," Lacy continued

"Oh, that's so nice, sweetie," Louise replied.

"But I'm going to have to get going today," Lacy said, looking sad. "I have some things I need to take care of at my apartment in the city and some errands to run as well. So, I'm going to be leaving in a little while," she continued.

"Oh, I'm sad to hear that," Louise responded, touching Lacy's hair along the side of her head. "I so enjoyed you being here. The house doesn't feel so empty with you here," she continued. "But I understand that you have things you have to do, and I hope you can make it back to visit again real soon," she added, leaning over and giving Lacy a hug.

"Oh, don't worry Mom," Lacy replied. "I'll be back before you know it, and of course, I will keep in touch in the meantime," she added.

"Yes, please do, I love to hear from you anytime," Louise responded, smiling at Lacy affectionately.

"I feel bad, because I know I told you I could stay longer, but I had forgotten about some important school work that I really need to attend to. I'm sorry," Lacy added.

"It's okay honey, I understand," Louise replied. "I want you to do well in school, and I'm very proud of you for what you are doing. Getting an education, especially for a woman, is very important. So I am happy you chose to do that for yourself," Louise added and smiled sweetly.

It wasn't long after breakfast before Lacy was packed up and was ready to hit the road back to the city. Louise kissed her on the forehead and hugged her tightly before she left to get into her car.

"Safe journey honey," Louise said as Lacy walked towards her vehicle.

"Don't worry Mom," Lacy said. "I'll be fine. I know this road like the back of my hand. I've driven it many times," she added.

"Yes, but be careful of the moose and deer, as they jump out quickly from the sides of the road, you know!" Louise warned.

"Yes, yes, I am aware, Mom," Lacy said, smiling while getting into her vehicle.

Louise waved goodbye and Lacy waved back as she drove out of the driveway.

Louise entered the house and started to clean up from breakfast, but she couldn't stop thinking about what Lacy told her as to where she was all that time and so late in the night and early morning, or why Lacy would opt to walk to the park and sit on a bench, especially in the pouring rain. It didn't make sense to her, but she was content at this point to just let it go and take Lacy at her word.

Lacy, on the other hand, was consumed in thoughts of her time with Frank. She wondered why she felt so attracted to him all of a sudden. "Sure, I dreamed of having sex with him when I was a teenager, but I never actually thought it would happen," she said to herself.

But for now, she did not want to analyze why she was attracted to him. She wanted to think about the actual sex she had had with him and how amazing it was. How it made her feel, and how she wanted more.

"I hope he calls me," she thought to herself. "I definitely want more of what he has to offer," she thought and smiled as she drove towards the city. And the more she thought about her sexual encounter with Frank, the more turned on she became.

"Oh my gosh, I am getting so turned on thinking about all of this," she said to herself. I have to stop thinking about it now, or I am going to blow my load right here while I am driving," she thought and laughed. "I will be home soon enough and if I still feel like masturbating over Frank, I can do it then in the privacy of my apartment," she thought, and she tried to focus on driving.

Once back at her apartment in the city for a time, she noticed she was having difficulty not thinking about Frank. She was tempted to call him just to say hi, but she did not want to appear needy, or too into him, so she opted to call her mom instead to let her know she made it home and was all good.

Still, it was not her mom she really wanted to call, it was Frank. "Maybe he will call me tomorrow or the next day," she thought. Maybe he will show up here and surprise me," she hoped. But she knew that was a long shot and that most likely she would not be hearing from him for a while. She tried to make herself busy by cleaning her apartment in an effort to distract her mind from it all.

Frank, on the other hand, was sitting at his kitchen table rolling a cannabis cigarette and sipping his freshly poured coffee. Life is good," he thought to himself, smiling. Life is really good, in fact," he smiled even wider. He could not believe he had had sex with Lacy, Louise's daughter.

"How did that even happen?" he wondered. But she was not a child anymore, she was a grown woman now and a mighty fine one at that, he reasoned. Still, it did not make sense to him, how Lacy suddenly came on to him at her mother's house that morning, and then how she showed up at his place wanting him to have sex with her.

"What is going on?" he wondered. And he told himself that he was not going to be having sex with her again due to the circumstances, no matter how much he had enjoyed it.

As he smoked his herb and sipped his coffee, he could not help but think about Lacy and how sexy she was, how he enjoyed having sex with her and how it felt, and this caused his manhood to respond in like manner. And, before he knew it, he was in the bathroom masturbating.

"I cannot be doing this," he thought. This is not right. She is Louise's daughter," he said to himself.

But he could not seem to help himself, much like he could not seem to help himself when it came to Rita. But he did not want to go there right now. Right now, he only wanted to focus on Lacy.

Just as he was finishing up from masturbating, a knock came to the door. He cleaned himself off, zipped up, and went to answer the door.

It was Louise.

"What a nice surprise," he said. "What are you doing here?" he asked in a surprised tone of voice.

"Oh, I was just feeling lonely is all and thought I would come by to see you for a visit. I hope you are not busy," she said.

"No, not busy. I was just in the washroom and heard someone at the door, but I was not expecting you because you have Lacy over," he said.

"No, she left this morning shortly after we had breakfast. She said she had to head back to the city as she had some things she needed to do for school. So I was feeling kind of lonely after she left, and I thought I would drop by and visit yea, but if you are busy,

I can leave, because I know I did not call first before showing up,"
Louise said.

"Oh no, not a problem. Come in and have a seat," Frank said,
motioning toward the kitchen table. Can I get you a coffee? I made
a fresh pot not too awfully long ago."

"Sure, that sounds great. I could use a cup of your delicious
coffee," Louise replied, smiling.

So Frank prepared Louise a coffee and brought it to her at the
kitchen table. Then Frank took his usual seat.

"Can you roll us a joint?" Louise asked. I could really use a puff
right about now," she continued.

"Sure," Frank replied, reaching for his bag of medicine and
papers. Hard morning, eh," he said while rolling the joint.

"Yea, it sure was," Louise agreed. I still do not understand why
Lacy walked down to the park and sat on a bench for all that long
time. Especially in the pouring rain. It still doesn't make sense to
me, but I have opted to just take her at her word and forget about it,"
Louise added.

Frank didn't respond. He didn't want to incriminate himself any
further than he had already. He lit the joint, took a couple of drags,
and passed it to Louise, who sucked on it hard and held in the smoke
as if she was desperately trying to get as high as possible. Then
suddenly she began to gag and cough while passing the joint back
to Frank.

"Are you okay?" Frank asked, as he took the joint back from her and continued to smoke it. But Louise was still coughing, so she just nodded her head indicating she was okay.

Once the joint was finished, Louise began to feel better about the situation with Lacy. In fact, she had forgotten all about it. Suddenly, she was now feeling horny. She looked at Frank sitting there, sizing him up and down. She realized what she already knew. "He is so damn handsome and sexy," she thought to herself. Then she started thinking about how good sex was between the two of them.

Knowing Louise very well, Frank sensed the rise in sexual energy that was now filling the room. "Oh no, she is wanting to have sex with me and I just had sex with her daughter this morning," he thought. "What am I going to do?" he asked himself. He had not expected Louise to show up that day, so soon after he had had sex with her daughter, and he wasn't sure how to handle it.

Just then, Louise reached over and began to touch his manhood. Frank didn't know how to respond other than to smile at her. He had to be honest; he didn't mind what she was doing. And before he knew it, his manhood was responding to Louise's touch.

"You're bad," he said to Louise, smiling as he spoke.

"I know," Louise replied. "But it's been a while since we had sex and I am feeling really horny for you right now for some reason," she said. "I tried to stay away since Rita and Joe left, but I'm not going to say it's been easy," Louise continued. "Nor was it easy when Rita was here and you and her were getting it on while her husband was asleep, or should I say drugged," Louise added.

"Shush, don't talk like that," Frank said. "Rita and I were strongly attracted to one another. It's no one's fault. You make it sound like a crime or something. It wasn't like that at all. We are just two people who found each other irresistible, is all. Yes, I know it was wrong on many levels, but we just couldn't help ourselves," Frank responded.

Louise smiled. "Okay, paint it any way you want, but you know it was wrong and I am glad they left and she is no longer a temptation for you. Let's just leave it at that and get back to where we were before I brought up all that crap," Louise continued, rubbing Frank's leg.

Due to Louise's comment, Frank now had Rita in his head. Frank thought Rita was the best sex he had ever had, and he was convinced she would be the best sex he would ever have. Even young Lacy did not come close to Rita when it came to sex, as with many other things. Rita was the be-all, end-all for Frank, but she was off limits, being married to his good friend Joe, and he was painfully aware of that fact.

As all of these thoughts were going through his mind, Louise had gotten up and undone her shirt, exposing her bra which she was about to take off. And if there was one thing about Louise that turned Frank on the most, it was her luscious breasts. She had big, voluptuous breasts, and Frank absolutely loved them. And before he knew it, Louise had her breasts out and was pushing them in his face. This made him forget about Rita and drew his attention to Louise, which is where Louise wanted it.

Louise straddled herself on Frank's lap and began grinding against his manhood. She moaned as she moved back and forth, pushing hard against his penis. The two of them were getting very excited when suddenly it occurred to Frank that he had not changed the bedding on his bed from when he and Lacy had had sex that morning. He wasn't even sure if there might be any evidence of Lacy having been there. Suddenly, he was filled with anxiety and wondered where he was going to have sex with Louise, as it was obvious she wanted sex from him.

"Think," he thought to himself. "Where are you going to do this?"

Then suddenly he realized he didn't have to take her to his bedroom, and could have sex with her right there in the kitchen, just as he had done with Rita. So, he motioned for her to get off his lap, and the two of them began to undress one another right there in the kitchen.

"Let's go to your room," Louise whispered in the heat of the moment. And before Frank even had time to think about it, the two of them were headed up the stairs to his bedroom.

"Did she read my mind?" he wondered as the two of them hurried up the stairs to his room. Frank was hoping that Louise was so hot and horny she wouldn't even notice that his bed was a complete mess from all the sex he had had there with Lacy. And he was right. Louise threw herself on the messy bed and grabbed Frank's hand to pull him close to her

"Give it to me," she said.

It wasn't long before the two of them had gotten each other off, and the sullen reality of the act being over filled the room. It was then that Louise noticed the state of Frank's bed and room.

"Wow, your bed looks like you've been having sex in it for days," she said and laughed. "Have you not changed your sheets since Rita left?"

"Yea, I've been a little busy and didn't really worry too much about it I guess," Frank replied.

"Oh wow," Louise responded. "You really need a good woman to take care of you," she continued and smiled.

Frank always knew that Louise wanted more from him, but he just wasn't there. He was happy and content to be friends with benefits, and that was as far as he wanted to go with the situation. It wasn't that Louise was not a fantastic woman, she was. Frank just didn't have that kind of attraction to her, was all. And Louise was content with their situation as it had been. She too did not want to be tied down to one man, and Frank was not the only man she had sexual relations with either.

But Frank was the man she liked the most, and if she were to settle down with one man, she knew she would choose him. But she also knew that Frank was not interested in taking their relationship to the next level. So she was well aware of where she stood in terms of any kind of lasting relationship of that kind with him. She was thus content to take what she could get from him when she could get it, which was most any time she wanted. All she had to do was show up and tempt him with her luscious breasts. It worked every time and she knew it.

"I should be going now," Louise said, getting up from the bed and putting her clothes on. "I hate to have sex and run, but I need to get some things done at home," she continued.

"No worries," Frank replied, smiling. "I'll see you to the door," he added.

Once Louise was gone, Frank sat back down at his kitchen table. He could not believe all that had just happened. "First Lacy shows up wanting to have sex with me and then Louise," he said to himself. "What in hell is going on? Why are all these crazy things happening in my life all of a sudden?" he asked himself, but he had no answers.

Chapter Eleven

The Plot Thickens

A week had passed now and Frank was starting to feel halfway back to normal again. He was back to his former routines and feeling better about his life in general. He hadn't spoken to Rita in some time because it was just too risky, and they had both decided to reduce the time they were talking on the phone. Also, emails were strictly out of the question due to their vulnerability of being seen. But that didn't mean they weren't in each other's minds. They both were thinking about the other many times throughout the day, wishing things could be different, yet realizing at once that they were not. It was a kind of limbo that didn't feel comfortable.

Lacy had not called or been around either, and Frank was relieved about that. Also, Louise was busy with work and had only called a couple of times since he had last seen her. So Frank was feeling like his life had finally gotten back to normal, and he wondered what all the situations he had just been through truly meant.

It seemed to Frank that in one day, when Rita and Joe showed up to be exact, his entire life had gone astray. And the situation with Lacy didn't help matters either. He'd never dreamed that the two of them would end up having sex, and he wasn't quite sure he couldn't believe it even now. Yet, he knew it was true and there wasn't a damn thing he could do about it. He just hoped that Louise never

ever found out, because he knew that would be the end of his longtime friendship and sexual relationship with her. He realized he stood to lose not only one, but two good friends due to his lack of sexual control.

Frank wanted to blame it on the women, but he knew he had to take responsibility for his own part as well. He didn't have to oblige them. And while there was a part of him that was sorry for what happened, there was another part that thoroughly enjoyed every minute of it. Thus, he figured it was better to just try not to think about any of it. So he tried to stay busy and keep his mind distracted, while at the same time moving his life forward and getting things done. He was doing fine and feeling good, but that wasn't to last.

Now, when the phone rang at Frank's house, feelings of anxiety would well up inside of him, and he always hesitated to answer any call. He'd look at the phone to see if he recognized the number and to see if it was someone he wanted to talk to or not. He'd answer if it was Rita, but he realized it could also be Joe calling. So he had to be careful in how he answered the phone when the number came up.

And Lacy had been calling, but Frank refused to answer, forcing her to leave a message. But then Frank realized that too was a bad idea since, by some chance, Louise might hear the messages on his answering machine. So he opted to delete all the messages on his answering machine just in case.

His sexual indiscretions had now complicated his life, and it was giving him the kind of stress he'd never felt before, and he didn't like it. He now felt like he was under some kind of pressure all the time, yet he knew logically that he wasn't. Still, he couldn't seem to shake the feeling. "One day at a time," he'd repeat to himself when he started feeling overwhelmed by it all. "One day at a time, one thing at a time," he'd say, and it helped him to deal with the task at hand.

So many questions were running through his head now. Why was Rita still keeping in touch with him? She was never going to leave Joe and he knew that. So what in fuck was he doing hanging onto that situation? "What is wrong with me," he'd say to himself. But he was short on answers, and his problem-solving skills were lacking when it came to dealing with the types of situations he now found himself in. "I'm a cheater now," he'd say to himself. He couldn't bear to think of himself in that manner. He'd always been a straight-up, honest kind of person, well respected by people and looked upon in a good light in the community. Now, if people knew what he had done with his friend's wife and his other friend's daughter, he'd not have such a glowing reputation. He felt shame and swore he was going to make some changes in his life before things like that ever got out of hand again. But he never imagined what was about to happen. There was no way he could have known.

While thinking about all these things, Frank was suddenly jarred out of his daydreaming by the ringing of the phone. He looked to see who was calling and saw that it was either Rita or Joe. So he picked up the phone.

"Hi Frank," Rita said. "You're not going to believe what has happened," she exclaimed.

Frank could tell by her tone of voice something was seriously wrong. "What's wrong?" he asked. "Are you okay?" he continued.

"No, I'm not okay. Something horrible has happened, Frank," Rita replied. Then she blurted out, "Joe is dead!"

"WHAT!" Frank exclaimed. "No, that can't be," he added. "What happened?" he asked.

"He went to sleep and never woke up," Rita said.

"Oh my gosh, that's horrible news, Rita. You must be devastated. I am so sorry this has happened, I don't even know what to say," Frank responded.

"Can you drive out here?" Rita asked. "You are his good friend, and I could really use your support right now," she added.

Frank hesitated. He felt a sudden block inside of himself because that was the last place he wanted to be.

"I don't think I can, Rita," Frank replied. "I have a lot going on right now and I just don't think it would be a good idea, but I'm here if you want to talk on the phone," he added. Then he continued, "You know yourself that it would not be a good idea for me to be there at this time."

Rita didn't speak, so Frank said, "Hey, are you there?"

"Yea, I'm here," Rita finally said. "But I'm not happy that you are not coming to help me with all of this. However, I admit it is probably best, like you say, that you are not here at this time," she continued in a sad tone of voice.

"I really have to go now, but I just wanted to let you know the sad news," Rita said. "I have a lot to take care of, and you might not be hearing from me for a while," she continued.

"I totally understand, Rita," Frank replied. "I will be thinking of you, and if you need or want to talk, I am here for you," Frank continued

"Thank you, Frank," Rita replied. "I may just take yea up on that, I'll see how things go and how I feel. Talk to yea later," she said and hung up the phone.

Frank's head was now swimming. "Is Joe really dead?" he said to himself. "How did he die?" he thought. "He was only forty-six years old and he died in his sleep. How strange," Frank said to himself.

Then, suddenly, he thought about Rita giving Joe her sleeping pills when they were staying at his place. "Don't even go there," he told himself. "I'm sure Rita had nothing to do with Joe's death," he told himself. "Get that right out of your mind," he said to himself whenever the idea came to him that maybe Rita did have something to do with Joe's death.

He couldn't bear to think that Rita would hurt or kill her own husband. If she was capable of such, hottest sex or not, Frank wanted nothing to do with her. "What if she decided she no longer loved me," he thought. "Would she off me?" he wondered. Yet, he couldn't see Rita doing anything to hurt Joe. Sure, she messed around on him, but she still acted loving towards him and the two of them seemed to get along quite well. Plus, Joe had provided Rita with everything she could ever want and then some. Surely, she appreciated all that Joe had given to her in love, Frank reasoned.

Then the guilt feelings started to come upon Frank and he couldn't bear to think about anything that had happened. However, his avoidance techniques were starting to fade the more that life piled on him. He'd try to stay busy and keep his mind distracted on other things, but the reality of his friend's death was something that just wouldn't stay buried. Memories of the two of them kept on popping up in his mind and he didn't mind that part. It was the shame he felt for what he had done to Joe, the betrayal and breach of trust. He couldn't believe he had allowed himself to fall into such a situation as that. He asked God for forgiveness and repented for the sins he had done against his friend. That was all he could do at that point, and he hoped that he would be forgiven.

Some time passed and Frank was finally starting to come to terms with the news of Joe's death, when the phone rang and it was Lacy. Frank opted to answer the call since she had called several times and his answering machine was no longer turned on.

"What can I do for you?" Frank said when answering the phone.

"Funny you asked," Lacy said in a sassy tone of voice. "I was wondering when you are coming to the city next and if you'd like to come and see me? I sure do miss yea," she said.

"Oh, I don't know about that," Frank replied. "I don't have any plans for going into the city any time soon," he added. "I am pretty well stocked up here now and I don't usually go into the city unless I need supplies," he added.

Lacy laughed. "You sound like such a recluse, Frank," she said.

Frank smiled "Well, thank you for the compliment," he replied.

"Sure, it's all good," Lacy said. "I just want some more of your sweet lovin' is all," she added.

Frank smiled. His ego welcomed Lacy's flattering tongue, but he also knew that obliging her request would not be a good idea. Still, for some reason in his mind he was suddenly entertaining the thought of taking her up on her offer. "Maybe going to see Lacy and having some fun with her would help me get things off my mind," he said to himself. "But what if it only adds to my state of stress and anxiety?" he thought.

The pull of her sweet voice and her insistence on seeing him for sex suddenly became too tempting for him to say no to her.

"Okay, okay, you win," Frank finally said. "I will come and see you sooner than later," he added. "I'll call you before I head into town and let you know I am coming, so you can be all ready for me when I get there," he added.

Lacy laughed. "I can't wait," she said. "Why don't you come over right now. I am getting hot just talking to yea and thinking about you coming over," she added.

"No, I can't come over right now, but I will come over soon," Frank replied. "Like I said, I'll call yea and let yea know," Frank continued.

"Okay, I guess I will just have to accept that," Lacy responded.

And with that they ended the call.

Frank sat down at his kitchen table and held his head in his hands. His mind was racing once again and he wasn't sure what to think anymore. "Should I go and see Lacy?" he asked himself. Then he questioned going to see her as he felt like maybe it was too big of a risk. "What's the point in continuing to have sex with her? She is way too young for me. Plus, her mother is my good friend," he said to himself.

But then his thoughts turned to sex with Lacy and he suddenly rationalized that it was just sex and there was no harm in it as long as Louise never found out about it.

All these thoughts were making Frank feel exhausted. "I just need to lay down and sleep," he thought to himself. "Tomorrow is a new day, and I just need to sleep now and forget about all of this."

But sleep wasn't going to come easy. He felt exhausted, but his brain was in full thought mode. So he opted to roll up some more herb and burn one down before going to his bedroom to try to sleep. Sometimes smoking some herb helped him to get to sleep, but tonight, he realized after smoking one, that this was not one of those nights. So, he opted to watch a movie instead and sleep on the couch.

"Maybe the movie will put me to sleep, or at least distract my mind for a while," he reasoned.

Frank finally fell asleep with the television blaring, and when he awoke in the morning, he felt much improved. "Today's gonna be a good day. I'm not going to think about any women, or any negative things at all. I am just going to concentrate on what I have to do and try to enjoy the day," he said to himself and smiled.

But he couldn't get Lacy's invitation out of his mind and he wanted to jump in his truck and head to the city. So eventually he stopped fighting the feeling and decided that was exactly what he was going to do. "She wants to see me and I want to see her," he said to himself. "I don't see the harm in going to see her," he thought.

He showered and cleaned himself up, put on his nice clothes, and headed towards his truck. Then he realized he had told her he would call before coming and let her know; however, he was now thinking it would be better to surprise her. Plus, he didn't want to waste any more time with making a phone call. He'd just leave. He was sure she'd be home, and she'd be more than happy to see him.

The entire drive to the city had his mind preoccupied with having sex with Lacy, and the closer he got to her apartment building, the more excited he felt about the entire situation. Once in the parking lot of the apartment building, Frank opted to sit in his truck for a few moments. Suddenly, it occurred to him that Louise might be there visiting her daughter. If that were to happen, how would he explain his being there? He was running over various possible scenarios in his mind, when he realized he was either going to go and knock on Lacy's door or he wasn't. So he got out of his truck and proceeded to the entrance of the apartment building.

He looked at the mailboxes in the lobby to see what floor Lacy's apartment was on. "First floor, number 189," he said to himself. So he took the stairs and walked the hallway until he found the right apartment.

There was a young man standing in the hallway outside of Lacy's apartment door, and Frank wondered if this was, in fact, the right apartment. "I'm looking for Lacy," he said to the young man standing there. "Do you know if this is her apartment or not?" he asked.

"Yea, this is Lacy's place alright," the young man responded, "but I'm next in line, just to let you know!" he added.

"What?" Frank said. "Next in line? What are you talking about?"

The young man smiled at Frank. "First of all, who are you? Do you even know Lacy? You look old enough to be her dad, are you her dad?" the young man asked.

"No, no, I'm a friend of her mother. I have known Lacy for years. I was in the city and just thought I'd come by to say hi. You know, to check up on her for her mother, to make sure she is doing okay. That sort of thing," Frank explained.

"Oh, well, obviously you do not know Lacy as well as you think you do," the young man replied.

Frank had no idea what the young man was referring to and was perplexed by the entire conversation. "Who is this dude standing in the hallway, advising me that he is next in line? Next in line for what? Was Lacy dealing drugs? What was he next in line for?" Frank wondered.

So Frank opted to just be direct and ask the young man what he was talking about. "What do you mean, next in line?" Frank asked.

The young man smiled a huge smile. "Come on man, figure it out for yourself. Lacy runs a business here and I have an appointment for 2:30 this afternoon, so you, my friend, are going to have to wait until my appointment is finished before you can have your turn. Get it?" the young man replied.

But Frank was still somewhat confused by the conversation, so he asked, "What is the appointment for?" He was thinking maybe Lacy had started a new business and had not yet told anyone about it.

The young man, still smiling, replied, "Man, are you truly that dumb? Lacy is a hooker. That's how she makes her money. That is how she is paying her way through college."

Frank was stunned by the young man's reply. "Lacy is a hooker" kept on running through his mind. "Is that really true?" he asked himself in disbelief. "It must be, the dude is standing there waiting his turn," he thought.

Frank was now at a loss for words, and the young man could see Frank was struggling with the news he had just provided him.

"Listen man," the dude finally said. "It's not a big deal. She turns a few tricks to make some cash under the table. Lots of people do it, men and women both; you have to get with the times, Daddy," he said. "Don't judge her, she's just doing what she can to help herself in this life, that's all. I'm a regular client of hers and I really dig her. She's a nice person and you shouldn't judge her based on what she does to make some cash on the side," the young man continued.

But Frank still couldn't get his head around it all and was still processing this new information when the apartment door opened and a dude exited.

"That's my cue," the young man said. "Talk to yea later, or never, as the case may be," he added, catching the apartment door before it closed. Then he turned around and looked at Frank. "Oh, did you want me to tell Lacy that her dad is here?" he said and chuckled.

Frank suddenly felt embarrassed, but he smiled and said, "No, no, that's fine. I'm going to leave now. As I said, I was just stopping by to see how she was making out. I learned more than I had anticipated, but it's all good," Frank said.

"Okay then," the young man replied and shut the apartment door.

Frank just stood there mystified and stunned by it all. He had no idea, and how could he, that Lacy was a hooker, a prostitute, selling sex for money. "If Louise ever found that out, she'd have a shit fit," he reasoned. And what was he to do now with all this new information, he wondered.

"No wonder she came onto me so hard," he thought. "She's a pro at this sort of thing," he reasoned. "Was she trying to catch me in a snare?" he wondered. "Like, offer me free sex to make me want it, and then charge me for it once I am hooked?" he thought to himself. "What is really going on here?" he wondered.

"I need to go back to my truck and think about all of this," he said to himself as he started walking down the hallway to exit the building. He had questions for which he had no answers, but he wanted answers to them now. Would he wait until buddy finished his 'appointment,' or would he just leave and call Lacy later on, or would he just forget the whole thing and not talk to Lacy anymore? He couldn't decide what the best course of action would be in the situation, but due to his time spent thinking about it all, he realized he had been sitting there for almost half an hour already.

So he reasoned he might as well just wait and go in and talk to Lacy face to face. "Face to face is always better than a telephone conversation," he thought. So, he kept an eye on the doors of the apartment building waiting for the young man he had met to exit the building. And it wasn't long before he saw the young man leaving the building.

Nervously, Frank got out of his truck and walked back to Lacy's apartment door. He lifted his hand to knock, but suddenly the door opened before he had a chance. It was Lacy. "I was just about to call you," she said. "Rob told me that there was an older man standing in the hallway looking for me and I figured it had to be you," she said, smiling. "I was going to go look for your truck to see if it was still in the parking lot here," she added. "Come on in, Frank, it is nice to see you and I'm happy you dropped by, but I thought you said you were going to call first before showing up, and it would have been better if you had," she added.

Frank was relieved that she was doing all the talking because he still wasn't sure exactly what to say to her or how to broach the situation of her being a prostitute. So as long as she was talking, he didn't have to speak.

Frank entered Lacy's apartment and closed the door behind him. "Excuse the mess," Lacy said. "I've been busy and haven't had time to clean up. If I had known you were coming, I'd have made time to clean up the place," she added.

"Oh, that's no problem," Frank replied. "I know from my own place how quickly a place can get messy if you're not able to stay on top of it all," he continued.

Lacy smiled. She appreciated Frank's non-judgment concerning her messy apartment. "Can I get you something to drink?" she asked. "Are you hungry?" she added.

"No, I'm all good," Frank replied.

There was an elephant in the room, but neither of them wanted to acknowledge it.

"I have to take a shower," Lacy finally said to break the silent awkwardness in the room.

"Oh, okay," Frank acknowledged. "Do you want me to leave and come back? Or just leave, or stay, or what?" Frank asked.

"No, I want you to stay, of course," Lacy said. "I won't be but a minute or two, I just want to freshen up for you is all," she continued, smiling at Frank.

"Oh, okay, I'll just sit here and wait then," he said, not knowing exactly what else to say.

So Lacy left to take a shower, and Frank took a seat and wondered what he should do. "Am I still going to have sex with her now that I know she's a prostitute?" He wasn't sure what to do in that moment, so he just sat there waiting for Lacy to get out of the shower.

It wasn't long before Lacy returned, and rather than getting dressed, she appeared back in the living room with a towel wrapped around her. As she approached Frank, she dropped the towel. "This is what you came for, isn't it, Frank?" she said, smiling. Then she straddled his lap and began to push her breasts against his chest.

It was strange to Frank that Louise, Lacy's mother, had done the same thing to him, even though she was dressed at the time, the last time he had seen her. "Like mother, like daughter," he wondered.

Lacy began running her fingers through Frank's hair while grinding on his penis. "You do want some lovin', don't yea, Frank," she whispered in his ear. Frank couldn't deny he was getting turned on, but he didn't answer her question because he wasn't yet sure what he wanted to do.

Suddenly, he blurted it out. "Are you a prostitute, Lacy?"

Lacy smiled a big smile, "So what if I am. Does that bother you? A girl needs to make money, you know, and if that is how I choose to do it, what business is it of anyone else?" she continued.

"What would your mother say if she knew you were working as a prostitute?" Frank responded.

"Who cares what she would think," Lacy replied. "She doesn't pay my bills and she has no say over my life choice. I'm a grown woman now, Frank, in case you didn't notice," Lacy added in an indignant tone of voice.

Lacy was starting to feel annoyed by Frank's line of questioning. She was determined not to feel bad about her choice to use sex as a means to make money. She had already convinced herself that it was not a shameful thing she was doing, and she was not about to let Frank, or anyone else for that matter, change her mind. She needed to keep her thoughts in check and objective, as it made her job easier that way. She thus didn't spend time debating with herself as to whether what she was doing was good or bad. She just did what she wanted to do and what she knew worked, and that was all that mattered. And Frank questioning her was now making her question her choices, and she didn't like the way it was making her feel.

"You have no right to question my choices in life," she finally said. "Do you want to have sex with me or not?"

Frank did not expect such directness from such a young woman, and he was taken aback by it and not sure how to respond. So he just sat there stunned, not really knowing what to say or do in the moment.

So Lacy got up off his lap, wrapped the towel now laying on the floor around her, and put on a sad face. "I take it you don't want to have sex anymore," she said.

Frank wasn't sure what to say, but something inside made him jump up from where he was sitting. He grabbed Lacy, bringing her close to him, kissing her passionately. Suddenly, he didn't care that she was a prostitute who had just had at least two other men in her bed earlier that day that he was aware of. Suddenly, it didn't matter that she sold sex for money. Suddenly, all he cared about was what he had come there for in the first place.

The next thing he knew, he was in Lacy's bedroom and the two of them were having wild sex. Frank was full of passion and nothing else was important in that moment. He reasoned he would make such sweet love to Lacy that she would forget about every other man she had been with. "I will make such amazing love to her that she will forget all the other men she has been with," he thought to himself. And with those thoughts in his mind, he made wild, passionate love to her as he had never done before. Sex had now become a competition in his mind, and Frank was determined to be the best. He would fuck her better than the others and thereby eliminate all competition.

The two of them had sex for what seemed like hours, because as soon as they were done with one round, it wasn't long before Frank was wanting more and Lacy was happy to oblige him. It was now starting to get dark outside and Frank realized he had been there too long.

"I have to go now," he said to Lacy.

"Ah, do you really?" she responded. "Can't you stay the night with me and leave in the morning?" Lacy asked.

"No, I really have to get going. I have things I have to do in the morning and I want to be home before it gets too late. But I will be back soon," Frank assured her.

"Okay then," Lacy replied. "I will be waiting for you," she added, smiling.

So Frank got dressed and washed his face quickly before heading out the door.

"Hurry back, Honey," Lacy said, giving him a kiss on the cheek.

"I will," Frank responded, tapping her ass as he opened the apartment door to exit.

She giggled a sexy giggle. Frank smiled and left.

As he walked back to his truck, he had to wonder what in fuck he was doing. Was he falling for her trap? Did she even have a trap? What was the point of having sex with her? Is this what he really wanted? These and so many more questions ran through his mind as he got in his truck and started it up to make the journey back to his house in the country.

As he drove, he kept on thinking about the fact that Lacy, the little Lacy he had known for years, was now a prostitute. It was hard for him to get his head around. He was trying not to judge her, but at the same time he strongly felt she was making wrong and bad decisions for herself regardless of her rationalizations. There were just so many things that could go wrong in that line of work. And he knew people generally did not look well upon those who chose that line of profession.

"Does she not realize she is ruining her reputation?" he thought. But he reasoned it was not like she was working the streets. She was doing it privately from her own apartment and thus fewer people would be aware of what she was doing to make money.

"Still, even in the privacy of her own apartment, she was leaving herself vulnerable to any wack job who made an 'appointment' to see her for sex. Was she not aware of these risks?" he wondered. "She must be aware of them," he thought. "How could she not be?" he reasoned

"Maybe the money was so good, she was willing to take whatever risks were involved," he said to himself. "Either way, or any way," he concluded, it was truly none of his business.

Chapter Twelve

So Many Questions – So Few Answers

Frank arrived home and was feeling frazzled. He dared not think too much about it all. He had gone to see Lacy in an attempt to get his mind off of Joe's death and his underhanded relationship with Rita. And while it had worked for the time he was away, the new information he had gained was not helpful in getting his head on straight. Now, he had to deal with the fact that he had had sex not once, but twice with a prostitute. It made him feel worried as to what the consequences of that might be.

What if he had gotten a disease from the sex he had with her, seeing as she had multiple partners and all. But he didn't want to think about any of what was happening in his world now. He just wanted to pretend none of it existed and his life was back to the way it had been before all of what had happened had happened. He was determined to forget about it all, even if at some level, he knew that was not really possible.

He told himself he would simply focus on what needed to be done at his place. He had lots of chores and things that required his attention around the house and land. He would keep himself busy and not allow himself to dwell upon any of it. "I will block out any and all thoughts that came up in my mind that reminded me of any of these situations. I will simply not allow those thoughts to enter into my mind," he said to himself. "If or when they do happen to enter my mind, I will quickly banish them," he added. "That is how I will deal with all of this mess," he confirmed as being the solution to the situations he now found himself in.

So, he took a quick shower and went straight to work on one of the projects in his barn that he had been putting off for a while. "I will tackle the roofing problem and finish it today," he said. "It shouldn't be that hard or take me too long to complete," he reasoned. Several holes had formed in the metal roofing on the old barn and Frank was determined to plug them all versus shelling out the money to put a new roof on. So, he gathered the tools he needed and proceeded to get to work on patching the roof. He reasoned that staying outside of his house was a good idea because that way if the phone did ring, he would not be tempted to answer it. And as long as he didn't answer it, he wouldn't have to talk to anyone. And he really didn't want to talk to anyone right now.

So, he kept on finding chores that required his attention that were outside versus being in the house. He would deal with the issues inside the house at another time, because right now, what he needed, he told himself, was to be outside working in the fresh air and not being around the phone.

Frank had not bought into getting a cell phone for that reason. He didn't want to be reached when he didn't want to be reached, and the thought of always having a phone on his person was not at all intriguing to him. He could see the usefulness of the cell phone in times when a phone was needed, such as breaking down on the side of the road, but he also knew that he, and everyone else, had survived without such for all of history. Hence, he reasoned it was not necessary now or ever. Plus, he didn't like the idea of everywhere he went being tracked, nor the constant invasion of his personal life via the data that would be collected continually on a cell phone if he opted to have one.

What felt like a few days had passed now, and neither Lacy nor Rita had contacted him, which he found rather strange. He wondered how Rita was making out with all the details surrounding Joe's death. He felt like he ought to call her, but inside, he truly didn't want to because he didn't really know what to say to her. And given the context of their relationship with one another, he felt it was almost inappropriate for him to be calling her at all. It was bad enough that the two of them had betrayed Joe, but now Joe was dead, and Frank still couldn't believe it.

He had so many questions regarding the death of his friend, but he had no one to answer them and he didn't want to call and ask Rita a pile of questions. It seemed inappropriate within the context. "Maybe in time I will ask Rita the particulars of how Joe died, but for now, I think it is best just to stay silent on the matter," he thought. "Just let it all go," he said to himself.

However, things were about to get far stranger than Frank could have imagined.

Continuing to work on the many projects Frank had on the go, he was content again with how his life seemed to be going. He knew there were things happening outside of his world that were connected to him, but for the past couple of days at least, he had not had to deal with them directly. He had just come in from doing work outside when the phone rang. He picked it up to see who was calling before he decided to answer. It was Rita and he knew he had best pick it up since he had told her to call him if she needed him, so he opted to answer the phone.

"Hey," he said. "How are you doing?"

Rita was crying and Frank didn't know exactly how to respond to that. He knew Joe had just died and it was expected that Rita would be crying and sad, yet Frank was at a loss as to how to respond.

"I'm so sorry for your loss, Rita," he finally blurted out, in an effort to try to make her feel better.

"I know you are," Rita replied, still sobbing. "And thank you. I am just so lost right now, Frank," she added, sobbing into the phone.

"It will all be okay in time," Frank replied. "Hang in there, Rita. Be strong, I know you are strong," he continued.

"Yes, I am, Frank, but there is more that is happening than you realize," she replied.

Frank was silent. "What could possibly be happening more than Joe's death?" he wondered.

Then Rita spit it out, "I am being investigated for Joe's death, Frank!"

"No, you're not," Frank exclaimed. "That can't be possible. Why would the police think you had anything to do with Joe's death?" he asked.

"It's a long story," Rita replied. "But it has to do with the sleeping pills Joe was always getting from me. The pills were my own prescription because Joe didn't want anyone to know he was taking sleeping pills. So, he would get me to get the prescription from my doctor and then divvy out the pills to him as he needed or wanted them. So, since the pills were in my name, the police seem to think I was feeding him pills against his will or something. I don't know. I don't know exactly what they think; all I know is that they told me I am being put under investigation as a possible suspect in Joe's death. I am beside myself right now," Rita continued. "I did give Joe pills, but he is the one who wanted them. It's not like I was forcing them on him. You know that, right Frank?" Rita asked.

"Yeah, yeah, for sure," Frank responded. "I know you would never do anything to intentionally hurt Joe, or at least not to kill him," he added.

"Thank you," Rita replied. "At least someone believes in my innocence in this situation," she added. "I just can't believe this is happening to me. It is bad enough that I have had to deal with Joe's death, which has been devastating to me, but now I am dealing with all of this on top of that. I just can't take it and I don't know what to do, Frank," Rita continued, still sobbing as she spoke into the phone.

Frank was not sure what more to say. His own head was swirling from all the information Rita was now relaying to him. "You need to call a lawyer," Frank finally said. "Call a lawyer right away. You and Joe must have a lawyer on retainer. I am sure Joe had that all set up for just-in-case situations. What you need to do is call him or her and let them know what is happening, and get them to advise you on how to deal with this situation. I have no idea how to deal with it, because I have never been, thankfully, in a situation like that in my life."

"Yes, that's a good idea," Rita responded. "I will do that first thing in the morning. I'm glad I called you and you told me this, as I wasn't sure what to do. I never even thought, for some reason, of calling our lawyer about this situation. Hopefully, the lawyer can advise me on what to say or do, or not say or do. I'm just so confused right now and I'm also very scared," Rita continued.

"Try not to worry about it," Frank said. "I know it is hard to do in the situation you are in, but worrying about it isn't going to make it any better," he added.

"I know," Rita replied. "But how can I not worry about it? The police think that I may have murdered my husband for God's sake. I can't believe this is happening to me," she said and commenced crying again.

Frank didn't know what else to say at that point, so he changed the subject and asked how things were going with the funeral and all the rest of it.

"There hasn't been a funeral yet," Rita advised. "They want to perform an examination of the body and get a report before Joe is cremated. They are doing a toxicology report to see what kind of drugs, if any, Joe had in his system and if he died as a result of a drug overdose. You know, the sleeping pills," she said, still sobbing.

Frank's mind went completely blank. Suddenly he was getting flashbacks to when he and Rita were making out in his bedroom, or the kitchen, while Joe was knocked out on sleeping pills. He remembered Rita assuring him that Joe would not hear them due to the effect of the sleeping pills, and he was at a loss for words. The silence on the phone lines at that time was deafening and he wanted to break it, but he just couldn't find the words.

"Are you still there, Frank?" Rita finally asked.

"Yes, yes, I'm here," Frank responded. "I'm just not sure what to say. I'm at a loss for words, Rita," he added.

"I know," Rita said. "I am as well."

"I'm really scared, Frank," she said. "Joe was on sleeping pills that night, just like he was on sleeping pills most nights. He used them to help him sleep after a long day at his office. He worked so hard, but he had a heck of a time getting to sleep. So, he would ask me for some sleeping pills to help him get a good night's sleep. I didn't think there was any harm in it. He's been taking them pretty much every night now for a couple of years. Well, ever since he started getting insomnia and was having trouble sleeping anyway, which has probably been at least two years ago now," she added.

"Well, that's not your fault," Frank responded. "If he was asking you to give him the pills, it's not like you were giving them to him without his knowledge. Right?"

"No, no, of course not. Joe would always ask me for them when it came time to go to sleep. I never gave them to him unless he asked for them, and he is the one who decided how many he wanted to take on any given night. I never gave the pills to him without his knowledge. But I'm afraid the police may not believe me and may think that I was giving them to him against his awareness and knowledge, that's the part I am scared about," Rita continued. "Because how can I prove that he was asking me for the pills, especially when the pills are in my name?" she said.

"I don't know, Rita," Frank replied. "That's why you need to call your lawyer first thing in the morning," Frank continued.

"You need to tell the lawyer everything you are telling me right now and get legal advice on what you should say or do. I have no idea what to advise you on this, Rita, I'm sorry. I'm sorry you are having to endure all of this on top of losing Joe. It must be so hard on you. I wish I could say or do more, but I just don't know what else to tell you," Frank continued.

"It's okay, Frank," Rita replied. Thanks for listening to me. I had to share all of this with someone and you were the only person I trust enough to share it with. Please don't say anything to anyone about all of this. I don't want people to know," Rita added.

"No, of course I won't say anything to anyone. You can count on that," Frank assured her.

"Thank you," Rita replied. It's all just so surreal to me right now. I just have to believe that the truth will somehow come out and that I will not be charged with murdering my own husband. I can't even bring myself to imagine going through such a situation as that," she said and started crying again.

"It will all be okay," Frank said in an effort to ease the burden he now knew Rita was under. Try to get some sleep and call the lawyer first thing in the morning, okay," he continued in a soft and compassionate tone of voice.

"Yes, I will for sure," Rita responded. "I'm going to let you go now and try to get some sleep. A couple of my staff are here at the house with me. I asked them to stay because I didn't want to be here alone," Rita continued.

"That's a good idea," Frank replied. "It is better to have people there with you, especially people you know and trust," he added. "Maybe they can help you if they were aware of the situation with Joe asking you for your sleeping pills. Do you think any of them knew?" Frank asked.

Rita was silent for a moment as if she was thinking about what Frank had just said. Finally, she said, "That's a good idea, but I'm not sure if any of them knew about the sleeping pills or not. I have to think more on that, but it is good you brought it up because it just may be that one of them was aware. And if this is the case, it could help to prove my innocence in this situation," she continued.

"Oh, how I wish Joe was still here," she said. "I am not used to dealing with heavy matters like this. Joe always took care of everything. I have been so sheltered from everything that now I am at a total loss as to how to deal with any of this. Thank God I have paid staff who I can get to do things for me. I don't know what I would do without the help of my staff right now," she added.

"Yes, it is good you have people there to help you. People that you know and trust," Frank replied. "I'm glad you are not there alone," Frank added. "You know I would be there for you if it were possible," Frank continued.

"Yes, I know you would be here if it were possible, but thank God you are not here at this time, as I have a feeling it would only make matters much worse than they already are," Rita replied.

Frank knew exactly what Rita was referring to, but he opted not to say anything over the phone for fear that someone may be listening, seeing as Rita was now under investigation for the murder of her husband Joe.

"I'm going to let you go now," Frank said. "Try and get some sleep and try not to worry too much about all of this. Things have a way of working themselves out," he added.

So, Rita and Frank ended their call and Frank sat down at his kitchen table.

Frank's mind was now swirling with all the information Rita had just given him. He couldn't believe all of this was happening, nor could he even imagine what the outcome was going to be. Then suddenly it hit him. "What if the police somehow find out that Rita and I were having an affair when she and Joe were here visiting?" he thought to himself, and he started to worry that maybe he, too, could be blamed in some way for the death of his friend Joe. Maybe he would be charged as an accomplice, he thought.

But then he reasoned that this could not be possible since he was nowhere near Joe or Rita at the time of Joe's untimely death. Still, it made him nervous to even think about such a possibility. Then, it also occurred to him that if the police knew of the affair between him and Rita while she and Joe were at his place visiting, that information could serve to further incriminate Rita in the situation she was now in.

So, he surely did not want Louise to find out, since she was aware that he and Rita were having sex behind Joe's back, even though Louise was just as guilty in one sense, as she too had joined in with sex between the three of them.

It all seemed so crazy now to Frank. How did his life turn into such a serious soap opera? And what was going to be the outcome of all of this? What if Rita were charged with Joe's death? Would she go to trial? Would she be found guilty and spend the rest of her life in prison? What if they found out she was having an affair with him? All these questions and possibilities were now running through his mind. He had no way of knowing the answers to any of the questions he had, and thinking about them was only making matters worse. He could only imagine what Rita must be going through, seeing that she was the one under investigation now for Joe's death.

"God, how did my life get so crazy?" he thought to himself. "I wish I had never invited Joe and his wife to come and visit," he said to himself. "Just look at all the mess it caused." But he knew he had no one to blame for his indiscretions and lack of sexual control regarding Rita. He felt great shame now for what he had done to Joe, who was his loyal friend. He couldn't believe he had crossed that line with Rita, and he wished he had exercised more control over his sexual temptations towards her. But she hadn't helped matters either by constantly flirting with him and dressing so provocatively in front of him all the time.

"Plus, giving Joe sleeping pills so she and I could have sex without Joe knowing!" he thought. And with that thought, it came into his mind that maybe Rita had murdered Joe. "Maybe she murdered Joe, so she could be free to go and be in a relationship with me!" he thought. "Oh my God, please don't let that be true," he said in a prayer. He could not bear the thought of that being true. "Surely, Rita would never do such a thing as that," he reasoned. "Yet it sure would serve as a motive if the police were ever to find out," he thought to himself.

"My lips are sealed," he thought. "I shall tell no one about any of this. I just hope it all blows over, and that the police find nothing to blame Rita and that she can get on with burying her husband and put this all behind her," Frank said to himself. He hoped that was the case, but from the looks of everything at that moment it was very unclear as to how things would pan out.

Frank opted to go to bed and try to sleep. There was nothing more he could do about any of what was happening. All he could do was hope that it all worked out somehow. He wanted to be there for Rita, but he knew that was impossible for him to do. He could not risk someone, anyone, finding out about him and Rita. It would make her chances of being found innocent all that much harder, and he surely didn't want that for her, or for him. He would have to just let it all go now and try to think positive about everything, for he dared not think in any other direction for fear it might come true.

He laid his head down on his pillow and thought of the times Rita had walked into his bedroom after Joe was asleep. How she had told him that Joe was on sleeping pills and thus would not hear them having sex. How he and Rita had wild sex for hours while her husband and his good friend lay sleeping just down the hallway from his room. And suddenly he felt sick to his stomach. How he could have ever let such a thing happen, he didn't know. He had always considered himself to be a decent person and a good and loyal friend; now that was all in question and he could no longer feel such goodness about himself. He had betrayed his friend, and now his friend was dead, and Rita was under investigation for his death.

"How in fuck can this all be happening?" he wondered as he lay there in his bed looking out the window at the sky full of stars shining brightly. "What will be my destiny now?" he wondered. "What will the future bring?" he asked himself. But he had no answers, and he sought sleep to help ease his troubled mind. Sleep was now his friend, but he wondered if sleep was also his enemy when he thought of how Rita had been giving Joe sleeping pills. Sleeping pills that may have been the cause of his death.

He tossed and turned and couldn't seem to get sleep to come to him. He tried to distract his mind and think about other things. He tried to think of Lacy and having sex with her as a means to get his mind off of everything that was happening, but nothing was working. When he thought of sex with Lacy, all it did was bring up more guilt and shame, and he couldn't bear to even think about it. He wasn't sure what to think about that would get this entire situation out of his mind.

Finally, he opted to go back downstairs and try to watch a movie. He would sleep on the couch and hope that the movie would distract his mind and put him to sleep. He looked through his movies, trying to find one that would not be a reminder of anything he was presently dealing with. Finally, he found a comedy he had not seen in some time and put it on to watch. He laid down on the couch, covered himself with the blanket, and tried to go to sleep.

The next thing he knew, he was opening his eyes and it was morning. The sun was shining through his living room windows and it must have woken him up. The television was still on, but the movie had long been over. He got up and shut the TV off and went to the kitchen to make himself a coffee. The situation of Joe and Rita came back up into his mind, but he pushed it out as quickly as it came in. "I just can't think about any of that today," he told himself. "I need a break from all of this. I need to find something to do to distract my mind," he thought. "I will have my coffee, smoke some medicine, and make myself a nice breakfast."

So that is what he opted to do, and then he went outside to see what project he could tackle next that would occupy his mind and keep it off the horror situation that was now his life.

 He couldn't talk to anyone about it, so he kept it bottled up inside and never mentioned a word of it to anyone, and even when it all was over, no one must ever know. "I must keep this secret until death," he told himself.

So he went outside and started doing some organizing in his barn in the hopes of escaping it all. He was working along when he heard a vehicle drive into the yard. He looked to see who it was, and it was Louise.

Louise parked and quickly jumped out of her vehicle. "Did you hear the news?" she asked, walking towards Frank. "No," Frank said. "What news?" "Rita," Louise replied. "She's been put under investigation for Joe's death! She never called you to tell you?" Louise asked.

Frank didn't know what to say, so he opted to remain silent. "I saw it on the national news last night," Louise continued. "I wanted to call you then to let you know, but it was late and so I decided to wait until this morning to come over and tell you face to face," she added. "What horrible news," Louise added. "I didn't even know that Joe had died, did you?" she asked.

Frank was stunned by all that Louise was saying. He had no idea it would be on the national news. Now he reasoned that everyone in the small town he lived in must know what was going on, and here he had sworn he would not tell a single soul. But he knew he had to respond to Louise's questions.

"Yes, I knew about Joe's death. Rita called me when it happened. It is very sad, he was only forty-six years old, you know," Frank replied.

"Yes, it is very sad indeed," Louise responded. "How did he die? Did Rita say?" Louise asked. "I'm not sure," Frank responded. "Rita didn't get into all the details. She just called to let me know that Joe had died and that is all I really know," Frank replied.

"Well, that's strange," Louise said. "Given how close you and Rita were when her and Joe were here visiting, I would think she would have given you all the details, especially seeing that you and Joe were close friends for many years. But she never told you any of the details? How bizarre," Louise continued.

"Nope, she only called to say that Joe had died and that is all I really know," Frank responded.

"Well, something must have happened a lot more than what Rita told you," Louise continued. "Because it said on the news that Rita is now under investigation for Joe's death! How could she be under investigation? Did she have something to do with his death?" Louise asked.

"No," Frank said. "Not as far as I know. Rita's not that kind of person, you know that. I am not sure why she is under investigation, but I am sure it is all just a big misunderstanding that will be worked out," Frank continued.

"I hope so for her sake," Louise added. "I have to get going," she said. "I have to get to work. I just wanted to drop by and let you know. I figured you already knew, but I thought I should come by and tell you just in case you didn't. And I'm glad I did, because apparently you didn't know," she added.

"Well, now you do. I'm sorry to bring you this information, but it is better that you know because Rita most likely will call you and tell you anyway," she added.

"Yes, thank you for dropping by and letting me know. It is all pretty crazy, but I am sure it will all work out in the end," Frank replied.

"It is good you are so optimistic," Louise responded. "I hope you are right," she added, getting back into her vehicle to leave.

Frank decided to return to his house. He suddenly needed another cup of coffee and smoke. His plan to keep quiet about all that was happening was now thrown out the window. "How many people in town realize that the people on the news are the people who had stayed here at my house?" he wondered. "Will it be on the news again?" he wondered.

He went and turned on his television and tried to find a news station with national news on it, but he was unable to find one that was airing news at that time, so he turned the TV back off and went back to the kitchen. He felt all he could do was pray now, and he didn't feel like his prayers would carry much weight seeing as all the sinning he had been doing. All the lying and cheating and sneaking around.

He couldn't believe the state his life and mind were now in, and he wondered how in hell he had gotten to the place he now found himself in. There was, he knew, no amount of positive self-talk or mind distraction that was going to take him out of the state he was now in. So, he opted to get as stoned as he could and as quickly as he could, hoping that being so stoned, he would not be able to think about anything except how stoned he was.

So, he proceeded to smoke one joint after the other until he was so stoned, he could barely sit on the chair, and he opted to go back to the couch and sleep some more. Sleep now was his best friend, for it was the only thing that could make his mind stop thinking about all that was taking place. "Tomorrow's a new day," he told himself as he shut his eyes and fell asleep stoned out of his mind.

Chapter Thirteen

Off The Rails

It had now been a couple or three days since Frank had heard back from Rita, and it was driving him crazy not knowing what was going on. He understood that Rita could not be calling him all the time, so as not to raise suspicion in regard to their affair, yet he so badly wanted to know the status of what was taking place. He reasoned that no news was good news, and that if anything bad had happened, surely Rita would have called him to let him know.

He had not heard from Louise either, since she had dropped over that morning to give him the news about Rita. He was relieved that Louise was leaving him alone about all of this, and he wondered if she was thinking about ratting him and Rita out in regard to their affair, or if she was telling anyone around town that the couple in the news were the same people who had stayed at his house. He prayed this was not the case, and he thought of calling Louise to let her know that she ought to keep her mouth shut about all of this, as she, too, was a party to some of the sexcapades that had taken place. And so she might want to think about that before she decides to open her mouth about it to people.

Frank had always detested gossip bags. He lived a very quiet life, and since he had moved to that small town, he made sure to keep his business to himself and avoid gossip in the town. Now, he realized, he might become the main subject matter for all the bored and inept people who use gossip as the glue for their popularity and friendships. Gossip being the main thing that tied them all together. The ones who loved nothing more than to hear some dirt on someone that they could spread around and add to the story.

He hoped this was not the case. He could not bear to think of being the center of people's gossip, nor to endure the looks of disdain when he had to go out into the community for something he needed. He knew what small towns could be like when someone was caught doing something wrong, and he didn't want to be the brunt of something like that. Yet, he knew it was a good possibility that he would be if this information were to get out and people realized he knew the people involved.

He opted to just chill. He made himself a fresh cup of coffee and sat down at his kitchen table to relax. He had to think all of this through, he thought to himself, and stop running. Stop the avoidance techniques he had been employing in an effort to keep his mind off of all that was now taking place in his life. "How in fuck did my life get into such a mess?" he said to himself. But he knew he wasn't ready to take personal responsibility for any of it.

The fresh cup of coffee tasted so good as he sipped it slowly and drew back on the joint he had rolled earlier and left on the table. "Ahhhh, that's better," he said to himself as he leaned back in his favorite chair and stared out his kitchen window into the nature that was his land. Suddenly, he felt very blessed to have all he had.

As he drank his coffee, he remembered Rita sitting there drinking coffee with him. "She must be under so much stress right now," he reasoned, and it made his heart sad to think of Rita in her current situation. He also felt very sad about Joe's death. But he couldn't let himself go there right now, it was more than he felt he could bear.

Just when he was thinking about all this, the phone rang. Frank picked up the phone to look and see who was calling. "Dam, it's Louise," he thought. "What does she want?" he wondered. He couldn't decide if he wanted to pick up the phone or not, but he finally opted to pick it up and say, "Hello," like he was unsure who was on the other line.

"Hey," Louise said. "Glad you are home. I was wondering if you minded me dropping by for a visit. I won't stay long, but I really have to talk to you about, you know!" Louise said.

Frank knew exactly what she was making reference to, but he wasn't sure he really wanted to talk with her about it, much less anyone else. Yet, he knew if he refused, it would most likely make things worse, so he agreed for Louise to drop by and hung up the phone.

Once off the phone, he opted to roll a couple of joints, figuring he was going to need them given the context of what was about to take place. What was he going to say to Louise? What did she want to know? He would just tell her the same thing he had told her that morning when she dropped by on her way to work, that he knew "nothing." But he wondered if that would fly with Louise, since she was one of the most intelligent people he knew or had ever known. He usually truly respected and greatly enjoyed her high level of intellect, but now it felt more like an enemy.

He was trying to prepare himself mentally for Louise's visit when he noticed that twenty minutes had already passed since she called. He looked at his phone just to make sure. It was unlike Louise to be tardy, and he had to wonder what was taking her so long. It was, at best, a five minute drive from her place to his. He hoped nothing had gone wrong. He felt he couldn't bear to hear any more bad news.

Just then he heard a vehicle pull into his driveway. "Oh, there she is now," he thought, and he stood up to straighten out his shirt in an effort to make himself look presentable. Louise knocked on the door and Frank let her in. She smiled a big smile and kissed him on the cheek. "You always look so damn handsome," she said, smiling. Frank smiled and thanked her for the compliment. "Was she here for sex?" he wondered, but he knew why she was there. He was just hoping that maybe her sexual drive was stronger than her need for answers concerning Rita and Joe. Yet, he knew that was most likely wishful thinking.

"Can I make you a coffee?" he asked. "Sure, that sounds perfect," Louise replied. "No one makes a cup of coffee quite like you, Frank," Louise said, smiling. "Yea, I was just thinking about Rita and how much she loved the coffee I made her," he said. "Well, she's not the only one," Louise blurted out. "I was having coffee with you long before she was, and I always complimented you on it," she reminded him. "Oh, I know. I didn't mean anything by what I said; I was just making conversation that's all. Your comment reminded me of how Rita always went on about how much she loved the coffee I had here, that's all," Frank replied. And with that, Frank was suddenly aware that Louise was jealous of Rita. "How could I have been so dumb not to realize that before?" he thought to himself.

So Frank made Louise a coffee and made himself another one as well, and sat down at the kitchen table with her. "Do you want a smoke?" he asked, handing Louise one of the joints he had rolled before she arrived. "No, I don't think I should right now," Louise replied. "I think what you and I have to talk about is too serious a matter, and I want to stay sober-minded," she continued. Frank didn't consider smoking the herb as something that made him not sober-minded, but he didn't want to debate the topic right at that moment. "Well, I'm going to burn one down, if you don't mind," he said, already lighting the joint. "Oh no, no problem. Do as you wish, Frank. This is your house and it is your pot." Frank smiled. "Yes, indeed it is," he responded. "But enough small talk, you said you wanted to come over to talk to me, so talk away. I'm all ears," Frank continued.

"Well, first off, have you heard from Rita?" Louise asked. "No, I've not heard from Rita since she called to let me know Joe had died. I was so devastated by the news, and then you tell me that Rita, of all people, is being investigated for his death. I am still having a hard time processing it all," Frank responded. "I imagine you are," Louise replied. "Must be feeling a lot of guilt, I would imagine," she continued. Suddenly, Frank felt a strong pang of anxiety run through his body. What was Louise referring to, he wondered, but he knew without asking, so he opted to remain silent as if he had not heard her.

"Why don't you call Rita and find out what is going on?" Louise asked. "After all, she is your good friend, isn't she? I mean the two of you were pretty close when she and Joe were staying here," Louise said and winked. "Oh, I don't want to call her," Frank said. "She has a lot going on right now, and I don't want to bother her. She just lost her husband of many years and now she is being investigated for his death. So, I don't think it would be cool to call her right now and ask her a pile of questions, when truthfully it is all none of my business, or yours for that matter," he added.

Louise was a little taken aback by Frank's response and she let Frank know by her facial expression. "Okay then," she said. "We'll just stay in the dark until she finally decides to call you and explain what is going on, I guess," Louise continued. "That's right," Frank said, blowing out smoke from the joint he was smoking. "It's none of our business, and Rita will advise what she wants to advise when she wants to advise it. That's the way I see it anyway," Frank continued.

"Aren't you curious?" Louise asked. "No, not really," Frank replied. "Like I said, I feel it is none of my business," he continued. "Well, I'm curious," Louise responded. "I'd love to know what is going on. How did Joe die, for example? Do you even know that much?" she asked. "I already told you that I'm not sure, Rita never got into any details," Frank replied.

"I find that very strange," Louise responded. "I figured she would have already called you and told you everything," Louise continued. "Well, I'm sorry to disappoint you, Louise, but Rita has not called much since she and Joe left here, and when she called to let me know of Joe's passing, the phone call was short as she was devastated and crying, and I really didn't know what to say to her in that moment. So it wasn't a long call. She just called to let me know that Joe had passed," Frank responded.

All the questions were making Frank feel sick to his stomach, and he desperately wanted to change the subject. Yet he knew that Louise had dropped by specifically to "discuss" the situation of Joe's death and Rita being investigated for it.

"Why would Rita be under investigation for Joe's death?" Louise asked.

"I have no idea," Frank replied. "It does seem rather strange," he agreed. Then he said, "Rita really loved Joe, and the two of them got along really well, from all I saw while they were staying here. I know Joe really loved Rita too. He could barely keep his hands off her when she was around, and he was always giving her compliments," he added.

"Well, if that's true," Louise replied, "why was she all over you behind his back?"

Frank could feel his face heating up with embarrassment, and he was at a loss for words. Finally, he blurted out, "I don't know why! Maybe I'm irresistible," he said, smiling a big smile.

"Oh, you are irresistible for sure," Louise replied, smiling. "But you should not have been messing around with your friend's wife, Frank!" she added.

There it was, on the table, full force, and Frank had nowhere to turn, nowhere to run and hide from it. He had to face it now, because Louise was not letting him do otherwise. "Why did I agree to let her come over here?" he thought to himself. "She is interrogating me over all of this, and I don't even want to think about any of it.".

Now the silence in the room was deafening, and neither Frank nor Louise seemed to know what to say next. The cat was out of the bag, so to speak, and Frank just wanted to put it back in.

"I'm sorry," Louise finally said. "I can see that this is really hard for you. I didn't mean to be rude, I'm just curious is all. I would just really like to know what is going on," she continued.

"Yea, me too," Frank replied. "But I've already told you everything I know. So there is really nothing more I can tell you until Rita gets a hold of me again, if and when she does," he added.

"You'll let me know if or when you hear anything, right?" Louise asked.

"Oh, for sure," Frank assured her. "No problem there. I will let you know as soon as I know, how's that," he continued.

"Okay then, you had better," Louise warned.

"Yes, yes, of course I will," Frank replied and smiled. And with that Louise got up to leave.

"I have to get going, but call me soon," Louise said, getting up from her chair. "I would like to have a 'stay over' night sooner than later," she added and winked.

"Yes, for sure," Frank replied, smiling while walking Louise to the door. The two of them hugged and Louise left.

Frank then sat back down at the table. Louise had been the only woman Frank had been with for years, and he wasn't even with her all that often, it seemed to him. But now he had Rita, Lacy, and Louise on the go, and the truth of that thought made his head spin. It seemed surreal to him that he had gone from barely having sex to having sex with three different women on what had become a semi-regular basis. But he swore he was not going to have sex with Lacy again, and he hoped he could maintain his stance on that, for he knew he was weak when it came to sex being offered.

And Rita was out of range, and he reasoned that was a good thing, especially now with Joe's death and her being put under investigation for it. He wondered how she was feeling and he reasoned she was under heavy stress. He felt sad and he wished there was something, anything, he could do to help her. Yet, he knew there was nothing he could do.

He knew the best thing for him to do was to stay away from her during this time so as not to raise any suspicions about the two of them. And so, he refrained from even thinking about her, as that might make her want to call him. Still, he wondered how she was coping with all that was happening.

He remembered Rita not wanting him to continue to have sex with Louise. He remembered how she told him she was jealous of Louise, and now he knew that Louise was also jealous of Rita. "What if the two of them knew about my latest sexual relations with Lacy?" he thought.

His life, he knew, was becoming, or had become, a tangled web of lies, and it bothered him greatly to face that truth. He had always prided himself on his high level of honesty, but now he saw himself as a liar and a fraud, and he didn't like the way that made him feel inside. So he opted to try and distract his mind with a movie.

He looked through the many movies he had to choose from and chose one that was not going to remind him of any of the situations he now found himself in. "I'll watch a comedy. That will help me to think happy thoughts rather than all the shit that has now become my life," he thought as he put the movie into his DVD player and laid down on the couch.

The movie was about three-quarters finished when the phone rang. Frank had fallen asleep and was aroused and annoyed by the sound of the phone. "Who in fuck is calling me now?" he thought, getting up from his comfortable position on the couch. "I don't want to talk to anyone," he said to himself, as he walked towards the phone. He picked it up to see who was calling. "Fuck, it is Louise again! What does she want now?" he thought.

"Hello," he said.

"Frank! You're not going to believe this! Rita has now been charged with Joe's death! She is being charged for murder, Frank!"

Frank just stood there dumbfounded, not knowing what to say.

"Are you there?" Louise asked due to the silence on the other end.

"Yea, yea, I'm here. I just can't believe what you just told me. Are you sure you heard that right? Where did you get that information?" he asked all at once.

"It was just on the national news, Frank! They said that Rita has now been officially charged for murdering her husband! I am beside myself. I can't believe this, and I am sure it is very hard for you to believe as well," Louise continued.

Frank was at a loss for words. He truly did not know what to say. He searched for words, but it was as if there were none to be found. His head was now swirling, and he felt like he was going to pass out.

"Are you okay?" Louise asked.

"No, I'm not okay," Frank answered. "I feel like I am going to be sick to my stomach. I'm going to have to let you go, Louise. I need to go and lay down. This is all just too much for me. I can't get my head around it all. I'm sorry, but I really have to go now," Frank said and ended the call without even saying goodbye.

"What the fuck is happening?" he though. "How can this be happening? Did Rita call the lawyer like I told her to? Why was the lawyer not helping her? What did they find out during the investigation that made them lay a charge of murder?" he wondered. So many things were now running through his mind. So many questions. "What if she is found guilty?" he thought. "Oh my God, this cannot be happening to me," he said to himself, and then he realized it was not happening to him. It was happening to Rita.

And suddenly his heart was breaking for Rita. He could not even imagine what she must be feeling, what she must be going through. He wanted to reach out and call her, but he was afraid to. He was afraid that someone would find out that he and Rita had an affair when she and Joe were visiting at his place. He feared being tied into the situation, and he knew if the truth came out, it would definitely make matters much worse for Rita.

He felt so sad, he began to cry. And crying made him feel worse, because he had been taught that crying was a sign of weakness. Yet, there he was crying like a baby all of a sudden, and he couldn't stop. It was as if a river of tears had been stored up deep inside him, and now it was coming out like a tsunami. "Get it all out," he said to himself, and he didn't hold back. He let the tears flow and felt like it was needed. He couldn't even remember the last time he had cried like he was now.

And while the big cry gave him some reprieve, the thoughts of what was happening just would not stop. All these various scenarios were now going around in his head. "What if this… what if that…" On and on and on the thoughts of the situation consumed him now. And he knew there was no amount of herb that was going to take them away. He thought of taking sleeping pills, and that made his whole body shiver in remembering the whole sleeping pill thing with Joe. Plus he didn't have any sleeping pills, so how was he going to take any? He would just have to endure it all the best way he knew how, and he wasn't at all sure, in that moment, what that was.

And if that wasn't bad enough, he suddenly realized that Louise knew the truth of everything. And he now knew she was jealous of Rita. And if Louise decided to tell anyone, he could be brought into this entire situation. The police might think he and Rita planned it all, if they ever knew of their affair. He realized he could be charged as well. And suddenly his heart began to pound within his chest. He started feeling like he couldn't breathe. His hands started to shake, and he could not stop them.

"What is happening to me?" he wondered, and he was sure he was about to die from a heart attack or stroke. He got up and walked outside. "Maybe if I get some fresh air it will help me breathe," he thought as he exited the house. The fresh air did seem to help somewhat, but he was still struggling to get his breath.

His chest was hurting, and pain was going across it now. He didn't know if he should sit down or keep standing. He didn't know if he should walk or stand still. He didn't know what to do at all. So, he just stood there, and then he began to pray and ask God to help him, knowing that he ought to have repented first for all the lying and cheating he had been doing. But, right now, all he could think of was begging God to help him.

And not long after he began to pray, a vehicle pulled into his yard. It was Louise, but this time he was relieved and happy to see her. At least there was someone there with him now in case he did have a heart attack or stroke.

Louise got out of her car and ran to Frank. "Are you okay?" she asked.

"No, something is happening to me, Louise. I don't know what it is," Frank said. And then he started telling Louise all the things he was experiencing.

"You're having a panic attack, Frank," Louise said in a sympathetic tone of voice.

"Are you sure?" Frank replied, still trying to calm himself down. "It feels like a heart attack or something of that nature," Frank continued.

"I know," Louise said. "Trust me, I've had them before. I know exactly how you feel," she continued.

"I have medication I can give to you if you want. It will help your nervous system to calm down. Do you want one?" Louise asked.

"Yes, please," Frank replied. "I'll take anything right now to help me get rid of this, whatever it is. I feel like I'm about to die," he continued.

"I know," Louise said. "It does feel like you're about to die, but you will be okay, I promise," she reassured him as she quickly dug in her purse for her bottle of medication.

She retrieved one and gave it to Frank. "Here," she said. "Put this under your tongue and let it dissolve. You will start to feel better in about twenty minutes," she continued.

Frank quickly took the small pill that Louise had given to him and did as she instructed. Then he grabbed Louise and hugged her. "Thank you for showing up. You're an awesome friend, Louise. I was praying and asking God to help me in this situation. I didn't know what was happening to me and I couldn't control it. I was scared. I am so glad you showed up when you did. Thank you so much," he said, still hugging her.

Louise had never seen Frank vulnerable like that before, and it made her heart hurt to see him in such a position. She was happy she had decided to drive over to his place after he hung up the phone without even saying goodbye. She knew the news of Rita being charged was going to be hard for him to hear, but she had no idea it was going to have such a devastating effect as she was now seeing.

She held him tight and tried her best to help him calm down. She touched the back of his head and patted his hair, whispering, "It's all going to be alright, Frank. Shuuuu," in her attempt to soothe what was obviously his very troubled mind and body.

"How long did you say it was going to take for this to go away?" Frank asked.

"It usually takes about twenty minutes or so," Louise responded. "But try not to think about that. Try to think about something totally unrelated," she said.

"I can't," Frank said. "I'm consumed by this right now. I feel like I am about to die. My heart is coming out of my chest. I feel very lightheaded and dizzy. Are you sure I am having a panic attack and it is not something more serious?" he asked.

Suddenly Louise realized that she may have wrongly diagnosed the situation, but she didn't want to say that to Frank. She didn't want to make his state of panic any worse than it was already. So she opted to just reassure him that he was having a panic attack and that he'd be okay in a while.

"Just try your best to think positive thoughts and try to relax as best you can. The medication will kick in soon," she reassured him.

"Are you sure, Louise?" Frank asked, looking at her.

Louise could not believe the state Frank was in. She'd never seen him in such a state as this. He looked so weak, so vulnerable, so afraid. It was breaking her heart to see him like that. He was always so strong, so self-assured, so confident; she could never have imagined seeing him in the state she saw him in now.

He was like a little child who needed help, and she was so grateful that she was the one who was there to help him, to save him. She was the strong one, the one giving him the comfort and help he needed. She was a good friend, the one who came to his aid in his time of trouble, she thought, and that made her feel good about herself.

Frank stood there leaning up against Louise, holding onto her like he was holding onto life itself. Finally, the medication Louise had given him seemed to kick in and he slowly began to feel his body calming down. He began to breathe more freely, and the pain in his chest began to subside a little. He had stopped shaking, and his head felt clearer and less dizzy.

"Thank God, I think this is starting to pass now," he said to Louise.

"Shuuu, just relax and try not to think too much. Just try to stay calm. Soon you will feel better," she reassured him once again.

So Frank leaned up against Louise and just waited there for the medication to fully kick in. He knew on one level that he should feel embarrassed by his current state, but he was too stressed out over what was happening to worry about it.

Finally, after about twenty minutes had passed, Frank began to feel somewhat back to normal. Louise helped him back into his house, and they sat down at the kitchen table. Louise held his hand

and talked softly to him, trying to soothe his nerves. Frank looked her in the eyes and said with all sincerity, "Thank you for coming over, Louise. I don't know what would have happened to me if you had not shown up. Thank you so much," and squeezed her hand in deep appreciation.

Louise smiled and reassured Frank that she cared about him and was happy to be there for him. That she was happy she had decided to drive over to his place to check on him after their phone conversation. "I'm just relieved you are all good now, or at least better than you were," she said.

Frank was now feeling the full effects of the medication Louise had given to him. He began to feel tired and drained. He was not used to taking medications of any kind, and it was a rare occasion that he would even allow himself to take an over-the-counter pain medication when needed. But this was something altogether different. He'd never experienced anything like this before. It scared him. He couldn't control what was happening to his body. He felt like he was dying. And then he realized it was best not to think about it, not to revisit how he had been feeling, for fear that it would trigger it to happen again.

Louise had just gone up a million miles in his "like" category. She was now his quasi-savior. And he wondered if God had not sent her, since he was praying for help not long before she arrived. "Maybe she's an angel and I just never realized it before," he thought.

"You're an angel, Louise," he blurted out. "I just never recognized it before," he added.

Louise smiled. "No, Frank, I'm not an angel. I'm just your good friend of many years who cares deeply about you, that's all," Louise replied. "I just happened to be here at the right time. And truly it was due to our phone conversation and you hanging up without saying goodbye. I got a sense that something was seriously wrong, and so I opted to drive over to see if you were okay. And you weren't okay, and I'm glad that I was able to help you. You mean a lot to me Frank, you know that right?" Louise continued.

"I do now," Frank said. "Yes, I have always known you cared for me, and I hope you know how much I care for you also. I know we have been sex partners for years and that maybe you wanted more, or maybe I did, I don't know. But the point is, we do deeply care for one another, and that's the truth of things," Frank continued, squeezing her hand once again and looking deeply into her eyes as he spoke.

The sound of what Frank was now saying was melting Louise's heart. Frank was not one for sharing his feelings and definitely not one for being mushy. So to hear him say those words to her was like heaven on earth.

"Please don't leave, Louise," Frank added. "I don't want to be alone right now. I'm afraid that thing, whatever it was, will come back over me, and I don't want to be here alone. Can you stay here with me?" he asked.

"Of course," Louise replied. "I wouldn't think of leaving you in the state you are in. I will even stay the night and as long as you need me to. Don't worry, Frank, I'm here for you always," Louise continued, leaning towards him and looking him directly in his eyes.

"Thank you, Louise. You're a true friend. I appreciate you very much," Frank responded. And with that knowledge, Frank opted to go and lay down on his couch. "Go ahead and put in a movie if you want. Pick whichever one you want to watch. Your choice," he said.

So Louise started looking through the piles of movies Frank had stacked up in front of his television and DVD player. She found a movie she wanted to watch and put it into the DVD player, then she sat in one of the chairs in Frank's living room. But Frank motioned for her to come and lay down with him on the couch.

"Come and lay down with me, Louise," Frank said, reaching for her hand. The couch wasn't that wide, but the two of them fit on it.

Louise was happy to lie beside Frank. To give him comfort and console him after his panic attack. She knew all too well what it felt like to have a massive panic attack, and thus she knew just how scary it felt when it came upon a person. Thus, she had great empathy for what Frank had just been through.

Louise had suffered through anxiety and panic attacks for years, but Frank had no idea. And most people didn't, because Louise hid it well. She always seemed so together, so solid and strong. And she was all of that, but she also had issues like everyone else. Thus, she always kept medication in her purse because she never knew when an anxiety or panic attack was going to hit her. She kept them close because she needed them when she needed them, and she couldn't imagine having to endure an attack without medication.

She knew what Frank meant when he said he felt like he was going to die, or that he was dying, because she had been there herself many times over the years. She was relieved that she had gone to Frank's place to check on him when she did and that she had medication to help him.

The two of them laid on the couch, and Louise pulled the blanket that was on the back of the couch over the two of them. Frank put his arm around Louise in a loving way. This was not sexual. No, this was friendship and love in truth.

Calm now filled the atmosphere and it wasn't long before Frank was fast asleep. Louise was comforted by Frank's arm around her, but she couldn't get to sleep as quickly as he had. He had taken medication which knocked him out cold, but she was still wide awake and still reeling from all that had happened. She kept thinking about how Frank looked when she showed up at his place. How she had never seen him like that before, and how it shocked her. Given the context of the information she had given Frank over the phone concerning Rita, she had been pretty certain it was a panic attack. Information like that, she knew, was enough to bring one on. She tried to focus on watching the movie, and it wasn't long before she, too, was fast asleep.

The sun came up and aroused them out of their slumber. It was cozy, if not crowded, on the couch with the two of them, and so Louise got up first since she was on the outside. Frank got up and grabbed Louise and hugged her.

"I'm so glad you are here with me," he said. "I really didn't want to be alone last night. I pray nothing like that ever happens to me again. I was certain I was dying," he added.

"I know," Louise replied. "Unfortunately, I have suffered with anxiety and panic attacks for years. I just don't talk about it," Louise added. "But I'm glad I was here and that I had some medication to give to you," Louise continued.

"You're glad! I'm ecstatic," Frank replied, smiling as if he never quite heard the first part of what Louise had just said. "I don't know what I would have done if you had not shown up, Louise. You saved me," he said, hugging her again.

"Stay and have coffee with me, Louise," Frank said as they entered the kitchen.

"Sure," Louise replied. "I have some time yet before I have to leave," she added, smiling warmly at Frank.

"Would you like me to make breakfast for you? As you know, I make a mean bacon and eggs," Frank said and smiled.

"No, I don't feel like eating right now, but thank you for the offer. I know you are an excellent cook," Louise replied, still smiling.

So Frank made coffee for the two of them, and they sat at his kitchen table consuming it.

"I was thinking of having a smoke, but I'm not sure if it's a good idea after what happened to me yesterday. I'm feeling kinda scared and shaky," he added.

"I get it," Louise replied. "I know how scary anxiety and panic attacks are, especially if you've never experienced one before. Like I said earlier, I've had the condition for several years, and still, when I have an attack, it feels scary. So I know what you mean, but you'll be okay," she continued. "Just try to keep your thoughts on the positive side. If you let yourself think too many negative thoughts, fear can set in and the next thing you know, you are having a panic attack," she added.

"What!" Frank exclaimed. "You've had this condition for years?" Frank added. "I had no idea," he continued, as if he was suddenly aware of what she had already told him.

"Yes, unfortunately, I have suffered from those kinds of attacks for a long time. And I have to tell you, they don't get any easier with time. You just get better at coping with them once you know what is happening. And the medication is a lifesaver," Louise replied.

"I'm so sorry to hear that, Louise," Frank responded. "From what I experienced, I would not wish that on my worst enemy," he continued.

Louise smiled and touched Frank's hand that was resting on the table. "Listen, I am here for you," she said, looking him directly in the eyes. "Try to stay positive in this situation. I know it is hard, given all that is taking place, but if you allow yourself to get consumed by it, it will only make matters worse," Louise continued. "Dwelling on it could cause you to have another panic attack, and I know you don't want that to happen," Louise advised. "No, I most certainly do not want that to happen again, and now I am feeling the fear of the possibility of it happening again," Frank replied.

"How can I stop that from happening again?" Frank asked. He was thinking maybe Louise had the answer, since she said she had been suffering with these attacks for years.

Louise had to stop and think about that question, as she was not sure how a person could stop the attacks from happening. She had not been able to do that in all the years she had suffered from the condition. So she opted to just be honest with Frank and to tell him exactly that.

"There's no way to really stop them," she finally said, with a sad look on her face.

"I'm sorry, Frank. I wish I had the answer to your question. Even though I've had this condition for years, I am not sure how a person can stop them. All I know is that when I feel one coming on, I take medication right away to try to lessen the impact, and it seems to work. But like I told you last night, and as you experienced, you have to endure the attack until the medication kicks in, and it usually takes about twenty minutes. So I just hang on and hang in until the medication kicks in. That's about all I can tell you about it. I'm sorry. I wish I had more information for you, but I just don't," she continued. "But you can't worry about it, because worrying about it could bring on another attack," she explained. "Just do your best to forget about it. Act like it never happened, and just live your life as you normally do," she added.

Frank wasn't sure what to think at this point. Now he was afraid another attack would come on him, and yet Louise was telling him that worrying about it could bring one on, and he surely didn't want that to happen. So he resolved to just do as Louise had told him and try to control his thoughts and forget about the attack and how it made him feel. He was determined that he was not going to let himself have another attack. They were way too freaky, and he couldn't imagine having that condition long-term like Louise.

It made him sad inside to think of it. "How has she been coping with these attacks for years?" he wondered. "How come he had never seen or realized she suffered from that condition all these years?" "How come she had never mentioned this to him ever before?" he thought. These were the questions now running through his mind. But he didn't want to ask her too many questions, as he didn't want to appear as prying into her personal affairs. Obviously, she did not want people to know about her condition, or she would have told him about it a long time ago. So he opted to just think about the questions but not to ask them.

They finished their coffee, and Frank offered Louise another. "No, I really have to get going, but thank you, and I will take a rain check," she said, smiling at Frank. Frank looked disappointed. He didn't want Louise to leave, but he knew she couldn't stay there with him forever. He knew he had to face being alone sooner rather than later, and it was strange to him because prior to having that attack, he had enjoyed being alone. Now, suddenly, he felt fear about it, and that bothered him greatly.

Louise sensed that Frank had fear about her leaving, so she again reached for his hand, looked into his eyes and said, "Listen, don't worry, you are going to be all good. Just try, as I said, not to think about all the negative that is happening. Thinking negative thoughts can cause an attack. So try, as best you can within the circumstances, to think about positive things. Distract your mind with something if you have to. Just try to keep your nervous system as calm as possible," she advised.

"Okay, that's what I will do," Frank agreed. Yet, he was unsure if it was even possible for him not to think about what was happening with Rita being charged for the murder of Joe, as well as the awareness that he could be brought into the situation. And with those thoughts, Frank suddenly realized that Louise was the key to keeping that from happening because she was the only one who knew about the affair between him and Rita.

He wanted to say something, but he wasn't sure what. He wanted to ask Louise to be quiet about the affair, but he was afraid to even bring it up for fear that somehow bringing it up could make it happen. He knew that was silly, yet it felt very real within him.

Regardless, he knew he had to talk about it with Louise, because once again, she had the power to save him from this situation, just as she had saved him from the horror of the panic attack he had the day before.

He sat there rubbing his chin and thinking. He knew he had to be quick about it if he was going to bring it up, as Louise was getting ready to leave and had gone to use the washroom before leaving. "How do I approach this subject? What do I say? How do I say it?" were now the questions running through his mind. He was starting to feel panic again, and he remembered what Louise had told him, how he had to keep calm and not get too excited or stressed or worried about anything. So he tried to erase the questions and not think of anything for fear of another attack.

"Is this something that is permanent now?" he wondered. "Do I have to concern myself with this all the time now?" he thought. So when Louise returned to the kitchen, Frank asked her more about it. "You are probably not going to have another attack," she said. "It was probably just a reaction to the news concerning Rita," Louise continued. "Chances are you will not have another one, but like I say, you have to be mindful of your thoughts and not get too overwhelmed by everything happening," she added.

Frank felt somewhat relieved by her words, but he wasn't convinced that it was never going to happen to him again. "Could you leave me a couple of your pills?" he asked. "Just in case I may need them. I think that would make me feel better," he continued.

"Just to know I have them if another attack does come upon me," he added.

"Sure, I can do that," Louise replied, digging for her medication and then putting three of her pills on the table for Frank. Then she took his hand.

"Don't worry, Frank, everything is going to be alright. I am sure Rita will be contacting you at some point, and she will explain everything that is happening. Just try not to dwell on it and trust that it will all work out. You know Rita better than I do, but I can't see her killing anyone," Louise said.

Frank knew he had to take this opportunity to bring up the affair between him and Rita because Louise was about to leave, and he didn't want to leave that conversation unsaid as he needed reassurance that Louise was not going to say anything. He also knew that Louise did not know the full story and that he had lied to her, saying he did not know anything about it. But chances were, he figured, that sooner or later she would find out the full story regarding the sleeping pills. So he forced himself to bring up the elephant in his mind.

"I know you have to leave, Louise, but I really have something I need to talk to you about," he said.

Louise was already standing and preparing to leave, but she sat back down at the table when Frank said that to her. "What's on your mind now?" she asked, smiling at him. She had no idea that Frank was worried about her saying something about his affair with Rita.

Frank sat there searching for the right words to express himself regarding the situation. He wasn't sure how to bring it up, but he knew he had to. Finally, he blurted out, "You know that Rita and I had an affair when she and Joe were staying here, and I'm just concerned about anyone finding out about it," he said. Then he reminded Louise that she too had slept with the two of them and that she too should be worried about it, providing her personal interests in not saying anything to anyone.

Louise was a little taken aback by what Frank was saying and she felt in that moment that she had to defend herself. "Yes, of course I obviously know about the affair between you and Rita. And yes, I, too, had sex with the two of you on one occasion. But Joe was not my longtime friend, and I didn't know him or Rita, really!" Louise continued. "I don't know how many times you had sex with Rita, because I obviously wasn't here all the time. I was only here on that one occasion, and I don't think one time really counts for much," Louise went on to say. "But yes, I am with you in keeping it quiet. God forbid that information ever gets out to anyone," she added.

"Thank you for saying that," Frank replied, reaching over to Louise and taking her hand. "It means a lot to me that no one finds out about Rita and I. I don't want to get drawn into this situation, and if anyone were to find out, it could easily be the case," Frank continued.

Louise was now confused. "What do you mean?" she asked. "How could you be drawn into this situation? I don't get it?" she asked. Frank realized he had said too much, so he tried to dismiss his comment, saying, "Oh, I am just worried, is all, and probably not really thinking straight right now," he added. Louise looked puzzled, but she took Frank at his word.

"Okay, we're all good then?" she asked, getting up from the table once again.

"Yes, we are all good," Frank said, smiling at her. He finally felt some relief in having brought up the subject with Louise and having heard her say that she was not going to say anything to anyone.

It was like a pound of weight had been lifted off his shoulders, and his body felt lighter all of a sudden. His mind, too, felt better and clearer because he had gotten it off his chest. Now, he felt willing to let her leave and get on with the day.

Frank stood up from the table and gave Louise a tight hug with feeling behind it. "Thank you again for staying with me last night. I truly feel like you saved me, and I want you to know how much I appreciate your friendship. You're a sweetheart, Louise, and I treasure our friendship. I just want you to know that," he said, still hugging her.

Louise was touched by Frank's words. She hugged him back just as tightly and reassured him once again that everything was going to be alright and to try not to worry. Finally, the two of them separated from hugging, and Louise left.

Frank sat there at his kitchen table. He was alone once again. He smiled as he rolled a joint and then opted to make himself a second cup of coffee. As he was making coffee, he couldn't help but think about all that had happened. He was having a hard time getting his head around the panic attack and how it felt, but he remembered what Louise had told him, and so he tried not to think too much about it. Instead, he told himself he would focus on the fact that he had brought up the subject of his affair with Rita to Louise, and she had confirmed that she was not going to say anything to anyone. "That information could be explosive," he thought.

Then suddenly it hit him that once Louise knew the full details of how Joe died and why Rita was being charged with his murder, she may change her mind about staying silent. And with that thought, he felt he was back at stage one again. How long could he maintain the silence of what had happened between him and Rita, he was not sure, but he prayed it would be forever.

Chapter Fourteen

The Uncertainty Of Life

While Frank had gotten Louise's assurance that she was not going to say anything to anyone about his affair with Rita, he wasn't sure how she would react if she were to find out that he had been having sex with her daughter, Lacy. He was also now aware that Louise was jealous of Rita, and he couldn't believe he had not clued into that previously.

In short, Frank was now a mess. His life was now a steady surge of anxiety at every turn. He hated what his life had become, and he resolved that he was going to change it and make it better, back to the way it was before any of what had happened had happened. Yet he wasn't sure exactly how he was going to do that, and he knew there was a distinct possibility that his life could yet get even worse. "If anyone finds out that Rita and I were having an affair while she and Joe were here visiting here, I am fucked," he reasoned. And the thought of that made his whole body shiver. Little did he know, he was right, because things were about to get much worse.

Just then, the phone rang, and Frank looked to see who was calling. "Oh no, it's Lacy! Thank God she didn't call when Louise was there. I'm not picking it up, I can't deal with her right now. I'll just let the answering machine get it," he thought. Suddenly, Lacy's voice was on his machine. "Heya Frank, it's me your little fuck bitch," she said and giggled. "I miss you, Frank, and I'm hungry for some of your sweet lovin'," she continued. "Why don't you come and see me, like real soon. You know you want to. I've been waiting for you. Please come and see me, Frank, I need you," she added and hung up.

Frank had to admit that hearing her voice and all the things she said was making his manhood react in a way he did not want. He wanted to delete the message right away, but he opted to listen to it one more time. As he listened to Lacy's message, he began to fantasize about having sex with her again. "No, you can't do that," he told himself, "it is far too risky." But his manhood was not complying with his thoughts. "I need to listen to it one more time," he thought. "Maybe, if I listen to the message one more time, it will be better," he reasoned. So he pushed play and listened to the message once again. "She is really horny for me," he thought. "Should I go and have sex with her again?" he asked himself, but he already knew the answer to that question. It was far too risky, especially now, for him to go and see Lacy. If Louise were ever to find out about the two of them, it would be the end of his strong friendship with her, and after all she had just done for him, he felt ultra guilty for even thinking of having sex with Lacy again. Plus, the last thing he wanted to do was turn Louise against him.

Yet he couldn't deny that he was tempted and turned on by the message Lacy left on his answering machine. "I'll think of Lacy and masturbate," he thought. "That will get rid of the tension and hopefully the temptation," he reasoned. So he opted to listen to

Lacy's message yet again and proceeded to masturbate, thinking of having sex with her. However, masturbation did not seem to help. Sure, he ejaculated, but he still felt horny, and the feelings of wanting the real thing were now even stronger. "What in fuck do I do?" he thought. "I have to get a grip on this. I can't go to Lacy's apartment. What if Louise were to show up? How would I explain that to her? She doesn't even know that I know where Lacy lives!" He was now in a state of confusion and fear again. He really wanted to go and have sex with Lacy, but he also knew it was a bad idea. "Why did she have to call me this morning?" he reasoned. "This is all her fault. She called and got me all horny for her," he thought to himself.

Just then, the phone rang again. "Who is it now?" he thought as he picked up the phone to see who was calling him. "Oh my gosh, it is Lacy again! What do I do?" he thought. Do I answer it, or do I let the machine get it again?" Frank didn't know what to do, so he picked up the phone without thinking. "Hello."

"Hey Frank, it's me, your sweet sex gurl. Remember me? I haven't heard from you in a while, and well, you know, I'm missing yea and I would really like you to come and see me," she said.

Frank couldn't help but smile, but he wasn't sure what to say, so Lacy opted to continue to speak sexy to him in an effort to get him to come and see her. "I'm really horny for yea, Frank. You've got the nicest penis I have ever fucked," she said. Now Frank was smiling from ear to ear.

"Stop it," he said laughing. "You've had a lot of them, seeing as to your business and all, so I doubt that mine is the nicest you ever had," he responded.

Lacy laughed, but then quickly returned to serious talk. "I'm tellin' yea, Frank, your penis is better than all the rest! And I'm not even joking," she said. Frank was now turning red in the face. He couldn't see the redness, but he could feel it on his face. "Stop Lacy, you're making my ego too big," he said, laughing. Truth was, he loved the compliment Lacy was giving him, and it was making him want to go and see her despite the circumstances and worry over the possible consequences of doing so.

"Come on Frank," Lacy continued. "You know you want to," she added.

"YES, YES I DO," Frank spurted out before he even knew what he was saying.

"You do?! Awesome, then come over right now," Lacy responded.

Frank was silent, he couldn't believe he had just agreed to go see her. "What am I thinking?" he thought to himself. "Ummm, yea, I can come over right now," he said, all the while being dumbfounded that he was saying such things. His mind was saying one thing, but his voice was saying something else.

"That's great Frank. How long do you think you will be? I just want to make sure I am ready for yea when you get here is all. I can't wait to see you. I've been thinking so much about yea and your delicious manhood. I am horny just thinkin about yea," Lacy replied.

Right at that point, Frank wished there was such a thing as time travel, because he wanted to be there in an instant after hearing Lacy's words. "Ummm, I just need to take a quick shower and I will be on the road," he told her.

"Okay, I am so looking forward to seeing you," Lacy replied.

"Yea, yea, me too," Frank responded. "Okay, soon," he said and ended the call.

"What just happened?" Frank thought to himself. "Are you crazy? Right out of your mind? What are you thinking?" were now the thoughts running through his mind. "You told her you were going to go and see her, do you realize what that could mean if you are caught?" he asked himself. But Frank chose to ignore all these thoughts and questions he was posing to himself. He was now on a mission to go and see Lacy. His sex drive was canceling out his better judgments.

He headed straight to his bathroom to take as quick a shower as possible and get on the road. He had visions of her waiting for him, as she had told him she was, while he was in the shower and masturbated once again, as he knew it wouldn't take long to ejaculate, as per his level of arousal. Plus, he wanted to make sure he had staying power for when he actually got to Lacy's place. He didn't want to ejaculate too quickly while having sex with Lacy and he figured that given his current state of arousal that might be the case. So he chose to take the extra time to masturbate as he felt it would be worth it in the long run.

Once showered and ready to go, he jumped in his pickup truck and headed to the city. As he drove, the previous thoughts of this not being a good idea started arising once again in his mind, but he quickly pushed them out. "Oh no, I'm going to see her. I have to, I just have to," he told himself. And with that, he increased his speed as much as possible in an attempt to get there faster. He couldn't wait to see Lacy and all he could think about was having sweet sex with her. His foot pushed down a little more on the pedal and he smiled a big smile. "I'm on my way Baby... I'll be there soon. Get yourself ready for me. It's gonna be a great time," he thought as he drove. And before long, he was parking in the parking lot of Lacy's apartment building, and not long after that, he was knocking on her apartment door.

Being at her apartment door, he couldn't help but think of the last time he'd been there and the man who was waiting to have his turn with Lacy. He'd chosen to forget the truth of what Lacy was doing to help put herself through college, and he didn't want to remember it now either. Just then Lacy opened the door. "Hey Frank," she said smiling. "What took yea so long?" she added and winked.

Frank was struck, not knowing what to do or say, as Lacy was naked underneath a see-through shirt that barely covered her private parts. Lacy could tell by the expression on his face that he was a little dumbfounded, so she reached out and grabbed his hand, gently pulling him into her apartment. Once inside with the door closed, she jumped up on Frank and wrapped her legs around his waist. "Take me now," she whispered in his ear. So Frank proceeded to the bedroom, laid her on the bed, and proceeded to get undressed as quickly as humanly possible. His penis was standing straight at attention, and Lacy was licking her lips in anticipation.

Frank climbed on top of Lacy on the bed. "Give it to me Baby," she said, smiling. "I've been waiting too long, and you know I have," she said, pouting. Frank was so aroused at that point, he thought he might explode right there and then. They were both enthralled in sex when suddenly Lacy's cell phone started ringing and distracted them.

Lacy had it set to voicemail so she could hear whoever it was if they left a message. It was Lousie. "Hey Lacy, I was just in town and thought maybe we could go for a coffee. I don't get to see you that often, but if you're busy, don't worry about it. I can stop by and pick you up if you like. Let me know okay. I'm going to be in town for about another hour. I'll wait to hear back from you, or maybe I'll just drop by. But I'm thinking you're not home, or busy since you didn't answer your phone. Okay, love you Bye."

Frank and Lacy were both stunned. The high level of sexual energy had now fallen to fear and complete silence. "Oh my God, Lacy, you have to call her back and come up with some excuse to get rid of her. If she finds out I am here, we are both done for!" Frank exclaimed.

Lacy and Frank untangled themselves from one another and Lacy sat on the side of the bed. "Just let me think for a minute," she said to Frank, trying to get him to calm down. She wasn't sure how she could dodge her Mom, and she was thinking about what she could say as an excuse for not wanting to go and have coffee with her. Her mind was swirling. "You have to think of something fast and call her right back. What if she decides to just come over here? Think Lacy... Think!" Frank said. "Okay, okay," Lacy exclaimed. "Calm the fuck down, Frank. It's not the end of the world. I'll call her! I'm just trying to think of a good excuse, is all," she added.

And just then, an excuse popped into her mind, and she picked up the phone to call Louise back. Louise answered in anticipation of making plans to hang out with Lacy. "I have bad news Mom," Lacy said. "I have to study for a big exam I have tomorrow. I'm really sorry Mom, but maybe next time you're in town we can hang out," she added. "Oh, that's okay Lacy," Louise responded. "Your schoolwork is important and I want you to study and do well. I'll reach out next time I am in town and good luck on your exam tomorrow. I'm sure you will do excellent," Louise continued, and then they ended the call.

"Now, where were we?" Lacy said smiling. But Frank was still reeling from what had just happened. The reality of what he was doing was hitting him full tilt in the face and he couldn't escape it.

Lacy picked up on his sudden change of mood and so reached for his penis and began playing with it. "It's all good now," she whispered in his ear. "You don't have to worry. She is gone and we are free to resume our fun," she added. But Frank was still having trouble getting his sexual drive back up and running. Lacy didn't know all the details of what Louise finding out about him and Lacy would mean for him, and he wasn't about to tell her.

Frank removed Lacy's hand from his penis and got up to go and use the washroom. "Where are you going?" Lacy asked. "You're not leaving now, are you?" she questioned. "No, I'm not leaving. I just have to go and use the washroom and splash some cold water on my face. I'll be right back," he replied, exiting the bedroom.

Once in the washroom, he looked at himself in the mirror. "What in fuck were you thinking you dumb bastard," he said to himself. He looked down at his penis and felt it was all to blame for the situation. "If only I could get more control over you," he said, grabbing his penis to take a piss. He splashed some water on his face and reasoned that since he was already there and Lacy was in the bedroom waiting for him, he might as well enjoy it and that this would definitely be the last time he would have sex with her.

When Frank entered back into the room, Lacy was still laying naked on the bed. Frank immediately felt his penis getting aroused, and the closer he got to her, the harder it got. Frank climbed onto the bed and began having sex with Lacy once again. The two of them seemed even more aroused than they had previously, but neither of them thought that was even possible. They were in complete ecstasy when the phone started ringing again.

"Oh no, who is it this time?" Frank wondered. "Just let it go to the machine," he said. Lacy groaned with enjoyment and acted like she didn't hear Frank's words or the phone. She pulled Frank close to her and began kissing him in an effort to shut him up.

Lacy usually didn't kiss the men she had sex with, as she felt kissing was too intimate for what she was doing. But Frank was different. She'd known him for a long time, and so she felt like she wanted to kiss him. Plus, if she was kissing him, he couldn't talk and interrupt their lovemaking session. She kissed him hard and passionately, and Frank was getting very turned on by it. He'd never had anyone kiss him quite like that before and he liked it. Still, he could not help but worry about who was on the phone, and he strained to listen to the person leaving the message.

"Hi Lacy. It's me Ziggy! Did you forget we have an appointment this afternoon? It's really important, as you know. So call me right back, okay, because it is 1:30 now. Okay, bye."

Lacy heard the message as well, and she suddenly realized that Ziggy and she had a date lined up with a man who wanted to have sex with two women. How could she have forgotten about that, she wondered. And what was she going to do about it now? She couldn't just leave Frank after she had practically begged him to come and see her.

"Who was that?" Frank asked finally.

"Oh, she's a co-worker of mine," Lacy replied. "You know.. my business and all," she continued.

"Oh, I see," Frank responded. "You and her are going to have sex? Do you have sex with women as well as men?" he asked.

"Yea I do," Lacy replied, smiling. "But this is a different situation. It's a date we have with a man who wants to have sex with two women. It's a big paying gig and I hate to have to tell her that I can't make it, but I don't want to leave you after getting you to come here. I don't know what to do," Lacy continued.

"How much do you get for that?" Frank asked.

"Oh, that's not important," Lacy replied. "I'll just call her back and let her know I can't make it and that I'm really sorry. I'm not going to take off after asking you to come all the way here. Plus, I want to have sex with you all day and night, if you want," she added, winking at Frank and smiling.

"Wait," Frank said. "Don't call her back just yet. I have a proposition for yea," he added.

"Okay," Lacy said, still smiling. "What is it?" she asked.

"Well, if it is not too much money, I was thinking she could just come over and join us. If that's okay with you?" he asked.

Lacy looked a little stunned. "Does Frank realize Ziggy is also a prostitute?" she wondered.

"Well, it's quite a lot of money Frank. To have two women at once, you're looking at eight hundred dollars for two hours. Is that something you are willing to pay for? I don't care about my half and I won't charge you, but Ziggy does this for a living and so you will have to pay her at least four hundred for two hours," Lacy replied.

"I can handle that," Frank said, all proud and smiling.

"Are you sure?" Lacy asked. "Because I will call her right now and get her to come over," she added, reaching for her phone.

"Wait, what does this Ziggy woman look like? Do you think I will be attracted to her?" Frank asked.

"Well, she has really big boobs, if that helps," Lacy said, laughing. "And men seem to fall all over her all the time," she added. "Put it this way, she is always busy and makes a damn good living off of her business. I wish I had as many clients as her, but I don't do it full-time like she does. I have to go to college, yet sometimes I wonder why, seeing as I can probably make more money doing what she does if I did it full-time," Lacy continued.

"No, it is good you are going to college," Frank assured her, but now his mind was focused on meeting Ziggy. "Yeah, call her and get her to come over then," Frank instructed.

So Lacy picked up the phone and called Ziggy back, explaining the situation to her and asking her to come over to her place. Ziggy agreed and said she would call the client and come up with an excuse and set another appointment with him in the near future. Lacy agreed and they ended the call.

"What did she say?" Frank asked in anticipation.

"Oh, she is on her way," Lacy said, smiling.

She could tell Frank was very excited about the prospect of having the two of them at once and she wondered if Frank had ever had two women at once before. Little did she know he had had Louise and Rita at the same time, not all that long ago, but he was content to let her think this was his first time.

He could feel his penis swelling at the thought of two women, one being a total stranger. The anticipation was killing him, and he couldn't focus on having sex with Lacy in the meantime.

"You're all fucked up over this, aren't you Frank?" Lacy said and chuckled.

"No, no... I'm not. I'm just saving my energy for the great sex we are all going to have, that's all," Frank responded.

Lacy was suddenly feeling a little left out. She didn't have any claims on Frank, she realized, but she kind of liked that she had him all to herself. Now she was going to have to share him with Ziggy and she wasn't sure she wanted to. But it was too late now, she had already made the arrangements and Ziggy was on her way. Suddenly, she was also thinking about how delicious Frank's penis was and how she really didn't want Ziggy to have a taste of it, so to speak.

She knew Ziggy was good at what she did, given the number of repeat clients she had, and she worried that Frank might fall for her and leave her out of the picture. But there was nothing she could do about it now. This was all her fault, she reasoned, for not remembering the appointment she and Ziggy had that day. She was so wanting to see Frank, she had forgotten all about it. Now she was in a situation she had not expected, and she wasn't sure she liked it.

It wasn't long before the doorbell rang and Lacy went to answer it. When she opened her apartment door, she was surprised to see Ziggy looking so sexy. She looked much better than the last time Lacy had seen her, which had been a little while. "Wow, you look great," Lacy said, giving her a hug and motioning her into the apartment. Ziggy was all decked out and looking fabulous.

"Where is he?" Ziggy asked.

"Oh, he's in the bedroom. He was here before you called. He is an old friend of the family, and he and I have had sex before. I don't think he has ever had two women before, so he proposed that he take the other dude's appointment rather than us losing money due to him being here!" Lacy advised.

"Well, that was sweet of him," Ziggy replied. "I am anxious to meet him. Is he cute?" she asked.

"Yea, he is handsome for sure," Lacy said. "And very sexy," she added. "My Mom has been fuck buddies with him for years!" she continued and laughed. "I've known him for a long time, just now I am a woman and well, you know, I wanted to fuck him myself," she said and continued laughing.

"You're bad," Ziggy responded, laughing right along with her. "Let's get to it then, shall we?" Ziggy said, putting her arm around Lacy and walking towards the bedroom.

Frank didn't know what to do with himself, and so he sat on the chair in Lacy's room waiting for the two of them. And when they entered the room, he was blown away by Ziggy's obvious beauty. Not to mention her huge boobs that were half exposed. His penis was immediately responding. Ziggy knew she commanded men's attention and that she held power over them in terms of her sexuality and beauty. So she smiled a big smile at him and took him by the hand to the bed. She then got on top of him and began to undress herself.

Frank just laid there mesmerized by Ziggy's huge breasts and sexy body. He couldn't believe his day had turned into the current situation. He thought he had died and gone to heaven. It was as if Lacy didn't even exist anymore, as he had forgotten that Lacy was even there in the room.

Lacy was now feeling very left out and wasn't sure what to do. "Frank is my friend, my client, my guy, not Ziggy's!" she thought to herself. "I made a huge mistake letting her come over here. Now she has taken over and is fucking Frank all to herself and leaving me right out of the picture.".

"This isn't usually how it is supposed to work when the two of us are doing one man. Usually, we take turns, but Ziggy doesn't seem to be following the rules," she thought. She wondered if she should just leave, go do something else, and just let the two of them have a time together, but she really didn't want to leave Frank alone with Ziggy for some reason. She felt that if she left Frank alone with her, it was like she was giving permission for the two of them to ignore her, and that was not okay with her. So she opted to just sit and watch the show instead.

She marveled at how Ziggy was fucking Frank like crazy and how she could maintain such stamina in the situation. "Is she on something?" Lacy wondered. "Because she seems to have more energy than normal," she thought.

And after what seemed to Lacy to be a long time, Ziggy finally got her rocks off and got off of Frank, who was lying on the bed looking worn out. Lacy couldn't help but giggle to herself, seeing him lying there all frazzled.

"Are you okay Frank?" she asked finally.

"Yea, yea, I'm good," he replied, smiling a huge smile. "That was something else," he said, looking at Ziggy.

Ziggy smiled. "Oh, that was nothing, Frank. I'm just getting warmed up," she added, winking at him.

But Frank was worn out and he realized that this was costing him a lot of money. Money he didn't really have to spend for such things. "Well, I may have to take you up on that another time," he replied. "Because I am a little short on cash today and I know you girls are expensive to have around," he added smiling.

When it came to sex and money, Ziggy was much more interested in the payout than she was the actual sex. "Oh, well that's a different story then," she replied, smiling.

Two hours had already gone by in what seemed like a flash, and Frank was cognizant of the time, seeing as he was paying dearly for it. So he got up from the bed and began to get dressed. He looked over at Lacy, who was still seated in the chair, and he realized he had not paid any attention to her during the whole sex session with Ziggy.

"I'm sorry," he said. "I hope you didn't feel too left out. It was just that Ziggy here," he put his arm around Ziggy. "Just took over, and well, what can I say?" he added, smiling.

Lacy forced a smile and looked down at the floor. She opted not to state how she truly felt. "Oh no, don't worry about it. I am just glad you had fun with Ziggy. I told you she was a rocket!" she replied.

Then they all laughed, and Lacy got up from her chair, and the three of them hugged in a circle.

"We will do this again soon, ladies," Frank said, putting on his coat to leave.

"We sure will," Ziggy said, kissing Frank on his cheek.

But Lacy was not so sure she ever wanted to share Frank with Ziggy again. She hadn't played by the established rules regarding the two of them having sex with one man, and Lacy was not happy about it. But Ziggy didn't even seem to notice, much less care how Lacy was feeling. She decided she wanted more of Frank, and she didn't care if Lacy was involved or not

"Would you like to take my number?" she asked.

"Sure, that would be great," Frank replied.

Ziggy asked Lacy for some paper and a pen so she could write down her number for Frank. Lacy was now feeling angry inside. She had not invited Ziggy over to give her yet another client. She already had more than enough clients, and in comparison, Lacy hardly had any. Now, Lacy felt like Ziggy was stealing one of her cherished clients, and she was not happy about it, but she opted not to say anything for fear of sounding jealous in front of the two of them.

Lacy left the room to get a piece of paper and a pen for Ziggy, and while she was gone, Ziggy opted to hug Frank and tell him how sexy she thought he was. She told him how much she enjoyed fucking him and how she could not wait to fuck him again. Frank was drinking in every word, and it was making his ego swell to hear such flattering words from such a knockout chick as Ziggy. He wondered if Ziggy was her real name and automatically assumed it was just a name she used for her business and not her real name. He wanted to ask her if that was the case, but he didn't want to make her feel uncomfortable, so he opted not to. He'd ask Lacy later, he thought to himself.

Lacy returned with pen and paper and Ziggy wrote down her number for Frank.

"Would you like my address as well?" she asked while writing down her number.

"Ah, yea sure," Frank responded "Why not!" Then he went on to advise that he didn't live in the city and that he was about an hour's drive away. "I try to avoid the city as much as possible," he continued. "I only come to the city when I absolutely have to, but I'll take your address just in case I am in here and would like to see yea."

Ziggy smiled at Frank's obvious naïveté.

"You have to make an appointment to see me," Ziggy said, smiling. "I'm a very busy woman, so you need to set a time if you want to see me," she added.

"Oh right," Frank responded. "I will make sure I call and set a time then, when I am coming into the city," he added.

Ziggy smiled and passed Frank the piece of paper with her contact information on it. "Here yea go," she said. "I hope to hear from yea sooner than later Frank," she added, smiling a big smile at him.

"Oh for sure," Frank responded. "You will be hearing from me again, don't worry about that," he added. "But I should be going now. I want to get on the road before it gets dark, as it is hard to see on those narrow country roads in the dark," he said.

"Yes, you had better get going," Lacy interjected, tapping his ass.

"Hurry back, I miss you already," Ziggy yelled as Frank was walking down the hall of Lacy's apartment building.

Frank looked back and smiled. "Later ladies," he said, waving his arm in the air as he continued walking.

Once out of the apartment building, Frank was suddenly hit by what had just happened. He had not expected any of it. The phone call from Louise was playing through his mind. "What the fuck," he thought to himself. "That was a close one. What if Louise had just shown up at Lacy's apartment?" he asked himself.

All the various what-ifs were now running through his mind, and he could feel a sense of panic suddenly welling up. "Stop thinking about that," he told himself. "Remember, Louise told you not to think negative thoughts and to focus your mind to positive, peaceful ones," he thought, and with that thought he attempted to change his train of thought. He didn't want to bring on another panic attack; that was for sure. So he opted to focus instead on the amazing sex he had had with both Lacy and Ziggy that day. Especially Ziggy, who was, he thought, drop-dead gorgeous and a hell of a lover.

He wondered how Lacy was feeling about the whole situation, since she was largely left out of the sex session between him and Ziggy, and he feared that he may have done wrong in not showing her more attention. But there was nothing he could do about that now. He just wanted to get back to his home in the country and relax.

Yet, he knew that his home was no longer a place of peace and relaxation due to all that was happening with Rita and the fact that Louise had the power to throw him under the bus if she chose to. He was still worried about that happening and realized that he was taking an awful chance in going to Lacy's apartment that day. "If Louise finds out I am having sex with her daughter, she is going to hate me!" he thought to himself. "And she would be so angry that chances are she would rat me out in regard to Rita and I having sex while her and Joe were staying at my place."

The mere thought of such a thing happening sent shivers down Frank's spine. "Oh, please God, don't let that happen," he prayed as he drove back to his house in the country.

Once home, it was just coming on dark and Frank looked at his house now in a different way as he pulled into the driveway. The house just didn't look the same to him. He used to love looking at the place when he drove in the driveway, but now his house looked dark, empty, and shabby. His yard looked a mess also and he realized that he had been neglecting taking care of the place due to all the drama that had now become his life.

He hated the fact that all of that had happened. He wondered why it had all happened, but he knew why. He knew it was wrong of him to sleep with his good friend's wife, no matter how sexy she was, no matter how she flirted with him, no matter how she dressed herself in a way that exposed her private parts and seduced him every chance she got.

"I'm just a man," he said to himself. "What was I supposed to do?" he asked himself. But he knew deep inside that being a man was a lame excuse for his betrayal of his good friend Joe, and he couldn't bear to think of the person he had become. He had always lived by strict morals when it came to loyalty, and now that had all been thrown out the window.

"Who am I now?" he wondered, but he didn't want to sink too deeply into that hole because he knew chances were good it would bring on another panic attack, and that was the last thing he wanted. "Thank God, Louise was good enough to leave me some of her pills just in case it did happen again," he thought.

Still, he didn't want to test the waters in terms of having another attack, so he opted to clean his house up and listen to music in an effort to distract his mind. "I need to let all of this go right now," he thought. "I will think about it all later, if I have to, but right now, I just want to give my mind a rest," he said to himself as he went about cleaning the house. "Cleaning the house will make me feel better about things," he reasoned.

He didn't have much company as he didn't really know many people in the small town. It was mostly only Louise who came by from time to time, but that didn't matter. Frank was cleaning the house for himself, not for possible company.

He hated cleaning the house, like everyone does, but he knew it would make him feel better to have a clean environment. So he went to town cleaning every room and doing as good a job as he possibly could until he was finally finished several hours later.

He sat at his kitchen table looking around at how much better his kitchen, and his entire house, looked now that he had paid it some attention and work. He opted to roll a joint and make himself a coffee as a reward for all the hard work he had just done.

"I could have a woman here," he thought. "And she would do all of that hard work for me," he reasoned. But Frank had never really wanted a full-time relationship and he wasn't sure exactly why that was. He just knew that having someone, anyone, full-time just wasn't his gig, even though he knew it was expected of him by society.

He had never felt the need to get married and have children and he was all good with that fact. He also had never been one to sleep around with various women, and the fact that he now had four women on the go was kind of blowing his mind.

It was as if a whirlwind had taken over his life, and he was caught in the middle of it somehow and didn't quite know how to get out. But he didn't want to think about all of that right now. Right now, he just wanted to enjoy his smoke and coffee and relax.

He put in a comedy movie and laid down on his couch, but it wasn't long before he was fast asleep. It had been a long day and one he had not expected. He went to sleep thinking of Ziggy sitting on top of him fucking his brains out, and he smiled and drifted off to la-la land.

Chapter Fifteen

The Rabbit Hole Is Deep Confusing

A few days had passed and Frank was once again starting to feel his life was somewhat back to normal. He had gotten back into his usual routines and had been able to control his thoughts somewhat better by pushing things out of his mind that might cause him to feel anxiety or worse, have another panic attack. But he was also aware that things were not settled and there would be more drama coming sooner than later.

Frank had not heard from Louise, Lacy, or Rita and he was happy and relieved about that. He didn't really want to hear from any of them. He knew Rita would not be contacting him due to the fact that she was now in jail awaiting trial. He still could not believe that Rita had been charged and incarcerated for Joe's death. "What if she is found guilty?" he wondered. "That would be horrible," he thought. But again, he chose not to dwell on thinking about it all.

He had finished his morning chores and was cooking himself a nice breakfast of bacon and eggs when the phone rang. At first he thought he would just let it ring and not bother to answer it, let the machine answer instead. But then he thought, "Maybe it is something important! I'd better go check to see who it is and then I will decide if I should answer it right now or not." So he went to the phone and looked to see who it was. It was Louise, and he wasn't sure if he should answer, but he opted to pick up the phone and say hello.

"Hey Frank," Louise said. "I hope I didn't wake you up. I know it is early in the morning, but I figured you'd be up since I know you like to get up early and get things done," she continued.

"No, you didn't wake me up Louise. What's up?" Frank asked.

"Well, I hate to be the bearer of bad news, but I just heard on the television news that Rita is going to trial for Joe's death!" she blurted out.

Frank was stunned. He didn't know what to say. He knew Rita's trial would be coming up soon, but he didn't think it would be that soon.

"What were they saying on the news?" he asked Louise.

"Not much really, just that the trial will be starting the first of next week, which is only three days from now," Louise responded. "I just feel so bad for poor Rita," she continued. "It must be horrible to lose your husband and then to be charged for his murder! I can't even imagine what she must be going through," she added.

Frank didn't know what to say, but he agreed with Louise that yes, it was all horrible indeed.

"Well, that's all I had to tell you Frank," Louise said. "I'll let you go now and get back to what you were doing."

Just then Frank remembered he was cooking bacon and eggs and he ran to the stove to check to see if everything was okay, only to realize that his eggs had overcooked while he was talking to Louise, but at least nothing was on fire, which was his main concern. The news about Rita consumed his mind so much that he had forgotten he had food cooking on the stove.

"Okay, I'll talk to yea later. Thanks for letting me know Louise, I appreciate it," he said, and they ended the call.

But the truth was, he would rather not have known that news. It wasn't that he didn't care about Rita and what she was going through; it was that he just didn't want to think about any of it. Now, with this news Louise had provided, it was front and center once again in his mind.

He loaded his overcooked eggs with the bacon onto his plate, poured himself a coffee from the pot that was half full on his kitchen counter, and sat down at his kitchen table to try to enjoy his breakfast. As he ate, he thought of Rita sitting in a jail cell in some prison somewhere and how horrible it must be for her. Tears welled up in his eyes and rolled down his cheeks.

"How in fuck did all of this happen?" he wondered. Suddenly, his heart felt great love and empathy for Rita and what she must be enduring. "Rita is a city girl. She is refined and educated. She doesn't belong in a prison," he thought to himself. And then he found himself praying to God and asking God to please help Rita in her situation. After praying, he felt a little better, but he still felt worried for Rita in that situation. Yet, he knew there was little to nothing he could do about it, and that made him feel so powerless and weak, neither of which, as a man, he felt good about.

The day was long for Frank that day. He tried to muster up the courage to do some work he had been putting off, but he just didn't have the energy. The news of Rita going to trial that coming Monday was more than he could bear.

"This isn't about me," he thought. "Why am I so fucked up over all of this?" he wondered. But he knew why. He loved Rita in a strange kind of way, and he didn't want to see anything bad happen to her. He also couldn't bring himself to believe that she had intentionally killed Joe. That was just too much for him to bear.

He opted to take a shower and try to erase it all from his mind, but when he took a piss before jumping in the shower, his penis hurt.

"What in fuck is wrong with my penis?" he wondered. "Why is it hurting now when I piss?" he asked himself.

He could feel anxiety welling up inside of him and the fear that he might have another panic attack consumed him now. "Don't think about it," he told himself. "Just let it go. It is probably nothing. Just take your shower and forget about it all," he told himself as he got into the shower.

As he showered, he examined his penis and didn't feel or see anything wrong, so he reassured himself that it was probably nothing and not to worry about it any further.

However, ignoring the situation was not going to work, and Frank quickly realized this fact when he continued to feel great pain every time he had to urinate. It became quickly obvious that something was seriously wrong and it dawned on Frank that he may have contracted a sexually transmitted disease.

"Oh my FUCK," he said to himself. "WHAT HAVE I DONE?" he thought.

Frank was now beside himself. He didn't know if he should stand up, sit down, go outside, stay inside, tell someone, or not tell someone. He was at a complete loss as to what to do, but he knew at once that he had to do something to address the situation. The pain was getting worse every time he had to use the washroom. So much so that he was trying to avoid using the washroom as much as possible.

In fact, every time he had to use the washroom, a great sense of fear and anxiety would overtake him. He was so afraid of knowing what he had contracted. "Is it serious?" What does it mean?" he asked himself

And all these questions were now running through his mind, coupled with the elephant in the room being his sexual indiscretions. His whoredom.

"Is this the price I am paying for having followed my penis instead of my intellect?" he wondered. "Sure, it was great having sex with Lacy, and especially with Ziggy too, but was it really worth it?" he was now asking himself. And the answer that came up in his mind almost immediately was, "No, it was not worth it at all."

Yet, Frank couldn't erase what happened. It happened, and now he would have to face the consequences. "How could I have been so short-sighted?" he wondered. "How could I have not realized that these women sleep with tons of men? How could I have been so fucking stupid? Am I really that fucking stupid?" he wondered.

Frank bent over, sitting on his kitchen chair, and held his head in his hands. He felt he had to hold his head now because it might explode from all the questions and thoughts going through his mind. He wasn't even sure he could sit back up straight or even get up from the chair. He felt stuck in that position. His entire body felt numb, like it had no feeling in it at all.

"Maybe it is better now if I did die," he thought to himself. "I have made such a mess of my life, I am not even sure who I am anymore." Sadness now consumed him and he wept like a man who had just lost his soul.

And just as he was enduring all of that, a loud knock came on his back door. The sound jerked him out of his enthrallment. He suddenly looked up as if the person had already entered the house. "Who could that be?" Frank wondered. "I don't want to talk to anyone right now. I am a complete mess. I don't want anyone to see me like this. Fuck that, I am not answering the fucking door," he said to himself, still sitting in the his chair.

He didn't even want to get up to see who was there. But the person knocking was not giving up, and the knocks seemed to be getting louder. So he finally opted to get up to see who was making all the racket and peeked out from behind the curtain in his dining room to look. It was Lacy!

"What in fuck is she doing here? Is she trying to kill me?" he thought. "She is putting me in harm's way! Doesn't she fucking realize?" But then he remembered that Lacy only knew part of the story and not the part regarding Rita and Louise, so he opted to give her some slack. "Still," he thought, "she should know better than to come here to my place. Louise just lives up the road!"

Frank didn't know what to do, as it was now obvious that Lacy was not going to leave. She knew Frank was home; his truck was right there, parked in the yard. So Frank opted to go to the washroom in an attempt to clean himself up and look more presentable before he went to answer the door. While washing up, he felt the welling of tears in his eyes. The feelings he was experiencing prior to Lacy showing up were just not going to magically disappear, he realized. But he would do his best to put on a strong face and deal with Lacy. "What in fuck does she want anyway?" he wondered as he walked to the door to open it.

Lacy was standing, leaning against the railing on the steps that led to the back door. "What in fuck is the issue?" Frank asked as he opened the door of his house. Lacy laughed and hit her leg. "Oh relax Frank. I was just in town and thought I'd drop by to see how you are doing, is all! And from the looks of it, you're not doing too well. What in fuck happened to you? You look like shit!"

"I'm just going through some things," Frank responded. "Thanks for the compliment," he added.

"Oh, I didn't mean anything by it Frank, I was just sayin. You know, or maybe you don't, but I really do care about yea," she added.

Right at that point, Frank didn't care if she cared about him or not. Someone, either her or Ziggy, had given him an STD, and he was not at all happy about it. And just then it occurred to him that if it had been Lacy who had given him the STD, she would not be at his door right now. Or would she?

"Maybe she knows I have an STD, because she has it or had it, and she knows she gave it to me. And that is why she is showing up at my door today!" he reasoned. Either way, Frank knew he had to get rid of her as soon as possible because it was far too risky to have her at his house with Louise just up the road. If Louise saw Lacy at his house, she would be full of questions as to why Lacy would be there, and Frank just couldn't deal with that on top of everything else he was going through.

"You have to leave now," Frank said to her while still standing in the doorway of his house.

Lacy smiled a big smile. "Don't yea want me to come in Frank?" she asked, pushing her breasts forward. Frank couldn't help but notice and looked directly at her chest, which was her intention, and instantly felt himself being sexually drawn to her.

"Stop it you fucking moron," he said to himself. "What are you thinking? He shook his head slightly as if to bring himself back to reality. "Listen, it is very important that you leave. I can't have you seen here. If Louise sees your car here, she is going to come right in and she is going to want to know what is going on and why you are here at my house. Don't you fucking understand? This is not a good situation, you have to go NOW," Frank replied.

Lacy was taken aback somewhat by the strict tone of voice Frank was now speaking in. She had never heard him speak like that before and it was kind of intimidating to hear.

"Are you rejecting me Frank?" she asked, pouting.

"No, I'm not rejecting you Lacy. The point of fact is, you shouldn't be here, and you know that as well as I do. You know Louise cannot find out about us! We agreed to that from the beginning right?" Frank replied.

"Yea, I guess so," Lacy responded. "But I really wanted to see yea. I miss yea. The last time you were at my place, you spent most of your time with Ziggy and I barely got to be with you. And you don't have to worry about Louise, she is at work. I wouldn't put you in harm's way. I know how to play my cards, Frank!"

"Fuck, this chick is insatiable," Frank thought to himself.

"What do you want Lacy?" he asked in a stern voice.

"I want you Frank. That's what I want," Lacy replied, licking her lips and trying to look sexy with her eyes.

"Lacy dear, this is not a good time, okay. I am going through some things and I am really not in the mood for company. It is nothing against you, it is just that I am having a hard day and I really just need to be alone, okay?" Frank said.

Lacy looked down at the ground and twiddled with the strings on the hoodie she was wearing. "So you don't want me?" she asked.

"I never said that," Frank responded. "I just said that today is not a good day for me, that's all." You should have called me first. I could have saved you the drive all the way here from the city," he added.

"I did call you Frank. You never answer your phone!" Lacy responded.

Frank had to admit that he sometimes did not answer the phone, but often it was due to not hearing it or even realizing someone had called until he checked to see.

Frank took a deep breath. He was tired and he didn't feel like arguing with Lacy at the back door of his house. That was when he suddenly realized his neighbors may have seen Lacy drive into his yard, and they may even be able to hear the conversation between the two of them.

"Oh my God," he thought, "I am doomed."

Right at that second, he wanted to push Lacy off of his back step and take her by the arm to her car, make sure she got in, and instruct her to fuck off out of his driveway and away from his house. But he knew he couldn't do that, as that would create a scene and would only serve to draw attention making matters worse than they already were.

Lacy could sense that Frank was now very tense and looking extremely worried. "Are you okay Frank?" she asked.

"No, not really," Frank responded. "I just realized that it is not only Louise I have to be concerned about, it is my neighbors as well. You know some of them are very snoopy and love to gossip. I am just wondering if they saw you drive into my driveway. If they knew your vehicle, and if they would recognize you as Louise's daughter. And if they might have heard our conversation here just now. So yea, I am not feeling too well at the present moment," he continued.

"Oh Frank," Lacy replied. "You worry too much about such dumb things. So what if they saw me drive in your driveway, or they know who I am! I can come and visit you. What's the big deal with that? And I doubt they could hear our conversation as we weren't talking loud or anything," she continued. "Goodness, they don't have ears that good, do they Frank?" she asked sarcastically and smiled.

"I don't know if they do or not! But what I do know is that they love to gossip about anyone and everyone, and it could easily get back to Louise that you were here at my house, and she would be wondering why and asking me a ton of questions about it. And I really don't want to deal with any of that. I am sure you can understand," he replied.

"Yea, I get it," Lacy responded. "But it doesn't make a lot of sense to me, to be honest," she added. "But I'll leave if that is what you really want. I just thought we could have some fun, that's all. Like I said, I miss yea and I was really looking forward to spending the whole afternoon with yea, free of charge even," she said, smiling and trying to look extra sexy.

Hearing those words somehow made Frank soften to the situation. "I could use some company right now actually," he thought. "Maybe it would be good to let her come in for a minute or two. Maybe there is no harm in it. If Louise does find out, I will just tell her that Lacy dropped by and had a coffee. She had come to visit her, but forgot that she was at work and just wanted someone to talk to about some guy she was having a hard time with. So she opted to come over to my place for a short visit is all," he thought. "Yea, that's a great excuse," Frank said to himself, and suddenly he felt okay about letting Lacy come into his house.

"What, you're all good now?" Lacy asked, sensing Frank's sudden change in attitude.

"Yea, come on in for a while. I don't see the harm in it, but I'm not going to have sex with you. I don't want to get caught with my pants down, so to speak," he added.

Lacy giggled. "Yea, like the first time I came here, we both almost got caught with our pants down, remember?" she asked.

"Oh yes, I remember," Frank responded. "How could I forget? It was an absolute freak fest," he added. So Lacy and Frank proceeded to enter Frank's house.

Lacy loved Frank's old house. "It's cozy and well decorated for a man," she thought. "Plus it is clean, which is unusual for most men," she said to herself. But Frank wasn't, she knew, most men. "Frank is the kind of man any woman would be lucky to have as a mainstay," she reasoned. "That must be why my Mom has hung by him all these years," she thought. She knew Frank had just said he wasn't going to have sex with her, but she also knew he was very weak minded when it came to such matters. She had already proven that much to herself.

"Would you like a coffee?" Frank asked. "I can make a fresh pot, if you'd like," he added.

"Yea, okay, that sounds good."

So Frank proceeded to make a fresh pot of coffee and sat down at the kitchen table with Lacy while it percolated. "Would you like to have a smoke with me?" he asked, reaching for his homegrown cannabis.

"Sure," Lacy replied. "That sounds awesome," she continued.

Frank smiled and proceeded to roll a joint for himself and one for Lacy. Once finished, he gave Lacy her joint and got up to make the two of them a coffee as it was now ready.

"What do you take in your coffee?" he asked, and then he prepared Lacy's coffee for her, bringing it to the table.

"I remember serving you coffee at Louise's place," Lacy said. "Do you remember?" she asked.

Frank smiled and assured Lacy that he remembered. "How could I forget? I was shocked to see how sexy you had become as a full-grown woman. I didn't realize how grown up you were until that day," he continued.

"Stop Frank," Lacy said, smiling. "You're making me horny for yea and you said we couldn't have sex," she continued.

"Oh right," Frank replied. "Yes, I can't be thinking or talking that way. Next thing you know, I will be getting myself into trouble again," he added and smiled, taking a drag off the joint he had just rolled.

"Don't you want to play with me, Frank?" Lacy asked in an innocent tone of voice.

"Of course I do Lacy," Frank replied. "But there is something I need to talk to you about."

"Okay, what is it?" Lacy asked. "Let's talk and get it out of the way, because I came here for some love," she added, smiling while reaching to unfasten Frank's pants

"Stop Lacy," Frank replied, pushing her hand away. "You don't understand. I really need to talk to you. This is not easy for me, okay," he continued.

Lacy was taken aback by Frank's reaction to her advancement, and she suddenly realized whatever it was Frank wanted to talk about, it was serious.

"Okay Frank!" she said. "Calm the fuck down man. Whatever it is, I am sure it is not that bad. Just spit it out already," she continued.

But Frank felt nervous as hell to talk about the situation. He wasn't even sure how to begin and he still wasn't sure he even wanted to tell anyone. But he knew he had to say something, as it was very unusual that he would turn down sex.

"Well, you remember the last time I was at your place and all that happened that day?" Frank said.

"Yes, of course I do," Lacy replied, smiling. "Oh, you want to see Ziggy again, is that it? What, you have the hots for her now and don't want to have sex with me anymore? Is that it?" Lacy asked in an accusing tone of voice.

"No, no, that's not it," Frank replied. "Listen, this is really hard for me to talk about okay. I have never dealt with anything like this before in my life. I don't even know what to say, much less what to do about this situation," he continued.

Lacy was now very curious as to what Frank was talking about. She couldn't make any sense out of anything he had said thus far.

"What in fuck are you talking about Frank? Just spit it out, whatever it is. I'm not going to judge you if that is what you are worried about. Look at me, who am I to judge anyone?" she replied and winked.

Frank took a deep breath. "You can do this," he told himself. "It might be good to talk to someone. Maybe Lacy will know what kind of STD it is! Maybe she can help you if you tell her what is going on," he thought. But he was still having a hard time getting the words out. It was as if he somehow couldn't bear to even speak of it. It was something he'd never dreamed would ever happen to him.

"These are the consequences of my poor decision-making," he said to himself. But there was nothing he could do about all of it now, and he knew he had to deal with his current situation as it was not something he could just ignore.

Lacy could tell that Frank was really struggling with whatever it was he wanted to tell her. "Come on Frank, just spit it out. It can't be that bad," she said. "Just say it, whatever it is. I promise I won't judge you and I won't tell anyone else if you don't want me to," she continued.

But Frank was still not sure he wanted to tell anyone, not even Lacy, who could be the source of his malady. He swore to himself he was not going to tell anyone, but now he was faced with a situation wherein he felt like he had to tell someone. And if Lacy was the source of his sudden malady, he needed to address the issue with her. Still, he felt like a puddle in the middle of the kitchen floor.

"How did I get here?" he thought. "This is not my life! Is it? Is this my life now?" he asked himself.

Lacy reached across the table and took Frank's hand. She looked into his eyes in a serious manner. "You can talk to me Frank. Whatever it is, just tell me. I can see you are very burdened by whatever it is. You will feel better if you get it off your chest, I promise," she continued.

"Okay, here goes," Frank finally said. "In simple words, I contracted an STD Lacy! I've never had such a thing ever before in my life, and I am beside myself in knowing what it is or how to deal with it. It is really messing with my head," Frank blurted out.

Lacy looked down at the floor. She was stunned by what Frank had just told her.

"How long have you had it?" she asked, finally looking up at him.

"I'm not sure," Frank replied. "I just know that it hurts when I go to the bathroom," he added.

"Hurts how?" Lacy asked.

"It just hurts," Frank exclaimed, like he was agitated by the question.

"Have you been to see a doctor?" Lacy asked.

"No, I can't get the courage up to go and see a doctor about it," Frank responded. "I don't want to go to my regular doctor here in town. I know it is supposed to be confidential, but I still feel worried that it might get out and become big town gossip," he added.

It seemed to Frank that Lacy was trying to pretend to be in shock and that was bothering him, so he said, "Why are you acting so shocked Lacy? You obviously knew I had this, whatever it is! I obviously got it from either you or Ziggy! So I am not sure why you are acting all innocent!" he added.

But Lacy was still in an obvious fog over what Frank had just told her. She acted as if she had not even heard what he had just said to her.

"Snap out of it Lacy," Frank said, snapping his fingers in front of her face.

Lacy looked startled by Frank's action, but it brought her out of the trance she seemed to be in after hearing what Frank had just told her.

"I'm okay Frank," she said. "I am a little shocked, to be honest, hearing this from you," she continued. "It must have been Ziggy that gave you the STD!" she added.

"Oh, so I take it you don't have whatever this is," Frank replied.

"No, no, I don't Frank. I am all clean. I get checked all the time to make sure nothing like that is present in my body. I know there are a lot of risks involved with my 'business,' so I always make sure I get checked on a regular basis, just in case. I would never give you something like that intentionally Frank," she replied, reaching over and putting her hand on top of his hand that was resting on the table.

"I'm so sorry this has happened to you Frank. I really am. But I am sure you can get help with it. You will get better, and then you can put it all behind you," Lacy assured him. "But you do need to seek the help of a doctor, and you should do it sooner rather than later," she added.

"So you have no idea what this thing is I have?" Frank asked.

"No, I'm not sure," Lacy replied, biting a little on her lip.

Frank wasn't convinced that Lacy was being honest with him. He had a feeling that she was lying and was trying to cover for herself, but he had no way to disprove what she was asserting.

"Are you sure you got the STD from either me or Ziggy?" Lacy asked.

"Yes, I am sure it was either you or Ziggy, Lacy!" Frank responded. "I don't sleep around with tons of women, you know! And plus, given that you both are prostitutes and sleep with tons of different men, I am pretty damn sure I got this thing from one of you!" he added.

The atmosphere in the room had now changed. Frank's libido was not interested in sex due to the seriousness of the conversation taking place between the two of them. Lacy was no longer putting out any sexual vibes towards him. In fact, she was thinking of just getting the hell out of there. She wasn't sure how to deal with the situation, and she didn't want to take any responsibility for it either.

"Maybe Frank did get this STD from me or Ziggy," she thought to herself. And the thought of it made her feel sad and ashamed, but she wasn't ready to admit to anything. Plus, she knew she didn't have an STD, so she was sure that he must have gotten it from Ziggy. Still, she felt rejected and dejected, and all her sexual power seemed to have instantly diminished. She had gone to see Frank in the hopes of having sex with him, but now she just wanted to get as far away from him as possible

She knew it wasn't his fault that he had contracted an STD, but she just couldn't bear to think that she was the one who introduced him to Ziggy.

"It's all fun and games until someone gets an STD," Frank finally said with a small smile on his face. He was trying to lighten the mood a little, but Lacy did not find his comment amusing.

Then, out of nowhere, Lacy looked Frank dead in the eyes. "I want to marry you Frank. I can make you happy, I know I can. We can have sex whenever and wherever you want. I will be faithful to you and I will take care of you. You are getting older now, and I am still young. I can take care of you in the future, and I want to. I need a good man Frank, and I think you are a really good man. I need to get out of this life I am living and I feel like I want to marry you. Would you consider marrying me, Frank?" Lacy asked.

Frank just sat there, stunned and at a loss for words. "Marry you! Are you crazy Lacy? Are you completely out of your mind now?" Frank replied. "Where is this coming from?" he asked.

"I don't know exactly where it is coming from Frank," Lacy replied. "I am just really feeling like the right thing to do is to marry you. If you will have me, that is," she said.

"Have you!" Frank replied. "I've already had you," he added, smiling.

"No, you know what I mean Frank," Lacy responded. "I need a good man. All the men I know are stupid and going nowhere in life. I need a man like you Frank. A strong man. A man who knows how to take charge and get things done. I know why Louise has been hooked on you all these years, it is obvious, you're a hell of a catch, Frank, and I'm actually amazed that you are still single," she added.

Frank was now smiling. He had to admit he loved hearing all these compliments, but the fact of the matter was, he was not interested in getting married to anyone. He had been single all these years out of choice and he aimed to keep it that way.

"I'm not a get married kind of guy," Frank replied. "Why do you think I have been single all these years?" he continued. "I have only slept with Louise these past few years, and I am not at all interested in pairing up with a woman or a man for that matter," he said and laughed.

Lacy put her head down and pouted. She thought that since she was so much younger than Frank that he would jump at the opportunity to marry her, but she quickly realized this was not the case.

"I thought older men dreamed of having a younger woman like me," she said.

At that statement, Frank burst out laughing. He couldn't help himself and he felt bad for laughing in her face, so he quickly corrected himself. Then, he took Lacy by the hand and looked her in the eyes.

"You're a sweet woman Lacy. You're sexy as hell and a great lay, no question. You're fun and you're funny. You have many great qualities. I am sure some young man will be happy to marry you at some point. If I were you, I wouldn't worry too much about it. There are plenty of men out there who I am sure would be happy to marry such a sexy thing as yourself," Frank said

"Just not you though eh?" Lacy responded.

"That's right," Frank replied.

Lacy looked down at the floor again and pouted. She wasn't sure what to do or say next. She felt totally and absolutely rejected in that moment and Frank also wasn't sure what more to say to her. So the two of them just sat there in silence for a time.

"Listen, I don't want to sound mean, but you really should be leaving. I don't want you staying here too long. I know you probably don't want to hear this right now, but it is the reality of the situation we have created," Frank finally said.

Lacy looked up, but she didn't look at Frank, she looked straight across the room at the wall. She suddenly felt like she was glued to the chair she was sitting on. Like she couldn't get up and leave, even if she wanted to, and now she didn't want to.

"I can't leave right now," Lacy replied. "I'm just not able to," she added. "I feel so rejected Frank," she said, and the tears started flowing down her cheeks.

Frank didn't know what to do. He couldn't stand someone crying in front of him. He was not good with human emotions of that kind. He instantly thought of Rita crying on the phone and how he didn't know what to say to her to comfort her and how lost and inept he felt. So he just sat there not knowing what to do or say.

Lacy put her head in her hands and continued to cry. Finally, Frank reached over to her from across the table and rubbed her back.

"It's all going to be okay," he said in a soft voice. "Don't feel rejected, Lacy," he continued. "I'm not rejecting you. Not at all. I am just being honest with you, is all. I'm a single guy for a reason. I have never wanted to get married to anyone. I've never met anyone that I've wanted to marry, and it's no offense to you, Lacy! Any man would be lucky to have you for his wife, and I am sure there are plenty of men out there for you to choose from. Choose wisely," he added.

"Maybe that is true," Lacy replied, looking up slightly. "But I want you Frank. You're the best man I know. Why don't you want to marry me?" she asked and sobbed.

Frank couldn't believe what was now happening. He had not seen anything like this coming forth that day. As if the day was not already drama enough, he was now being faced with this young woman, his friend's daughter no less, who was quite literally begging him to marry her! He felt like he was living in some kind of twilight zone.

So he reached over and touched Lacy's chin, softly raising her head.

"Listen Lacy, you're a hell of a catch, don't get me wrong okay. I am not rejecting you whatsoever, it is not about rejection okay! It is who I am. Who I have always been. It's not about you at all. So please stop playing the victim here. There is no victim here. I am just a single guy, who has been a single guy and who wants to remain a single guy, that is all there is to it, period," Frank said

"Now wipe your tears and realize that this is not in any way about you," he added.

"I can't," Lacy replied. "I can't just let it go," she sobbed. "I really feel like I need you to marry me," she said, looking at Frank with as much pity as she could muster in the moment. "I really feel like I need you, Frank, and I don't see why you just won't let me come and live with you and be your wife. I just don't get it," she added. "I will do whatever you want, whenever you want. I will have sex with you at the drop of a hat. All you have to do is say you want sex, and I will obey," she added.

"I will cook and clean and take really good care of you. If you want me to be naked, I will be naked. If you want to see my breasts, I will let you. I will do ANYTHING you want me to do. You can tell me how to dress and dictate my life to me and I will obey you. I will be totally submissive to you Frank. Like TOTALLY submissive. Wouldn't you want a woman like that Frank? Someone at your beck and call at all times. Totally submissive to you at all times. Hey, doesn't that sound intriguing to you at all?" Lacy asked.

Frank had to admit at that moment that it did sound somewhat intriguing on the one hand, but on the other, it sounded strange to him. He wasn't sure he wanted a woman who had no mind of her own who would just follow him around like some kind of robot that had to be told what to do and when to do it. He liked to have intelligent conversations, and while he felt like he had become a whore as of late, it was not something he planned on continuing long term. Plus, Lacy was a lot younger than him and from a totally different generation.

"How much could I truly have in common with her?" he wondered.

Finally, he said, "Listen Lacy, that does sound like it could be a lot of fun, but I don't think that kind of a relationship is something I would want."

"What! Are you kidding me right now?" Lacy responded. "Do you know how many men dream of having a woman like that? Someone who will allow themselves to be dominated one hundred percent without question? Do you Frank? Do you know and realize that this is every man's dream!" she added.

Frank smiled a big smile. He couldn't help but be amused at Lacy's insistence on knowing what every man dreams of, and it struck him funny that she was convinced she did.

"Not every man dreams of such a relationship, Lacy," Frank responded. "Sure, there are no doubt some men who do, and power to them if that is what works for them and the woman, but it is not a relationship dynamic that I am interested in. I need a woman who is strong and able. Someone I can share deep thoughts with and have intellectual discussions. Someone who has wisdom and can help me understand things. You know, a woman who knows her own mind and is not afraid to share it. I am not interested in having a robot, so to speak," he added. "I do well to keep myself on track, let alone taking on the responsibility of having to care for and instruct someone else's life," he continued. "Sorry, but that kind of situation is just not for me. But I do appreciate the offer, Lacy, and I can see how some men would jump on such an offer. But I am just not one of those men," he added.

Lacy was dumbfounded and at a loss for words. She couldn't believe that she had just offered to be Frank's sex slave and he had still turned her down. Suddenly, she realized that the woman Frank was describing sounded a lot like her mom.

"Oh, I get it," she replied. "You're talking about Louise! Do you plan on getting married to her?" Lacy asked.

And with that comment, Frank broke out laughing again. "No, I am not planning on marrying anyone. I told you, I'm a single guy and I plan to remain that way," Frank replied. "Why is that so hard for you to grasp and accept?" he asked.

"Oh, it's not hard to grasp or accept," Lacy responded. "I'm just curious how any man could turn down such an offer as the one I just put on the table," she continued.

"Yea, I have to admit," Frank replied. "It is a heck of an offer indeed," he continued. "But it is just not something that would work for me, is all. I know who I am and what I need, even though my decisions as of late are making me wonder about that!" he added. "I just know that having some kind of 'sex slave,' as you put it, would be fun for a while; but I know I would grow tired of it rather quickly," he added. "You know I love having sex, but sex will only take a relationship so far. It needs a lot more substance than just sex," he continued. "Don't get me wrong, sex is important. I'm just saying it's not everything," Frank added.

Lacy wasn't sure what more to say. She felt like she had laid bare her soul and offered up her body and mind to this man who couldn't care less about either. She had been almost certain that once she had made her offer, Frank would be down on one knee proposing to her in an instant. Now, she was faced with the reality that Frank was not interested, and she wasn't quite sure how to deal with it.

Just then, she thought of something. "Well, you know I am smart Frank," she began. "I am currently in college, you know!" she added. "And I am strong and able, and I can have deep conversations with you. I'm not stupid Frank!" she continued, suddenly looking serious and strict thinking Frank wanted a more serious type of woman.

Frank smiled. "You don't give up easy, do you?" he said. "So, you want to be my 'sex slave,' do you?" he continued, still smiling. "Come here then and undress. Show me what you got," he added.

So Lacy jumped up from her chair and started undressing as instructed. "See Frank, see how easy that was," she said while taking her clothes off.

"No, stop," Frank said. "I was just messing around to see if you would actually do what I told you to do. I can't have sex with you right now, and you know why," he continued. "Until I get this STD thing taken care of, I'll not be having sex with anyone, quite obviously," he added. "I certainly don't want to give anyone whatever it is I got, and I hate to sound mean, but you really do have to leave now," Frank continued. "You've been here way too long, and I am sure the neighbors are keeping tabs on the time frame. We really don't want to start any rumors around here, especially seeing as your mom would be very upset by such. I know you understand what I am saying!" he added.

"Yea, I guess you are right," Lacy replied in a sad tone of voice. She was now resigned to having to leave, not having gotten any sex and having her marriage proposal outright rejected. She was now feeling both rejected and depressed, and she couldn't understand how an older man like Frank would not be jumping all over a proposal from a sexy young woman like her, especially given the great offer she had made to him in being his submissive sex slave. "What man could refuse such?" she wondered.

But she knew, because one such man was sitting right across the table from her. Still, she could not help but think that Frank was just bullshitting her. "There is no way he could be serious," she reasoned. Yet, she had no choice but to take him at his word.

"I've planted the seed now," she thought to herself. "What I said to him will go round and round in his mind, and sooner or later, he will succumb to my offer. I will just bide my time now, and I won't give up either. I will keep on reminding him of what he could have, if he chose to take it," she thought, getting up from her chair to prepare to leave.

As she dressed, she noticed that Frank was staring at her, so she acted more sexy than usual putting her clothes back on.

"I know what you are trying to do, Lacy," Frank said and smiled. "You're trying to turn me on," he continued. "I get it, and yes, I think you are very sexy, no doubt about it," Frank continued while watching her. "And I love having sex with you for sure, but you know I can't have sex with you today, and you know why. So I feel you are just teasing me now," he added.

"I'm not teasing you Frank," Lacy replied, bending over in a sexual position as she spoke. "I'm just trying to show you what could be yours, all the time," she said as she stood back up and smiled.

"Just think Frank, you could be horny in the morning, in the afternoon or in the evening, or even in the middle of the night, and presto I would be right there. Doesn't that sound like a great deal," she added.

"Well, now that you put it that way," Frank replied and smiled. "It does sound rather intriguing for sure," he added and rubbed his chin at the thought of what Lacy was saying. "But it sounds more like a fairy tale than reality," he continued. "Life, I don't think, is like that, Lacy," he added. "Life is a lot more complicated than that."

"Well, maybe so, Frank," Lacy replied. "But it doesn't have to be," she continued.

Frank wasn't sure what more to say. It seemed to him that Lacy had an answer for everything. Every objection he had spoken, she had squashed with her offers of submission. He had never had a woman speak to him like that before. He had never even entertained the idea of having a partner who was a self-professed sex slave at his beck and call. He had never even considered such a proposal as the one that was before him now, and he wasn't quite sure how to deal with it.

On the one hand, it was as intriguing as hell, but on the other hand, it was not intriguing at all.

"What's a man to do?" he thought. "How do I appease her so I can get her to leave?" he wondered, looking at the clock on his kitchen wall and realizing Lacy had been at his house now far too long for comfort.

"Maybe I will just agree with her somehow, and then she will be willing to leave," he thought to himself.

"Okay Lacy, you win," Frank said, smiling.

"What, you mean you are willing to marry me?" Lacy exclaimed.

"No," Frank replied. "I told you, I am not the marrying kind and I really need you to leave now! You've been here far too long and this is getting more concerning by the minute. You know you shouldn't be here, and I don't know why you are being so damn difficult in terms of leaving. Are you trying to get us both in trouble? Is that it?" Frank asked.

Lacy smiled. "Alright Frank, have it your way. I will leave, don't worry. And I won't bother you any more either," she said pouting.

"I didn't say you had to leave and never come back, I just said you have to leave because you've been here too long. We can continue this rather strange conversation some other time, okay!" Frank replied. "But for right now, I really need you to leave," Frank added.

So Lacy got up slowly from her chair at the kitchen table, put on her coat, and proceeded towards the door with Frank following right behind her.

"Sure you won't reconsider Frank?" she asked, smiling as she reached to open the back door of Frank's house.

"How about this, I'll think about it and let you know for sure, okay?" Frank replied and smiled.

Lacy was happy to hear this response, and she kissed Frank on the cheek.

"Think hard on it," she said as she walked towards her car.

Frank watched her leave out his driveway and they both waved to one another as she drove away. Frank shut the door, locked it and proceeded back into his house.

He sat down at his kitchen table and tried to grasp all that had just happened and was happening in his life. He knew he had to deal with his medical situation but he really didn't want to go to the only doctor in town, and he didn't want the staff that worked there to have access to that kind of information on him.

"I'll go to one of those walk-in clinics in the city," he thought. "I'll get up early tomorrow and drive into the city and be there when the clinic opens. That way, I will be sure to get in to see someone tomorrow, because I can't let this go. I don't even know what it is and Lacy wasn't any help at all," he said to himself.

Then Frank rolled himself a joint and poured the last of the coffee that was left in the pot on the kitchen counter.

As he sat down at his kitchen table drinking his coffee and smoking his cannabis, he thought about all that had happened around that table. "If this table could talk," he thought to himself, but he was relieved and happy that that was not possible.

As he sat there, his mind wandered to Rita. "How must she be coping with all that she is going through," he wondered. And he suddenly felt a lot of sadness in his heart. Sadness for Rita, sadness for his friend Joe who had died, and guilt for the way he had betrayed him.

He wondered if Joe knew before he died about the affair between him and Rita. He wondered what had happened the night Joe died. He wondered if Rita would be found guilty of murdering Joe. But it was all too much for him to contemplate at that moment. He didn't want to think about it all, so he tried to distract his mind with other things. Still, the reality of it all was not easy for him to escape, and he knew there was truly no escape from it.

Sure, he could distract his mind for a time, but he knew it was only for a time.

As he looked around his kitchen, he had visions of Louise, Rita, and now Lacy all naked in that very room, and it kind of blew his mind.

"How in fuck did all of this happen?" he thought to himself. But he knew how, and that made him all the more angst and sad.

Chapter Sixteen

Oh What Tangled Webs We Weave

The next day, as planned, Frank was up early and on his way to the medical clinic in the city. As he drove, a thousand things were running through his mind.

"How am I going to talk about this to the doctor?" he wondered. "What will I say? Do I tell him I slept with two prostitutes?" he asked himself. Just then it occurred to him that the doctor might be a woman, and his anxiety increased even more. "It's one thing to talk about such matters with another man," he thought, "but having to tell a woman doctor would be really unnerving," he said to himself.

The possibility of a female doctor was not something he had considered, and realizing the possibility in that moment gave Frank even more anxiety than he was already feeling. "Oh God, please let the doctor be a man. I cannot bear to talk to a woman doctor about this situation. Please God, make it a male doctor," he prayed as he drove towards the city.

Reaching the city, Frank found the clinic without issue and pulled into one of the many parking spaces. "One good thing about being here early is that there is no problem finding a parking space," he thought. The only people in the parking lot were there early, like him, in an attempt to get in to see a doctor at the clinic. And while there were quite a few of them, Frank still felt he had a good chance to be one of the ones who would be counted in the day's patients for the clinic. There was a cut-off number, and if you were not there early, chances were you were not going to get seen by a doctor that day.

It wasn't long before the door opened for the clinic and people quickly began to line up outside the door. Frank wasn't too far down the line of people waiting and thus he was almost certain he would be counted among those who would be allowed in to see a doctor that day. And sure enough, the lady passing out tickets to people who fit within the cut-off number passed one to Frank and smiled.

"Thank you," Frank said, taking the ticket from her.

His heart was now beating fast and he could feel anxiety rising inside his body again. He wanted to ask the woman passing out tickets who the doctor was, but he couldn't bring himself to do it.

Soon the people who had gotten a ticket were seated in the small waiting room, while others were still lined up outside the door of the clinic. The rest were told to go home and try again tomorrow.

As Frank sat there in the waiting room, he tried to think of what to say to the doctor when his name was called. His anxiety had not subsided much and he wondered if the people sitting in the waiting room with him could somehow tell he was nervous. If they could somehow tell he had an STD he was ashamed of. But he knew that was not reasonable thinking, for there was no way for them to know such information. Still, for some reason, he felt nervous as hell about sitting there.

Time passed and finally his name was called. A woman led him into an empty office and asked him to have a seat. She had a notepad and clipboard. Frank had already provided his personal information to the receptionist in the waiting room, but now the woman in the room with him wanted to know why he was there to see the doctor.

"So what brings you here today?" she asked him

"Ah, ah, I'm having problems with my private part," Frank replied, not looking the woman in the eyes.

"Your private part," she said and smiled. "Which private part are you referring to?" she asked.

"Ah, my penis," Frank replied.

"What is the problem with your penis?" she asked.

"It hurts when I have to use the washroom," Frank said.

The woman wrote down the information Frank provided to her.

"Anything else you'd like to add?" she asked.

"No, thank you," Frank responded.

"Okay, the doctor will be in to see you shortly," she said as she exited the room.

Frank sat in the sterile room, looking around at all the things in the room in an attempt to distract his mind. "So far so good," he told himself. "Talking to that lady wasn't that bad," he told himself.

It seemed like a long time before the doctor finally arrived to see him.

"Hi Frank, I'm Doctor Liam," the doctor said upon entering the room.

Frank was relieved and grateful that the doctor was a man. "Thank you God," he whispered in his mind.

"What seems to be your problem today?" the doctor asked. But before Frank could answer, the doctor continued. "It says here on the chart that you are having pain with urination, is that correct?"

"Yes sir," Frank responded.

"How long have you been having this problem?" the doctor asked.

"Ah, about a week or so now," Frank replied.

"Do you have any idea how you might have gotten this issue?" the doctor asked.

Frank could now feel his face turning red and his blood pressure increasing. "Ah, yea, I had sex with a couple of ladies of the night," Frank said, putting his head down and not wanting to look at the doctor when he answered.

"Ah, I see," the doctor responded. "Have you had any discharge from your penis?" the doctor continued.

"Yes," Frank replied.

Then the doctor instructed Frank to undress from the waist down and to lay down on the examination table, and he would return momentarily.

So Frank stripped off from the waist down and laid down on the examination table as instructed, covering himself with the thin sheet there for that purpose.

It wasn't long before the doctor was back, and Frank was nervous as hell as the doctor examined his penis. Finally, the doctor said, "I think we should take a urine sample just to be sure. It could be an STD, but it also might be another kind of infection. So just to be on the safe side, I am going to get you to pee in this cup and bring it back."

So Frank went to the washroom and urinated in the cup provided. Then he gave it to the woman who was waiting for him to exit the washroom. "You can go back into the examination room now," she instructed him.

It wasn't long before the doctor came back into the room.

"Well, it is not another kind of infection Frank. It looks as though you have contracted gonorrhea, Frank!" the doctor advised.

Frank was devastated. "What is that? Is it serious?" he asked.

"It is a sexually transmitted disease that seems to be on the rise these days," the doctor advised. "And yes, it can be very serious," the doctor continued. "It is good you did not let it go any longer, and that you came to get help with it, because these types of STDs can lead to very serious health problems if not addressed," the doctor added.

Then he got out his notepad and said, "I'm going to give you an antibiotic. Make sure you take all of it and take it as instructed on the bottle. It is very important that you take all of it, Frank, because you want to make sure you rid your body of this infection, okay."

"Yes, yes, I will make sure I take all of it, and thank you," Frank responded.

"No problem," the doctor advised, smiling. "And stay away from ladies of the night Frank, it is not a good idea to have sexual intercourse with people who are having sex with multiple partners," the doctor added.

"Yes, yes, I know that now," Frank replied, taking the note from the doctor with the prescription written on it.

Frank noticed his hands were now shaking as he looked down at the piece of paper the doctor had given him. "Oh my goodness," he thought to himself. "How is all of this happening?" he said to himself. He felt like he was going to cry as he exited the medical clinic to return to his vehicle. "I need to find a pharmacy and get this prescription filled right now," he thought, and he tried to think of a pharmacy that was close by.

It was then that he realized there was a pharmacy right in the same building as the medical clinic, and so he opted to get back out of his truck and head there to get his prescription filled. As he passed the prescription paper to the woman at the counter, he felt a sudden surge of anxiety. "Is she going to know what this antibiotic is for?" he wondered. But the woman didn't appear to have any reaction, so Frank figured if she did know, she wasn't showing any judgment.

And chances were good that the antibiotic was for any number of possible infections, he reasoned.

"It will be about twenty to twenty-five minutes before your prescription is ready," the woman advised.

"Okay, thank you," Frank responded as he left the counter. He would walk around the store and maybe buy some things he needed, if he saw anything he needed, that was. He needed to distract his mind while he was waiting for the prescription to be filled. He looked at his watch for the time, so that he would know when to return to the counter.

As he walked around the store looking at various items for sale, the time seemed to pass quite quickly and he was back at the counter. The woman passed him a bag with his prescription in it.

"Have you ever taken this medication before?" she asked.

"Ah, no, no, I haven't," Frank replied.

"Well, there is a pamphlet inside the bag that advises of possible side effects that you should watch out for. I suggest you read it so you know what to look for, just in case you have an adverse reaction to the medication," she advised.

"Oh, okay," Frank responded. "Thank you, and have a nice day," he said, as he turned to leave the pharmacy.

As he exited the pharmacy, he suddenly felt hot all over, like he was having a hot flash of some kind. He quickly returned to his truck and once seated inside he just sat there thinking. He noticed his hands were shaking again as he opened the bag to examine the bottle of pills he was going to have to take. He hated taking any kind of medication. The only medication he felt good about was the cannabis that he grew himself. Other than that, he rarely took any kind of medication. An aspirin or Advil when he absolutely had to was all Frank was used to taking.

Now, he was forced into taking this antibiotic and he felt fear about it, yet he knew he had to do it. He opened the bottle and examined the pills inside. There seemed to be a lot of them, and they seemed unusually big to Frank. "I don't even know if I can swallow these things," he thought to himself, and feelings of anguish welled up inside of him.

Then he read the directions on the bottle. *Take one tablet three times a day until gone. Take with meals,* it said. Then he opened the pamphlet regarding possible adverse side effects and began to read it, but he quickly put it back in the bag.

"I can't read that stuff," he said to himself. "It will just make me more apprehensive about taking this shit. I just need to take it and that is all there is to it. I will force myself to take it," he said, and he closed the bag back up and laid it on the seat beside him. Started his truck and headed out of the city.

"I just want to get back home," he said to himself. "I just need to rest and take care of this thing," he continued. "I am never going to sleep with another prostitute again," he told himself.

And with those thoughts, he remembered the proposal Lacy had made to him and how she offered to be his submissive sex slave. He couldn't help but smile when he thought of her sitting there in his kitchen practically begging him to marry her. "What in fuck is she thinking?" he wondered. "Was she actually serious?" he questioned. He wondered what Louise would think if she were ever to find out that he had sex with her daughter. But he didn't want to think about any of that right now.

As Frank drove into the driveway of his home, he swore he had never felt such relief to be home again. He now looked at his home and property as some kind of safe haven where he could hide from the world, and he felt deep gratitude for all he had managed to attain in his life thus far. Even the house now looked so lovely to him as he gazed upon it and all the land surrounding him, he suddenly felt great appreciation.

It wasn't that he had not felt all those things before in regard to the house and the land he had acquired; it was just that now, he felt those feelings even deeper than before.

"Home sweet home," he said as he exited his vehicle and walked towards his house.

Once inside his house, he put on a fresh pot of coffee and made himself a grilled cheese sandwich. As he sat at his kitchen table drinking his freshly brewed organic coffee and eating his sandwich, the phone rang.

"I'm not answering it right now," he said to himself. "The machine can get it. I don't want to talk to anyone right now. I just want to enjoy my sandwich and coffee.".

And while he opted not to answer the call, he could hear the answering machine from where he was sitting.

"Hi Frank, remember me? It's Ziggy! I got your number from Lacy. I hope you don't mind. Lacy said you lived out in the country and I was thinking on coming out to see yea, if you want to see me that is," she said. "Give me a call Frank, I'd really love to see yea again." Then she spoke out her phone number. "Okay bye for now," she said and ended the call.

"Oh my goodness!" Frank exclaimed to himself. "These women have a lot of nerve," he thought. "How can she call me and want to come and see me? Does she not realize she has an STD for fuck sakes?" he wondered.

He wanted to call her back and tell her off, but he felt too nervous to do so. He noticed his hands were shaking again and he knew his nerves were on edge. "Maybe I should take one of the pills Louise gave to me. Maybe taking one of those pills will help me deal with all of this, I don't know," he thought.

And he opted to go and get one of the pills that he had stashed for safe keeping in case of another panic attack. He looked at the pill. It was so tiny. He remembered Louise saying the medication would make him tired and how he had fallen asleep not long after he took one the first time. But he knew he also had to take one of the antibiotics he had gotten for the STD.

"Gonorrhea," he thought to himself. He had heard about such horrible sexually transmitted diseases, but he had never dreamed he would actually ever have one of them. He opened the bottle and took out one of the pills, which seemed huge in size. He popped it into his mouth and took a drink of coffee.

"How in fuck did I get in this place," he thought as he swallowed the pill. Yet, he was thankful that he had opted to go and see the doctor and that the pills the doctor gave him would be the cure to his issue.

"It could have been a lot worse," he thought to himself. "I could have contracted something that was not curable," he reasoned. And with that he felt a sense of relief, but he didn't want to take the medication Louise had given him, just in case the two medications had a reaction to one another inside his body.

So he opted not to take one of the pills Louise had given him and to put it back with the others he had stashed for safe keeping.

"I will just have to suffer through this," he said to himself. "It's my own stupid fault. What was I thinking having sex with two women I knew were prostitutes! What did I expect to happen?" he asked himself.

His head was now swirling as he sat there at his kitchen table.

"What happened to my serene life? What happened to the man I used to be?" he asked himself. "I used to love myself. I was a good person. I did the right things. Now I feel like a whore, a cheat and a deceiver," he said to himself.

And the tears welled up in his eyes and feelings of deep guilt gripped him hard. He held his head in his hands with his elbows resting on the table. The tears ran down his cheeks like a river.

"Just let it all out," he said to himself. "You will feel better if you just let it all out," he said, and so he just sat there sobbing and crying for all that had happened and was happening in his life.

"I've made such a mess of things," he thought as the tears flowed.

As he sat there crying in a complete state of misery, the phone rang again.

"Oh no! Please just leave me alone," he thought as he heard the phone ringing. "Is it Ziggy again?" he wondered. He wasn't going to answer, regardless of who it was, he said.

Soon the answering machine picked up, but this time it was Lacy.

"Hiya Frank," she said, "I miss you. I hope you don't mind, but I gave Ziggy your number. She called me and asked for it. She wants to see you again Frank! I never told her about our conversation and I never mentioned what we talked about to her. Anyway, I hope you are okay. Call me," she said and ended the call.

Frank just sat there staring into space. He wasn't going to call her, or Ziggy. He had just gone to the doctor because of the two of them, or at least one of them, he wasn't sure which one. He wanted nothing to do with either of them now, he reasoned.

"Why are they calling me? What? They want more of my money? They already got enough of my money. Fuck them," he said to himself, determined not to give in to calling either of them. "Sure it was fun at the time, but now I am paying for it dearly," he continued. "I paid four hundred dollars to have sex with them and ended up with gonorrhea. That doesn't seem like a very good trade-off to me," he added.

But he knew Lacy well enough now that she would most likely not give up that easily. Still, he was determined not to talk to either one of them ever again. He had never had an STD and the fact that he had one now was devastating him.

"I'm going to go and lay down. Watch a comedy movie. Hopefully that will take my mind off of all of this," he said to himself. "This day will end sooner or later," he thought. "And one day, I pray I will have my life back to normal again."

He picked out a movie, put it in the machine, and laid down on the couch. He covered himself with the blanket that was there and made himself cozy. He needed to be kind to himself now, he reasoned. He had been through a lot and while most of it was all of his own doing, he at once felt sorry for himself regardless.

And it wasn't long before he fell asleep. When he finally awoke and got up from his slumber, he could see the light beeping on the answering machine. "Fuck off," he said to himself as he walked passed the machine. "I'm not even going to listen to any messages right now," he told himself as he sat down at his kitchen table and rolled a cannabis joint. "I'm gonna smoke this joint and then I'm going to go for a walk on my property. That will help clear my head.".

But once the joint was half smoked, his curiosity started getting the best of him. He didn't want to hear, but he did want to hear who left messages and what they had to say. So reluctantly he got up and went over to his answering machine. Still hauling on the joint as he pushed the play button.

"You have six new messages," the machine said.

"What!" Frank exclaimed. "Six messages. Who in fuck called me that many times?" he wondered. But two of the messages were from before he had fallen asleep, so really it was four new messages, he realized. Still, that was a lot of messages, he thought.

He skipped the first two messages as he had already heard them, then the third message started to play.

"FRANK... I know you are there. Now pick up the damn phone!" It was Lacy again. Just as he expected, she was not going to give up bugging him. "I'm not going to stop calling you until you pick up! If I have to drive back down there, you know I will," she added. "And I know you don't want Louise to hear me on your machine, or worse see me at your house again. So answer your damn phone Frank," Lacy demanded.

Hearing this made Frank feel sick inside. If Lacy didn't stop, he knew it would only be a matter of time before Louise found out he was having sex with her. He couldn't bear the thought of that happening and knew it had the potential to cause grave harm in his life. Louise could turn against him and rat him out to the police for having been in an affair with Rita, which could then drag him into the whole trial as a possible witness or worse.

"Oh my God, this is horrible," he said to himself. "What have I done?"

Then the fourth message began to play.

"FRANK, it's me again. ANSWER THE PHONE FRANK!" Another message from Lacy.

Then the fifth message.

"Frank, come on. I just want to talk to you. Please answer the phone Frank, I need to talk to you. I was thinking about our conversation and I think maybe I can help you. I think maybe I know what is wrong with your, you know! Call me, we really need to talk, okay. Please."

Then the sixth message started to play, Lacy again.

"Frank, I want you to think about the proposal I made to you. I was dead serious you know! And I can help you with your problem, I now know what is wrong. So call me Frank. I'll be waiting for your call," she said and ended the call.

"Should I call her back?" Frank asked himself. He reasoned he might as well call her back since he knew she was not going to let up until he did. So he picked up the phone and called Lacy.

"Hey," she said. "I'm so happy and relieved you called," she added. "I was worried about you due to all the stuff you told me when I was at your house," she continued.

"Hey," Frank responded. "Yea, I got all your messages. Sorry, I fell asleep watching a movie and didn't hear the phone. But I'm okay. I went to the city this morning and saw the doctor at the walk-in clinic. He gave me an antibiotic to take and I have taken one since I got home," he told her.

"Oh, that's good Frank. I was going to tell you that you needed to get to a doctor right away. I spoke to Ziggy and told her about your situation. I hope you don't mind Frank, but I had to find out what it was! I guess you know now what it is," she added.

"Oh yes, I know what it is alright," Frank responded. "And it is horrible," he continued.

"I know, I know," Lacy replied. "I'm so sorry this happened to you Frank," she continued.

"Ziggy didn't know she had that STD. She only found out recently and she feels terrible about transmitting it to you. She wanted your number so she could call you, so I gave it to her. I hope you're not mad at me about that," Lacy continued.

"No, I'm not mad at you, but don't give my number out to anyone ever again. You know how much I love my privacy," Frank responded.

"Yes I do Frank, and no, I won't give your number to anyone else, I promise," Lacy responded.

"Did you talk to Ziggy?" Lacy asked.

"No, I didn't talk to her, but she did call. She left a message on my answering machine, but I've not called her back. And truly, I am not going to call her back. I don't really want to talk to her. I have nothing to say to her," Frank continued.

"Okay Frank, I understand," Lacy replied. "I am so sorry this happened to you Frank, but remember it was your idea to invite her over that day!" Lacy continued.

"Yes, I am well aware," Frank said. "And now I am paying the price for it, on top of the four hundred dollars it cost me that day. I feel stupid as fuck for my behavior as of late, but that's a whole other story," he added.

"I hate to bring this up right now Frank, but have you thought any more about my proposal?" Lacy asked.

Frank smiled. "No Lacy, I've not had time to think about your so-called proposal. I've been consumed dealing with this STD situation and it has caused me a lot of stress and anxiety. It's been all I've been able to think about as of late," he continued.

"That's understandable," Lacy replied. "But please think about my proposal. I really meant what I said," she continued. "I am more than willing to be your submissive sex slave," she added and giggled a little.

"Okay Lacy, that's great; but I'm not sure I want a submissive sex slave for a wife, and what is more, how would Louise feel about you and I getting married? Hey, have you thought about that?" he asked her.

The phone went silent.

"Are you still there?" Frank asked.

"Yea, yea, I'm still here," Lacy replied.

"I thought I lost yea there," Frank said.

"No, you didn't lose me Frank. I was caught off guard by what you said about Louise. To be honest, and I'm not sure why, but I hadn't thought of that aspect of my proposal. And now that you have raised the issue, I can see that it might be a huge problem I had not even considered," she replied.

"See," Frank responded. "It's important to think about all aspects before you commit yourself to things. Trust me, I know all about it," he added.

"Okay, I have to go now Frank, but I'm glad you called me back and we had a chance to talk," Lacy said, and they ended the call.

All of a sudden Lacy was struck by the fact that her mom had been so into Frank for many years. She knew if her mom knew she was with Frank, it had the potential to cause irreparable damage to their relationship and she didn't want that to happen. She loved her mom and she hadn't meant to cause her any harm. "She doesn't know about Frank and I, and so I think Frank is right, we need to keep it that way," she said to herself.

She was suddenly amazed that she had not even taken her mom into consideration when she opted to seduce Frank on that first day at her mom's house when Frank had shown up there to visit her mom.

"What was I thinking?" she said to herself. "I love my mom. My mom doesn't deserve this from me! She's been nothing but loving and supportive my entire life," she suddenly remembered, and deep feelings of guilt washed over her. She couldn't believe that she had put her own sexual desires over the importance of her relationship with her mother, and it hit her deep within.

Memories now flooded her mind of all the times her mom had shown up for her, showed such deep love to her, and with those thoughts, she began to sob. The mere thought that she could have completely destroyed the relationship with her mother now devastated her to the core of her being.

"He's just another stupid man, but one I know, my mom is really into," she said to herself.

She hung her head in shame and could not look at herself in the mirror that was right in front of where she was sitting. Now, she wished the mirror was not there because she was having a hard time picking her head up knowing she would be looking directly at herself.

She sat there for a time, holding her head in her hands, crying her eyes out.

"How could I have been such a bitch to my own mother," she said to herself. "And why did I not truly consider all of this before I decided to make Frank one of my clients? Am I that unaware? That selfish?" she asked herself.

She then got up from where she was sitting without looking in the mirror and moved to another chair in her bedroom. Then she thought about her proposal to Frank and she suddenly felt completely embarrassed of herself.

"I offered to be his submissive sex slave," she thought. "What was I thinking?" she asked herself. "I'm an independent woman. I take care of myself. I don't answer to anyone. I don't have children and I don't want to have children. It's just not for me," she continued. "Why would I offer to be his sex slave?" she asked herself again.

But she knew why, because deep inside she had always felt this competition with her mother. She knew it was wrong to feel that way, but she couldn't deny it. She wanted what her mother had, but she didn't feel she had the parts her mother had to make it happen. So, seducing Frank on some level was to one-up her mom, even though luckily her mom knew nothing about it. She wanted to see if she could seduce Frank and get him to have sex with her now that she was a grown woman, and she had been pretty sure she could. So she did.

"Men are soooo easy. You can literally lead them around by the nose!" she thought and smiled. "So pathetically weak," she added.

"No wonder men are compared to bulls. They all should have a ring in their nose," she added. "Then you could just lead them around by the ring. Drag them around," and with that thought she began to laugh uncontrollably.

"Fucking dicks," she said, still laughing. "Anyway, he is not my mom's official boyfriend. Never has been. As far as I know they are just fuck buddies," she thought to herself. "So really, I mean, did I really do anything wrong?" she asked herself.

"If Frank wasn't so weak and easy, I could never have fucked him. He was so easy it was pathetic," she said to herself. "Show some tit and they will follow yea anywhere," she thought. And with that thought she again began to laugh uncontrollably.

She was laughing so hard she was crying from the laughter, but she knew, in truth, this was no laughing matter.

"I'm an f'ing snot," she said to herself, but she just didn't want to think about it all anymore. She now understood why Frank just wanted to be left alone. She got it. And she opted to commit to herself that she would never have sex with him again.

"Sure, he has a nice dick, so what!" she reasoned. "He's just an okay fuck. I've had better and I've had worse, but yea, he was pretty decent. At least he could last longer than five minutes," she said to herself, and once again she started to laugh.

Blaming Frank and laughing about it was her way of coping with the situation, but she knew it was no excuse for what had happened between the two of them.

"Oh, it's as much my fault as it is his. Just let it go and move on," she said to herself. "There's no point in dwelling on it," she thought. "I can't change what happened now, so what's the point in torturing myself with all of this?" she reasoned.

"Louise doesn't know anything about it and if I stop this situation now, she never will. I can't believe the chances I was taking in having sex with Frank," she thought.

The mere thought of it all made her feel sick to her stomach. "If I lost my mom, I don't know what I would do. She's been my biggest support my entire life. She took good care of me and has always been there for me. I couldn't even imagine my life without her in it," she thought. "She's my mom," she said to herself, and with that she began to cry once again for the guilt she was feeling for having betrayed her mother.

"But she will never know," she thought finally, wiping the tears from her face and reaching for a Kleenex to blow her nose. "Frank is not going to tell her, that is for sure. He wants to continue fucking her! Fucking whore bitch that he is," she said to herself in an attempt to soften the blow of the deep betrayal she knew she had committed against her mother.

"He is just as guilty as me," she reasoned. But she knew her betrayal was much deeper than Frank's. Louise was her mother. She had much more to lose if Louise were ever to find out than Frank did," she reasoned. Yet, she wasn't aware of all Frank had to lose if Lousie were ever to find out.

"I'm so sorry Mamma," she said out loud, as if Louise could hear her. "I never meant to hurt you Mamma," she continued. She was apologizing despite the fact of Louise being unaware of the betrayal. Somehow, speaking an apology to her mom out loud made her feel a little less guilty.

"I am, right now, putting all of this behind me. If Mom wants Frank, she can have him," she said to herself. "Sure, I can't deny that he was fun to fuck, but a fuck is not worth my relationship with my mom. Plus, truly, he is way too old for me," she continued. "Sure he is handsome and all and a good person for sure; but he is not more important to me than my mom," she thought to herself.

And with all of that, she took the piece of paper she had with Frank's number on it and ripped it into tiny pieces, letting the pieces fall to the floor. "That's it for that," she said to herself. "I will never ever betray my mom like that again in my life," she thought. Yet, little did she know, Frank had a lot stronger hold on her than she cared to admit.

Frank had returned to sitting at his kitchen table following his telephone conversation with Lacy. "She's crazier than a hoot owl," he said to himself and smiled as he rolled another joint. "What is she thinking?" he asked himself. "She wants to be my submissive sex slave," he said to himself and laughed.

"I think I really messed her up when I brought up Louise in the conversation though. She went completely silent there for a minute and she wasn't very talkative afterwards either," he thought.

"Wonder if she is contemplating that realization now?" he asked himself. "I hope she is thinking about it," he thought. "She has a lot more to lose than I do if Louise were ever to find out about her and I," he reasoned. But then he remembered that Louise also had information on him that would be explosive and devastating if exposed. Yet, he knew Lacy was unaware of that aspect.

"How could she have not even taken all of that into consideration when she opted to be a little slut with me?" he questioned.

And then the thought ran all the way through him. The realization of what he had done with Lacy gripped him. "Louise has been my good friend for many years. The fact that we have sex together from time to time is really a moot point. She has been there for me when I needed her and she helped me most recently with that violent panic attack. I don't know what I would have done if she had not shown up right when she did. She was an angel to me in those moments," he thought to himself, and he suddenly felt great guilt and shame over his betrayal to Louise.

"Man, I have screwed things up royally," he said to himself, but then it occurred to him that Louise did not know about him and Lacy, and as long as Lacy stopped being an idiot, she would never know," he reasoned. "I hope and pray that Lacy snaps out of it," he said to himself. "I really don't want to hurt Louise. That's the last thing I want to do," he said, getting up from the kitchen table

He was now going to take the walk he had planned to take before talking to Lacy. So with his joint in hand and a bottle of water, he left his house to go walk in the forest that was his backyard.

As Frank walked deep into the forest on his property, he felt a surge of gratitude for the fact that he owned the land he was walking on. He looked around at all the beauty of the natural world of creation that surrounded him.

"I still can't believe I own all of this," he thought to himself and smiled. "Thank you God," he said out loud. "And please forgive me of all my horrible sins as of late," he added.

When he reached the river bank he sat down on the bench he had built. He pulled out the joint he had rolled and, lighting it, he gazed at the beauty of the river and all the nature that surrounded him.

"I am one lucky bastard," he said to himself, dragging back on his cannabis cigarette. "Life is damn good," he reasoned and smiled a big smile. "Wonder what the rich folks are doing?" he said to himself and laughed.

Frank saw wealth differently than most people in society. To Frank, he was far richer than any millionaire or even billionaire. "What I have right here," he said to himself, "is worth more than all their money combined," he reasoned and smiled a huge smile as he continued to smoke his homegrown organic cannabis.

"This is the life," he said, taking the last toke off of his joint. "I am so fortunate and so blessed," he added while standing up to stretch.

He raised his arms above his head and just when he did he saw a huge eagle flying directly over top of where he was standing. The sight of the eagle hit him hard for some reason. He'd seen eagles down by the river before and even had a feather from one of them that he had found one day, but today, this eagle seemed different somehow.

"Maybe it's a message," Frank thought as he watched the eagle disappear high into the sky. "What must it be like to fly like an eagle," he wondered. "Such a majestic bird," he thought. And then he felt curious as to what the message was, and in that same moment it occurred to him that the eagle was a sign of freedom.

"Ah, I know what the eagle's trying to tell me," he said to himself. "I am supposed to remain free! That's it. Cool," he said to himself and smiled.

And while it had always been Frank's intention to remain free, he had gotten himself tangled into webs as of late that had the potential of tying him down.

He walked along the shoreline of the river and looked back to where he had been sitting. Just then the image of Joe and Rita popped into his mind. He could see the three of them all sitting there enjoying the day. And he remembered Rita flirting with him behind Joe's back. He also remembered how she had her breasts partly revealed and how damn sexy she was. How he wanted her so badly and how he could not control himself when it came to having sex with her, despite the fact that she was married to his good friend Joe.

Joe, who was now dead! He still couldn't believe that was true. Just as he couldn't believe that Rita had been charged with his death no less. Thinking of such was all too much for him and he immediately tried to rid his mind of all of it.

"Don't think about all of that right now," he said to himself. "You were enjoying the day and now you are bringing up all kinds of misery. Stop it," he told himself. "Get back into nature again," he said to himself in an effort to rid his mind of all those horrible thoughts.

So he grabbed a stick and threw it in the water. "I really should clean this area up down here," he thought, and with that, he began to pick up sticks and put them in a pile in an effort to distract his mind by keeping himself busy.

As he worked cleaning up some of the dead wood his mind wandered back to Lacy. "She's way too young for me anyway," he thought to himself. "What does she want with an old man like me?" he asked himself and laughed. He knew he truly wasn't that old, but he felt old in comparison to Lacy, who was only in her early twenties.

"I'm old enough to be her dad," he said to himself, and with that thought he felt creepy and gross. "But I'm not her dad, of course," he reasoned, "and so get that thought out of your mind," he told himself. Then he thought about her proposal and wondered how that would work if he were to take her up on it.

"So, she wants to marry me and be my submissive sex slave," he thought to himself. "Humm, that could be interesting indeed," he said to himself.

He opted to sit back down on the bench and seriously contemplate Lacy's proposal as she had asked him to. "Just imagine, you've got this sweet young thing that wants to be at your beck and call. Who will have sex with you at the drop of a hat. Anywhere and anytime. Who will wear what you want, or wear nothing at all. All at your command," he thought.

And he had to admit there was a part of him that was greatly intrigued by it all. He'd never really thought of women as mere sex objects, but Lacy's proposal was now making him think that way about her all of a sudden.

He imagined in his mind he and Lacy being married and her having sex with him whenever and wherever he wanted. "Fuck, that does sound good," he thought, rubbing his chin.

He thought about how sexy Lacy was. How, because she was so much younger than him, other men his age would be jealous when they saw him out and about with such a young wife. Then he thought about how annoyed women his own age would be for the same reason. He could just imagine the look of complete disdain on their faces in seeing him with such a young woman, and he laughed at the thought of it.

And the more he thought about it, the more intriguing it became to him.

"Fuck, I think I want to marry her," he said to himself and laughed. Then, he began to masturbate.

However, once he had ejaculated he wasn't so sure it was such a good idea as he suddenly remembered why he needed to stay away from Lacy. He didn't want to ruin his relationship with Louise. It was bad enough that he had already betrayed and lost one good friend, he really didn't want to lose Louise's friendship too. He also didn't want to make Louise his sudden enemy for obvious reasons.

He got up from where he was sitting and began walking back to his house. The ejaculation and the joint were both working to make him feel tired now. As he walked back to his house he thought about all that was going on and wondered how it would all work out in the end.

Chapter Seventeen

Things Are Not as They Appear

Life, once again, seemed somewhat back to normal at Frank's house. He had taken all of the antibiotic the doctor had prescribed to him and his penis seemed back to normal again. He was both relieved and thankful for that fact, and he swore he would never sleep with another prostitute again, including Lacy. Even though, at this point, it seemed it was Ziggy who had given him gonorrhea and not Lacy. Still, he reasoned that they both were prostitutes and he thus needed to follow the doctor's orders and stay away from both of them. He hadn't heard from Lacy, and Ziggy hadn't called again either, and he was thankful for that.

"Maybe the two of them will leave me alone now," he thought as he went about his morning routine. "I can only hope that is the case," he said to himself, thinking about the horrible STD experience he had just endured. How it had hurt so much just to urinate, how a horrible discharge came from the tip of his penis, how his testicles were swollen and sore. It was one of the most horrible experiences Frank had ever had in his life and he didn't want to ever go through such a thing again. As he thought about these things, he reached down and touched his penis "I'm so glad you are all good again," he said and smiled.

He made himself a pot of coffee and sat at his kitchen table. "Wake and bake," he said as he reached for his bag of organic homegrown sitting there and began to roll a joint. Frank didn't always smoke cannabis first thing in the morning, but that morning he felt like he wanted to.

As he sat there drinking his coffee and smoking the cannabis cigarette he had rolled for himself, a knock came on the back door of his house. "Who could that be?" he wondered, as he got up from where he was sitting and went to the dining room to peek out from behind the curtain. "It's Louise. Wonder what she is doing here so early in the morning?" he thought as he quickly went to answer the door.

"Good morning sunshine," he said smiling as he opened the door to Louise. But Louise didn't look happy. In fact, she looked disheveled and worried.

"Frank, I have some bad news,"

"Well come on in and talk to me," Frank said, motioning her inside his home. "Have a seat. I just made a fresh pot of coffee, would you like a cup?" Frank asked.

"Yes please," Louise replied. "Two cream, one sugar in case you forgot," she added.

"I didn't forget," Frank replied, looking over his shoulder at Louise. "I've made coffee for you enough times now that I know what you take," he continued and smiled.

So Frank made Louise a coffee and brought it to her at the kitchen table. "Here you go, sweet thing," Frank said as he set the cup down in front of her and took a seat himself.

Frank was almost afraid to ask Louise what she was obviously so upset about, but he felt he had to. "What's up?" he asked.

But before Louise could even answer, Frank asked her if she wanted him to roll her a cannabis cigarette.

"No, I'm good, but thanks," Louise responded. "I want to be sober-minded when I tell you what I have to tell you. It is not easy for me to tell you this," she continued.

Suddenly Frank felt a surge of anxiety run through his body. He felt fear as to what Louise was about to tell him. "Did she somehow find out about Lacy and I?" he wondered. "Oh God no, that can't be it," he reasoned. Then it dawned on him that it was most likely about Rita, and he wasn't sure he even wanted to hear what Louise had to say.

Louise took a sip of her coffee and looked down at the table. "I think you know what this is about Frank," she said, looking up at him slightly.

"Is it Rita?" Frank asked.

"Yes it is Frank," Louise replied. "Rita has been found guilty, Frank!" she continued.

"WHAT!" Frank exclaimed. "That can't be. How was she found guilty? I don't understand this! There is no way she could have murdered Joe! Her own husband, for goodness sake!" Frank responded.

"I know," Louise agreed. "It's hard to grasp for sure. I heard it on the news just this morning and I thought I'd best come and tell you right away," she continued.

The two of them sat there at the kitchen table in complete silence as if neither of them knew what to say next. Frank leaned his elbows on the table and held his head in his hands. Finally, he looked over at Louise, who was just sitting there looking down at the table.

"What the fuck," Frank blurted out.

"I know," Louise agreed.

"So tell me more," Frank said. "What exactly did they say on the news?"

"Well," Louise replied. "They really didn't say all that much. Just that Rita had opted to plead guilty to the lesser charge of manslaughter," Louise continued.

"Oh my God," Frank said. "This is crazy. I mean, this is completely crazy," he added.

Frank's mind was now swirling with what felt like a thousand different thoughts. "Why would Rita plead guilty?" he wondered. "None of this makes any sense," he reasoned.

"I hated to come here this morning to tell you all of this Frank, but I felt at the same time that you needed to know," Louise said.

"Yes, I did need to know and thank you for coming over to tell me. Even though it is news I would rather not have heard," he continued. "I just don't understand why Rita plead guilty!" he added.

"I don't either," Louise replied. "None of this makes any sense," Frank responded.

"I know," Louise agreed, reaching for Frank's hand across the table. "Maybe there will be more information in time," Louise continued. "Because you are right, none of this makes any sense," she continued.

"Are you okay Frank?" Louise asked.

"Oh, I'm okay I guess," Frank replied while trying to force a small smile on his face.

"I know this must be really hard for you to hear," Louise continued. "I wanted to be the one to tell you versus you hearing it on the television or radio news," she added.

Just then it occurred to Frank that this was going to be all over the news and people in the area where he lived would all see and hear about it, and great fear began to well up inside of him.

"Oh my God Louise, this is too horrible for words," he said, suddenly feeling a sense of panic coming over him.

At that, Louise reached into her purse and retrieved her bottle of anti-anxiety pills. She opened the bottle and retrieved one.

"Here Frank," she said, passing him the pill.

"Oh thank you," Frank replied. "I really do need one right now. I still have a couple left of the ones you gave me. I almost took one once, but if there was ever a time when I needed one, it is right now," Frank continued, holding his hand out to receive the pill.

"Thank you so much Louise," Frank said as he put the pill under his tongue. "You've always been such a dear, sweet, and good friend," he continued, getting up from his seat to hug Louise while she was still sitting down.

"It's okay Frank," Louise replied. "That's what friends do. They help and care for one another," she added while smiling and engaging in Frank's embrace.

Frank sat back down in his chair and rubbed his chin. "I think I need another smoke," he said, reaching for his bag of cannabis and his papers. "Are you sure you won't join me?" he asked.

"No, I can't right now," Louise responded. "Like you, I am feeling a lot of anxiety over all of this. I am sure it is not the level of anxiety you are feeling, but yea, I am feeling anxiety over it all for sure," she added.

Frank rolled himself another cannabis cigarette and began to smoke it. He didn't usually smoke so much early in the morning, but he now had a good excuse in his mind to smoke more than he usually would. As he hauled back on his cannabis cigarette, he realized his coffee cup was almost empty and the coffee that was left was now cold.

"I'm going to make another pot of coffee," he said, getting up from the table and walking towards the kitchen counter.

"Yes," Louise responded. "I'll take another cup too if you don't mind," she said and smiled.

"I don't mind at all," Frank replied.

He thought he could feel the medication Louise had given him kicking in, but he wasn't sure if maybe he was just getting high from the cannabis he was smoking. Then he remembered Louise telling him that it takes about twenty minutes for the medication to kick in, so he reasoned it was the joint that was making him feel more relaxed.

Rather than going back to sit down at the table to wait for the coffee to brew, Frank just stood there at the kitchen counter, hands on the counter, head down, watching the coffee machine brew the coffee. He was taking the time watching the coffee brew to try to clear his mind of the news Louise had just relayed to him. He felt like his mind was being blown and his brain just could not accept the information Louise had told him.

"Is she sure that is what she heard?" he wondered. "I hope and pray she is wrong about this," he thought. "This is so wild. I can't even get my head around it," he said to himself.

But he knew Louise, and he thus knew that she would not lie to him about such a thing, so he reasoned that yes, it was true. Still, he couldn't understand how or why.

Soon the coffee was ready and Frank served Louise first. "Here yea go," he said, setting the fresh cup of coffee on the table in front of her.

Louise looked up and smiled. "You're the best Frank," she said. "Thank you," she added.

Then Frank got his own cup of coffee and sat back down with Louise at his kitchen table once again. He wasn't sure what more to talk about. They didn't have enough information about Rita's situation to have a real discussion. Plus, Frank wasn't even sure he wanted to talk about it at all anyway. In fact, he was quite sure he didn't want to talk or even think about any of it.

And it wasn't much longer when the medication Louise had given him had started to work and he suddenly felt totally and absolutely relaxed.

"The medication you gave to me is kicking in now," he told Louise.

Louise smiled. "Happy to help Frank," she said.

"Yea, I am feeling very relaxed now," Frank added.

"Good," Louise replied. "I knew this was going to be really hard for you to hear. That is why I came over to tell you myself and to be here with you. I knew this news might send you into another panic attack and I wanted to be here in case it did," she added.

"You are such a good friend," Frank responded, looking very serious and reaching for Louise's hand across the table. "I don't know what I would ever do without you Louise," he said while squeezing her hand a little. "I want you to know you mean the world to me," he continued. "You've always been such a good friend for all these years I have known you," he added.

Louise suddenly felt shy and nervous and looked down towards the floor. She wasn't good at taking compliments, and Frank's words made her feel embarrassed for some reason. She could feel her face getting hot and she knew it must be turning red.

"Are you embarrassed?" Frank asked her, noting that her face was now red as a beet.

"Yea, a little bit I guess," Louise said, looking up slightly at Frank and smiling. "I'm not good at taking compliments," she continued. "But thank you," she added.

"It's all true Louise," Frank replied. "You're a really good person and I am so glad and blessed to have you in my life all these years. I know you probably wanted more from me in terms of a relationship, but I feel our strong bond of friendship is even more special than anything like that," he continued.

Louise didn't respond, she just smiled. Frank knew she had always wanted more from him and he oftentimes wondered over the years why she had stuck around all this time. He knew the relationship between the two of them was not what Louise desired, but it was all he had to offer her, and he was happy that she had accepted it.

"Maybe I will have a smoke now," Louise said smiling.

"Really! Okay, good," Frank said, reaching for his bag of cannabis and papers. "I will get right on that then," he added as he began to roll a smoke for Louise. He was happy Louise was now opting to smoke with him, and he opted to roll himself yet another joint as well.

"Wow, I am really smoking them back this morning," he said smiling as he rolled a joint for each of them.

Louise giggled. "That is not like you Frank, is it?" she asked.

"No, no, not at all. I don't usually smoke this much this early," Frank replied and smiled.

And so the two of them sat there at Frank's kitchen table, each smoking their individual joint and not really saying much of anything.

"I really enjoy your smoke," Louise finally said as she exhaled the smoke from her mouth.

Frank smiled. "I'm glad. I really enjoy it too," he agreed, and the two of them busted out laughing.

"Only problem is," Louise added. "It has a tendency to make me horny when I smoke it," she added, looking at Frank and smiling.

"It's my secret weapon," Frank said, smiling a big smile. "Oops, I guess it is not secret anymore," he added, and the two of them started laughing again.

Louise lightly slapped Frank on the leg. "You're silly," she said, smiling.

"I know," Frank replied. "That's why you like hanging out with me," he added and smiled.

"That and your delicious penis," Louise replied.

She couldn't believe she had just said that. And with that, Frank now had a shocked look on his face but he was still kind of smiling.

"Say what?" Frank asked.

Then the two of them started laughing once again.

"Are we having a good time now?" Frank asked.

"We sure are," Louise replied while grinning and taking another deep haul.

"Do you want to have some fun Frank?" Louise asked, looking down at her large breasts and shaking them a little, which took Frank's attention directly there.

"This is perfect," he said to himself. "Making out with Louise will get my mind off the news about Rita. Plus I've not had sex with Louise in awhile now and I miss it," he reasoned.

"Take me Frank," Louise said. "I'm all yours baby," she added, smiling a big smile and pushing her breasts forward. Louise knew that above all Frank loved her breasts.

"Ummm," Frank thought and licked his lips while gazing at Louise's breasts.

"I'll take you, no problem," he replied, getting up from his seat and taking Louise by the hand, leading her upstairs to his bedroom.

However, halfway up the stairs he remembered the STD and wondered if he should even be having sex. "What if the STD has not totally cleared up yet," he thought. And even with the medication Louise had given him, he started to feel a ping of anxiety.

"Come on," he told himself, "you know it is gone now. You took all the medication like the doctor told you to. It has not been hurting to pee. You don't have any gross discharge coming from your penis and your testicles are no longer swollen and hurting. You know it is gone," he reminded himself.

Still though, he was feeling very apprehensive. "I am now thinking I should call this all off," he said to himself. "I may be cured of that horrible STD, but what if I were to give that to Louise?" he thought. "I could not bear something like that happening," he said to himself.

And his penis that had been hard and at attention had suddenly gone soft. In fact, his penis now felt like it was shrinking. Sweat began to form on his forehead and his head began to swirl.

"What do I do now?" he asked himself. "Louise is wanting and expecting to have sex with me. I can't just turn her down, can I?" he thought. "What possible excuse could I tell her?" he asked himself, and he found himself not having a clue as to what to do next.

Then just as they were about to enter Frank's bedroom, he realized that Rita's panties were laying on his bed.

"Wait here for a second," he told Louise. "I just need to tidy up the room a little before you come in," he continued.

So Louise did as Frank asked and stood outside his bedroom door.

Frank picked up Rita's underwear with one finger and held them up in the air. He remembered Rita giving them to him as a reminder of her that morning before Joe and her left. He remembered how happy he felt to have them and how he had sniffed them over and over after she was gone and jerked off with them laying on his face.

By impulse he smelled them once again. "Oh Rita," he thought. "I so wish none of this was happening to you," he said to himself. "I miss you and I pray that things turn around for you," he continued. He sniffed the underwear once again and placed them back inside the drawer and just when he did he saw his clean pillowcases laying there. And so he proceeded to change the pillowcases on his bed.

"There," he finally said to himself. "My bed is clean and fresh again."

But he still hadn't decided if it was a good idea or not to have sex with Louise. "How long has it been since I completed that medication?" he thought and he realized it had only been a couple of days.

"Oh man, what do I do now?" he said to himself. "I don't want Louise to feel rejected. That's the last thing I want! But I am quite sure she will feel rejected if I suddenly tell her I can't have sex with her! She is waiting to have sex with me!" he thought. "What in fuck do I do now?" he asked himself. But he had no immediate answer.

Just then Louise yelled from the hallway.

"Frank, are you okay? What is taking you so long?"

Louise was growing impatient at what seemed to her to be taking too long to tidy up his room.

"It's all good now. Come along," Frank yelled back.

As Louise entered Frank's bedroom she had a sense that something wasn't quite right. Something just wasn't the same. "Something feels off in here," she said.

"What? Off! What do you mean?" Frank asked. "It's my bedroom, you've been in here many times," he continued, now taking her by the waist and kissing her neck.

"Yea, I know I have been in here many times, but the air or something in here smells different and the atmosphere just seems different," she continued.

Frank immediately thought of the rotten smell of the discharge that had come from the end of his penis. He wondered if that might be the strange smell that Louise was smelling.

"Well, the sheets are all clean," he said smiling and putting his hand out towards the bed. "And I even changed the pillowcases," he added, smiling.

"Okay Frank," Louise replied. "Maybe it's just my imagination or something. Maybe it has been too long since the last time I was here in your bedroom, and that's why it feels off to me," she added, winking at Frank. "Shall I get undressed for you?" she asked.

"By all means, please do," Frank responded, and with that he laid down on the bed to watch Louise get undressed.

Louise was trying to be sexy in the way she undressed herself in front of Frank, and Frank was staring at her intently while she did. And even though he was smiling at her at the time, his mind was still caught up in the fact of his recent case of gonorrhea.

"Get that shit out of your mind you dumb ass. You're not going to be able to even have sex with her if you keep thinking about that shit," he told himself.

But Louise didn't notice. She was caught up in undressing herself for Frank and looking as sexy as possible. And the more she exposed herself, the less Frank was preoccupied by the worry of the recent STD situation.

"Come here you," Frank said, reaching for Louise's hand and pulling her down on the bed on top of him, and the two of them started making out with each other.

They had sex and then suddenly Louise realized the time and said she had to leave.

Frank really didn't want Louise to leave. He didn't want to be alone with his thoughts, and he felt that if Louise was there, he could be distracted by other things. But he understood that Louise had to leave, and so the two of them said their goodbyes at the back door of Frank's house, and Louise commenced walking toward her vehicle.

"Listen, if you hear any more about, you know, let me know okay!" Frank yelled as Louise departed.

"Yes I will Frank. Don't worry, okay, and try your best not to think about it too much," she added. "Remember what I told you about controlling your thoughts in terms of panic attacks," she continued, looking back slightly at him standing in the doorway of his house.

"Yes, I remember," he replied smiling. "I will do as you told me, or at least I will try to," he added.

Louise got into her vehicle and waved to Frank as she exited his driveway. Frank waved back and smiled, still standing in the doorway watching her leave. Once she was out of sight, he shut the door and walked back into his kitchen, which suddenly felt very empty. But it wasn't only his kitchen that felt empty. He felt empty as well.

"You just had great sex with Louise and now you feel empty," he said to himself. "How can that be?" he wondered.

It was at that moment that fear suddenly gripped him and he realized he had wanted Louise to stay because somehow he felt that would ensure she did not get the horrible STD that he had had. "That makes no sense," he said to himself, but regardless he was feeling it anyway. He felt that somehow if he kept her there with him, she wouldn't contract the horrible virus.

"Am I going crazy?" he asked himself. "This is not reasonable thinking," he said to himself and shook his head in an attempt to get his thoughts straight again.

"Should I smoke yet another joint?" he asked himself, but at the same time he really didn't feel like smoking a joint right then and there. "Maybe I should go put in a movie," he thought. "Maybe that will help distract my mind from all of this," he said to himself.

It was just then that he remembered he was all out of cream for his coffee and that he would have to go to the store. "I don't want to leave the house," he thought. "I have no desire to go out into the community. What if people have seen the news and realize that is the couple who were here visiting at my house just a short time ago," he thought, and with that thought the idea of having to go to the local store to buy cream felt like a monumental task.

Yet, he knew he had to do it. It was either that or go without cream in his coffee, and he didn't even want to think of that prospect. Frank loved his coffee and he had to have all the right ingredients in his home at all times.

He sat there at his kitchen table and it felt to him, once again, that he was glued to the chair. "I have to get up and get ready and go to the store to buy some cream," he said to himself. "Come on, you can do it," he told himself.

And slowly he got up from where he was seated and went to the bathroom to inspect himself before leaving the house. He fixed his hair, threw some water on his face and dried it. He fixed his clothes and went to put on his jacket.

"You can do this," he told himself once again as he exited the door of his house and headed towards his truck parked in the driveway.

Once at the local store he could tell from the number of cars parked in the parking lot that quite a few people from the community were inside the store and this made him feel even more anxious.

"Just focus on what you need to get. Go straight to where the cream is located, get it, pay for it and get out of there as quickly as you can," he told himself as he parked his truck in one of the parking spaces and turned off the ignition.

Fear was now gripping Frank, but he knew he had to push through it. He didn't want to sit there in the parking lot in his truck. He figured that would only draw more attention to himself, as people might wonder what he was doing just sitting there.

So he put his hand on the door handle, opened the door and exited his truck.

Walking towards the store he kept on repeating, "Just stay focused. You can do this. Try to act normal."

He noticed he was walking unusually fast and so he immediately slowed himself down to a normal walk as he entered the store.

As soon as he entered the store it seemed to Frank that everyone turned and gawked at him, but he pretended not to notice and went directly to where the cream was located.

"Just ignore everyone. Pretend like you don't even see them," he said to himself as he took the cream down from the shelf.

"Maybe I should buy two of them, or even three so that I don't have to go through this again for a while," he thought. And so he opted to buy two because he reasoned that if he bought three, the third one might go bad before he had a chance to consume it.

As he walked down the aisle toward the checkout, he noticed there was a line of people waiting to be checked out. One lady he observed had a huge cart full of food, which he knew would take a long time to process.

"What do I do?" he wondered. "I don't want to stay in this store any longer than I have to.".

And just then, another cashier opened up shouting, "I can help someone over here," she said, raising her hand in the air to alert people. Frank quickly started walking toward the newly opened checkout, but to his dismay other people who were closer had already gotten in line.

It was then that he noticed one of the town's biggest gossip bags standing last in the line. "What luck is that?" he said to himself, but he had no choice but to stand directly behind her, for he thought if he didn't it would look suspicious and he didn't want to raise any suspicion.

As he stood there in the line, he noticed the magazine rack situated along the line of the checkout, and right on the front page was a picture of Joe and another picture of Rita. The headline read, *"Found Guilty for the Murder of Her Husband."*

"What the fuck," Frank thought. "This is too bizarre," he said to himself, and he tried not to look at the magazine for fear that the woman in front of him would notice.

But it was too late. She had already noticed him looking and she reached over and grabbed the magazine, taking it out from the rack.

"Well look at that," she said, not looking up when she spoke, her eyes fixated on the pictures. Then she lowered the magazine and looked directly at Frank.

"Isn't that the couple that stayed at your place?" she asked.

Frank's mind went completely blank. He just stood there not knowing what to say.

"I know it is the people that stayed at your place," she continued, putting the magazine back in the spot she took it from.

Frank was still silent. He felt like he couldn't speak.

"What's the matter?" the woman asked. "Cat got your tongue,?" she continued and smiled. "Everyone in town knows that they were the people that stayed at your house!" she added, implying to Frank that there was no point in him trying to deny it.

Finally Frank found his voice. "Ah yea, that's right," he responded. "They are the people that stayed at my house. Yup! It's a very sad and unfortunate situation," he continued. "Not sure too much about it, but I don't think this is the truth of it all and that is all I have to say on the subject," he added, trying to force a smile.

"Yea, people in town also think there's a lot more to the story," she said, winking at Frank.

"Oh God, what does she mean by that?" Frank wondered, and he felt strong anxiety suddenly welling up inside of him.

Just then it was time for the woman to put her items on the counter to be counted and paid for, and so she was distracted from further conversation. Frank was relieved that she could no longer question him or torture him with her gossip. Once she was finished paying for her items, she looked back at Frank and smiled a snotty smile

"See yea later Frank," she said as she walked away to exit the store.

Frank wanted to buy a copy of that magazine, but he didn't want to draw any more attention to the situation than already existed. According to the woman he had just spoken to, everyone in town was already aware that Rita and Joe were the people who had visited him. So he opted not to buy the magazine.

"Maybe I could drive to the city and buy it there," he reasoned. But he wasn't sure he wanted to take the long drive into the city just to buy the magazine. Just then he thought of a possible solution. "I'll get Louise to come over here and buy it. Sure, people know Louise and I are friends, and no doubt they assume more is happening between us as with all the gossip and rumors; but they don't know that Louise knows Rita and did know Joe," he thought to himself

And with that he paid for his items and exited the store.

As he drove back to his home he wondered about what that woman had said. "Does everyone in the town know that Rita and Joe are the people that stayed at my house?" he wondered.

"Fuck, I hope not," he thought. "But even if they do, it's no big deal. They are just people I know! What happened has nothing to do with me!" he reasoned, in an effort to calm his troubled mind.

"The important thing is, no one knows about the affair between Rita and I, thanks be to God," he said to himself. "Now, that would be really bad and I may have to sell my house and leave here if that were ever to get out," he thought.

And the mere thought of anyone knowing that truth made him feel weak and unstable in his body.

Once at his house he quickly parked and exited his truck as if he was afraid someone was going to see him. He entered his house and put the cream he had purchased in the fridge and sat down at his kitchen table.

"I could make a fresh pot of coffee now," he said to himself, but suddenly he felt really tired. So tired in fact, he wondered if he even had the energy to walk upstairs to his bedroom, so he opted to only walk as far as the couch. He laid down on his couch and thought about getting up to put in a movie, but he just couldn't bring himself to get up off the couch to do it.

He grabbed the blanket that he kept on the back of the couch and covered himself up. "Just go to sleep," he told himself. "This too shall pass," he thought. He was worn out by the news Louise had given him that morning, plus the medication she had given him. It had all caught up with him now and he was feeling totally exhausted, so he quickly fell asleep.

Frank wasn't sure how long he had been sleeping when he was awakened by the sound of the telephone ringing. He pulled himself out of his sleeping posture and got up to check to see who was calling. It was Louise, so he opted to pick up the phone.

"Hey!" he said, answering the phone.

"Hey," Louise responded. "I was just calling to check up on you. Just wanted to make sure you were okay," she said.

"Oh yea, I'm okay," Frank replied. "I was just sleeping," he continued.

"Oh, well I will let you go then so you can go back to resting. You probably need rest," she added.

"No, I'm good now," Frank replied.

Just then Frank remembered the magazine. "Hey, I have a favour to ask of you," he said.

"Oh, what's that?" Louise asked.

"I had to go to the store this afternoon for some cream and when I was there I saw a magazine on the rack right by the checkout line, and you're not going to believe this, but the situation between Rita and Joe is the headline on the rag!" he continued.

"Oh my," Louise responded. "I had no idea!" she continued. "But it makes sense really!" she added. "After all, he was a big-time businessman and all!" she continued.

"Yea, I guess eh," Frank said. "I'd never really considered their social status I guess. I just always knew Joe as my buddy and never thought about his life in terms of the big picture," Frank continued.

"But anyway, I was wondering if you could go over there and buy that magazine and bring it to me? I will pay you for it," Frank asked. "I didn't want to buy it when I was there as I didn't want to draw any attention, if you see what I mean," he added.

"Yes, I can do that for you, but it won't be until later as I am in the middle of something right now," Louise replied.

"Oh, no worries," Frank said. "Just when you get a chance. I would really appreciate it," he added. And at that, the two of them said goodbye and ended the call.

Once off the phone, Louise was curious about what Frank had just told her, and even though she had told him she was busy at the moment, she opted to drop what she was doing and go directly to the store to buy the magazine.

Once in the store Louise went directly to the magazine racks. She looked on the first rack at the first checkout station, but she didn't see anything there. So she kept on walking past each checkout to see if she could find it and then suddenly she saw it.

Upon seeing the front-page pictures of both Rita and Joe separately and one of them together, along with the headline *MURDER,* her eyes grew wide with shock even though she knew prior to seeing it. She quickly grabbed the magazine from the rack and proceeded to the checkout.

The cashier picked up the magazine and rang it through, pretending not to notice what was on the front of it. "That will be five dollars and sixty cents," she said, holding out her hand for the money to pay for the magazine.

Louise had put the money to pay for the magazine directly in her pocket before she entered the store so that she would not have to dig in her purse for it, and so she passed a ten-dollar bill to the cashier.

"Do you need a bag?" the cashier asked, suddenly smiling.

Louise wasn't sure how to respond. It was obvious she didn't need a bag.

"No, that's fine," she said, trying to force a smile back at the cashier.

"Oh, I just thought you might want to hide that magazine cover," the cashier said, passing the magazine to Louise.

"Oh my God," Louise thought. "She knows these are the people who stayed at Frank's place. I wonder if Frank knows that people in town know that Rita and Joe are the people who visited him?" she wondered.

Louise took the magazine from the woman, forced a half-smile, and exited the store. All the way driving back to her house she wondered what was written about the case inside that magazine. She knew she was supposed to take the magazine directly to Frank, but she just didn't want to. She wanted to take it home and read it first.

As soon as she was in the door of her house she sat down at the kitchen table and looked up the article inside the magazine. The index said to go to page two for the story, and so she did, and there it was. A full two-page article on the case!

Louise sat there mesmerized by all the information written there on the pages. The article gave background information on both Rita and Joe, but mostly on Joe since he was a big-time wealthy businessman. Louise was astonished to find out just how wealthy Joe and Rita truly were. Frank had never told her how economically well off they were, and she wondered why.

The article then went into the case against Rita and how Joe had died of a sleeping pill overdose and how the prescription for the pills was in Rita's name. Upon seeing this, Louise was in shock and she wondered if Frank already knew this information, and if he did why he had not told her.

Then she continued reading. The article spoke of how Rita's lawyers argued that just because the prescription was in Rita's name didn't mean that Rita had given the pills to Joe, and that Joe had a habit of taking Rita's pills in order to sleep. However, the prosecution argued that Rita had been drugging Joe for some time and that she had intentionally given him too many pills that night as she intended to murder him by doing so.

They said her motives were that she would inherit all of Joe's wealth and life insurance money, which was in the millions of dollars, plus that her motivation was one of revenge and greed as Joe was married to his work and had hence neglected Rita much of the time. The article also said they had testimony from some of the house staff that supported their allegations, as well as hard evidence to prove their case. But the article neglected to state what the hard evidence was that they had.

"Wow," Louise thought. "Who knows if all of this is even true," she thought, once she was finished reading. "These rags make all kinds of claims," she added. But at the same time, it all seemed pretty legitimate and reasonable, she had to admit.

"I had better take this magazine over to Frank," she reasoned. "He will want to know this information," she added. Still, she couldn't quite grasp the entire situation and she began to think back to when Rita and Joe were at Frank's house.

"Was Rita drugging Joe when she was at Frank's place?" she wondered. And the mere thought of that sent shivers down her spine. "Was Joe drugged the night we all had sex together?" she asked herself, but she already knew the answer to that question as it had come out while she was there that night.

"Oh God, this is horrible," she said to herself. And guilt suddenly came over her like a river. "Was I part of this whole thing?" she asked herself, but she could not bear to answer the question she had just posed to herself.

Her mind now was fixated on the cause of death and she once again wondered if Frank knew the details of Joe's death as described in the article. She had asked him early on what he knew about the situation, but he had told her he didn't know anything. However, Louise was now questioning the validity of what Frank had previously told her.

"If he spoke to Rita, chances are he knew a lot more than he was letting on to me," she reasoned. And she wondered why Frank would keep that information from her, if he did know. "Why would he not tell me those details?" she questioned.

Then it dawned on her that Frank didn't want to bring up the sleeping pills. "Oh, now I know why he didn't tell me," she said to herself. "And truly, it's just as well," she thought. Since she herself had engaged in sex with Rita and Frank that night while Joe was drugged on sleeping pills just down the hall in another bedroom. She shuddered to even think about it.

"Pull yourself together Louise," she said to herself, now sitting up straight in the chair and fixing her hair. "You have to be strong for Frank. You can't go over to his place in a big mess. That is not going to help him or you," she told herself, getting up from where she was sitting and going to look in the mirror in her bathroom

"Okay, you can do this," she told herself, looking in the mirror, and with that she grabbed the magazine, her keys, and her purse and headed out the door to go to Frank's house.

As she pulled into the driveway of Frank's place she suddenly wondered if she should have called first since Frank could be sleeping. He had been sleeping when she had called him earlier, and she knew the medication she had given him made people sleepy.

"I'll just knock lightly," she thought to herself as she parked her vehicle and walked toward the back door of Frank's house. "If he doesn't answer right away, I'll just leave and come back later," she reasoned.

But Frank was up and around and heard Louise's knock on his door right away and, without even thinking about who it was (which was unusual for Frank these days), he went straight to answer the door. Frank was happy to see it was Louise and he smiled a big smile. He also immediately saw that she had the magazine in hand.

"Here yea go, Frank," Louise said, passing him the magazine.

Frank reached out and took the magazine. "Thanks so much, Louise, I really appreciate it. What do I owe you?"

"Oh, it was around five dollars, but don't worry about it. You can buy me a coffee sometime," she replied, smiling.

"No, no, I want to pay you for it. I'm the one who asked you to go get it for me," Frank responded. "Come on in and have a seat and I'll get the money," Frank added.

And so the two of them entered into Frank's kitchen and Louise took a seat at the kitchen table while Frank went to retrieve the five dollars he owed her for the magazine.

"Here yea go," he said, passing Louise a five-dollar bill.

Louise took the bill and smiled. "You really didn't have to pay me for it," she replied, smiling. "I can afford five dollars, you know," she added and laughed a little.

"Oh, I know you can," Frank replied. "But that's not the point. The point is, I am the one who asked you to go and buy it and so yeah, I feel like I need to pay you for it," he continued.

Louise put the money in her wallet. "Yea, I get it, Frank," she said. "Don't worry about it," she added.

"So did you read the article in the magazine?" Frank asked her, smiling.

Louise looked kind of shocked, but then she opted to just be honest with Frank that she had taken the magazine home first to read it prior to bringing it to him.

"I figured as much," Frank said, smiling. "And I don't blame yea. I probably would have done the same," he added. And the two of them started laughing. Yet, they both knew at the same point that this was no laughing matter.

Louise really wanted to ask Frank if he knew that Joe had died from a sleeping pill overdose, but she wasn't sure it was a good idea. She was thinking it could stir things up for her as well as Frank and she didn't want to do that. So she opted instead to say, "I think you will find the article very interesting."

"Oh yea!" Frank replied. "I hope it's not too interesting though," he continued.

Louise wasn't quite sure what Frank meant by that comment, but she opted not to question it.

"Yeah, for one thing, I had no idea how wealthy Joe and Rita were!" she replied. "Apparently, they were rolling in the dough," she said, smiling.

"Yea, yea, for sure," Frank responded, smiling back at her. "I always just saw Joe as Joe. You know, my good buddy from University days. I guess I never thought of his big life in the city and the fact that he was filthy rich," Frank added, smiling. "I mean, I always knew he was not in any way hurting for cash, I just never saw him as anything but my buddy, I guess. If that makes any sense," he added.

"Coming from you, Frank, it makes perfect sense," Lousie replied, and smiled. "Most people would have been bragging about their rich and quasi-famous friend, trying to make themselves look like better people from having such a friend as that. But not you, Frank. I know you're not like that. You just take people as people and that is one of the sweet things about you," she added.

Then she went on to say, "Plus you're not one for bragging about all that you have accomplished in your life, and all that you have as the result of your hard work over many years," she continued.

Frank just sat there listening to her. He wasn't used to people acknowledging his accomplishments or his hard work over the years. People rarely ever complimented him on his achievements or having reached his goals, so the words Louise spoke felt kind of foreign to him, as if she was maybe speaking about someone else.

"Even my own family don't acknowledge those things, Louise," Frank replied. "So thank you so much for saying that. It really means a lot that you notice and acknowledge that," he continued, getting up from the table to give Louise a hug.

Louise had no idea that her words would mean so much to Frank. It was as if she had just told him something major, when in her mind it was just common knowledge and truth. Yet, she could tell from Frank's response to her words that Frank had deep wounds about such matters, and she suddenly felt pain in her heart for him.

Louise then realized that she had never considered that Frank might have such wounds. She had always seen him as this very strong and accomplished person, who was totally self-assured, highly intelligent, responsible, and ultra-stable. Now, she was seeing yet another side of him and it hurt her heart to see and feel his obvious pain.

"Some people are dumb," Louise finally said in a strong tone of voice, as if reprimanding those who had not been kind to Frank.

"It's okay, Louise," Frank replied, smiling. "I've learned to deal with it over the years by just staying away from people. It's all good," he added. "I realized many years ago now, that what people say and do is on them, not me," he added.

"No, it's not alright," Louise replied. "It is mean and hateful," she added. "And I believe the reason people act like that is because they are jealous of you," she continued.

"Yea, maybe," Frank replied. "But I really don't want to talk about it all right now. I try not to think about it. I let go of it all a long time ago," he continued. "But yea, obviously it still hurts at points," he added.

At that moment, Louise felt great compassion for Frank. She realized that while she had known Frank for many years, she only knew him in the context of their relationship and the truth of that struck her deeply. She wondered if her entire relationship with Frank had not just been this superficial sex thing with no real depth, and the mere thought of that made her feel sad. But then she remembered all the times that she and Frank had had deep discussions about many different subjects, and that even though she maybe did not know him as deeply emotionally as she would have liked to, she was positive that they had a friendship that was deeper than just casual sex. And with those thoughts, she felt somewhat better about the situation.

"I'd love to stay and hang out with yea, Frank, but I really have to get going," Louise said, looking at her watch.

"Oh, no worries," Frank replied. "Thanks for coming by and bringing me the magazine," he added, smiling.

Frank was itching to read the article in the magazine, so he was happy that Louise had to get going.

Frank walked Louise to the back door of his house and just as she was exiting the house, he grabbed her and hugged her once again.

"Thanks again, Louise, for acknowledging me, my worth, my achievements, accomplishments, and hard work. It really means a lot to me," he said.

Louise hugged Frank tight. "I meant every word of it," she said. "It's all true and you know it's all true. Be proud of yourself. You deserve every good thing you have and will have," she added.

Frank squeezed Louise one more time in their embrace and then the two of them separated.

"I'll call you later," Louise said as she walked down the steps towards her vehicle.

"Okay, please do, if you have time that is and feel like it," he added.

Frank shut the back door of his house and quickly returned to his kitchen. "I'm going to make a fresh cup of coffee and sit down here and read this article," he said to himself.

But he couldn't wait for the coffee to brew before he opened the magazine and began to read the article. As he read, he realized that Joe was far more successful than he had realized, and he saw where the prosecution was zeroing in on Joe's wealth as part of the motive as to why Rita had murdered him.

The feelings of shock ran through his body. "Rita wouldn't kill Joe for his wealth," he reasoned. "Why would she do that? She had access to all his wealth regardless if he were alive or dead," he thought to himself as he read.

He saw where the prosecution were accusing Rita of having drugged Joe intentionally, arguing she had given him an overdose of sleeping pills. Suddenly, his mind went back to when Rita and Joe were there at his home. How Rita gave Joe sleeping pills to knock him out, so the two of them could have wild sex without worry of Joe hearing them, or worse catching them in the act.

And suddenly he felt sick to his stomach and ran to the bathroom to puke.

As he returned to the kitchen, he made himself a coffee and sat down once again to finish reading the article. "This is insane," he said to himself. "Maybe she is guilty," he reasoned. "Maybe she did kill Joe on purpose!" he thought. But the thought of that possibility was too much for him to bear.

"Did I have sex with a murderer?" he wondered, and he just couldn't bring himself to believe that Rita was capable of such a horrible thing as murder. "Despite Rita's actions while she was here, I think she did love Joe. She seemed to love him," he reasoned. "Sure, she flirted with me and had sex with me behind his back, but I still think she loved him," he thought. "And I never had any feeling, nor did I see any evidence, that she wanted to murder him," he continued.

It was at that moment that the thought occurred to him that maybe Rita murdered Joe so that she could be with him. And with that thought, he spit his coffee out all over the magazine article. He jumped up and grabbed some paper towel from his kitchen counter and dabbed it on the magazine in an attempt to dry up the coffee before it ruined the page and the article. He wasn't sure he wanted to keep the magazine, but for now he at least wanted to finish reading it.

He managed to get the coffee off of the magazine article and continued to read. "I don't think Rita had a very good lawyer," he said to himself. "Surely, there is evidence the lawyer could have used to clear Rita from this horrific allegation and charge," he thought. But the more he read, the more he was convinced that Rita was going to jail for a long time, whether she was guilty as charged or not. And the thought of that distinct possibility made him feel tremendous sadness inside and he began to weep, and the tears rolled down his cheeks like a river that was turning into a flood.

Frank was crying not just because of the situation with Rita and all that surrounded it. He was crying for everything that had happened from the time Rita and Joe had come to visit. He tried to stop crying and pull himself together, but it was no use. The tears just kept on coming and coming, and it seemed there was nothing he could do to stop them.

It felt strange to Frank that he was crying so hard and for what seemed to him to be so long, as Frank was not a person to cry easily. In fact, he rarely cried, so this situation felt very strange to him. Yet, due to all that had been happening, it seemed he had been crying a lot in the past while. And in this context, he reasoned he was crying for good reason and he opted to just let it happen, since he realized there was truly no way to stop it.

Just then the phone rang and startled Frank out of his deep emotional state. He looked up from where he was sitting over to where the phone was. "Do I answer it?" he thought. "No, I can't answer it right now," he said to himself. "I'm a mess and I can't bear to speak to anyone right now," he added. So he put his head back down and continued to cry.

The answering machine came on, but Frank couldn't hear what was being said or who was saying it because of the sound of his fervent crying. "I'll listen to it later," he thought, and with that he continued to cry. He cried so much and for so long, he felt that there was no water left inside his body. It seemed to him that hours had passed by while he was sitting there crying, when in reality it had not been all that long.

He felt drained and exhausted from all the crying, but he wanted now to check to see who had called and what their message was on his answering machine. So, he got up from where he was sitting and walked over to his answering machine and pushed the play button.

"Hey Frank, it's just me, Louise. I was just calling to check up on you. I know the information in that article is hard to take. It bothered me too when I read it, so I can only imagine how it is making you feel. I hope you are okay. And I also have more news, but I don't want to say it on this machine. So call me when you get this message, okay," and with that she ended the message.

Frank wasn't sure he wanted to hear any more news regarding Rita and Joe. In fact, he knew he didn't, but curiosity got the best of him and he picked up the phone to call Louise back.

Louise answered on the first ring, as if she was right there waiting for Frank to call her back. "Hi Frank," she said as she answered the phone. "Are you okay?" she asked before he even had a chance to speak.

"Yea, I'm okay I guess," Frank responded. "You are right though, reading that article took a lot out of me. I'm kind of ashamed to say it, but I've been sitting here crying up a storm," he advised.

"Awe, I'm so sorry, Frank," Louise replied in a compassionate tone of voice.

"So what's the news you wanted to tell me, Louise?" Frank asked.

Louise took a deep breath. "I'm not sure that now is a good time to tell you. You sound like you are already in a state and I don't want to add to it," she replied. "Maybe you should take another one of the calming pills I gave to you," Louise suggested. "I'm okay, Louise, just tell me. You have me all curious now. Just spit it out," he responded.

"Okay then," Louise said. "It's more news on Rita, Frank. The sentencing has just come out on the news and the judge in the case has sentenced her to ten years in a maximum security prison!" she continued.

"Ten years!" Frank exclaimed. "Wow, she must be beside herself right now!" he added.

And at hearing that news Frank almost dropped the phone.

"Are you still there, Frank?" Louise finally asked after a few seconds of silence.

"Yea, I am here," Frank responded, but he wasn't truly sure he was still there. He felt like he had somehow left his body and was floating above somewhere.

"I can come over, Frank, if you need me to," Louise offered.

"No, no, I'm okay," Frank replied. "I think I just need to lay down and maybe I will take another one of those pills. I am not feeling well at all," Frank continued.

"Okay, go and get some rest, Frank, and yes take another one of those pills. Don't worry about taking them, I have lots and I can give you more if you need them," she added.

"Okay, thank you, Louise. Thank you for everything. You are a great friend," he added. And with that, the two of them ended their conversation.

Once off the phone, Frank went immediately to where he had stashed the pills Louise had given him and retrieved one of them, popping it into his mouth under his tongue to let it melt. "Come on pill, melt," he said as he pushed the tiny pill with his tongue in an attempt to make it melt faster. He then looked at the clock to see how long twenty minutes was from that point so he could know how long he had to wait for the effects of the pill to kick in.

It would be a long twenty minutes, as Frank sat there feeling like he was going to die at any second. Finally, the pill started to kick in and he began to feel calm inside. "Thank God Louise gave me those pills," he said to himself. "I wonder how I would cope with all of this if I did not have those pills to help me navigate this situation," he reasoned. And he felt grateful to have a friend like Louise, even though thinking such also brought him a great sense of guilt in knowing he had also betrayed her with her own daughter.

"I am such a failure," he said to himself, now holding his head in his hands while sitting at his kitchen table. Thoughts of all the things he had done wrong were now swirling through his mind. "STOP," he told himself. "I can't bear to think of all those things right now," he added as he got up to go into his living room and put on a movie. "Please let this movie, along with that pill, take my mind off of all of this. I cannot bear to think about all of this right now."

He laid down on his couch and began watching the movie he had chosen out of his pile of movies. He'd seen all the movies he had more than once, but he didn't care. He just felt he needed to distract his mind from all the shame and guilt that was now consuming him.

As he laid there, his mind began to wander back to all the horrors of the past while, but Frank refused to let his mind wander and he tried to maintain his focus on the movie even though he already knew what was going to happen in it. Finally, he fell asleep. Sleep was now Frank's best friend, as he didn't have to think when he was sleeping.

Chapter Eighteen

The Way Back

A week or so had passed since Frank had gotten the news of Rita's sentence for the murder of her husband and his good friend Joe, but Frank had not been able to put any of it out of his mind for too long. He had tried to keep himself busy with work he had to do around his home, but the thoughts were intrusive into his mind when he would least expect them to be. He felt shame like he had never felt before in his life, but he couldn't bring himself to examine his own choices and behaviors. Every time the thoughts of what had happened came up in his mind, he quickly pushed them back out. He knew he was just avoiding his emotions, but he didn't feel strong enough to deal with them.

He reasoned that Rita's sentence of ten years would not actually be ten years and that she would most likely be eligible for parole in three to five years. Maybe even sooner with good behavior. After all, Rita was not a criminal. She had no criminal record and she was a refined woman from a good family. Hence, he reasoned that she'd not be in prison all that long and he was almost sure of it. And these thoughts made him feel somewhat better within the context.

Frank understood now why Rita had pleaded guilty to the lesser charge of manslaughter. "There was just too much evidence against her," he thought. "She was probably wise to take the plea bargain," he said to himself. Then he thought about how it said in the article that her house staff had turned against her and gave statements that supported the case of the prosecution. And he thought ill of those people and questioned their motives and loyalty to Rita, who had given them jobs, paid them well, and treated them with kindness, he was sure.

"That's how people are," he thought. "You can't trust them. You treat them well and then they turn on yea," he said to himself. And in that moment, he realized that is exactly what he himself had done. He had betrayed his long-time loyal friends and now one of them was dead and the other was unaware of his betrayal. He wondered again if Joe knew before he died about the affair between him and Rita, and he shuddered at the thought of Joe knowing he had betrayed him in the worst possible way.

Sadness consumed Frank, as it now did on a daily basis. He felt that his life had become meaningless. He went through the motions of what was required for his survival, but that was about all he could muster. His home was a filthy mess and he felt it was an accurate reflection of his life. "I don't care about any of this anymore," he thought to himself. "What is this life anyway?" he questioned as he looked around at the dirty dishes stacked on his kitchen counter and on his stove. "I don't care about any of it," he told himself. "And no one cares about me either, and that's okay, because I don't deserve anyone's care," he added.

Frank barely left his house now but for when he had to go and get supplies or take care of bills and such. He hated to leave his home because it was the only place he felt safe. "At least Lacy and Ziggy are now leaving me alone," he said to himself. "Thank God for that," he added. "Those whores can play with someone else, they are not playing with me anymore," he continued. "That bitch Ziggy, as sexy and pretty as she is, gave me that horrible STD. I will never forget that," Frank thought. Yet, he knew that it was his decision to have sex with Lacy and Ziggy, and that he was the one who had initiated the entire situation concerning Ziggy. Still, he didn't feel like taking personal responsibility for any of it and was thus content to continue to blame them for the choices he himself had made.

He now dragged himself around his house as if he was in some kind of zombie state of existence. He ate, smoked cannabis, and watched movies, which had now become his daily and nightly routine. He didn't even care anymore about how he looked and had to force himself to take a shower now and then due to the fact that he could smell himself and he didn't like the odor. Even still, it was extremely hard for Frank to even take a shower.

He'd taken all the pills that Louise had left for him and he wanted to ask her for more, but he hadn't done so because he didn't want Louise to know the state he was in. Just thinking of Louise now made him feel deep regret and shame. She was yet another of his victims, he reasoned, and he couldn't bear to ask her for more pills. "Thank God she never found out about Lacy and I," he thought. "That would be more than I could bear right now," he reasoned. But he still wasn't sure that Lacy wouldn't opt to be vengeful and rat the two of them out. "She had better not say anything," Frank thought. "If she does, I am going to tell Louise the truth. That she seduced me and pushed herself on me and that hence it was her fault all of that happened, not mine," he said to himself, even though he knew if Louise were to find out, there would be no forgiveness and no way of talking his way out of the situation. "She won't say anything," he reasoned. "Because she has as much to lose, and really more to lose, than I do if she does," he thought. And that thought gave him some comfort in the situation.

Louise had been calling to check up on him, and Frank had opted to talk to her on occasion just to ensure she didn't end up at his door. He had assured her every time she had called that he was "all good" and for her not to worry about him, even though he knew that was a complete lie. He didn't want to burden her with his current emotional state and he couldn't bear to see her knowing what he had done to her behind her back. "Here she is being all sweet to me and concerned and I have been a rotten friend to her. If she only knew what I have done behind her back, she'd never speak to me again," he reasoned. And the realization of that thought just made him all the sadder.

It had been awhile since Frank had gotten his mail from the community mailbox because he was afraid he would run into someone from the community while there and they would question him about the situation regarding Rita and Joe. But he knew he had to go and get his mail at some point, so he waited until late in the evening one night and went and retrieved his mail. He didn't look at the mail, he just grabbed it and threw it all on the front passenger's seat beside him. When he got home, he gathered it up and took it all into the house. There was a huge stack of mail from the fact that he had neglected to go and get his mail for some time. As he went through the various pieces of mail, he sorted out what was junk mail and what was mail he needed to pay attention to. Then suddenly he saw it – a letter from Rita! "What the fuck," he said to himself. "Why is she writing to me? Is she crazy?" he wondered. But then he remembered that no one but he, Rita and Louise knew about the affair and that it was okay that she wrote to him, or at least it seemed like it might be.

Frank slowly opened the letter as if he was afraid there was something inside the envelope that was going to hurt him. He wasn't even sure he wanted to read it. "What would Rita have to say to me now?" he wondered. "I don't want anything to do with her, doesn't she get that?" he continued. "She may have murdered my good friend! Does she think she and I can still be friends?" he wondered as he pulled the letter from the envelope and slowly unfolded it to see what was written there.

"Hi Frank," the letter started out. "As you no doubt know by now, I am in prison for the murder of Dear Sweet Joe. I have no words to describe what this whole experience has been like, but suffice it to say, it has been like a really bad horror movie," she wrote. "I just thought I would write to you to let you know how I am doing, in case you still care, that is," she added. "But I'm pretty sure you don't care and that you probably want nothing more to do with me, still I hold out hope that that is not the case," she continued. "I hope you're not mad at me for writing to you, but I just needed you to hear my side of the story," she added.

"I'm not sure how much you know about the case, but I want you to know I didn't murder Joe, Frank. I'm not guilty of the crime I am now in prison for. I opted to plead guilty to the lesser charge of manslaughter because my lawyer said that even though I am innocent of the crime, a trial judge and jury would most likely find me guilty due to all the circumstantial evidence they had against me. So he strongly suggested I take the plea bargain and so I did," she continued. "But I kind of wish I hadn't because it feels very wrong to be in prison for something I know I didn't do," she added.

"You know Joe took sleeping pills to sleep. He had been taking them for years, but he never wanted to go and get the prescription himself as he didn't want his rich clients to find out he took them. Not sure how he thought they would ever find out, but it was something he just didn't want to do. So he always got me to get the sleeping pills from my doctor and then I would just give them to him," she added. "But now, because the prescription was in my name, the prosecution has blamed me for him taking an overdose that night! And there is really no way for me to prove I had nothing to do with it, besides my word. And they did not believe me, quite obviously, when I told them the truth. So here I sit for the next who knows how many years! I was sentenced to ten years, but my lawyer says with good behaviour, and since I have no criminal record, I could possibly be out in two to three years. But I can barely get through a day in here, so I have no idea how I am going to endure being here for even that long," she added.

"It's been a horrible ride," Rita continued. "I never got to give Joe a proper burial or anything," she added. "It is all just so unjust, Frank. The house is just sitting there with everything still in it. Luckily I had savings in my account and so I am able to make the necessary payments on things through my lawyer until I can get out of this hell hole," she added. "I don't really care about all that material stuff anyway. It's more the principle of the matter. Joe worked hard to have all that he did and he had a lot, and I am not willing to just let the State take it all," she continued. "They think I killed Joe for his material wealth and hefty life insurance policy, but that could not be further from the truth. I no longer care about material things. I just want my freedom back," she wrote.

Frank could see flaws and inconsistencies in what Rita had written, but he opted to overlook them and to just continue reading. "I was in complete shock when they charged me with murdering Joe. I couldn't believe my ears," Rita continued. "It was surreal to me when they put handcuffs on me and took me off to jail to face these horrible charges," she added. "And I was in mourning for the loss of my husband on top of it all," she continued. "I don't want to lay all of this on you, Frank," she added. "I am just writing to explain my side of the story so that you know the full story and not just what the media is saying happened. I am sure you have heard the story the media is putting out there because it has been all over the news and rag magazines have picked it up the stroy as well. Joe was a big-time business man and so I guess this makes for good gossip, apparently," she wrote.

Frank immediately thought of the article he had read in the magazine. He had to agree with Rita that they had made her sound like a complete monster in their account of the situation, and he felt sad for Rita in that manner.

"So here I am now, in jail," she continued. "I hate this place with a passion already. The women here are mean and nasty and not the kind of people I am used to being around. Even though the rich people I had to associate with are cold-hearted and mean, snobby and bullies, at least I didn't have to worry about them physically attacking me like I do the women in here," she added. "I am thinking of asking my parole officer if I can be put in solitary confinement because I am afraid to even leave my cell," she added. "One of the women in here told me that I can request to be put in solitary if I fear for my own safety and so I am thinking that is maybe what I should do. I don't know if I could handle being in solitary though, that is the problem. Being alone in a cell twenty-four hours a day might not be something I could handle," she added.

"I guess they do let people in solitary out into the yard for one hour a day, but still, I don't think I could handle being in such a confined space for twenty-three hours a day. I think it would make me crazy," she added. "So I think I am just going to have to learn to cope in this situation somehow, but I am really not sure how. Because I have huge anxiety every time I have to leave my cell for anything," she added. "I guess this situation will either make me or break me," she continued. "All I know is that I cannot wait to be free from this place and to have my life back. Two to three years, if I can even get out in that time period, cannot pass soon enough as far as I'm concerned. I have always hated to wish time away, but now I am wishing it away like no tomorrow," she continued.

"On another subject, how is Louise doing? Have you seen her much?" she asked. "I wish I was free, I would come and visit again. I really enjoyed my visit there and Joe did as well. It was our last really good time together," she added.

And with that, Frank started to feel anxiety welling up inside of him. He knew Rita had been jealous of Louise and had asked him to stop having sex with her, so he wondered what angle she was coming from in stating such in the letter. And even though he was assuming she was disguising what she really wanted to say, as per the context of where she was writing him from, he was still amazed that she would even suggest coming to visit him in the letter. And the line, *"It was the last really good time together"* hit Frank hard, because he knew, as did she, that they had both betrayed Joe behind his back during the time the two of them were there. So Frank failed to see how such a situation would constitute a good time for Joe, but he kind of understood what Rita, he thought, was trying to say.

"Oh Frank, this place is so horrible. It is cold and damp and a most hateful place," Rita continued. "I cry every day. I don't know what to do with myself or if I can even endure two or three years in this hell hole," she added. "The women here are vile and are more like pig men than they are actual women," she added. "But maybe I can find a friend here, who knows. There must be some women here who are more like me. I am sure there must be other innocent women in here as well. I just pray that I meet some good ones, because so far all I have seen are these really tough looking ones that scare the living crap out of me," she added.

At reading that, Frank wanted to tell Rita to toughen up and never to act like she was afraid, because he reasoned that if a bully knows you are afraid they will come after you all the more, and he thought of writing Rita back just to let her know that truth. But he quickly realized he could not write Rita back for fear of anyone seeing the letters and for fear of anyone making the connection between him and Rita. Still, he wished there was some way he could tell her that, because he feared for her safety.

Rita was a small refined woman who had lived the good life and had never had to want for anything. Plus she was highly educated and Frank knew that most of the women inside that prison could not relate to the life that Rita lived and that they would most likely be jealous, envious, and mean towards her for having lived a life they could only dream of. So he wanted to tell her not to tell the women in the prison who she really was and to pretend she grew up poor and that she was uneducated just like they were. But again he had no way of letting Rita know these things.

He thought of asking Louise to write to Rita to advise her on these important matters that Frank felt were essential to Rita's well-being and maybe even survival inside the prison; but he wasn't even sure he wanted to tell Louise that Rita had written to him. And then there were the postal workers who would know that letters were being exchanged between the three of them, and that was not something he wanted to take a chance with.

"You could write to her and mail it from the city," he told himself, but he wasn't sure it was even a good idea to write to Rita at all. "I may mention it to Louise to see what she thinks," he said to himself. "Because Rita really does need to know this information. It could help her a lot in coping with being inside that horrible place," he told himself as he continued to read.

"I really miss you Frank," Rita wrote, and when Frank saw that his heart began to beat fast. "Oh no, don't write things like that, Rita!" he thought to himself. "What in fuck are you thinking in saying such a thing?"

"Please write back to me, Frank. I'd love to hear from you. I could really use a good friend right now," she added. And while Frank understood what she was saying, the fear of what she had written about missing him and wanting him to write her back gripped him hard and he dropped the letter on the table.

"I need to stay out of all of this," he told himself right away. "Yes, I could help her by telling her what to say and how to act inside of there; but at what cost to myself?" he reasoned. "I just have to let all of this go. I just can't be involved in any way, shape, or form," he told himself. "It's far too dangerous," he reasoned as he picked up the letter from the table once again to finish reading it. "Anyway, I hope all is well with you. And I do hope you will think about writing me back. I am very lonely and alone in this horrible place, Frank. I hope you can find it in your heart to reach out to me here. I know you are probably busy with things in your own life and that you might not want to be involved in any way with this situation, but I do pray that you can find it in your heart to write me a note. I would really appreciate it. I hope to hear from you real soon," then she signed the letter, *Love Rita* and put x's and o's beside her name.

Frank's eyes grew wide when he saw how Rita had ended the letter. "She is fucking crazy," he thought to himself. "I can't write her back! What in fuck is she thinking?" he said to himself. And he crumbled up the letter and threw it immediately into the garbage can as if the letter somehow was making him guilty of something just by him having it in his house. His level of anxiety was now rising higher and higher and he thought, "No, the garbage can is not good enough. I need to burn this letter right now," he reasoned.

And so he retrieved the letter from the garbage can and took it into the bathroom. "I'll burn it here in the sink," he said to himself. "Page by page, until it is gone," he added. And he proceeded to take his lighter and burn the pages of the letter in his bathroom sink. Once all the pages were burnt, he cleaned out the sink and swiped his hands together. "There, that's the end of that," he said as he exited the bathroom and returned to his kitchen table.

And just then he noticed that the envelope the letter had come in was still sitting there on his kitchen table and he noticed that the address of the correctional facility where Rita was being incarcerated was written on it. "How in fuck did all of this happen," he thought as he picked it up and put it away with his other mail. "I'll deal with that later," he told himself. "The important thing is, the contents of the letter are gone. Who cares about the stupid envelope," he reasoned. "It's an empty envelope so it would hardly serve as any kind of evidence," he thought as he shoved the envelope into the bottom of the stack of other envelopes sitting there that he had yet to open.

Just then it occurred to him that the women at the local post office must have all seen the letter from Rita as with the address of the correctional facility on the envelope as well. "Oh my gosh," he said to himself. "Is all this shit ever going to end?" he wondered. And he began to feel anger towards Rita for having dared to even write to him knowing that he lived in such a small town. "She must have known that the community here and the people that work at the post office would see this," he reasoned, and anger welled up inside him against Rita for what he saw as her grave lack of good judgment and ultimate stupidity.

"Maybe she is guilty," he thought. "Look how she acted when she was here!" he said to himself. "She was a complete whore," he added. "All that happened was her fault," he thought. "She is the one who dressed like a whore. She is the one who seduced me behind her husband's back. She is the one who gave Joe the sleeping pills to knock him out so she could sneak behind his back and have sex with me," he reasoned. "Yes, it was all her fault!" he now determined. "If she really loved Joe, she could not have done any of those things," he thought.

"Maybe she is not who I thought she was at all," he questioned. But he knew deep inside that none of that really mattered anymore. Joe was dead and while Rita was part of the betrayal, he knew he too was a participant in all of it. And the thought of that truth made him feel weak in his knees. He wanted to blame it all on Rita. He wanted to justify it all by putting all the blame on her, but he knew he too was at fault and that he had to own his part in the situation. Still, he really didn't want to. It was too much for him to bear that he had betrayed his good friend Joe who had been nothing but kind and loyal to him over all the many years of their friendship.

"I'm a real piece of shit," he said to himself. "I used to think I was such a good person. A person with good morals and high standards, but now I just see myself as a worm. A maggot even. I am a worthless human being," he said to himself, and he hung his head in shame for all that had happened.

As the days passed, Frank's depression got worse and worse. He was now at the point where he didn't even want to eat anymore. Smoking cannabis used to make him feel better, but now that wasn't even working. He would just stay in bed and only get up when he had to use the washroom. His clothes were dirty and he had not done laundry in weeks. His house was a mess and smelled bad, his bed was dirty and stank, and he stank as well, but he just didn't care.

He now rarely left his house and only went out after it was dark. If he needed anything, he ordered it online from his computer. He tried watching movies but even that did not help. He had no more pills left from the ones Louise had given him, and he really felt he needed more of them, but he could not bring himself to face Louise either, or even to ask her over the phone. He just laid in his bed drowning in his sorrow for what seemed to be days on end.

Until finally one day he decided it was time to end his misery and that he was going to end his miserable life and be rid of all the guilt and pain he was feeling once and for all. So he made a plan on how he would end his life, and he wrote it down to make sure he did it right because he didn't want to mess it up and end up still alive.

"How am I going to do it?" he asked himself, and then the idea of hanging himself came to his mind. He knew he had lots of rope in his shed and he reasoned he could hang himself out in the shed.

But then he worried that Louise would be the one to find him hanging there, and he didn't want to do that to her.

"Where can I hang myself?" he thought, but nothing was really coming to him, until he thought about going deep into the woods on the land behind his home. "I can hang myself from a tree out there in the woods," he said to himself, looking out into the woods from the window of his bedroom. "Yes, that will work. I will hang myself out there and the animals will eat my body. That is perfect."

He managed to get out of bed and he began to gather all the things he would need in order to carry out his mission. He wanted to do it sooner than later because the pain and deep sorrow he was feeling was more than he could bear now. So he reasoned the sooner he could do it, the better it would be.

He gathered up the materials he thought he needed and sat down at his kitchen table. He was low on food as he had not left his house in days, if not weeks. He still had a tiny bit of his organic coffee left in a tin, and so he opted to make himself one last cup of coffee before he headed out to do the deed. And just as he was waiting for the coffee to brew, a knock came to the door.

"Who in fuck could that be?" he questioned as he went to peek out from behind the curtain in his dining room window. But he wasn't sure who it was as he could only see the back of the person standing there. It was a man, he knew that much, but beyond that he wasn't sure.

"Maybe I had better go and answer it," he thought. "It might be something important," he reasoned. But then he realized there was nothing important to him now, and he might as well just not answer. So he sat back down at his kitchen table and waited for the person to leave.

After a short time he got up to see if the person had left, and to his surprise the man was still standing there. "Who in fuck is that?" he asked himself. "And why are they still standing there?" he wondered. "I'm going to have to go and answer the door apparently," he thought to himself, "as this person, whoever it is, is just not going to leave!" So he got up and went to answer the door.

Upon opening the door, Frank realized it was his longtime friend who he had not seen in years standing there. "Hey Frank, long time no see," his friend said, smiling. Frank was a little shocked since he had not expected a visit from anyone, let alone Chris, who he had not seen in he didn't even know how long.

"Wow, good to see yea, buddy," he said to Chris. "Good to see you too, Frank," Chris replied. And the two of them embraced in a hug.

"Come on in," Frank said. "Don't mind the mess in here. I've been a little under the weather as of late," Frank continued, trying to explain the mess his house was in.

As Chris entered into Frank's house, he was shocked at the mess he saw. Dirty dishes were stacked all over the place and there was a strong stench in the air, but he tried to pretend not to notice.

"What's been going on with yea, buddy?" he asked Frank, taking a seat at Frank's kitchen table.

"Oh, not much," Frank responded. "Just haven't been feeling well these past few days, or maybe weeks, I'm not sure how long," Frank replied, trying to force a smile.

Then Chris noticed the pile of stuff in the middle of the kitchen floor. The rope stood out to him and so he asked Frank, "What are you planning to do with all that rope?"

Frank looked down at the pile of stuff he had prepared, sitting there in the middle of the kitchen floor. "Oh that, ah, well, I was…" and then he stopped talking. He wasn't sure how to explain what the pile of rope was doing there, as with the other items.

"You were what?" Chris asked.

"Oh, it's not important," Frank responded. "Just forget about it," he added. "Tell me what's been going on with you," Frank said in an attempt to change the subject.

But Chris wasn't having it. He now knew that something, or maybe many things, were not quite right in the situation, and he feared the worst.

"Are you okay, Frank?" Chris asked.

"Oh yea, I'm all good," Frank responded. "I know my house is a mess, and I look like a mess. As I said, I've been under the weather lately and just haven't been up to par. I usually keep my house pretty clean and all, but you know, I just haven't been feeling well lately," he added.

"Are you sick, Frank?" Chris asked.

"No, not exactly," Frank responded. "I've just been having some troubles and making dumb decisions and choices as of late is all," he added.

Chris then leaned across the table and looked Frank directly in the eyes. "Tell me what is going on here, Frank," he said in a serious tone of voice.

"What do you mean?" Frank responded.

"I can tell something is not right here," Chris replied. "I can tell that you are not well, Frank," he added. "Now tell me what is going on," Chris continued.

And with that, Frank began to crack and broke down crying. "I can't talk about it all, Chris. I just can't. It is too much and I don't want to tell anyone. I just want to end it all. Do you understand? I need to get away from all that is around me now," Frank said.

Chris sat back in his chair. He was shocked to see Frank in such a state and even more shocked to hear what he was saying. He suddenly realized what the pile of rope laying in the middle of the kitchen floor was for.

"Frank is planning on committing suicide. "What in fuck do I do?" he asked himself.

And just then he thought of the Priest at his local church. Chris didn't know the Priest all that well, but he knew he had to try to do something to help his friend.

"You really need to talk to someone, Frank," Chris finally said.

"It's no use, Chris," Frank responded. "I've ruined my life now. I just want to die and get it over with. Just let me carry out my plan. No one will ever know you were here. Trust me, I need to do this," Frank said, sobbing and hanging his head.

"You're in bad shape, brother," Chris replied, reaching out to touch Frank's arm that was resting on the table. "It's going to be okay, brother," he said, gently rubbing Frank's arm. "I can help you, and I want to help you," he continued.

"I know someone you can talk to who is confidential. You can trust this person. He is bound to confidentiality and no one will ever know what you tell him," Chris added. "Let me call him and see if I can bring you over to talk to him, okay!" Chris got out his phone and proceeded to find the number for the church.

"No, Chris, I really don't want to talk to anyone. I can't even talk about all of this with anyone. I don't care if it is confidential or not, I just can't!" Frank responded.

But Chris ignored Frank's words and proceeded to contact the Priest.

Finally someone answered the phone at the Church.

"I need to speak with the Priest, it's urgent," Chris said to the person on the other end of the line.

"Okay, one moment please," the woman said and put Chris on hold.

"It's going to be okay, buddy," Chris said to Frank, who was sitting there with his head hung down and tears flowing from his eyes.

Just then the Priest came on the line. "Hi, this is Father Smith, how can I help you?" the man said.

"Ah, hi, my name is Chris. I have attended your church a few times, but you probably don't know me. I have a friend here who is in really rough shape and I believe is planning to end his life, and I was wondering if you could make some time to talk to him if I bring him over to the Church?" Chris said.

"Of course," the Priest replied. "Bring him right over. I will be waiting for you. You know how to get here, right?"

"Yes, yes I do Father," Chris responded. "And I will try to get him to come and talk to you as soon as I can. He is hesitant to go and speak with you, but I have assured him that anything he tells you is strictly confidential," Chris added.

"That's right," Father Smith responded. "Just bring him along. Don't, whatever you do, leave him alone. If he refuses to come here to speak with me, call me back and I will get the address and come to where the two of you are, okay," the Priest added.

"Okay Father, thank you," Chris said and hung up the phone.

"The Priest wants to see you, Frank," Chris said once off the phone. "He is waiting there now for us to come over so you can talk to him. Please come with me and go and see the Priest. You need someone to talk to, Frank. You need help, Frank," Chris continued.

Frank was consoled by the words of his friend. He could feel the compassion and love Chris had for him in his situation, but he wondered if Chris knew the whole story, if he would still feel that way.

"I'm not worthy," Frank said. "I've made a mess of my life and really the world would be a better place without me in it," he added, with tears rolling down his eyes while he spoke.

"That's not true, Frank," Chris responded. "Please just come with me and go and talk to the Priest. If after you talk to him you still want to end your life, I won't interfere," Chris said in an attempt to get Frank to go with him to see the Priest.

"What good is talking to a Priest I don't even know going to do?" Frank asked. "I haven't been to Mass in I don't even know how long," he added. "And why did you show up here today anyway?" he asked.

"I think talking to the Priest will help you a lot. You can get whatever is eating you alive off of your chest for one thing," Chris replied. "And for another, the Priest can give you some good guidance on how to help yourself in whatever situation you are in," Chris added.

"As for me showing up here! I can't really tell you why. I just had it in my mind to come and see you today, that's all I know!" he said. "Maybe it was God," Chris added. "Maybe God told me to come and see you today because God knew you needed a friend right now," Chris continued.

And just when Chris said that, Frank realized that he had forgotten all about God. He had forgotten the social belief that if someone killed themselves they cannot go to heaven. He had forgotten to pray and even ask God to help him. And he suddenly felt even more ashamed than he already had.

"I'm not leaving here until you come with me to talk to the Priest," Chris said. "Come on, what do you have to lose?" Chris added.

So Frank finally agreed to go and speak with the Priest even though he really didn't want to. He knew that Chris wasn't going to leave until he agreed to go with him so he figured he might as well just agree and go.

"I'll go and talk to this Priest. I know it is not going to do any good, but at least it will get rid of Chris and then I can carry out my plan in private," Frank told himself. "I shouldn't have answered the fucking door," he thought to himself. "But now that I have, my plan is all messed up!" he thought. "And what's more, now another person knows what a messed up piece of shit I am," Frank reasoned as he got up from his chair and went to the washroom to try to make himself look halfway presentable to see the Priest.

"I really need to take a shower, Chris," Frank said in an attempt to stall time.

"I can wait," Chris replied. "Go ahead if you want to take a shower," he added.

But Frank didn't have the parts to even get into the shower at that time and so he opted to just comb his hair, brush his teeth and throw some water on his face before heading out with Chris to go see the Priest.

"I'm going to drive my own truck over to the Church," Frank advised once they were outside the house.

"Are you sure?" Chris asked. "I don't mind driving you over," he added.

"No, no, I want to take my own truck," Frank replied. "Don't worry, I'm not going to back out on yea. I'll follow you over because you know where to go and I really don't. As I said, it has been a long time since I have been to Mass or any Church for that matter," Frank added.

So Chris agreed and they both got into their respective vehicles and headed down the road toward the Church where the Priest was waiting for them.

Frank saw that the Church was huge as he pulled into the parking lot behind Chris. The Priest's house was just beside the Church and the Priest came out and waved the two of them over to his house.

"I'm not going to go in," Chris said after they had both parked and had gotten out of their vehicles. "Unless you need me to, or want me to," he added.

"No, I think I'm good," Frank responded.

"Okay brother," Chris said, putting his hand on Frank's back. "You've got this, okay!" he added, trying to encourage Frank. But

Frank didn't even respond, he just walked toward the Priest who was standing in the door waiting for him.

"Hi, I'm Father Smith," the Priest said, holding out his hand to Frank.

"Hi Father," Frank said, extending his hand as well. "My name is Frank. And I have to be honest, I've not been to Mass in a long time," he added.

"That's okay Frank," the Priest replied and chuckled a little. "Don't worry about that, God has lots of children who do not attend any Church, of that I am sure," he continued, smiling at Frank. "But that's not to say you shouldn't come to Mass," the Priest added, still smiling.

"Yes, I know Father," Frank replied. "Maybe if I had been going to Mass all of this horror my life has become would not have happened," Frank added.

The Priest didn't respond, he just smiled and led Frank into his home.

"Have a seat in the living room, Frank," the Priest instructed. "Would you like a drink? A coffee, tea, or a glass of pop?" the Priest asked.

"Yea, I'll have a soda if you don't mind, thank you," Frank responded.

And so the Priest prepared a glass of soda for both he and Frank and sat down in the chair near the couch where Frank was seated.

"What seems to be the problem, Frank?" the Priest asked.

"I don't even know where to start," Frank replied.

"Your friend I spoke with on the phone seemed to think you were contemplating taking your own life," the Priest said.

"Honestly, yes I was," Frank responded.

"Well, what can be so bad as to drive you to that decision?" the Priest asked.

"I've committed many sins, Father," Frank replied. "I've committed so many horrible sins that I feel I am no longer worthy to walk this earth," Frank continued.

"We are all sinners, Frank," the Priest said. "Even me," he added. "No one on this earth is perfect, Frank," the Priest continued.

"Yes, I know Father," Frank replied. "But I have committed grave sins that I am not even sure God can forgive me for, or will forgive me for," Frank said, and with that he began to weep.

"Oh come now Frank," the Priest replied. "God forgives all sins but one and I am quite sure you have not committed the one sin God does not forgive," the Priest added.

"What is the one sin God does not forgive?" Frank asked.

"Blaspheme of the Holy Spirit," the Priest said.

"Oh okay, I don't think I committed that sin," Frank said. "At least I don't think I have," he added.

"I am sure you haven't," the Priest responded. "So talk to me Frank and tell me what is causing you such deep sorrow as you are now experiencing. Maybe I can help you unburden yourself," he added.

Frank took a deep breath and started recounting to the Priest the whole story of all that had happened. And as he spoke and told the Priest, he noticed that the Priest was not looking at him with scorn or judgment. In fact, the Priest seemed to have compassion even though he was not saying much and rather just listening to Frank's account.

Frank went on for what he felt like was a long time, because it was, after all, a long story. But the Priest did not seem to get bored or impatient with him, he noticed. He cried through most of what he told the Priest and once he had finished telling the Priest everything, he said, "Now you see why I am worthless and why I need to end my life, right Father?"

The Priest smiled at Frank and put his hand on Frank's hand.

"The truth is you have made some grave errors, it is true. You have done some things that involved very poor judgment and you have hurt other people and you've obviously deeply hurt yourself as well," the Priest continued. "But none of that means you are a horrible person, Frank," the Priest said.

And with that, Frank was shocked as he was convinced he was rotten to the core. Then the Priest continued.

"I want you to reflect on the wrongs you have committed and now that you have confessed your sins and taken ownership of all of them in doing so, I want you to pray to God and ask God for forgiveness of those sins, Frank," the Priest advised. "If you want me to pray with you or for you, I am more than willing to do that," the Priest added.

"Yes, please," Frank responded.

So the Priest began to pray.

Most Holy Father, Creator of Heaven and earth and all that is, we come before you now with sorrowful hearts. My brother Frank here, who is also your Child, is in grave need of your love and your forgiveness. He has confessed his sins as the teaching in Holy Scripture advises us to do and he has repented of those sins. Please cleanse him now of all unrighteousness and forgive him his sins in the Holy Name of Jesus. In the Name of the Father and of the Son and of the Holy Spirit Amen.

Frank had always known, but had somehow forgotten, the awesome power of prayer. He had closed his eyes while Father Smith was praying and when he opened them the room appeared to be full of a mist. He could feel the Holy Spirit and it both gave him comfort and made him nervous at the same time.

"Do you see a mist in the air in here, Father?" Frank asked.

The Priest smiled. "That is God's Holy Spirit Grace, Frank," the Priest said smiling. "God has forgiven you and God wants you to be free now. God doesn't want you to dwell on those sins anymore. He wants you to learn from them and never to do them again. He wants you to be mindful of your actions and how they affect other people. He wants you to be a wise and healthy Child of His. He doesn't want you to be lost and alone. He wants you to be happy and fulfilled in your life. He wants you to do good and to show love to others," the Priest continued.

"Can you do that, Frank?" the Priest asked.

"Yes," Frank responded. "I can surely do that, or at least try to," he added.

The Priest smiled. "You're not a bad person, Frank. You made some very poor choices and decisions and look where it has brought you. Today you were ready to end your own life, Frank. Do you see the serious consequences of your sins?" the Priest asked.

"Yes, I do Father," Frank answered.

"Good," the Priest said and smiled. "Just as it says in the Holy Scriptures, we are all sinners and we all fall short. The point is to confess our sins and to learn from them and grow in our spiritual walk with the Lord, Frank," the Priest continued.

"Yes Father, I understand now," Frank responded. "And I have to say Father, I feel so much lighter now. I feel so much better. I feel like the shackles that were binding me hard have now been broken," Frank responded and with that he burst out crying, but this time it was in gratitude and joy and not in pain and sorrow.

"I hope those are tears of joy, Frank," the Priest said smiling.

"Yes, they are," Frank responded. And they both rose from where they were sitting and Frank reached out and hugged the Priest. "Thank you so much, Father," he said to the Priest, hugging him and still weeping.

"You are most welcome, Frank," the Priest said.

Frank let go of the Priest and started walking towards the door to leave.

"You are all good now, right Frank?" the Priest asked.

"Yes Father, don't worry. I am all good now and I can't thank you enough. I have been in such a deep dark hole for a while now and finally I can see the light again," Frank said. "And it's all because of you, Father, so thank you so much. I can't thank you enough," Frank added.

The Priest smiled. "Don't thank me, Frank, thank God. God is the one who forgave your sins. God is the one who extended His Grace upon you. God is the one who sent His great love down upon you. I am just the vessel, that is all," the Priest replied, still smiling.

"Yes, right," Frank responded. "And I do, I thank God. I thank God for you, Father. For you helping me today. I could be dead in my sin right now and I realize I have much to be grateful for," Frank added.

"And what of your friend? I forget his name now. The one who called me earlier and asked me to speak with you," the Priest said.

"Oh right, his name is Chris," Frank responded. "And the strange thing is, Father, I'd not seen him in I don't know how long and he just showed up at my door today. I asked him why he showed up and he said he didn't know why! Then he said maybe God sent him to my house today. Now I am thinking he was right. God most definitely sent him to my house today. Because if he wouldn't have shown up right when he did, I'd be hanging dead from a tree in the woods behind my house right now!" Frank added.

"Well, praise be to God," the Priest said, smiling. "You see, Frank, God cares about you and He sent your friend to you today because He knew what you were planning and He knew you needed help. That is the great and wonderful God we serve," the Priest added.

"Yes indeed it is," Frank responded, now smiling a big smile. "God really does love me," Frank thought, and with that thought a great surge of love flowed throughout his entire being.

"God loves me," he repeated over and over and with each time he said it to himself, his smile got even bigger. As Frank exited the Priest's house he felt like he was walking on air. He had not felt so good, so free, so light in a very long time, if ever.

"If I have ever felt this before, I don't remember when it was," he said to himself as he smiled the biggest smile and walked towards his truck parked in the parking lot.

Just as he approached his truck he saw what looked like a dog standing there. "Whose dog is that?" he wondered as he got closer to his truck. "Hey pooch, what are you doing here all alone?" he said to the dog who was just standing there looking at him. Frank checked to see if the dog had a collar or tags so that he might be able to identify who the dog was and who owned it; but the dog had no collar or tags.

Then Frank noticed that the dog looked rather ragged and unhealthy and he reasoned he must be a stray, but he wasn't sure what to do. As he looked at the dog he noticed the dog's eyes were very sad and that he was looking at Frank as if he needed something, but Frank had no idea what and Frank didn't quite know what to do. So he walked back to the Priest's house and knocked on the door.

The Priest came to the door. "Is everything okay, Frank?" the Priest asked.

"Yea, everything is great, but the strangest thing just happened when I left your house. When I walked to my truck there was this strange dog standing there! I checked but the dog has no collar and no tags and he looks like he might be a stray or something, I'm not sure. I was just wondering if you know the dog and if you can give me some guidance on what to do, as I am not sure," Frank said.

The Priest then peered out to see if he could see the dog and upon seeing the dog the Priest realized he had not seen that dog before. "No, I don't know the dog," the Priest said and just then it hit him and he said to Frank. "I think I know who put the dog there, Frank."

"You do!" Frank exclaimed. "You think someone put that dog there?" Frank continued.

"Yes, I do," the Priest said, smiling. "I think God put that dog there, Frank. I think that dog needs you, Frank, and I think you need that dog," the Priest continued.

All of a sudden tears started to roll down Frank's cheeks. "You think God put that dog there for me, Father?" Frank asked.

"Yes, I do, Frank," the Priest replied. "Now go and take that dog and take it home with you and take care of it and it will take care of you, okay Frank," the Priest said smiling.

Frank grabbed the Priest and hugged him once again. "Thank you, Father Smith. You have no idea what all of this means to me," Frank said, still hugging the Priest.

The Priest smiled. "Again Frank, thank God. God is the one who put the dog there, not me," the Priest said, still smiling.

"Okay Father, I got yea," Frank said, letting go of the Priest. "I want to keep in touch with you, Father," Frank continued.

"Good," the Priest replied. "I hope you do. I look forward to hearing from you and seeing you at Mass," he added, still smiling.

"You will Father, I promise. I will contact you and I will start going to Mass again," Frank said, smiling the biggest smile.

Then Frank walked back to his truck. The dog was still standing there with its sad eyes looking up at Frank. "Well, I guess you're my doggie now," he said to the dog, reaching down and patting its head. "I've not had a dog since I was a child, so you're gonna have to bear with me until I get used to taking care of a dog again," Frank continued as he opened the passenger's side door of his truck and motioned for the dog to get in.

Suddenly the dog looked happy and with its tail wagging wildly it quickly jumped into Frank's truck. "I don't know who you belonged to before today, but whoever it was, they didn't take good care of you obviously," Frank said to the dog, patting the dog on the head. "I'm going to take good care of you now, boy," he told the dog. "God sent you to me, so now you are my doggie," Frank told the dog.

Frank rolled down the window for the dog to stick its head out and headed on down the road to return to his home.

The day seemed surreal to Frank. He had started out the day with a mission to kill himself. He had a plan and had gathered together all the materials he needed to carry it out. Then out of the blue, his friend Chris showed up and talked him into going to see a Priest Frank had never met before! And now he was headed home with a dog!

"Wow, life is so strange," he said to himself as he looked over at this dog that was now in his truck beside him. "I don't even have food for a dog," he suddenly realized. "How am I going to take care of a dog?" he reasoned. Yet he felt deep gratitude for all that had happened that day.

Frank stopped in at the first store he saw on his way home and bought a big bag of dog food, plus a bag of chews and some dog treats he saw in the same area. "That should do it," he said to himself as he headed to the checkout to pay for his items.

The woman cashier smiled at Frank as she passed his items through the scanner. "That will be fifty-five dollars," she said, holding her hand out. So Frank passed her a fifty and a five, smiled at her, took his items and exited the store.

"I've got some good food for you now, buddy," he said, putting the items in the back of his truck. "Everything is gonna be okay. I'm gonna take real good care of yea," he told the dog. And the dog seemed to understand what Frank was saying as it wagged its tail and looked to Frank to be smiling.

Frank also noticed that the dog's sad eyes he had seen when he first saw the dog seemed to now be looking less sad and more happy. This made Frank feel good inside. "Finally," he said to himself, "I feel like I am doing something right for a change." And with that thought, he smiled a big smile, patted the dog's head, and headed down the road towards home.

As he pulled into the driveway of his home, he remembered that his house was a complete mess and that the items he had gathered to commit suicide that morning were still in a pile in the middle of his kitchen floor, and the thoughts of all of that made his heart sink. "I don't even want to take you into my house right now," he said to the dog. And he could feel strong emotion welling up inside and tears began to run down his cheeks. The dog suddenly looked bewildered and sad again. "Don't worry boy," Frank said to the dog. "It's all going to be okay fella," he added, patting the dog's head and then hugging the dog around its neck.

Frank got out of his truck and let the dog out. "This is your new home buddy. Feel free to roam all you like, but don't go too far," he told the dog. But the dog just stood there staring at Frank as if waiting for Frank's direction on what to do next. So Frank started walking towards the back door of his house and the dog followed.

As he entered his house he could hear the phone ringing, so he hurried to try to answer it before it stopped. He got to the phone just in time. "Hello," he said without checking first to see who was calling.

"Hey Frank, I'm just calling to see how you are doing." Then Frank realized it was his good friend Chris.

"Oh hey Chris, I'm doing a lot better thank you, and you are never going to believe what happened," Frank continued.

And just then Frank noticed that his house was all cleaned up! The items he had placed in the middle of the kitchen floor were gone! All his dirty dishes were washed and the place looked much improved from when Frank had left to go and talk to the Priest.

"Did you clean my house?" Frank asked in a surprised tone of voice.

Chris laughed at Frank's reaction. "Well, not just me, my wife came and helped me, but yea the two of us cleaned up your house a bit while you were gone. I hope you don't mind. You didn't lock the door when you left, so I asked my wife to come and help me and she agreed and so we did some cleaning. I figured it would help you if you didn't have to look at all of that when you got back from talking to the Priest," Chris said.

"Wow Chris, thank you so much my friend, and tell your wife I said thank you too," Frank responded. "To be honest, I was dreading having to come back home to see the items I had piled in the middle of the kitchen floor ...” then Frank went silent.

“It’s okay Frank,” Chris replied. “You don’t have to explain. I understand,” he added.

“Thanks for being such a good friend Chris,” Frank said.

“Oh, don’t mention it,” Chris replied. “I’m just happy that I went to see you today and that I was able to talk you into going to talk to the Priest,” he added. “Speaking of which, how did you make out talking to the Priest?” he asked.

Frank was silent. He didn’t quite know how to explain all that had happened during his visit with the Priest.

“Are you okay Frank?” Chris finally asked.

“Ah, yea, no I’m better than okay Chris,” Frank responded. “I’m just having a hard time finding the words for what happened while I was at the Priest’s house. It was all kind of surreal,” Frank added.

“You don’t have to explain,” Chris replied. “I just wanted to make sure you are all good now and that you are not going to do anything stupid,” he added.

It now seemed strange to Frank that he had planned on ending his own life just that morning and he wasn’t quite sure how to respond.

“I’m not going to do anything stupid, don’t worry,” Frank finally said. “But it wasn’t stupid to me when I was thinking of doing it,” he added.

"No," Chris said. "I'm sorry! Maybe that was a bad choice of word to use," he added.

"It's okay Chris. I have never felt that down and lost before in my life and it was a very serious matter. I was so depressed and I just couldn't seem to shake it," he continued.

"I understand Frank," Chris replied. But Frank was pretty sure that no one understood, yet he didn't want to argue the point and so he didn't really respond.

"Well okay then!" Chris replied. "I'm so glad you are feeling better and that things went so well at the Priest's house. I don't know the Priest well, but I've heard nothing but good things about him," Chris added.

"Yea, he is a really swell guy," Frank replied. "He really helped me a lot and I can't thank you enough for pushing me to go and talk to him. It literally saved my life," Frank said.

"I'm glad the Priest could help you. I figured it would help and that is why I suggested it," Chris responded.

"Yes, and you were right Chris. It helped me more than I have words to explain," Frank added.

"That's great Frank," Chris said. "Okay, I'll let yea go now, unless you need or want to talk more," he added.

"No, I'm good now," Frank replied. "But you are never going to guess what happened when I left the Priest's house," he added.

"Oh, what's that?" Chris asked.

Then Frank began to tell Chris about how this strange dog showed up out of nowhere and how he went back to the Priest's house to see if the Priest knew the dog and/or who it belonged to. But the Priest didn't know the dog and that the Priest told him God had put the dog there for him.

"Wow," Chris said. "That is strange, I have to agree. So what did you do?" Chris asked.

"Well since the Priest said that God had put the dog there for me and that the dog needed me and I needed the dog, so I opted to bring him home with me," Frank said, smiling and looking at the dog who was now laying on his kitchen floor

"Wow Frank, that is awesome," Chris exclaimed.

"Yea, it is very awesome," Frank agreed.

"I have a dog now Chris," Frank said laughing.

"That's great," Chris responded, laughing along with him. "Did you give it a name yet?" Chris asked.

"No, not yet," Frank responded. "Come to think of it, I'm not even sure if it is a girl or boy. I've never even checked yet. I've been calling the dog boy so I hope it's a boy," he said laughing.

"Well that is something else Frank," Chris responded.

"Yea, it sure is. This whole day has been so surreal," Frank replied. "And you were a huge part in all of it Chris," Frank continued.

"Awe, well I am happy that I opted to go and visit you and that I was able to get you to go and talk to the Priest. It sounds like it was the right thing to do and I am so happy you are feeling better Frank and that God sent you a dog," Chris responded.

"Me too," Frank said.

"God works in mysterious ways," Chris added.

"He sure does," Frank agreed.

"Well, I'll let you go now, but if you ever need to talk, please call me," Chris added.

"Will do brother," Frank responded. "Will do! And thanks again for all your help today. You literally saved my life brother and I will never forget you for that," Frank added. "And thank you to you and your wife for cleaning up this mess of a house," he continued.

"Don't mention it," Chris responded. "I'm just relieved and happy you are all good now," Chris added.

And with that they ended their conversation and Frank went over and laid down on the floor beside the dog, putting his arm around the dog. "Everything is gonna be okay buddy," he said to the dog. And as the two of them laid there on the kitchen floor, Frank closed his eyes and gave thanks to God for all that God had done for him that day and his heart felt more free and happy than it had in years. Feelings of deep gratitude surged through his body and contentment and peace now consumed him.

And with that, Frank started a brand new chapter in his life. He now spent his days with his dog and his life was more fulfilled than it had been in years, if ever.

THE END